ITALIAN BODIES OF CHANGE

Other Books by Tina Assanti

Italian Bones of Contentions

The Kingdom of God and Playboys

ITALIAN BODIES OF CHANGE

MARIA'S SECRET IS OUT... AND IT'S A KILLER

BY TINA ASSANTI

Italian Bones of Contentions
Pride Series Book Two

Tina Assanti Books

Library of Congress Number: 9781777177416
Library of Congress
US Programs, Law, and Literature Division
Cataloging in Publication Program
101 Independence Avenue, S.E.
Washington, DC 20540-4283

Paperback ISBN: 9781777177416
Cover designed by Rade Rokvic and Willow Publishing

www.tinaassantibooks.com

I thank my family for their patience,
my partner for his love and light,
and my children
for the special people
they have become.
To my editor, Vic Schukov, thank you
for your wonderful sense
of black humour.

Tina Assanti

This book is dedicated to Anthony (Tony) Nauss.
Tony, you were a warrior for the rights for all
and for those who suffer.
You loved everyone equally with respect and dignity.
You are sorely and terribly missed.

April 23, 1998 – November 3, 2018

CHAPTER ONE

November 1983

"Maria, get out of that friggin' coffin."

Ten-year-old Maria, a tomboy awkward in her frilly dress and socks, looked over her shoulder at Andy, her mother.

Andy sat fidgeting in the front row, frowning at Maria, then looked down at her well-manicured hands clasped in her lap. She was in her late thirties, trim and dressed elegantly in her blacks, with auburn-dyed shoulder-length hair disheveled enough to reflect the frantic state of mind Maria knew her mother was in. Maria noticed a run in her mother's silk black stocking.

"I just wanted to make sure he's really dead."

"Oh, he's really friggin' dead, all right," said Andy. "That friggin' Anita made sure of that. Take my word for it."

Maria stubbornly turned and leaned back into the coffin until her chin caressed the scratchy, white satin lining. She touched her nose against her *Nonno's* folded waxy hands. Cross-eyed, she studied the hair that oddly looked alive on his grey sausage fingers. She reached out and gently squeezed his cold powdered nose. She sniffed him, noticing he had lost that familiar, comforting, medicinal garlic smell. Instead, her nostrils filled with the aroma of fresh carnations, dust, and stale make-up.

Nestled inside, her over-large ears no longer heard the hustling noise—mostly snickers and laughter—from the hot, over-packed room of well-wishers and curiosity-seekers. In the silence within her *Nonno's* cocoon, she strained to hear his usual soft, raspy breath. But there was only the maudlin sound of a piano coming through the tinny ceiling speaker in the drop ceiling above her. Well, that and her own open-mouthed, raspy breath.

She looked at his purple eyelids and, having overheard eyelids were sewn together, wanted a better look. She searched with her toe for something to push against, and felt a vase that overflowed with white and pink carnations next to her, give way and topple.

"Maria."

Maria sighed and straightened up. She pushed her bundled-up skirt down and studied the carnation arrangement now sprawled like a flattened dead bird. It reminded her of a dehydrated and headless white dove she had seen under a juniper bush at the graveyard once, its neck encrusted in blood, its feathers spread in a strangely regal manner.

She quickly bent down to right the urn. There, something caught her eye at the bottom of the coffin: The tip of a tie. She shot up and looked at her *Nonno's* tie. Not the same. She bent down, lifted the tie's end and eyed the slit in the wooden coffin from where the tip extended.

"Maria."

Maria dropped the tie and scurried back to her seat between Andy and her father, Stefano Giordani.

Forty-year-old Stefano sat quietly with his mitts for paws resting peacefully on his muscular thighs. He raised them to encircle Maria's shoulders as she squirmed closer to him. He patted her and smiled, winking.

"Dad?"

He shushed her and held a finger to his lips.

She looked down at his well-creased pants, always surprised to see how he transformed into one of her Ken dolls when he dressed the occasional time in a fine suit instead of his customary red plaid lumberjack quilted jacket and work boots, or fresh T-shirt and jeans after his evening showers after work.

She leaned in and upwards and held up a hand to her mouth. "You look handsome," she whispered.

His thick eyelashes lowered over his brilliant eyes and he smiled slightly, pleased.

"But Dad, I see a tie," she tried again.

A sturdy finger at the lips and a shake of his head made her stop. She thought she'd try her mother. She turned and looked at the tie before gently tugging at her mother's long sleeve. "Mom, I saw a tie."

Andy turned to her sister-in-law, Sandra Giordani, who sat quietly behind them. "When's *Zio* Leo coming?" asked Andy, glancing at her gold watch. She looked at the ceiling and shook her head in disapproval. "And what's this crap playing?"

Sandra looked at her husband, Peter Giordani who happened to be the funeral director. He nervously hovered at the end of their row, keeping a steely eye on everyone.

The room was full of grieving and respectful Calabrian *famiglia* and old friends of Fabrizio di Giovanni, Maria's grandfather. The room had a disturbing air of aloofness—almost a sense of joviality. To make matters worse, Constable Stan, their local *ghoul in blue*, was watching over the gathering, so, they couldn't afford to slip up.

Peter nervously looked at his watch.

"Peter."

Peter jumped, startled by Sandra, her eyebrows raised.

Sandra pointed with a manicured finger at the drop ceiling. "What's playing now, Andy wants to know?"

"It's called, *The Day Thou Gavest, Lord, is Ended.* Good funeral stuff. People lap this shit up."

"*Nonno* always liked Culture Club," Maria offered from her chair, impatiently kicking her feet.

"We are not going to play Culture Club at your *Nonno's* funeral," Andy announced, pressing her hand firmly on Maria's legs to stop her kicking.

"Mom, there's a tie…" Maria pointed.

Stefano nudged his daughter gently. "*Si*, Maria, *Nonno* like'a your Culture Club."

"Dad, I saw something."

Her father sushed and winked at her lovingly.

"Give me a break. *Nonno* was as deaf as a doornail. He only pretended," Andy muttered.

"Mom, you're not hearing me."

"Maria, shut up," said Andy.

Maria eyed her father, looking down at her from under his lids. He wagged his finger at her in warning. She crossed her arms and pouted.

Andy leaned over Maria to look at her grieving mother at the end of the row, a small, petite, veiled woman clad in black, leaning silently against a wall. "Ma, what do you want for music?"

Claudia di Giovanni sniffed and shrugged. "Fabrizio, he alway' love'a *Ave Maria*." She raised a lace handkerchief to her nose and reached past Stefano to pat Maria's hand. "*Nonno* like'a you *Caughtcha Club'a*."

"*Culture Club*, *Nonna*. And *Nonna*, I see a tie," Maria said.

Standing in an aisle, Peter leaned in. "What did Claudia say?"

"*Ave Maria*," repeated Sandra.

Peter quickly motioned to an adjacent minion. "Ditch the music and play *Ave Maria* for Claudia."

The minion nodded and hurried off.

Someone suddenly howled mournfully from the back. Maria craned her neck to look at a gathering of another grieving throng out in the main lobby of the elegant Vindenza Funeral Home.

"Hey, who are they here for?" asked Andy, twisting in her chair.

"It's Tomasino Valpaccio," Peter muttered. He jiggled change in his pocket.

"Tomasino died?" Andy whispered, appalled.

"No, his son." He coughed into his hand and waved a weak-limped wrist.

"That's not nice," Sandra whispered, shaking her head. She was the only one in the family who wasn't wearing black; Orange, for some reason.

"What do you mean?" said Andy, mimicking the limp wave. "What's this?"

"You know…" Peter bent down with a grim face as all around him leaned in to hear.

Andy covered Maria's ears.

"His son was killed." Peter straightened and nodded. He wiggled his eyebrows.

Gentle harp strings of *Ave Maria* floated down.

"Oh my god, not Vitorino." Andy let go of Maria's ears.

"What, Mom?"

"What happened, Peter?" Sandra shifted her buttocks and twisted to better look back into the lobby.

"He committed a heinous crime."

"What the hell did he do?" Andy said. "He was so young."

Maria climbed onto her knees on the chair to also get a better look at the curious group out back. People were stepping into view. There appeared to be a slight altercation amongst the men.

"He became Vitarina." Peter tapped the side of his nose.

Everyone frowned, confused.

"He changed his name...?" Sandra tried to cross her legs in a tight dress and gave up.

"He changed everything, if you know what I mean." Peter flicked a look at Andy.

"Shit," said Andy.

"What does that mean, Mom?"

Stefano shot up from his seat. He moved past Maria and Andy, and stood next to his brother in the aisle. His eyes nervously flashed at the back throng. "Pietro, talk'a to me."

"The kid was found in the dumpster back of our mall."

"What?" asked Andy. "*Our* mall? When?"

"It happened the day after Fabrizio died," Peter said. He motioned to his *Zio*'s body in the coffin.

Stefano grabbed Peter's arm and moved him away from the women. He looked back at his little daughter, then jerked his head at Peter questioningly.

"Stef, the kid was found with his *stugats* in his mouth. I mean, he was wearing girl's clothes, had lipstick and full make-up." Peter frowned and shook his head. "Stupid kid. He came out of the proverbial closet."

Stefano shivered. "Who did this? *I Siciliani*?"

Peter nodded, then shook his head, and shrugged. "Maybe. Or their West End Gang." Peter looked around. "Or could be anyone of us. Some people like to do this kind of shit."

Stefano clenched his jaw. He looked at Andy, and his eyes squinted at Maria.

Maria innocently pursed her lips at her father. She blinked, her eyes large and questioning. "What?"

Andy wrapped her arm around her daughter and pulled her closer.

"Mom, that hurts." Maria gazed at the tongue of the tie again. Blue stripes. *Familiar* blue stripes. Maria frowned.

Stefano nervously adjusted his own tie and pushed Peter out of the way to hurry up the aisle to the lobby.

Peter grabbed Stefano's wrist. "Where are you going?"

"*Per porgere le mie condoglianze.* Is what we should do."

"I already did for the family when I made their funeral arrangements," Peter said, letting go the wrist.

"Why you no say somethin' to me?" hissed Stefano.

Peter shrugged and motioned to family members. "You were all caught up with Fabrizio's death. I wasn't' gonna bother you with this shit. Why are you so upset? It's just a screwed-up kid."

Stefano looked at Andy watching them, craning her neck. She shifted her weight and let go of Maria. She climbed on her knees on the chair and reached out toward Stefano, motioning for him to come back to his seat.

He didn't budge.

She stood up. "Wait, Stef, I'll come with you, then." She rubbed down the creases in her skirt and noticed the run in her stocking. "Shit."

Stefano didn't wait for her. He quickly moved through mourners and onlookers in the aisle to the back doors. Suddenly, through the crowd in the lobby, a blonde apparition in black filled his consciousness. Anita Taylor appeared in the doorway. He stopped and looked at her short, slim figure and her finely chiseled face, his heart pounding.

Anita's eyes widened as she saw his handsome face. "Stefano, I'm so, so sorry about Fabrizio." She had been crying, her mascara smudged and dried. She looked as if she hadn't slept for days. Her eyes darted to the front of the room where Andy stood watching. She noted the look of hate. "I know Andy hates me now, Stef. I'm so sorry. Maybe I shouldn't be here."

Stefano shook his head, and his hair fell over his broad forehead. "Is'a accident. Is not your fault."

"I feel I need to give my condolences, though, especially to Claudia. I need to explain why I jumped and fell on him..."

Someone nearby broke out laughing.

Stefano quickly turned and saw three of Fabrizio's old friends, all balding, grey, grizzled, and bent, jovially smiling at Anita and him. One elderly toothless gentleman grinned through his gums, apparently enjoying a joke Stefano knew was at his father-in-law's expense. He overheard the words "boobs", "*seni*", and "suffocating."

Anita looked at them, appalled and humiliated. "I didn't know Rose was crossing right in front of him. I just wanted to kill her. I didn't intend for us to fall on Fabrizio in his wheelchair. I didn't know what I was doing, I was so stupid crazy. It's this thing about Jack missing and him having an affair with her, that's got me confused, Stefano. That woman wore *my fur coat*, Stef. He gave *my coat* to her." She covered her eyes and shook her blonde curls. "I don't think I'm right in the head, anymore. Jack is driving me nuts."

He reached out and squeezed her arm.

"Stef, I just saw red." She broke into tears and covered her eyes. "Oh, how awful, how terrible. Poor Fabrizio. Sick and on oxygen. He didn't deserve that." She wrung a damp tissue.

Stefano cradled her against his chest. He glanced back at the front row to see Andy angrily watching them. He gave her a warning look. "Shhhh, Anita. Is no your fault."

"Oh, Stef, I also lost my job because of this."

"At the radio station?"

She pulled back, pushed blonde tendrils out of her face, and sadly nodded. "Remember? Everything was live and on-air, as part of your mall's Grand Opening celebrations. It was a big deal. That whole fight, everything I screamed, was caught on the radio." She looked at him. She smiled grimly, "I said the 'F' word and more than once.

A big no-no on air." She furtively cocked her head. "Have you seen or heard from him, Stef? Anything at all?"

"Jack?" Stefano inhaled deeply, raised his chin and looked over the throng. He saw Tomasino Valpaccio, standing next to his bent wife, glaring at a man who was reprimanding him, threateningly wagging a finger in Tomasino's face. Stefano's senses prickled. He dragged his piercing eyes away, lowering them onto Anita's own grey-blue peepers. He shook his head. "No. I no'a hear from Jack. And Peter say he no hear from him since before." He motioned at her and at the coffin in their room.

Anita gently pulled at Stefano's suit collar, straightening it out a little. "Stef, I need to talk to you. Jack's going to kill me when he finds out. I think I'm—"

"Get your fucking hands off of my husband." Andy screamed from the front of the room.

Everyone went dead quiet in the sweltering lobby. For a moment, everyone could hear the angelic singing and harp of *Ave Maria*.

"Fight," someone joked.

Someone else giggled.

Stefano glared at Andy. She stood with clenched fists, glaring back.

He looked down at Anita whose face had turned white. She was about to walk away, when he grabbed her arm. He took a deep breath. His nostrils flared. He angrily looked around.

In fear or respect, many looked away. The formidable Stefano Giordani was the *famiglia Zio*, after all, the head of the local 'Ndrina.

"Come," Stefano said quietly, taking Anita's elbow, guiding her to the front. "You go see Claudia."

An elderly woman in an aisle seat grabbed Anita's winter coat as they passed. Anita stumbled to a stop and sadly looked back.

"You'a find you'a *marito*, Jack?"

Anita shook her head. "No, Mrs. Santorino. Not yet. No one knows where he is."

Mrs. Santorino smiled kindly and winked. "You'a find him. You're a beautiful wife. He come back, no worry."

Anita bent down and allowed Mrs. Santorino to peck her on her tear-streaked cheek. She stood back and wiped her cheek.

"AS IF SHE WAS THE ONLY WOMAN in the world whose husband runs off on her. What a friggin' martyr." Andy angrily hissed. She wanted to wallop Anita. *What the hell was she doing here at the funeral?*

"Go easy on her, Andy." Peter gave her a warning look, as Stefano and Anita approached.

Peter gently gave Anita a hug, and kissed both sides of her face. "I know you feel terrible. He was on his last legs, anyway." He shrugged. "You actually gave him a happy send-off. That's how you should think about it. He was smiling, for Christ's sake, with boobs on his face."

"Don't be so crass," said Sandra from her chair in the second row.

Andy snorted. She watched Anita smile faintly at Peter. "You're the reason why my father is in that box." Andy spat at her and pointed at the coffin.

Still sitting on her knees, Maria jumped up off the chair and pushed her mother aside. She lunged at Anita and grabbed her midriff. "Anita. I missed you."

Anita tousled Maria's cropped hair. "I'm so sorry about your *Nonno*, Maria. It's all my fault, I'm afraid."

"God dammed right, it's your fault." Andy stood, her arms crossed in defiance.

"Oh, Anitaaaaaaa."

Andy watched her mother stand up from her chair near the wall, and hobble toward Anita, arms outstretched.

Andy dropped her arms. "Ah, Ma. Give me a break."

Claudia ignored her daughter and continued towards Anita, sobbing, allowing Anita to wrap her arms around her. They stood and rocked together.

"Oh, for frigg's sake," muttered Andy. Disgusted, she flopped into her seat. Her nostrils flared. Her eyes rested on the urn by the coffin. She blinked, and looked at the scattered petals on the floor. She was about to get up and clean the mess when she suddenly spied the tip of a tie and fell back down. "What the…?" Andy slowly rose, stepped toward the coffin, and sunk onto her haunches to yank at the tie. Her stocking run crawled all the way over her knee. "Fuck," she muttered, as she looked at her knee. She re-focused on the tie and pulled at it. It gave an inch and stopped. She stood and looked into the coffin, at her father's tie. She touched the knot, then looked back at her brother-in-law. "Peter. What the fuck?"

Peter's face dropped. "What are you doing, Andy?"

She frantically motioned at him, pointing at the tip of the tie on the floor.

He stood on tiptoes and looked. "Shit." His eyes widened. His face went pale, then instantly red, and he desperately looked around the room.

"I tried to tell you, Mom," Maria protested, looking at her mother from where she stood, squished between her *Nonna* and Anita.

"Tell'a you Mamma what?" Maria's *Nonna*, Claudia, asked. Both Claudia and Anita looked curiously at Maria, then Andy. Then they looked down to where Andy was looking. They saw the tie. "Who lost'a dat tie?" asked Claudia, stepping away from Anita, toward the coffin. She stopped and stared, as Andy fought with the large urn of flowers, to hide it from others.

Andy grunted. "Help me, Ma. We have to hide this."

"*Che?*" Claudia asked, open-mouthed, and raised her eyes to look at the tie her husband wore in the coffin.

Peter hurried over. "Quick, Andy. Hide it." Peter shot a glance at Constable Stan nearby.

Andy looked at the cop as well. "Shit, Peter. This is shoddy." They struggled with the urn, then both straightened out only to see Constable Stan frowning at them, as if he read their minds.

Andy looked away. "Oh, shit, Peter. Don't look now." She heard a gasp and looked to see Anita rush toward them and drop at Andy's feet.

Andy viciously kicked at her. "No, Anita. No. Get the hell out of here."

"But that's Jack's tie," whispered Anita, as she frantically fingered the tip of the tie. "I bought it," she said, loudly.

Andy kicked her again. She swallowed hard, and her eyes went back to Constable Stan. "Anita, for Christ's sake, listen to me. Now's not the time. Get up." She clawed at Anita's back.

Anita slapped her back. "What do you mean, now's not the time? I wanna know why Jack's tie is sticking out of this coffin."

"Shut up." Andy grabbed Anita's hair and tried to pull her to her feet. The two women began a slap fight next to the urn, causing more pink and white carnation petals to sift and flutter to the ground. "Leave it," yelled Andy.

STEFANO FROWNED AT THE SIGHT of the two women, wondering why the very best of friends were fighting like two irate lionesses. Curious, he stood on tiptoe to see what they were fighting over. On the floor amongst the flower petals and the women's feet he saw the tie. He cocked his head and squinted. It sure looked familiar. Stefano swirled around and grabbed Peter by the collar. "Tell me is'a no Jack in dere…"

Peter tried to pull away. "I'm sorry. It's Jack this time, Stef. Something shitty happened, and I didn't know what else to do." He shrugged. "And, it's what I do, Stef, right? I get rid of bodies. So how was I *supposed* to get rid of him?"

Stefano's face paled. He clenched his jaws. "In Fabrizio's coffin?"

Peter jiggled his head. "The others were taken."

Stefano noticed Constable Stan moving slowly toward them. "Who did this'a? Venezuela? *I Siciliani* in Montreal?"

"Nope, not them. You'll never believe who did." Peter fidgeted with Stefano's knuckles at his neck. "It was Nancy. Jealous rage over that Rose."

Stefano glanced at Anita, now on her knees crying and clawing at the coffin above the tie. He fumed. *That goddamn Jack couldn't keep it in his pants.* Stefano pulled back a fist at Peter, and hesitated while his fist shook in mid-air. "How'a can you do this'a to Anita?"

Peter put up his hands. "Not the face, Stef. Not the face."

Stefano landed a full punch in his brother's face, launching Peter back into the front row.

Sandra, appalled, stood up and looked down at her beautiful husband's classic nose bleeding over his white collar, silk tie, and thousand-dollar suit from Rome. She struggled out of the tight row of chairs and heaved herself at Stefano, knocking over an end chair.

Stefano brushed off her punch.

Andy, startled, backed against the coffin at the sight of Sandra attacking Stefano. She pushed Anita over onto her side against the urn, toppling it again. She flew to her husband's side, screeching like a banshee. With a grunt, Andy pushed her sister-in-law away from Stef.

Sandra, her tummy and breasts jiggling like Jell-O, toppled backward over her husband, digging an Italian stiletto-heeled shoe into his bony shin and blood splattered pant leg.

Peter howled.

Stefano watched Peter's funeral minions rushing over to help. Then, they stopped when they saw his threatening glare, warning them to stay away. They stood confused, as if they did not know how to intervene in a fight between the two most powerful brothers in Canada's notorious *'Ndrangheta*— the Calabrian Mafia of the Eastern Townships of Quebec. Suddenly, Stefano felt his sleeve tugged. He looked down at a disturbed Maria.

"Daddy. Is *Zio* Jack dead, too?"

A gunshot ripped through the packed lobby, and people screamed.

"Oh my God, it's Tomasino Valpaccio. He's dead," someone howled.

More people screamed. Another shot rang out. In shock, Stefano almost pushed his little daughter to the ground in his haste to rush back to the lobby, a gun drawn from his jacket.

Maria watched her father brutally push people out of the way, as he rushed with Peter to the lobby. Everyone scattered. She looked around. Absolutely no one took notice of her anymore. Maria pouted and left the world of adults to their own craziness, and trudged back to her seat. She flopped down and angrily crossed her arms, staring at Anita crying over the tie on the floor. "Oh, brother. People keep dying around here."

CHAPTER TWO

January 1984

S TEFANO STOOD SHIVERING but kept his senses sharp. He waited patiently in the crisp, biting wind which pummeled him from across the rolling fields.

He threw up his suit collar against the cold and dug his paws deeper into his pockets. He peered at the sky. Hidden above a low ceiling of linen-colored clouds, the sun burned like molten steel. He looked around. The light cast a bright silver hue over the flowing Quebec landscape.

There was almost complete silence, save for the soft hiss of dead cornstalks in the fields and the rattle of ice pellets racing across his driveway.

He glanced back at the barn. No animal or chicken in sight. Not even a sparrow in the bare sycamore trees that lined the wall of snow piled along the driveway.

He looked down and stomped his feet. Suddenly, he heard a squawk. He looked up to see a black crow land with a clatter on the edge of his garage's rain gutter. The crow's head bobbed in quick succession. Then, it flapped its wings up into the air and shifted and circled above his head. It cawed loudly before swerving to the road and over the landscape until Stefano could no longer focus on its image.

Stefano had carefully chosen these 200 acres, years before. The land was close enough to Vindenza, within an hour of Montreal, yet still very secluded, and out of the way of regular traffic. His nearest neighbors were out of sight, and he had specifically built his home on top of a small crest giving him a clear view in all directions.

Agitated, he blinked back tears caused by the wind, and glared when he spotted the glint of a shiny, black car appear in the distance. It disappeared into a gully and reappeared again, slowly, steadily, spewing dry snow and ice pellets in its wake.

He pulled out his calloused hands, blew into them, and rubbed them together quickly. He calmly watched the car, a black Mercedes, slow down and turn into his driveway.

Bile rose in his throat, as he thought of his brother. That Peter was held without bail in jail didn't bother him in the least. In fact, it was probably the safest place in all of Vindenza—probably the entire world, at this point. What Peter faced through the justice system was nothing compared to what he faced with those higher up. Peter had broken an *'Ndrangheta* rule. He and a non *'Ndrina* member, the now dead Jack Taylor, had gone rogue.

It was Jack's influence, Stefano damn well knew. His little brother, Peter, didn't have it in him. But there you go. He did something bad, and he was caught. Now big brother had to figure out how to save his life, their *'Ndrina* reputation, and perhaps the lives of their families. The only way was to face the dragon, himself—the chairman of the North American *'Ndrangheta* out of Venezuela, Jorge Pesseck.

Stefano swallowed hard.

The Mercedes crawled up the driveway and came to a stop in front of Stefano. Its engine clicked, hissing, hot metal against frozen air. A dark, good-looking young driver with black curly hair that whipped in the wind, opened the door and stepped out. He stood tall, slender in black leather jacket and gloves which he pushed down tighter over his fingers as he looked around. He was exotic-looking, Stefano thought. Italian with a touch of ebony.

The driver turned to Stefano, and nodded deferentially. He took long strides to open the back-passenger door. The driver scanned the landscape, his eyes keen and focused, then nodded at the passenger. He held out his hand. A much older man took his hand and stepped out and looked over. The passenger wore sunglasses against the glare, thick black gloves, and a quilted black coat. He wore a grey fedora—a hat strikingly out of place in this frigid environment. He grimly looked at Stefano. He stepped past his driver and waited for him to close the door and lead him away from the car.

Stefano noticed his shoes were brightly polished, black patent leather. He wore black dress pants, finely pressed. The material too thin, Stefano imagined the wind cut right through the fabric. It was a lousy time of year to have to fly all the way from Venezuela, for a meeting in Quebec in the middle of winter. But these, he knew, were extraordinary circumstances. He breathed deeply with resolve through his nostrils, and stepped forward, hand outstretched.

"*Benvenuta, Signor* Pessek."

The man shook his hand briefly as he tightened his collar around his neck.

"Stefano Giordani," Stefano said, bowing slightly. "How was your trip from Venezuela?"

"Far too long. I was just here two months ago and the jet lag was a bugger. Didn't look forward to this." He looked around the fields. "But call me Jorge, Stefano. Leo's a good friend of mine. I understand your wife is his long, lost niece."

"*Sì,* she is'a."

Jorge shivered and motioned to the young man behind him. "This is my son, Alessandro. He's accompanying me on this trip. I'm grooming him for better days." Jorge Pesseck smiled, and a gold tooth glinted in the light.

Stefano nodded at Alessandro.

"Nice to meet you, Mr. Giordani."

Stefano stared at him for a moment. A fine son. Polite. He seemed to have it together. He shook Alessandro's outstretched hand, then turned to lead Jorge quickly out of the wind to his open garage. "You wan' I give him something to drink?" Stefano motioned back at Alessandro.

"Nah, he's okay. I told him to stay with the car unless I call for him. Is Leo here already?"

"*Sì.*" Stefano pushed a button at the side of the front door to close the garage. As the heavy doors noisily clattered shut and echoed with a bang, he motioned to a large hole in the cement floor. Light and steam emanated from the depths below. This access to a secret room was customarily hidden under a tarp and a large metal slab slid, now to the side. On top of that, always stood Stefano's Cadillac—a car he treasured but rarely used. Today, the Cadillac was parked to the side, where Andy usually parked her Volvo.

Jorge walked up to the *caverna* opening and leaned on the top of a sunken ladder to peek inside. "Hey, you ol' bugger. Are you there? Show me your ugly snout." Jorge laughed at his own joke.

Stefano listened to Leo's roar with laughter from the bowels of the *caverna*. He walked over and stepped in front of Jorge, to go first. Six rungs. He looked up the ladder and motioned for Jorge to follow.

At the base of the ladder, sat Leo Mangione, perched on a wooden crate and smoking his proverbial Cuban cigar. Off to the side, on stools, sat Stefano's cousins Mario and Guido.

Jorge looked at the scene below him, from the garage floor.

"Jorge, come on down and join us. It's warmer down here, and we'll close the hatch," said Leo.

Jorge pulled off his gloves and timidly reached for the ladder. He put a polished shoe gently on the first rung. Leo stood up opposite Stefano, and reached up. The two men gently kept their palms on Jorge's back as he slowly lowered himself onto the concrete floor.

He planted both feet on the ground, turned with a crunch and nodded at Mario and Guido.

They stood and nodded defentially. The top of their hair brushed the bottom of the steel rafter above them.

"Mario, Guido."

"Mr. Pessek'a," mumbled Mario, nodding once again.

"Jorge." His gold teeth glinted in the candlelight. He looked around, allowing his eyes to adjust to the faint light. In front of him was a small table with three burning candles. On the floor, was a rusty floor heater; its luminescent red and orange elements hummed and rattled as the fan roared hot air around their feet.

Small, thin, bat-like cadavers of sausage and teardrops of cloth-covered cheeses hung from the steel rafters, looking as if they danced with surrounding shadows. Against a wall stood a wooden rack. A spider web swayed in the currents of air. Each shelf in the rack was packed with reclining bottles of homemade wine, *grappa*, vinegars and olive oil.

Beside the rack, was a door that led into the basement through Andy's laundry room. It was slightly ajar to let heat into the *caverna*. From the depths of the sacred hiding spot, they could just make out faint music playing off a radio in the house.

"Sit, Jorge, please. We have a nice warm heater here by our feet. Not as warm as Venezuela, I know." Leo slapped Jorge on the back and motion for him to sit on a cushion-covered stool. Everyone took their seats.

"Invigorating, this cold," Jorge said, breaking into a smile in Leo's direction. "I didn't quite acclimatize last time I was here."

Stefano reached up and unhooked two small doors from below the garage floor and locked them in place.

Between them, the air quickly started to warm.

"Listen, I'm sorry you had to come all the way back again so soon," Leo grunted. "Look at you, you're still shivering."

Jorge rubbed his hands.

Stefano pushed the space heater toward Jorge who thankfully leaned toward it, hands outstretched.

"You got any *grappa*?" asked Jorge.

Stefano smiled contentedly and reached for a green glass bottle and a ceramic cup. He poured a hefty amount and handed it to Jorge. Stefano topped up everyone else's cups. "I make'a dis *grappa*," he said proudly, softly. He smiled at Jorge.

"Ah, home-made. *Grappa* always reminds me of my mother," Jorge said. He pulled out a tissue and wiped his nose before holding the cup up. "My Dad was German, but my mother is Italian. She lives with us. I don't know what I'd do without her cooking."

"Don't get me started on food," Leo laughed. "Wait till you taste my Yvonne's cooking. My café drew clients and fishermen from along the Georgia and South Carolina seaboard before it was destroyed by a twister." Leo shifted and raised his cup. "But first..."

Everyone raised their cups.

"*Faccio un brindisi,*" he announced. "To your health and a safe return."

Jorge took a sip. He closed his eyes. "Aaaaah."

Stefano watched Leo's smile fade quickly. He steeled himself for the verbal showdown—the news from the rest of the Consortium.

"Now to serious business," Leo said.

Stefano looked down into his cup. The Consortium in Venezuela, Stefano already knew, wanted Peter's head. Jorge, though the Chairman, was only the go-between and not the arbitrator. Precisely because Leo was a good friend of Jorge, there was a sliver of hope they could save Peter's life.

Jorge motioned for Leo to continue.

"We got the missing money, as you know. That's why you're here."

"Where is it now?" Jorge asked.

Stefano turned to face Mario who bent and picked up a heavy, bloodied canvas bag and handed it to him. Peter had found it hidden under Rose's apartment floorboards, at the same time he discovered Jack's body. It was a godsend that Jack was killed before running off with it. Stefano took the hefty bag and set it at Jorge's feet.

"And we gotta appease everyone so that we can preserve Peter's life," Leo said, pulling out a new cigar. "Yes, he shouldn't've let this Jack Taylor, who was his partner in a plastics company, do what Peter was *assigned* to do. By you. He was being lazy."

"Plastics. That was the connection with this Jack Taylor?" Jorge asked. He looked down at the cigar offered him by Leo and thankfully took it. He bent over as Leo nodded and lit it for him.

"Now, as you know, Jack Taylor was not *famiglia*." Leo said. "He and Peter were buddies from school and did guy things, you know. Like goin' on Las Vegas junkets together. They frequented the race-track. They even owned a racehorse together. But this, I know, was unforgivable in itself. We're sorry. We apologize. Also, sending Jack to Venezuela instead of himself to deliver the money to the Consortium in Venezuela—that was disrespectful. Not that anything different may have happened if Peter went instead. Getting kidnapped by merce-naries in Venezuela was something nobody expected, but somehow Jack escaped with the money and came back here to Vindenza; I think his brush with death was why he was emboldened to try and figure out how to keep the money. Can you blame a guy like that? I wouldn't do it. But a snot-nose like him?" Leo shrugged. "He had no honor to begin with. Weak. I know Peter wouldn't have done that." Leo flicked the ash from his cigar into a coffee tin half-filled with cigarette and cigar stubs.

"That's why you sent me to assassinate him," Jorge said.

Leo pursed his lips and nodded. "He was going to run off with this dame—"

"Rose," Jorge offered, smiling slightly. He tapped his cigar against the edge of the coffee can. "I've gotten to know Rose quite well. She's in Venezuela, in my home, as we speak."

Stefano blinked.

Leo did, too. "You, old dog."

Jorge smiled and took a sip of *grappa*. "I got to know her quite well. She told me she liked monkeys, you see, and I asked her if she wanted to see some in Venezuela. For some reason, she accepted."

Leo slapped his knee. "Just like that."

"Just like that. But I don't understand how you people can live in a country like this when you have the whole world to choose from. People die in this freezing cold."

"I live in the South. I don't do this shit," said Leo.

Jorge looked at Stefano, who shrugged and grinned. "Is'a home."

"Home. Vindenza. Quebec, Canada." Jorge sat back and unzipped his coat. He started to take it off, and Leo helped by pulling at the neck. "This little town, Vindenza," continued Jorge, "It's not a bad little place, but it has only one dumpy motel."

"The Nova Vida Motel," said Leo.

"Yeah, and there was this guy who kept singing opera at the top of his lungs. At all hours, keeping me awake."

Leo burst out laughing and pulled out a tissue. He had to wait to catch his breath and wipe his eyes before he was able to speak. "That was me. I was trying to get to you before you knocked off Taylor but couldn't find you. You mean you were right under my nose all that time?"

Stefano cleared his throat and leaned toward Jorge and waited until Jorge looked at him.

"Jorge, *per favore*. I have a proposal for the Consortium. As a penitence'a for Peter, we pay half as extra on top'a of this money." He put his large hand on the canvas bag. "This is'a five million American dollars. So, another two million and a half from'a my own pocket. We ask'a for Peter to be safe. We are small here. 'N Peter, he take'a care of maybe thirty of the business we have, so we need him."

Leo said, "'N if you need more sweetener, I'll throw in that much more. Whatever it takes. Listen, Jorge, these businesses are mostly small. Funeral parlor, flower shop, a couple of pizza joints, ladies' shops, a couple of other restaurants, but they add up. Right now, we're waitin' to see what Peter's going to be charged with. At first, they tried to pin the murder on him. As you know, it was the other mistress, Nancy who admitted to killing him out of jealousy over Rose."

"Ah, yes. Rose," said Jorge, smiling.

"At worst, I think, he'll be charged with unlawfully hiding a dead body by trying to get rid of it under my brother's body in his coffin."

Jorge looked amused. "May God rest his soul."

"Well, it's something they do here as a service for the others," said Leo.

Mario and Guido chuckled.

Leo pointed to the two cousins. "These guys here usually do it, but Mario's been out West workin' and Guido's been busy with other stuff so Peter had to do it on his own. Whatever, whoever and why, it was shoddily done. Jack's tie stuck out. Dead giveaway." Leo shrugged and made a face.

"What's happening with Taylor's widow? What does she know?" Jorge asked.

Stefano shifted his bulk. He suddenly felt overheated. "Anita, we take care of. If'a Jack was *famiglia*, she would get money from the *famiglia*. But he wasn't so, I'a, I will make'a sure she's okay."

"Why? What's she to you? She's not *famiglia*."

Stefano looked at Jorge. He knew he could never explain what Anita meant to him. "She'a Adriana's best friend." He turned and pointed at Mario and Guido. "I have Mario keep'a watch on her. She know'a nothing."

Jorge nodded. "Who is taking Peter's place in the businesses while he's indisposed?"

"Sandra, his'a wife. She's smart'a. Good worker."

"And another thing, Jorge. Tell 'em we got plans—big ones." Leo raised his cigar in the air. "We're expanding. Now that I've found a family I didn't know I had, thank *Santa Maria*, we got a whole tribe here. We're going to work together, expand south 'n maybe west and east. Personally, I have dibs on hundreds of acres in the marsh just outside of Myrtle Beach, South Carolina. I'm doin' a theme park, restaurants, rides—great ways to wash money. The accounting will be a cinch. Stef, here, is going to do the construction part. We can launder money through the process easily and immediately for you. You know, the usual; hire people who don't work for us. It'll cost us a hell of a lot more on the books to build everything." He sat back and looked pointedly at Jorge. "I'm offering 30% ownership of my theme park to the Consortium in return for giving us all another chance, and to keep Peter alive."

Jorge sat back, deep in thought.

Stefano tried to read what he was thinking. He had to accept only Jorge could know what the Consortium was likely to do. They were like whimsical gods. He had heard terrible stories of what happened to people who messed with them over the years.

Jorge pointed at Leo and the others. "You must remember. No secrets that can raise their ugly heads and bite us in the ass later. You've got secrets, they get in the way, and you're in deep shit."

"Secrets?" asked Leo. "What kind of secrets?"

"Anything that can upset the apple cart."

Stefano cleared his throat nervously. He thought about the upset caused by Tomasino Valpaccio's son's secret. The rift caused by Tomasino's son's personal challenges and his consequent torture and murder started a turf war in the other township. Not only was Tomasino killed, but several of his family members. It even got into the news. He thought of his own special Maria and broke out into a cold sweat. He took out a handkerchief from his pants and dabbed his clammy forehead.

"We don't have secrets." Leo raised his shoulders and looked at Stefano, Mario and Guido. "What's there to be secret about? We're completely transparent. What you see is what you get. And we are offering the best from here on in."

Jorge grunted and changed the subject. "Who's your lawyer?"

Leo turned to Stefano.

Stefano looked back at Leo. They had this discussion during the previous few days. Stefano wasn't too happy with the one they had now.

"Right, we'll find a good one for you," said Jorge, not waiting for an answer. "You should have a trusted *'Ndrina* lawyer handy in the *famiglia*. I'll send someone your way."

"I've actually looked into that for future business," said Leo. "I'm sending Willie, my stepson-to-be, to study law. He's very bright, and I trust him with my life."

"That's good. A lawyer in the direct *famiglia* is a must if you want to expand as grandly as you plan." Jorge's eyes moistened. "You getting married, Leo? Stepson-to-be?"

Leo grinned. "I'm marrying my *bella* Yvonne. The most beautiful and big-hearted woman I have ever known. She's changed me for the better, Jorge. She told me she wanted nothin' to do with me if I kept killing people. That's why I chased you up here from Georgia to stop you from killin' Jack Taylor. She would've seen it as blood on *my* own hands." He tossed his cigar stub into the coffee tin and clasped his hands together, leaning his elbows on his knees. "'N if it wasn't for her putting her foot down, I wouldn't have found my *famiglia* here in Canada." He lowered his head sadly. "I only got a glimpse of my brother, Fabrizio, moments before he died. But now." He looked at Stefano with dewy, bloodshot eyes. Leo reached out and grabbed Stefano's left hand. He squeezed tightly.

Stefano was suddenly overwhelmed with emotion.

"Now, I am blessed with nephews and nieces, distant cousins," Leo motioned back to Mario and Guido. "And also great-nephews through Peter and a great-niece, Maria, with Stef." Leo pulled another cigar from an inside pocket. "And all this miraculously happened because of a tornado destroying all I had going in Georgia. And, I tell you, Jorge, I didn't care about all that when it came right down to it. It takes something like having the world torn apart around you to know what's important in life."

"What happened?" Jorge asked.

"I was sittin' on my chair at the counter in my café. I was on the phone when everything exploded around us. It was a twister. Before I knew it, I woke up at the docks in the middle of my destroyed boat facing this little statue I have of *Santa Maria* glued to the helm of my boat. Is that a message or what?" Leo shook his head, amazed. "At that moment, all I cared about was Yvonne and her son, Willie. I prayed to *Santa Maria* and promised I would never lay a hand on another human being again if She would save them." He raised his shoulders and held his palms up in the air. "They just disappeared. I didn't know if they were dead or alive. Somehow, later, I found them in Darien and I knew I had to fulfill my promise to *Santa Maria*. I dropped everything in Georgia to race after you to stop you from doin' the hit up here. And here I am. *Santa Maria* answered my prayers and more. I'm now getting married, and I have an entire *famiglia* I never knew I had." Leo stopped and suddenly covered his eyes.

All the men reached and patted him.

Leo sighed and looked up. He smiled sadly at Jorge. "So, Jorge. What do you think? Can we create another miracle and save my nephew's life?"

Jorge pursed his lips. "I will take your proposal straight to them. You're offering a fairly good cut from this new venture in Myrtle Beach." He motioned around and cocked his head. "You're adding half again on the money owing. And offering more. Thirty percent of the expansions." He shrugged and made a face. "It's better for them in the long run, that's obvious. 'N I'll tell em so. They trust me."

"What about Peter," asked Stefano.

"That, we'll see," said Jorge smiled. "I will let you know."

ANDY'S VOLVO crept into the driveway and came to a stop a short distance from the Mercedes. As they approached, Andy and Maria watched a young, well-dressed man step out of the car and lean back against the back-passenger door to watch them park.

Andy turned off the ignition and looked over at Maria, who sat in her burgundy parka with raggedy fur-trimmed hood. She wore torn khaki pants under her school uniform skirt and had rested her boots, wet and encrusted with road salt, on top of the dirty dash. Today, she sported a cut across the top of her cheek.

Maria looked out the window at the young man, and then sideways at her mother, questioningly.

"Don't look at him. He's business. Take your friggin' boots off the godamn dash."

"Business?" Maria's eyes widened, as she struggled to lower her boots. She looked at the handsome young man again.

"Oh, for crying out loud, I told you not to look at him."

"Why not?"

"Cause you never know who's trouble." Andy wagged a finger at her. "It's time you behaved yourself, missy. Still getting into fights. One of these days you're going to be expelled." She undid her seatbelt and opened the door. "Right. Never mind. Don't forget your backpack."

Maria undid her seatbelt and stared at the man again.

The man watched her with amusement. He crossed his arms over his leather jacket and squinted at her.

Maria closed her mouth, and leaned into the back seat for her backpack. She watched her mother go up to the young man.

"You need anything while you wait?" Andy asked.

"No, thank you, Ma'am. I'm all right."

"What's your name?"

"Alessandro Pesseck. Are you Mrs. Giordani?"

Andy shook his hand. "Yes, but call me Andy. This is our daughter, Maria."

Maria twisted back, cradling her backpack. She blinked at him. Suddenly, the sun broke through the clouds and Maria watched as sunbeams lit up his face. She could see sparkling gold in his dark brown eyes.

Alessandro smiled at Maria and pointed at his cheek where he had a scar. "We match."

Maria shyly looked away and smiled. "You should see the other person."

"Same here." He laughed.

Andy looked at Maria and shook her head. "She's always in a scuffle at school."

"It's that Selena Ryan," Maria said. "She's a bully."

Andy raised her voice. "Since when are you the Archangel Michael?" Not waiting for a reply, she turned back to Alessandro. "Feel free to come to the front door if you need anything, Alessandro. Or come in and stay warm."

"I'm fine, thank you, ma'am."

Maria climbed out of the car. Her mother turned to her. "Let's go, Maria. Front door. *Caverna's* occupied today."

Maria shut the door. She pushed back her fur-trimmed hood and blew her bangs out of her eyes to better see the young man. She was curious. He seemed exotic. Not dark like *famiglia* but a different dark. She looked at his black Reeboks and raised her eyebrows. *Cool*, she thought. She passed him, following her mother to the front walk to the door, and noticed how he watched her closely. Their gaze locked for a moment before she turned and shuffled her heavy boots along the icy walk to the door. Before she closed it behind her, she looked back, one more time.

Alessandro gave her a little smile.

She cocked her head slightly. Then, she stuck her tongue at him and slammed the door behind her.

CHAPTER THREE

April 1984

ANDY SUCKED AT A CIGARETTE, in the kitchen, by the open window over the sink. She took in the fresh spring air, and listened to the animals outside. Goats bleated, lambs called, chickens cawed and the rooster crowed. Birds chirped gaily in the bushes at the side of the barn and dog kennel. "What a noise," she muttered. She took another drag, waved the smoke away, and flicked the ash out the window. She leaned over the sink, and looked out the window to watch the ash drop. She watched with satisfaction as some cackling hens rushed to the little ash bits in the wet grass. "Schmucks," she muttered. She tipped her head back and inhaled the air, heavy with luscious scents left by an April rain. That, plus sheep manure.

She coughed. "Lovely," she said to herself, flicking ash one more time, before turning on the tap to wet the cigarette. She tucked the wet butt under garbage in the can under the sink. She slid the window closed against the raucous animal noise, only to become more aware of the racket coming out of Maria's bedroom.

She leaned back against the counter and thought of the phone conversation she had earlier with Father Carloni. What a conversation. Happy news. She had waited so long. His news hadn't sunk in, quite yet. She couldn't think straight, with all that noise coming from Maria's room

"Maria. Stop that racket."

She listened to the god-awful tinny version of Italian Rag Time which played since she brought Maria home from school, a half hour earlier.

Maria was moody these last few weeks, and Andy thought perhaps she was still grieving the loss of her *Nonno*. Claudia bought Maria the music box of evil in an attempt to cheer her up.

Andy ran through the kitchen into the hallway leading to the bedrooms. She leaned against the handrail and eyed fresh streaks on the wall leading up to the landing. She bowed her head to the stairs and shook her head. She raised her head and quickly rubbed the streaks with the tea towel, but gave up. She slapped her forehead. "Go on, drive me crazy," she yelled.

The tinny happy-go-lucky beat went on and on.

Dah dah dah dah dah dah dah,
DUHDUDUHDUH…

"All right, already then." Andy stomped up the stairs, down the hall, causing the shag rug to crackle with static from her stockinged feet. She pushed at Maria's closed door, and touched the doorknob. She squealed when she got a shock from the door handle. She flapped her hand. "Shit." She opened the door. She stood in the doorway with her hands on her hips and feet wide apart. She saw Maria sitting cross-legged on the carpet, turning a little metal handle on a jukebox, her face hidden by her hair. Andy said, "Kiddo?"

Maria didn't look up, nor stopped playing the tinny ragtag. "Maria."

Maria kept turning that handle.

Andy came over and grabbed Maria's hand.

Maria pushed her mother's hand back. "No."

Andy yanked the music box away.

Maria reached for the music box. "Give me."

"What? *Give me*? You're four years old, now?" Andy kept the box out of reach. "Listen, kid, we all die one day. Your *Nonno* had a good run."

Maria kicked the rug under her and scrambled onto the bed, burying her head into a pillow which muffled indecipherable words.

Andy placed the music box on top of the bookcase with tattered Bert and Ernie dolls perched on children's books. On the wall hung Maria's favorite Culture Club poster. Andy looked at it briefly and sniffed. A gift from Anita. She came over to the bed and sat on the edge of the cover, touching Maria's back. "Shhhh. It's okay. I miss your *Nonno*, too."

Maria lifted her moist face and frowned. Her hair hung in her eyes and stuck to her mouth. "Miss, who?"

"Your *Nonno*, of course, who do you think? The man in the friggin' moon?"

"No. Not *Nonno*. I knew *Nonno* was going to die. He was a sick old man. It's Anita. I found out she sold the house and moved away today. I'm going to miss her." She fell face-first on the pillow sham. "I want her back."

She just ruined my day, thought Andy and stood up and smoothed down her skirt. "Anita, Anita." She raised her voice and dramatically pointed to the carpet. "I told you I didn't want to hear that name around here ever again."

Maria shot back. "It's not her fault *Nonno* died. It was that woman who stole her coat and stole *Zio* Jack from her. He died, too. She had to find him in someone else's coffin. You never think about *that*. Anita lost her husband, Mom. And I never hear you say how awful that is for her. She was fun to be with. I *never* have any fun around here anymore."

The late afternoon sun burst through the dusty bedroom window. Andy sniffed and blinked. It was a goddamn soap opera: Anita loses her husband, Jack, who flees with *famiglia* money; then Nancy, Peter's secretary, has an affair with Jack. Then Nancy discovers Rose, the red-headed bimbo from the school board who was also having an affair with Jack. Then Nancy kills Jack in a jealous rage. If she was really honest with herself, Andy would've done the same thing. She would have jumped off that fashion runway at Rose, who stupidly wore Anita's fur coat to the Grand Opening fashion show. But she would've knocked Rose's head off, not thrown her boobs first onto her father's face, or cause Rose to land on the crotch of an older man on oxygen. It was so friggin' horrific, and embarrassing. All the old geezers making fun of how her father died. The funeral ended up a comedy roast, a farce, a fiasco. Peter's arrest and two men shot dead in the lobby will be what everyone will remember of her father's funeral. Suddenly, Andy felt a familiar low rumble vibrate through the floor and walls. It signaled Stefano's truck rumbling up the driveway. Andy went into gear. She slapped Maria's thigh. "Come on, get up. Your father's home. Clean yourself up."

Maria sat up, wiped her eyes. "Dad misses Anita, too."

Andy paused. She wanted to scream at Maria to shut up about Anita. But it was what she feared—that her husband, Stefano, would miss her, too. Her best friend. Well, once upon a time, her best friend. "Yeah, right. Just what I needed to hear." She turned and left the room. Andy bounced down the stairs and reached the kitchen stove just as Stefano opened the door from the garage. "Stef, ten minutes."

Stefano liked to have his supper on time, minutes after taking a shower and a shave in his basement bathroom. "*Si, dieci minuti,*" he repeated. She heard him slowly take his tired bulk down the steps to the basement.

Almost immediately, Andy heard the back door smash open, and her mother screaming, "Adriana, I'm 'a heeeere."

Andy, holding a spoon, yelled back. "Maaaaaaaa, I can heeeaaaaar you." Andy heard bangs and scrapes from upstairs, and Maria appeared, sliding along the ceramic floor through the kitchen doorway, just as her *Nonna* reached the few steps up to the top from the family room. Maria flew at *Nonna's* neck.

"Maria, be careful with *Nonna.*"

Nonna, dressed in widow's black, heartily hugged the child who almost catapulted her back down the stairs.

"Nonaaaaaaaaaa."

"Mariiiiiaaaaaaa." Claudia leaned back and took a long look at her 'big' angel's tear-streaked face. She touched her face gently. "You' a still cry fo' you *Nonno, Bambina?*"

Maria nodded, wide-eyed.

Andy saw through the lie, and rolled her eyes. "Suck up to her, why don't you," she mumbled, turning back to the stove.

Maria sniffed and pulled away from her *Nonna*. She looked at her mother, out of the corners of her eyes.

Andy, feeling it, looked back, and their eyes met. Slowly, Maria's tongue peeked out between her lips.

Andy held out the spoon threateningly. "Don't you dare."

Maria quickly straightened up, took *Nonna's* hand, and led her to her usual spot at the kitchen table. She helped her sit down and gently took her light spring jacket.

"Ooo, *grazie*, Maria."

Maria smiled contentedly.

Andy turned away from the sight and poked at a home-made sausage in a frying pan. Tonight's dinner was bone soup, Stefano's home-made sausage, tortellini with a light tomato sauce—canned by Stefano—and some crunchy Italian buns to dip into the olive oil and balsamic vinegar. She thought of how comfortable the routine was, how she timed herself by Stefano's noises: First, the rumble of the truck into the driveway; then the slamming of the truck door; then the rattle of the garage door; the side door to the house would crash open; and Stefano would kick off his work boots. That was the 10-minute warning for dinner. She would hear the shower in the basement run, as she raised the heat on the food one last time. The shower stops as she takes buns out of the oven. If there is a salad, she tosses it then and brings it over to the table. By the time Stefano made his way back up the basement stairs, squeaky-clean, she would have everything on the table save for the *vino*. She then would wait for him to sit at the head of the table, by the kitchen window before she finally set the carafe of watered-down *vino* (as ordered by their doctor) in front of his plate.

Stefano, cleaned, brushed, shaven and face aglow, lumbered into the kitchen and wordlessly looked out the window over his domain, before sitting down in his spot. Maria quickly slid over, clung to his neck, planted a big fat kiss on his cheek, and sat back down beside her *Nonna*.

Stefano flashed a happy smile at his princess.

As Andy came to the table holding the soup pot, she reviewed her family. She suddenly stopped ladle in hand. She had a flash of something strange. Something extraordinary. Was it happiness she felt? No, relief. It was relief. She ignored the ladle dripping broth over the bowls, and looked over at her daughter. The emotional storm of the past 12 years of not knowing whether there was an inadvertent mixing of the same bloodlines with Stefano, finally came to an end with that afternoon's conversation with Father Carl. It had taken him over a year of searching what church records he could find in Calabria, to finally locate and receive word from a distant relative of Stefano's; one single elderly lady. It was she who finally confirmed that morning with Father Carl, that Stefano was not in any way related to her. She gasped for air. It was as if she suddenly woke from an ongoing nightmare to find it wasn't real, after all. She shakily put the ladle down with a clatter.

"Are you alright, Mom?" Maria asked, waiting with her spoon by her bowl.

Andy looked at her. Her eyes glistened. She looked at Stefano who held up his glass for wine. She picked up the carafe and poured him his watered-down wine. "Talked to Father Carl today," she said, smiling at him.

"*Sì?*"

"*Sì.*"

"He'a fine?" asked Claudia.

"He's super fine," Andy quipped, finishing the ladling of soup. "He solved a puzzle for me."

"I like puzzles, Mom."

"Believe me, it ain't that kind of puzzle." Andy sat and reached for Stefano's wrist. She patted it, then grabbed her napkin. Andy blinked back tears of relief, because what Father Carl had told her that afternoon was there was no way in Hell that Maria's unusual birth and unforeseen physical anomalies were caused by incest. It was just darn old Mother Nature. She looked sideways at Stefano. Could it be that Andy could finally return to Stefano's bed after 12 years of sleeping in the guest room? She coughed and touched the back of her neck. She wondered if it was too late to be sexy. To be enticing. What if she had dried up like a prune? She looked at Stefano, wide-eyed, almost frightened of the prospect of being in his arms. Then, just as quickly, through a strange form of thought association, Andy jealously thought of Anita in his arms. Whether her suspicions were true or not, the thought disturbed her greatly. She looked angrily at Stefano and thought of what Maria had said earlier, that Stefano also missed Anita. And her own daughter had the audacity to suggest she should feel sorry for poor Anita because she had lost her husband and had to sell everything to move far away. She haughtily picked up a piece of bread and tore it apart. "Who gives a shit," she muttered, as she dabbed oil and vinegar on her plate.

CHAPTER FOUR

May 1984

SELENA'S TREE TRUNK OF A KNEE got in the way as it dug into the small of Maria's back. Gravel cut into Maria's right cheek as she grabbed the long red ponytail from underneath her ribcage, but there was no squiggle room to yank it through her legs. She couldn't breathe with Selena's fat arm firmly across the back of her neck, forcing her head down. Maria was choking. Shoot. There was no way Maria was going to let Selena get the better of her. Maria had a well-earned reputation for winning scraps, and this one was a fight between good and evil. Besides, her entire ball hockey team cheered her on, along with other students in the yard. She didn't want to let them down. Maria smiled, despite her lips picking up dirt. She loved this. The worse it got, the more at peace she felt inside.

"Say sorry," demanded Selena. Blood dripped from her nose onto the side of Maria's cheek. "Say sorry, or you die."

Maria laughed, though it sounded more like a choke. What an asinine thing to say. *Say sorry, or you die.* Maria struggled under Selena's weight, testing angles she hadn't yet explored. Maria could see Selena's cohorts cheering Selena on, squinting past the gravel by her nose. She tasted Selena's blood. Or was it hers?

Earlier, Maria had been playing ball hockey when she witnessed Selena pushing a third-grader so hard that the girl fell face-first against the fence post by the gate. She immediately ran howling like a banshee at Selena with her stick in the air, and whacked her in the back with all her might, breaking the stick in half. Selena had howled and turned, and as she did, Maria grabbed her by the shoulders and flipped her over her head, as she dropped down and somersaulted backwards.

Selena landed with her nose against her kneecap. The only reason Selena got the better of her was because her two cohorts jumped on Maria and brought her down, giving Selena time to pull herself together. When Selena discovered her nose was broken, she roared. She pulled her cohorts away and jumped with her full weight on Maria.

Maria felt a sharp jab in her lower abdomen, but she didn't have time to worry. She'd been there before, and knew success was inevitable. She just had to figure out how to get there.

Selena shifted her weight just enough for Maria to feel that long hair suddenly hang limp in her hand. She instinctively nudged up with one hip and turned Selena enough to pull her hair between her legs. At the same time, Maria curled up into a fetal position. By doing so, Selena ended up sliding slightly off Maria. Maria then twisted her other leg underneath and pushed off from her knees, bodily lifting Selena up and over. With a yelp, she quickly straddled Selena and grabbed her pudgy little thumb and squeezed down as hard as she dared; a neat little trick Anita had taught her. Maria knew she had the power to break Selena's thumb, but Anita had warned her not to go so far. A little pressure went a long way in disabling some culprit.

Selena's eyes popped under the pain. She winced and wailed in shock. "Owowowowowowowow. Le'go. Le'go."

Maria stood up stiffly, still holding Selena's thumb. Maria's hair hung over her eyes, and her face was streaked in blood and dirt. She licked at the blood as she stood catching her breath. Then, as she grinned, she looked around, and wiped the gravel and dirt off her face and clothes. When Selena's cohorts made a move, Maria simply pushed down on the thumb to get another wail out of Selena. "Don't, or I'll break her thumb."

They stopped.

She looked at the cowering little girl by the fence, still holding her nose. "She won't bother you no more," Maria yelled happily. She bent down and bellowed, "Right, Selena?" For effect, she pressed down on the thumb again.

"Yes, yes, yes, yes. Stop. I won't do it no more." Selena started to blubber and cry.

A few of the students cheered Maria on, and she gave them a royal wave, then bowed. She looked down at Selena writhing at her feet. "Hey, big baby? Why'd you pick on that little girl, anyhow?"

Selena remained quiet except for her raspy breath.

Maria looked at Selena's cohorts. One of them eyed the little girl. "Why did you pick on her?"

The girl sneered at the cohort and spit on the ground.

Maria pushed down on Selena's thumb again.

Selena howled. "Okay, okay, okay," said the tall, gangly girl, holding up her hands. "She looks like a homo, okay? She looks like Vitorino."

"Homo, eh?" Maria looked at the little girl. Indeed, there was vagueness in how she looked. Short black hair, freckled nose, feet slightly too big. Pretty, tomboyish. Big ears. Very unfair. Maria raised her eyebrows. That girl looked a bit like she did at the age of six. She gazed down at Selena. "And that's coming from somebody who looks like a butch. That's not very nice. Say you're sorry, Selena."

"I'm sorry. I'm sorry. I won't bug her no more."

With disgust, Maria let go of Selena's thumb and stepped away.

The students milling around, all in their school uniforms, split apart to let Maria limp through to the fence. Maria's skirt was torn, and her school sweater had split under the arms. She didn't care one iota.

Maria reached out, and protectively wrapped her arm around the little girl. "C'mon, let's get outta here." Maria led the waif back through the crowd to the side door of the school. When they reached the door, Maria opened it for her.

Just then, the bell rang, and classrooms vomited students into echoing hallways. Some stopped and stared at the two warriors and their disheveled and bloody appearance.

"Not again," said one.

"Holy crap, look at Maria."

Maria grinned and gave them the finger.

"Hey, Maria. Are you still coming to the pajama party Saturday?" someone asked.

"I wouldn't miss it for the world," Maria said, giving a friend a thumbs-up. She hurried the little girl down the length of the hallway and kicked open a washroom door. She led the girl to the sinks and tried all the taps to find one working, and turned it on to warm. There was no paper towel in a broken dispenser, so she slammed one of the toilet cubicles open and yanked at the toilet paper. It coiled and draped onto the floor like an albino snake. Maria rolled it up in a ball, and returned to the sink. She stuck it under the running water, let the water run hotter, then turned and dabbed the girl's swollen cut eye and bloody nose. "What's your name, kid?"

"Francesca." The little girl's voice was so little. She had a thick accent. French-Canadian.

"Hi, Francesca," Maria held out her hand.

Francesca looked at the hand, blankly.

Maria grabbed Francesca's hand and shook it. "My name is Maria. Next time anyone bugs you as that dork did, you just call me. Or put a note in my locker. I'll show you where it is, okay?"

Francesca smiled and nodded.

Maria stood back. This little girl had black hair like herself, a short cut just below the ears, just like hers. Yes, she had a look of being boyish. A slightly large nose. A skinny little frame. Oversized feet and hands. "Why'd Selena pick on you, eh?"

"She say I look like a stupid boy."

"Look at me. I look like you. Do I look like a boy?"

Francesca hesitated, then nodded and giggled slightly.

Maria shrugged. "So?"

Francesca grinned shyly. "So, I kick her." She pointed to her knee. "'N I tell 'er I tell *mon pere*."

"You kicked her in the knee? Hahaha." At that moment, a deep searing pain in her groin came so suddenly it took her breath away. It felt like a knife was twisted and shoved into her lower abdomen. She dropped the wad of toilet paper and wrapped her arms around her belly. Another jab bent her over. It knocked the breath out of her. "Wow," she gasped

The door to the washroom banged open. "Maria, out."

Maria, hunched over, looked up to see her history teacher, arms crossed, standing in the doorway. Behind her, Maria saw students peering in. Maria tried to straighten up but couldn't. "Selena was picking on her and pushed her into the fence post," she croaked.

"Did it ever occur to you that maybe Selena was suffering? Maria, have mercy. Her father was just brutally killed a few months ago. Give her a break."

"Huh? Why'd he get killed?"

"Never mind. Out. To the principal's office. I'll take care of this." She waved to Francesca. "Come." The teacher kept the door open with her outstretched arm. She motioned impatiently at Francesca. Obediently, Francesca walked out into the hallway and turned back to look at Maria.

"But Selena broke her nose," said Maria.

"I can see that, Maria. But I believe you may have broken Selena's nose, as well. And these things are not always for you to fix. The principal's office, now."

Maria looked at the waif. She grinned at her and winked but suddenly had to bend over the pain again. Maria forced a few steps towards the teacher. Suddenly, she vomited. Maria tried to wipe her mouth but then fell over onto the cold linoleum. She curled up into a ball. Slowly, as she writhed in pain, a deep growl rose from deep within, like a primitive yowl. She could not bear the pain any longer. Maria passed out.

ANDY HEARD THE PHONE inside as she struggled with groceries in the garage. She rushed, because they didn't have one of those flashy answering machines. As far as Andy was concerned, people were crazy to want to know everything they missed, anyway. If something was that important, people could damn well keep calling until they reached her. She pondered whether she should hurry to catch it. Usually, it didn't ring long enough, and she'd get to the phone just as they hung up. That always boiled her blood. But Lord, this time, the phone kept right on ringing.

"What is it. The end of the world? Shit." She juggled too many bags, with too many fingers looped into too many plastic grocery bag handles. As she turned to move away from the car, a bag collapsed under the weight of three cans of olive oil. They clattered onto the garage floor. One of the cans burst, and premium virgin olive oil spilled across the garage floor, splattering the old Volvo's tire, her nylons, and her expensive suede shoes. "FUCK." She bent into the back seat of the Volvo and rolled the other plastic bags off her fingers. She turned and slid across the green oil slick, arms whirling around for balance, until she finally body-slammed against the door to the house.

Ring. Ring. Ring. Ring ...

Shut the f ..." She yanked at the door and stumbled over Maria's Sunday shoes, Stefano's work boots, her fancy leather boots, *Nonna's* extra slippers, and one of Maria's many backpacks. "Hell, hell, hell." She kicked off her shoes.

Ring. Ring. Ring. Ring ...

Andy reached the family room, almost fell, and clamped onto the handrail for the few steps up to the kitchen.

Ring. Ring ...

She slid on her oily stockinged feet across the ceramic tile, leaving a trail of olive oil. Again, she body-slammed the kitchen door trim into the hallway. She grabbed the phone off the wall. It flipped out of her hand. "Fuck." It landed with a plastic *whop* onto the floor, cracking the shell of the receiver. She bent down, grabbed and steadied it against her ear. Her hair billowed around her face. "WHAT?" She listened. "Oh shit. What the hell did Maria do now?" She straightened up with a gasp. She quickly hung up, and dialed a number. She listened, and paced back and forth as far as the coiled line would allow. She banged her forehead into the door jamb. "Pick it up. Pick it up. Stefano, be there. Pick it up." Someone answered. "Yeah. Guido. Get Stefano on the line. What the f--. Italian? You understand English well enough, just get me, my husband. You little ..." Andy made a fist with her free hand and pretended to threaten Stefano's cousin, Guido. "Yeah, Stef. Listen. It's Maria. She was in a terrible fight with that Dunie Ryan's daughter, Selena. She's in the hospital again."

A PIERCING SCREAM echoed through the ICU hallway at St. Joseph's Hospital. Pairs of squeaky shoes hurried past Andy, sitting impatiently, flipping through the same magazine she'd been looking through for 20 minutes. She leaned over and looked around the corner of the doorway.

"I wonder who that was?" she mumbled.

Stefano, big enough to fill the room by himself, didn't answer and looked queerly uncomfortable sitting in his quilted red lumberjack shirt, plaster-covered work pants, and steel-toed boots in a rickety plastic seat.

Maria was curled up on the gurney under a thin sheet, facing the wall and moaning softly. She had been given a sedative and appeared sleepy.

Stefano watched Maria's breathing while he rested a hand lovingly on her head. In response to every moan, his fingers caressed the hair that matched his own. He shifted his weight slightly, his shirt ballooning out over the armrests of the chair.

Andy looked at Stefano, then down at the chair. She looked back at the magazine. "That looks like one of those chairs you broke once. Goddamn, they're cheap here." She shook her head and reached out with a manicured hand to hold onto his forearm. It was like feeling a tree trunk. She patted his arm gently, then took her hand away. She looked down at the chair once again and prayed it would not collapse under his weight. "Flimsy chairs."

"*Perdono?*"

"Nothin'."

Maria moaned.

Andy giggled and shifted in her seat. "Okay, I got a joke. A man was taking tests in a hospital. A nurse asked him to take a bottle to the bathroom and bring her the result. When he came out, he asked his wife to return the bottle back to the nurse. 'Is this urine? asked the nurse. 'No,' his wife says, 'It's his'n.'

Stefano shook his head and smirked.

Andy leaned in to touch Maria's back. "Get it?"

Maria started to snore softly.

"No respect. I get no respect around here." Andy suddenly realized something. "Stef, you know, now that I think of it, it's probably her, well, you know," Andy tapped the side of her nose, "first time of the month thing comin' on. She's almost the same age I was. Well, younger, maybe." She went back to flipping the magazine. "You could blame all those steroids they put into burgers these days."

Stef swiveled his gaze from his daughter to his wife. His face turned a deep crimson. He withdrew his hand from Maria and squeezed his manly nose. He sighed loudly. He shifted his weight, farted, and sighed again.

Andy shook her head. "Stef."

"*Scusate.*"

"Yeah, right." Andy lifted her arms and fluffed up her teased hair. She looked down and studied her mohair sweater and plucked at imaginary lint. Not her best color but tradition is tradition. With her father's death, it was a must. Oh well, there were worse things in life than having to wear black for a year.

Maria groaned and Andy looked over. *My little girl*, she thought proudly. She leaned into Stefano's muscular shoulder. "Our daughter is becoming a woman, Stef." Smiling sweetly; an unusual act for her facial muscles.

Stef turned to her. He grinned and blushed.

Then for a moment, she felt terrible. Now with her angst over an inappropriate union with Stefano lifted because of Father Carl, she realized what a shit she had been with Stefano throughout their marriage. In spite of that, he spoiled her rotten. He worked so very hard—not only at *Giordani & Sons Construction*, but also at home, on the farm and in the fields. He had hired help, but he was right in there, up to his arm pits, shoveling shit, feeding animals, and wrangling them for butchering. Plus, he was the head of the *famiglia* in Quebec. The *'Ndrina famiglia*.

Stef's group was small. The only blood Stefano had in the Eastern Townships were his two cousins, Guido and Mario, and his brother Peter. Now, of course, Sandra had taken over for Peter and was a soldier, too. A vice *capo*, one of the things that set the *'Ndrangheta* apart from the Sicilians—women took over for their men. Though, as with the Sicilians, wives didn't typically know much about the *famiglia* business, but Andy knew enough to realize not all the money flowing into their home was just from building boring suburban ranch homes and strip malls.

Suddenly, there was a commotion in the hallway. Andy could hear her mother talking to the nurses in the hall.

"Tereeeeeeesa. *Come va? Dov'e* Maria? Is'a my Adriana here?"

"Ma's here," she mumbled to Stefano.

Stefano nodded, and chuckled. He got up. "She'a sit here. I go."

"Why, Stef? Don't go."

"I come back." He lumbered out of the room, his shoulders barely fitting through the door frame.

"*Stefaaaaaaano. Dov'e Maria?*"

Andy listened as Stefano explained to her mother.

"Ah, *Si*. She is'a becoming *una donna*."

Andy raised her chin. She waited for her mother.

Claudia hustled her little self into the examination room. The little human spinning top raised her little bejeweled hands at the sight of Maria under the thin blanket in front of her. "Ah, Mariiiiaaaaa."

"Hi, *Nonna*," Maria said.

"She's a *donna* now, Adriana." Claudia clapped her little hands and beamed.

"Yeah, yeah. Enough, Ma. The whole world is going to know. Speak a little louder, will ya?"

"I no'a care," beamed Claudia. She stepped past Andy and plunked down into the seat still warmed by Stefano. She reached over to the back of Maria's head and tickled it. "*Sono fiero*," she sang. "I'm a so'a proud."

Maria struggled onto her back and twisted to look at her *Nonna*. "What's so wonderful about this? I hate it. I can't move, it hurts so much."

"Is'a only for now."

"Yeah, it will pass. Believe me," Andy said. She looked down at her hands and played with her gold rings. She thought of how very special Maria was and how what a gift she was after all those miscarriages; they didn't give a hoot about the strange things Maria was born with. She had miraculously survived and was perfect in their eyes. And nature was confirming her female identity. They weren't sure if Maria actually had all the workings until now. Another weight off her shoulders. Life was good.

Maria suddenly groaned. "Why are we here so long, Mom? I wanna go home. "N I gotta get better. I have that pajama party to go to on Saturday."

"Is that this Saturday?"

"That's what I said."

Claudia reached out and made little kissing sounds. "Soon you go out, Maria. Soon'a."

"What would you know, Ma? And, where were you? I called everywhere. We've been here two hours already."

Claudia raised her little shoulders. "I was at'a church with *Padre* Carl."

Andy gave her mother a weird look. "You were in church for two hours in the middle of a weekday? What the hell, Ma? You have that much to confess?"

Claudia shook her little salt and pepper curls. "No'a. I was'a helping Mrs. Carlucci with the festival *Autunnale Italiano*. We'a make'a decorations for da tables."

"Ma, it's May. We have other festivals before that."

Claudia shrugged. "We'a ready."

"Wow, what would you do without all those festivals, huh, Ma? What a godsend. Did you do them all by yourselves?"

"No'a. Dere was," Claudia counted her little fingers. "Patricia, Phillipa, Roberta, Josie, Antonia—"

"How is her Tony? Is he still in the hospital? She whacked him in the head with a frying pan, didn't she? She thought she'd killed him, took a bottle of sleeping pills, and called the cops?"

"No, he is'a okay. He always okay ma he lost a tooth."

"ALL RIGHT," Maria suddenly yelled. "That's enough talking."

Andy and Claudia sat upright and looked at her in surprise.

Andy threw up her hands. "Don't you talk like that to us."

"It's taking so long," Maria complained.

"Goddamn shit," Andy looked at her Giorgio Armani watch. She dropped her hands on her bony knees and stood up. "Stay here, Ma. I'm going to make some heads roll." She straightened her sweater over her black wool skirt. She looked down and realized she still wore her olive-oil-stained suede shoes.

"Sit, Adriana." Claudia insisted as she patted Andy's chair. "Dey'a busy."

"No, Ma. While you were playing arts and crafts with your little friends, we've been here for hours waiting like a bunch of losers. I want to take her home. It's only a period, for crying out loud." She walked to the doorway and looked down the hallway for a nurse. She shook her head. "All that blood on her face, I thought I was going to die."

"Blood?" Claudia snapped. She reached out and caressed Maria's pale face. There was blood still in the creases of her nose. "How you'a get blood'a?"

Maria grinned. "It wasn't mine."

"Ooooooooh. You fight'a still?"

"I rescued a fair little maiden, like a knight in shining armor."

Claudia laughed. "But you no'a man. Man is'a knight, *Si*?"

"I pretend." Maria raised her hands and clenched them into fists. "*Nonno* would've been proud of me." She feigned punching someone.

"Stop bragging," Andy said. She leaned against the door jam. "Geez. I thought her ribcage would've snapped under the weight of that fat cow."

"Who fat cow?" asked Claudia.

"Selena Ryan. She's just like her father and two brothers. Bad news. He's dead, you know."

Claudia raised her eyebrows. "Who?"

"Dunie Ryan. Remember? The West End Guys? Someone whacked him, looking for his stash. He didn't believe in banks."

Maria curled up and moaned again.

Andy came over and patted her on the head. "Maria. This ain't no game. Selena's godfather is now the head of the West End Gang. You don't want any trouble there. No more fighting that bitch, okay?"

"Mom, this pain, it's like someone has a knife sticking in my gut."

"Believe me, that pain? It's just the beginning, kid. You wait." Andy laughed.

Stefano loomed in the doorway. He looked to see what he missed and was satisfied; there was nothing. He looked down at his knuckles.

Andy studied him for a second before she looked back at Maria. She patted her on her shoulder. "Hang in there, kid. I'll be right back." Andy tried to step past Stefano. He grabbed her arm.

"You leave'a dem alone."

"Ah, Mr. *Giohdani?*"

Stefano and Andy, surprised, looked down to see a little doctor with a clipboard standing behind Stefano.

Stefano jumped back. "Oh, *si.*" He jerked into the far corner by a small sink. He leaned back and crossed his massive arms.

The doctor walked in, bowed to Stefano, then to Andy and Claudia.

Andy did a double-take at the doctor. "Hey, you are the same doctor who saw my Dad last year."

"Ah, I am Dr. Yin." He nodded profusely, his round lenses bobbing up and down on the bridge of his nose. He offered his hand. "Mrs. *Giohdani…*"

"Mrs. Giordani. With an 'r'."

Dr. Yin gulped and pulled back his hand. His face went pale. "Mrs. Giordani." He looked back at Stefano, leaning patiently against the sink. Then, he looked over at Claudia, and then at Maria. He adjusted his glasses and looked down at his clipboard. "Ah, yes." He pushed up his glasses and squinted at Maria. "I remember. Maria."

"It's that time of life in a young girl, isn't it, doctor?" asked Andy.

Maria let out an intense, elongated groan.

Dr. Yin closed the door. He cleared his throat, then very gently began to coax Maria to sit up. She allowed her legs to be slowly moved over to the end of the gurney. He gently placed his fingers on both sides of Maria's chest and watched her expression. "No broken *libs.* I am now goin' to press down on your abdomen, Maria. Okay?"

Maria, her eyes shut with pain, nodded.

Andy's hand went to her mouth.

Claudia looked over at Andy.

Stefano looked down at his feet.

Dr. Yin touched the lower part of Maria's abdomen. He frowned, as Maria twitched and moaned. Then he went lower and pressed on both sides. Maria jumped and let out a scream. Dr. Yin jumped back and pushed up his glasses. "Ah, I will need to look at Maria's lower abdomen. I seem to feel an *anomary* and need to do some tests."

"A WHAT?" yelled Andy.

Maria shot up. "AN ANOMARY, MOM. A FUCKING ANOMARY. Are you DEAF?"

Andy reared. "Who the FUCK do you think you are TALKING to?"

Maria tilted her head and screamed.

Dr. Yin yanked the door open and pushed two nurses apart as he rushed through. "We need to give her rest now. Come. We talk."

Stefano pushed away from the corner and grabbed Andy's upper left arm. He maneuvered her out of the examination room and motioned for Claudia to follow. He waggled a finger at Maria, and nodded reassuringly, before closing the door behind them.

AN HOUR LATER: "YOUR DAUGHTER HAS Congenital Uterine *Anomary*." Dr. Yin sat on the edge of the examination table.

Maria had been given more painkillers prior to a lower abdomen MRI. Afterward, with results in hand, Dr. Yin pulled the curtain around Maria to examine her more thoroughly. At that point, Andy had surrendered to the fact that Maria's secret had now fully been exposed to the doctor and technicians. She had never found the time to tell Maria she was special, that she was different from other little girls. Maria never knew that she was special, but Andy kept putting it off simply because she didn't entirely understand everything herself. Besides, she thought, perhaps nature would one day correct itself.

But here it was—bad news, whatever it was. *Congenital what? Is that a form of cancer? Is she dying?* Andy fretted as she clutched Claudia's hand. *Mother Mary of God, I finally have an angel, and I can only have her for 13 years? Are you holy fucking serious?*

"I see in your daughter's files when she was born, she was the second of twins. The first one unfortunately died, but she survived. This is after many miscarriages." He looked up from his clipboard and gave Andy a gentle gaze.

Though sedated, Maria's eyes zeroed in on her mother, her father, her *Nonna*, and then at the doctor. "Wow, Mom. I was a twin?"

Andy nodded slightly and looked away.

"And no one ever told me?" Maria lifted her head to get a better look at her mother. "What else don't I know? What happened to my twin?"

"Doctor, the scoop. Give us the goddam scoop," Andy demanded, ignoring Maria.

Dr. Yin turned to Maria and patted her knee. "Your twin was dead before you were both born."

Maria's face slowly twisted.

"Oh, for f-," Andy fumed.

Maria broke out into tears.

Dr. Yin sighed and cleared his throat. "Maria, you were bo'n with an *anomary*. You have what we call *Pseudohermaphrodites*. That mean' you have gonads of one sex 'n an *anomary* of the external genitalia of the other sex."

Maria stopped crying and struggled up onto her elbows for a moment before dropping back down. She covered her face with her hands. "I knew it. I'm a freak. A freak."

Andy stood and looked down at her. "What the hell are you talking about." She turned to Stefano pleadingly. "What the hell is he saying?" Her eyes danced from Stefano to the doctor, and then to Maria again.

Claudia shifted in her seat and pulled at her daughter's sweater. "What?"

Claudia motioned to the chair beside her for Andy to sit.

Andy sat stiffly and refused to look at Dr. Yin. Then she stood up, bent over her crying daughter, and gently lifted Maria's fingers off her face. "Come on, Maria. Shhhhh. You know you're not a freak. Everyone's slightly different. And I'm sure when you get older, we can correct whatever it is that makes you feel bad. You'll be right as rain. You'll be just as beautiful as you are now, honey. You are already growing up to be a beautiful woman. Your Dad and I are so very, very proud of you."

"*Nonna* too'a." coo-ed Claudia, nodding and beaming from her seat.

Maria threw her hands up and pushed her mother away. "Mom. Are you deaf? He said I am a, a—"

Dr. Yin offered, "A *pseudohermaphrodite* with gonads of one sex 'n the exterior of a—"

"Mom, I am a *pseudohermaphrodite* with *anomaries*. I am a boy *and* a girl." Maria, in a fit, curled up and faced the wall.

Stefano came over and put a gnarled hand on Andy's shoulder. He stared at his little suffering princess, who lay facing the wall, emotionless and resigned, as Dr. Yin continued to explain her anomalies. Maria robotically continued to translate what Dr. Yin said into a form of layman's English her parents and *Nonna* could understand. Finally, the room quietened down. No one dared breathe. They waited for Dr. Yin's final stunning announcement about what happened to Maria that unforgettable day.

Maria's *testicoli* had dropped.

CHAPTER FIVE

April 1986

STEFANO CALMLY watched a German Shephard sniff the tires of his Cadillac. It was a new procedure at the Établissement Archambault prison in Sainte-Anne-des-Plaines. Lately, there'd been more media coverage about drugs being smuggled into Quebec jails, so car and body searches were implemented ahead of visits. Ironically, the guards focusing on his car could never have guessed Stefano was the reason for all this hype. He stood by benignly, smiling and feeling quite untouchable.

As he waited, he shot his sleeves and adjusted the crisp collar on his dress shirt. He knew he didn't have to wear a suit, but it was important to look trustworthy. Friendly. Clean cut and beyond any suspicion. And he liked to show some respect both for the system and for those who were incarcerated. After all, in addition to his brother, Peter, a few of their other guys were waiting out their time in the prison.

The dog stopped briefly at the rear bumper and Stefano saw the guard take a second look at the license plate: ZIO. The guard briefly glanced up at him, then motioned for the dog to continue to sniff. It suddenly stopped at the passenger side and obediently sat down. Stefano smiled and walked over. He opened the door, and the guard allowed the dog to climb partially into the car. Its keen nose found a paper-wrapped, oblong object.

"Sir, do you mind opening that package for me?" the guard asked politely.

Stefano smiled and leaned into the car and retrieved the package.

The dog's sturdy tail started to whack the pavement.

Stefano chuckled. "Is'a sausage. For my brother."

"Open it, please, sir."

Stefano unwrapped the sausage and held it out for the guard to see. "Is'a homemade." Stefano's nostrils twitched contentedly at the wonderful aroma of garlic and spices that wafted about. He watched the dog lick his chops, staring at the sausage intently.

"All right, you can wrap it up again."

"Can'a I give dog'a a piece?" Stefano offered, grinning and holding out the sausage.

"He's on a strict diet," joked the guard.

Stefano patted his own gut, hidden by his dress coat. He laughed. "Me'a, too."

The guard pulled away the dog who clearly did not want to go. He yanked at the collar, and gave Stefano the clear signal.

Stefano smiled as he walked back to the driver's side. He slipped back into the cream leather interior of his Cadillac, carefully folding his coat around his legs. Every year he bought a new Caddy. It was, other than his annual moose hunt, the one luxury he allowed himself. Always black, with that perfect amount of chrome and with his ZIO license plate. Though catching the eye of any onlooker went slightly against his Calabrian grain, it was prudent to have an impressive car for special occasions. He inhaled the new car smell and congratulated himself for otherwise having such a strong sense of self-discipline. It disturbed him to see his Sicilian peers flash their wealth by building homes on Millionaires' Row and driving around in fancy sports cars. Their ostentatiousness was a dangerous animal. He knew it eventually took on a life of its own and led to carelessness and pride—death was always the outcome.

All the more reason what Peter did was unforgivable. *Che palle.* To Stefano's horror, his brother's name and photo ended up in the Quebec papers. Jack's death and his suspected connection to dirty money and Peter's attempt at hiding his body was all over TV and radio; sensationalized both in English and French. Fortunately, Peter was no longer a suspect, which was his *botta di culo.* That narrative died with Jack. It made it appear that he was working on his own.

Peter may not be so lucky next time, either with the authorities, the Venezuelan Consortium, *or* the Sicilians.

Stefano slowly drove through the first electric gate to a vacant parking spot. He checked his rear-view and side mirrors, then looked at his gold watch and saw he was a little early. He pushed a button on the side of his electric seat and reclined it further, allowing his long, muscular legs to stretch. He leaned back with a sigh and adjusted the rearview mirror so he had a view of the prison's gate and guards.

He reached to pick up the loosely-wrapped sausage and held it to his nose as he pondered how his *Zio* Leo was now fully in charge. He took stock of his immediate *famiglia* soldiers: Peter, his younger brother, unfortunately in jail, Peter's formidable wife, Sandra, doing a great job taking over for Peter, Mario and Guido Giordani, his orphaned cousins who he sponsored from Italy, six years before, and who were dedicated to the *famiglia*. Once there was Fabrizio, his deceased father-in-law who had the privilege of sitting in on the meetings in the *caverna* but had no real role to play. And Sandra's father? Well, he got his hands dirty once in a while, but only when they desperately needed help. And now they had *Zio* Leo, Leo Mangione, a superior warrior and soldier, the patriarch of their 'Ndrina.

They were quite small in comparison to other *'Ndrina famiglias* in North America, so they weren't worth the trouble for either the authorities or the Sicilians. But there was a distinct possibility that was going to change: it wasn't Stefano or his *Zio's* intention to stay small. They were aware of the challenges that lay ahead, especially as Stefano set his eye on the lower outskirts of Montreal as a possible immediate expansion, even though he knew it was Sicilian Mafia territory.

He heard the Sicilians were getting nervous because everyone knew Leo Mangione was one of the most prominent Calabrian *'Ndrina* heads in North America. And now he was the head of the Eastern Townships *famiglia*.

Stefano glanced at his watch. He moved his seat back into position. He checked the mirrors one last time. He opened the car door and stepped out. He bent back into the car, retrieved the sausage, and locked the car. A few drops of rain fell. He squinted at the low ceiling of gray clouds, then looked at the top floors of the surrounding stone walls of the century-old building, noting the green painted bars in all the windows. He'd never seen the inside of a cell and didn't plan on ever getting put in one and have to see that same sky from behind bars. He shuddered and scrambled to the glass entranceway, in a sudden downpour.

He stopped just inside the vestibule and took a moment to pull out a handkerchief to dab his wet face and hair. He shook out the handkerchief and stuck the soggy material back into his jacket pocket. He took off his coat and shook it before folding and hanging it over his arm. As he went through a metal detector, he mentally went through the points of the upcoming conversation with Peter. He had a lot to share with his brother.

PETER'S FACE WAS BLOATED and gray. He looked like he had just woken up. His head appeared oversized, perched on top of his bony, narrow shoulders. He yawned and leaned on his elbows over the scratched table bolted to the floor.

Stefano looked closely at his brother. He was usually quite dapper but, already into the first year of his three-year sentence, Peter had lost control of his physical health and welfare. "You no take care of yourself."

Peter made a face and shrugged. He always wore the best, the most expensive clothing a man could possibly find to wear. All of it ordered from Italy through one of their respective businesses—a tailor shop called Scorsese's' on Main Street. "It's hard getting excited about looking good around here, Stef," he said, motioning at his grey sweat pants, sweat shirt and white sneakers. "No one to impress around here." Peter scanned the visiting room.

Stefano did the same. Visitors were gathered at little tables. All quietly huddled together. Peter was a married man but the anticipation of a pretty face always prompted him to dress sharply. Here, there were none. Stefano sat back, readjusted his suit jacket, and wiped some imaginary lint off his knee.

"You got a shave and a haircut, I see," Peter said. He rubbed his own chin. "The tables are turned, dear brother."

Stefano saw someone he recognized at one of the tables and motioned toward him with his chin. "Remember him? Dat's'a Dominico Alvare. He took'a da fall."

Peter observed a squat man sitting opposite a woman and two children. "Yeah, I know. We talk sometimes. I think he's a good guy. *Buono come il pane.* So, he said he did the dump into the ditch? He lied for us, saying he wanted to get to the strip club where his girlfriend worked and dumped the stuff to get there in time."

"*Si.*"

"So, this has to do with that toxic waste contract you're goin' after?"

"*Si. I Siciliani*, dey in the way."

"You know that ditch was Sicilian territory."

"I wan' it to look like'a they did it," said Stefano. "Cause a little trouble." He had his eye on that lucrative business in Montreal. "I put in a tender next time'a."

"And that's his wife and kids?"

Stefano crossed his legs. "*Si.* I take care'a of them until he come'a home."

"Nick Rizzuto's in charge now and he's not so easy to get along with, Stef. Why don't we try Trois-Rivières instead of going for Montreal?"

Stefano shook his head. "I think'a I get dat contract, too."

"What if they get back at us?"

Stefano shrugged. He knew it always took time to raise their ire and figured he could get away with a two-year stint. He needed to make money quickly. Because of Peter. "I make'a deal. Leo is now our *capobastone* 'n dey know. We can do stuff for 'em," Stefano watched the visitors around them. He gazed at a middle-aged woman with a young man and a girl in a school uniform like Maria's. The girl was rather large, with a long messy, red braided pigtail. He squinted. She looked familiar.

"You're right, he comes with a lot of great resources and connections." Peter eyed his brother and tapped him on the shoulder to get his attention. He leaned in and whispered. "Even so, maybe we don't need to wake the giant."

"Let *I Siciliani* have da contracts later again." Stefano watched a gangly, red-haired man in his twenties enter the lounge. The young man headed toward the woman, young man and girl, and sat down at the same table.

Stefano uncrossed his legs and sat up straight. His nostrils flared.

Peter caught the reaction. "What?" He quickly stole a glance over his shoulder. "Oh shit." He turned back to face Stefano. "Dunie Ryan's widow and kids. His eldest son's doing petty time here for a hit and run."

Stefano looked at the young girl. "Selena."

"What?"

"Selena. Dat's her name. The young girl. She go to Maria's school." Suddenly, he felt sucked of all strength. This problem with Maria was a dilly. He looked down at his hands and frowned. His fingernails were dirty.

"Stef?"

Stefano looked back at Peter. "Oh, sorry. *Mi dispiace.*"

"What's wrong?"

Stefano continued to study the dirt under his fingernails. "Maria, as you know'a, was born, um, a little different from another baby girl, *si*?"

Peter bent closer to Stefano. "Yeah, I remember. You said she seemed to have a little—" He waved his little finger.

"*Si.*"

"But she was still, um, a little girl, so to speak."

"*Si.*"

"Okay. Something happened?"

"*Si.*"

Peter wiped his mouth. He was drooling as he pressed his chest into the edge of the table.

Stefano leaned on his elbows, his hook nose almost touching Peter's. He glanced at a guard giving them the hairy eyeball. He sat back a little. "Maria, she'a had a *mal di stomaco.*"

"A stomach-ache."

"*Si.* She was in a fight'a wid dat girl." Stefano pointed at Selena.

"Maria's always in fights."

"*Si*, but dis girl she jump'a on Maria, full weight."

Peter winced, looking at Selena. "She's twice Maria's size."

As if knowing they were looking at her, Selena glanced at Stefano and Peter. She paled and quickly looked away.

"They're big trouble, especially now that they're under the protection of their godfather, Allan 'The Weasel' Ross. Some say he hired Hells Angels to knock Dunie off. No one can prove it, though. In the end, Dunie and those guys were blown up together."

Stefano looked away from the red-haired family and leaned toward Peter. "But'a it was not'a her *stomaco*. She had…" Stefano looked down at the smudged table top.

"She had what?"

"*Testicoli*, they'a dropped." Stefano felt slightly nauseous.

Peter shot back in his seat. "What?"

"*Si*."

Peter leaned in again and rubbed his eyes. "I can't get my head around that. Maria? With *stugats*?" Peter's whisper seemed to ricochet around the visitor's lounge.

Stefano winced. He leaned in with lowered voice. "I no'a like'a dat you say *stugats*. I no know'a what to do'a. I—"

"Wow."

"'N I think I know'a why."

"You mean, why she was born this way?"

Stefano nodded.

"Did Andy take drugs or something? You know, like that thalidomide stuff that deformed babies in the sixties?"

Stefano shook his head. "No. Is'a because'a—" Stefano slumped in his chair. He couldn't help but think back to the year before, just after Fabrizio died. Leo had spent hours in Stefano's *caverna* scheming over new ventures and smoking cigars with him while they waited out Peter's court proceedings. Somehow, they stumbled upon a massive skeleton in their proverbial closet. Leo figured out that he was a brother to Stefano and Peter's mother, making him their uncle. But he had already established he was Fabrizio's brother, as well.

"Our mother had died giving birth to your mother when I was four," Leo had told him through a *grappa* haze, "and Fabrizio was only two. Our grandmother and father took care of us, but in 1922, just after the first world war, Mussolini founded the Fascist Party of Italy and took over as Prime Minister. He spilled a lot of blood, and our father ended up dead on the street, along with hundreds of others in the village. Our grandmother couldn't handle the three of us alone, so Fabrizio was farmed out to a relative in another village, and then I lost contact. I was only a little boy, myself."

Stefano shrugged after reiterating Leo's words to Peter.

"Stef, that means you married our cousin, Andy."

Stefano shivered as he sat back.

"No wonder you guys couldn't have babies," Peter said. "Oh shit. Andy deserves to know the truth, Stef. And Maria should know, don't you think?"

Stefano leaned over and lifted the Italian sausage hidden by his feet. "They opened it to make sure there were no'a knives." He forced a smile.

Peter took the package, buried his Giordani nose into it, and inhaled the warm, garlicky aroma. "Hmmm. Oh, my God, do I miss that smell. Thanks, Stef. But I mean it. Don't change the topic. Maria. She has to know, right?"

Stefano didn't answer.

Peter picked at the sausage. He turned slightly red and said, "I mean, what is she going to do? Still wear dresses? What about bathing suits and shit? I mean, how will that look?"

Stefano stared at Peter's fingers picking at the sausage.

"What are you going to say to the other guys? To the *famiglia*? Oh fuck, I just remembered Tomasino's son, Vitorino. Stef, how are we going to hide this?"

Stefano slammed the table with one hand. Quickly, he looked at the guard, who was coming toward them. He held up his hand, grinned, and shook his head.

Peter looked over and grinned as well, shrugging his shoulders. "We're just foolin'. Brother stuff." Then he dug into the sausage again. He took out a piece and held it in the direction of the guard. The guard looked the other way.

Stefano sat quietly, as his brother continued to pick at the meat. He knew precisely what Peter meant. Neither the Sicilian Mafia nor the *'Ndrangheta* had any empathy for what they called "queers." But what was he to do? Hide Maria in the cellar? Then he remembered a great aunt who had wisps of a beard and had to shave regularly. She was ugly as hell, for a woman, and always hid away. Never married. Died without having a life.

"*Pietro*, do you remember, *Zia* Amelia?"

"Great aunt, Amelia? Yeah, I do. She gave me nightmares."

"You think'a she maybe was like'a Maria? Hermaphrodite'a?"

Peter frowned. "Wow. She never got married or had kids. You know what? I bet you're right. I bet she was partly man."

Then Stefano wanted nothing to do with the subject. It was too much for him.

"Couldn't you just take the *testicoli* away?"

"Is'a more complicated den dat." Stefano said.

Peter offered a small chunk of Italian sausage. Stefano held up his hand and shook his head. Peter pulled his hand away, Stefano decided to take it. He grabbed and stuffed it into his mouth. He closed his eyes as he chewed. He remembered what Dr. Yin had said. That puberty was when the body established itself and no one could control it. "No'a. Dr. Yin say da body still wouldn't stop. She'a still will be'a *per lo piu un omo*."

"So, she's turning into more of a man. Wow."

Stefano watched Selena turn in their direction.

Peter rewrapped the sausage and put it to the side. He wiped his mouth with his sleeve and looked at Stefano. "So, what do you do to stay sane, Stef? I mean, you look good, right, but all this that's going on?"

Stefano tapped his temple. "I plan." He motioned Peter to come closer as he outlined what he and Leo had done to date, their acquisition of the marshy acreage just outside of Myrtle Beach, and of the plans for draining the land and breaking ground. He also had a plan for Maria and her protection.

The ten-minute buzzer went off. Stefano looked at the clock on the wall. Then he looked at his Rolex. He shook his wrist, covering his watch with his sleeve cuff. "I have to go'a." Stefano's eyes sparkled. Sharing the plans for Leo's theme park invigorated him. It refreshed him.

"We have much work to do," said Peter.

"*Si,* feels good'a." He got up and gave his brother a bear hug. He slapped his shoulders, then stepped back and shook his hand. No guard protested.

SELENA SAT QUIETLY, as her brothers and mother stood to say their goodbyes, and watched Stefano leave. Then she looked over and watched Peter rewrap his sausage, then slowly turn, chewing as he left the visitor's lounge with a guard. She breathed heavily as she pondered what she was sure she had overheard. She could feel her eyeballs heating up. Suddenly, someone slapped her across the back of the head.

"Selena, git up. I said it was time to go." Her mother yanked her heavy sweater before letting her go, so she could stand and say goodbye to her older brother.

"Selena, I'll be out soon, so pay no mind. Before you know it, I'll be yanking your pigtail again over breakfast. So, don't look so sad." Her brother yanked her pigtail. "I'm the head of the household now, so whatever you need, you just say. Understand?"

"No, godfather is," she said, stubbornly.

Her brother frowned. "No, I am. You remember that."

Selena nodded sadly.

"Don't be sad."

"I'm not sad, and I don't care when you git home."

"That's no way to talk to yer brother, Selena girl," shouted the mother.

"Well, it's the truth."

"It's da troot, is it? Well, you wouldn't feel that way if you ever lost 'em."

"That would be the day." Selena got another wallop across the back of her head. Selena felt her head and frowned angrily.

"Don't push me, Selena. Now wit yer father gone, I need you to be strong for me and your brothers."

Selena pouted. She looked down and thought of Maria. Ever since Maria broke her nose, she'd been itching to find a reason to get back at her. What she overheard was just snippets of information, disjointed enough that she couldn't really understand the whole picture, but she heard enough so she had a plan. Suddenly, the world seemed like a brighter place. She had something to look forward to. She grabbed her coat and caught up to her mother and brother as they left the lounge. She leaned forward and grabbed her younger brother's jacket and yanked it. "Brian, hold on," she called.

Brian stopped and turned. His freckled face took on a quizzical look.

"Can you take me to school in the morning? I need to do something on the way."

"What do you need to do?" demanded her mother.

Selena looked at her mother's gray face, her nicotine-stained fingers and wiry hair. She had no feelings for her mother, but needed to be wary. Lies were always better than the truth. "I left a school book at a friend's and she's sick and won't be at school tomorrow. I said I'd pick it up in the morning."

Her mother nodded. "That's a good girl, Selena. You hit those books and you'll get somewhere. Anywhere but here. I spend far too much time between you father and brothers comin' here t'visit."

Brian reached out and gave his sister a high five.

Selena gleefully slapped his palm, enjoying the opportunity to try and sting him.

He winced and shook his hand, smiling. "You're a regular Irish warrior, you are, Selena."

"You better believe it."

Chapter Six

"MARIA, OPEN THE DOOR."

Maria stood in her pajamas by her bedroom window, sadly watching the sheep frolic in the small pen around the pond out back of the house. At the sound of her mother's voice, she scrambled back into bed and pulled the covers over her head.

"Maria, I'm telling you, today you're going to school."

Maria threw the covers off, grabbed the other pillow on the floor, stuck it on her head, and blindly groped for the covers again. She threw them back over the pillow and her head.

ANDY JIGGLED THE DOOR HANDLE and considered getting the sledgehammer to break it down. She was at a loss as to what to do. Almost. She bolted down the hall, scrambled down the few steps, and slid through the front entrance into the kitchen. From there, she slid towards the few steps leading into the family room and did a tight turn down into the basement.

She went into Stefano's sacred area, where he kept most of his tools. She reached up in the dark to find the bulb that hung from the rafter, and found the chain. She yanked so hard, the chain came off, but the light turned on. There stood what she was looking for; an old, extendable stepladder splattered with years' worth of paint and plaster. She reached for it and grunted. It hardly budged. "Holy crap, you're friggin' heavy." She'd never used a ladder in her life, but this was an emergency. She lifted it, again, and scraped one of the bottom supports against her nylons. She felt a run snake up her shin.

"Nylons are gone. All gone." She struggled to keep the ladder balanced. The legs scraped against cement, brick, then rafter, then floor, then her head, then her foot. Eventually, she dragged it through the door into the basement. She looked at the stairs going up to the family room. Then she looked at the slanted ceiling over the stairs and realized that the ladder was probably going to dig into that, and that would piss off Stefano. She carefully laid the ladder down flat on the stairs, and then bent down to push the thing up. But the sharp edges on top of the stepladder caught into shag rug. She stood up and slapped her head.

"Fucking moron."

She dragged the ladder toward the basement door that led out into the backyard; the door Stefano always used when he had to go in and out, to and from, the barn. It suddenly occurred to her that she may have only used that door half a dozen times in over twenty years, the few times she bothered to barbecue a summer meal at the picnic table Stefano had built when Maria was finally born. Funny, how you can live in a house and not see parts of it for years. That thought struck Andy as really funny. She thought of all the small pets Maria had over the years that mysteriously disappeared: a turtle, a frog, a gerbil, and a guinea pig. She shivered at the thought of little skeletons hidden in corners of areas of the house she never frequented.

She reached behind her, as she balanced the ladder and groped for the doorknob. She turned it. Nothing. She yanked at it. It wouldn't open. She looked back and glared at the door. It had Stefano's dirty handprints all over it. "What the hell." She noticed it was double-locked. She reached over to unlock the top lock. It was stiff, but she managed to put her weight into it. "What are you, Superman? Why's this so stiff?" she muttered to herself.

Finally, she unlocked and opened the door. She made sure that the lock was off on the adjoining screen door, then turned to grab hold of the ladder. She stepped back a bit, pushed on the screen door with her behind, but almost let the ladder fall sideways. She took control of the ladder, again, then pressed against the screen door with her butt. The door closed on her, again. She reached for the handle but couldn't find it. The ladder felt like dead weight. She hefted it up a bit, and a sharp edge caught the weave of her 300-dollar sweater, sent to her direct from Italy, by her shop owner friend in town.

"Frickin' fart. Fick, fick, fuck." She glared at the pull in her sweater. Her heart beat fast. She took some deep breaths to control herself. Very carefully, she hefted the ladder again. She leaned back to search for the handle. Finally, she felt it and pressed with her thumb to release the grip. She broke her thumbnail.

"What?" She pulled her hand back and studied her thumbnail. She looked at the ceiling. She imagined stomping on Maria as she lay in her bed. Through clenched teeth, she focused on the door handle. As she pulled the stepladder through the doorway out into the frigid air, she stepped off backward in her stockinged feet, and stepped into chicken shit.

She made a small choking sound.

Suddenly, Stefano's lone hunting dog, Luna, broke out in bays, whines, and barks from her kennel. "Quiet from the peanut gallery," she shouted over her shoulder, but Luna didn't listen. She kept on barking.

Andy slowly lifted her heel and tried to scrape her foot against the edge of the doorstep. She did her best to stretch her leg as far back as she could to bypass the chicken shit. She dragged the ladder; it banged and bumped and scraped until finally, she pulled it free of the doorway. The feet dropped to the ground. As she happened to look past the doorway, she'd come through, she just caught sight of the interior door shutting itself. She heard locks click into place.

"Shit." She dropped the ladder, and it landed with a clatter on the bony part of her foot.

She howled, cursed, and swore—so loud, in fact, she could hear her echo over their fields. The chickens, sheep, and goats joined her and cackled, cried, barked, and howled along with her and Luna.

MARIA THREW OFF THE PILLOW and blanket and listened to the animals complaining back of the house. She heard banging and her mother cursing. She stared at the ceiling, as she tried to understand what her mother was screaming. "Mom?" She rolled out of bed and jumped to the window.

Out by the pond, she saw barn animals congregating around the gate, watching some activity below her window. She was about to hike herself up to lean onto the window sill and look down, when something strange caught her eye. She stood back and focused on the back of the barn. She could swear she saw something move too fast, too surreptitiously.

"Mom," she yelled at the window glass. Was that her mother at the barn? She turned to her door, unlocked it, and ran down the hallway to the stairs. She raced through to the kitchen, her bare feet gripping the ceramic tile. She hurried through the family room to the garage door. She threw the door open and stuck her head into the garage. "Mom?" Her eyes darted across the two cars: her father's Cadillac and her mother's Volvo. She withdrew and slammed the door shut. She turned and ran to the stairs leading to the basement.

ANDY STOPPED YANKING at the back door. "Fart."

She dragged the ladder under Maria's bedroom window. She grunted as she raised the top half, the tip teetering tall up to the sky. She rocked the ladder from side to side, walking it closer to the wall. Finally, she let the ladder flop against the house. The top end smashed the window and shattered the glass.

"Whaaaaaaaaat?" she screamed. She covered her head against the falling shards of glass. "Why you—"

Determined like heck, she brushed the first step of the ladder free of glass and carefully climbed up in her stockinged feet, her jaw set, her teeth clenched. She stopped halfway up when she caught a scent. Something was burning. She frowned and thought back on what she may have had on the stove. She had nothing on the stove. She shook her head, hoisted herself up, and grabbed the brick windowsill to look through the shattered window. She saw that the bed was empty and the door was open to the hallway. "Mariiiiiaaaaaaa. Where the fuck are you?"

"I'm here, Mom."

Andy looked down. "Maria. What the f—? Look what you made me do." She motioned to the broken window.

"I'm sorry," Maria said, frowning.

"Well, hold the ladder so I can get down."

"Mom, something's burning."

Andy strained to look at Maria. Then behind her. She saw smoke billowing from the barn and she jerked in shock. She tried to climb down fast, but the sudden shifting in her weight was sufficient to tip the balance.

The ladder wobbled and fell backward.

CLAUDIA SAT WRINGING HER HANDS. Her eyes were wide, with deep, dark circles. Next to her in the tiny rickety plastic seat sat Stefano looking queerly uncomfortable in his usual work pants and lumberjack jacket. Calls for doctors and nurses continuously echoed through the faulty speakers outside in the hallway.

Andy lay stretched out under a thin sheet on the gurney, staring up at the ceiling and cursing under her breath. She winced from the pain in her broken leg. She was sedated and appeared to be comfortable, but her whispered language was foul.

Maria stood by the door looking on. She bit her nails, staring at her mother. They'd been at the ICU Department at St. Joseph's Hospital for two hours.

Stefano's eyes rested on Andy. He reached out to touch her messy, auburn head.

She viciously swatted his hand away. He shifted his weight slightly, as Dr. Yin showed up at the door beside Maria. He heard his chair crack just before it shattered under his weight.

THE GARAGE DOOR slowly opened and came to a rackety stop, shimmying in its tracks as it settled into place.

Claudia pulled her turquoise Omni into the spot where Stefano's truck usually sat; the tires' indents in the surface of the driveway, having created crevices, now filled with rain water. She turned off her ignition, looked at the open garage door, and glanced in her rear-view mirror. She turned to Maria sitting next to her in the passenger seat.

Maria shrugged.

Stefano fumed quietly, squished into the back corner behind Maria.

Andy had fallen asleep with her head resting on Stefano's shoulder. Jammed in front of them were four crutches.

Stefano sighed deeply.

"Should we wake Mom up, Dad?"

Stefano looked down at the top of Andy's head. He bumped into her with the side of his body.

"Wha—?" Andy lifted her head. "Where are we?"

"We're home, Mom. You need some help getting out?"

Andy looked out the window at the open garage door, then down at the cast on her leg. "What do *you* think?" She did a double-take when she saw the wrapping around Stefano's ankle. She looked at all the crutches. She looked at Stefano's crimson face. "What happened to *you*?"

"Fabrizio, she'a sprain his foot'a. Remember?" Claudia looked at Andy.

"Fabrizio foot'a?" quipped Andy.

"*Nonna*, you said Fabrizio," Maria said.

Claudia looked askance at Maria. "Fabrizio? I say'a Fabrizio?"

Maria nodded. "Yeah, *Nonna*, you did. You said *Nonno's* name."

"*Mamma mia*," muttered Claudia.

Maria patted her shoulder. "That's all right, *Nonna*. A lot of weird stuff going on."

"*Si*," said Claudia. She looked toward the scorched barn.

Andy woke up a little more. "How the hell did you sprain your foot?"

"Guess," Maria said, biting her lip. She tried not to smile.

Wide-eyed, Andy looked at Stefano. Despite all the pain, doziness, and the stupidity of the situation, a smile slowly widened, splitting her face. "The chair." She held up her hand to do a high five with Stefano.

Stefano eyed her raised hand. He looked out the car's windshield at the deep tire marks dug into the soft ground where firetrucks and an ambulance had cut into the wet grass. It was a mud field, full of soot and debris. Then he looked over at the scorched barn and sighed. He glanced at her hand and shook his head. As if surrendering, he held up a massive paw and let her do the high five against his fleshy palm.

STEFANO REFUSED TO FOLLOW the doctor's orders to stay off his foot and keep it elevated. Instead, he decided to go check on the damage to the barn.

Carefully placing the crutches onto solid-looking patches in the grass, he slowly made his way to his dog kennel. It was time Luna had a good run around the property, and he wanted to see if she would come up with any traces of smells. There was nothing in the barn that could've possibly started the fire; he *knew* someone had to have started it. He leaned on one crutch as he unlatched the gate into the kennel.

Luna, happy to see him, jumped on her hind legs until the gate was open. She raced through the opening and did figure eights through the charred and muddy grass. But, just as suddenly, she stopped to sniff the ground. Stefano watched Luna follow a scent back to the house and to the top of the driveway. She stopped and sniffed the air, then disappeared down the driveway out of sight.

Stefano lifted his crutches and made his way across the destroyed grass to get a better look. He stopped to see Luna sniff at the bottom by the gravel road. She put her nose to the ground and retraced her steps to Stefano. She passed him toward the barn, straight to the paddock gate. She sat, staring at the lock. Stefano felt a tingling sensation climb up his spine. Luna had a lead.

He carefully hobbled along the grass, reached the gate, and opened it for Luna to continue her path to the back of the barn. He hopped past the gate, closed it, and followed Luna.

At the back, he saw where the fire had originated. There was a substantial burn in the hay cleared out of the sheep and goat stalls. He had piled the hay underneath the eaves, where it was kept until needed to fertilize acres of garden. The back wall was burned away, and part of the overhanging roof was missing.

Luna continued to sniff around the burnt hay, then came to Stefano. She sat on her haunches and expectantly looked at him.

He patted her robust head. He loved his hunting dogs and grieved the loss of the male, Dante. But this female, younger and more vigorous, still had a few years of hunting ahead of her. But this time, Stefano sensed it wasn't moose Luna was going to hunt this season. It was something more akin to a human being.

He looked over his domain. He searched the small clusters of forest and the tilled, colorful rows of seedlings: cucumber, tomato, radicchio, squash of various kinds. He looked over at the paddocks where his sheep and goats frolicked and munched at the terrain. He saw the migrant workers in the distant fields. He intuitively knew they had nothing to do with the fire. He looked around for footprints in the blackened ground. If anyone were to start a fire in his barn, they would either come up the driveway from the road or across his property. Either way, there was no way to come close with a vehicle. Someone, somewhere, would have to be quite determined to cover the distance on foot.

He thought of Nick Rizzuto. Perhaps this threat came from him?

He rubbed his nose with a thick thumb as he turned to retrace his steps to the front of the barn. He looked at the back of the house, and then around. He was leaving, the next morning, with some heavy equipment to South Carolina, and knew what he had to do before then. He looked back at the barn. First, he had chores to do.

An hour later, Stefano, leaning on one crutch, hauled up the last bale of hay, manhandling it between the rafters to block the wind from coming through the damaged wall. The odd water droplet fell occasionally from the waterlogged rafter, drenched by the firefighters, but some of the hay stacked in the middle was still dry. At first, he thought to get plywood to close the back gap but realized it was best left this way. It was all he could do, for now, with his limited mobility. He decided he'd pull one or two of his men from another project to come and rebuild the barn while he was away. He patted the stacked hay and removed his ratty work gloves.

He looked over at the sidewall. It was scorched but still standing. Every time he faced this wall, he thought of Anita. He couldn't fathom how it all happened that fantastic day. He was a loyal husband—he never strayed. Up until Anita, he never even looked at another woman, despite Andy making it almost impossible to live under the same roof through years of frustration. He shrugged. It happened with Anita; once. He was a man, after all. But that one time changed his life. He looked forward to every letter and photo Mario sent back to his office, with word about how she was doing and what she was up to. In the last photo, she stood in a grocery store. She looked like she had gained a little weight. She looked sad, but Stef knew that as long as he kept a watchful eye on her, nothing bad would ever happen to her.

He turned awkwardly, pulled up an old stool and gingerly lowered himself onto it. He winced as his swollen ankle banged against one of the lower bales of hay.

He settled down and thought about the last time he saw her that day, at court, when Nancy sat in the witness box. Murder charges were initially laid against Peter, but Nancy admitted to the crime. Anita was the beautiful, suffering widow, crying as she listened to Jack's mistress describe how she killed Jack in a jealous rage.

Stefano sighed and thought of Nancy. She was being held at the Penetanguishene Jail for the Criminally Insane in Ontario. He heard they had the best view of Georgian Bay from a high cliff. Good hunting and fishing there.

Stefano shifted his shoulders to loosen tension in his muscles. He frowned. He remembered looking over at Anita, when Peter received the lesser charge of unlawfully disposing of a body. She didn't look angry with the charges. She understood Peter's predicament. But it was Jack's body; her own husband. She must have felt very alone. Stefano wanted to go and hold her, to comfort her, but with Andy there, it was an impossibility.

His heart and body ached for her.

He picked up a long straw and twirled it between his fingers. He had to call Guido to tell him he was helping take the heavy machinery down the next two days as scheduled. There was no way he was driving. He looked down at his grotesquely-swollen ankle.

A noise attracted his attention. He looked through the barn doors at the house. He saw his chickens peck at the slowly-drying ground, their bottom feathers covered in black soot from the fire off the grass. He watched his new rooster strut its stuff. Stef chuckled at his antics, pretending he was hot shit.

Suddenly the kitchen window, above the birds, flew open, and *Nonna's* little hand waved a white handkerchief. Supper was ready.

His heart skipped a beat. He coughed. He tried to get up, but wasn't able on first try. He held onto one of the crutches and pulled himself up. As he balanced between the two crutches, he thought of Maria, his precious daughter.

Daughter?

His stomach turned. What do you call a daughter who is slowly becoming a young man and still maintains part of her womanhood? This was the part that drove him crazy. No one ever talked about these things. The worst part was the dangerous bigotry of their culture. He thought of Vitorino, Tomasino's poor son, and wondered what *their* story was? What made their son want to be a girl? Did he have an *anomaly*, too? He used to think there was something wrong with guys who wanted to act like girls—it was unnatural, weird and sinful. He was taught it was evil and an abomination. He remembered in school the story of Sodom and the Sodomites.

He felt nauseous at the thought of others thinking that way about his little princess, his angel of a daughter. She was born this way. The poor child certainly didn't ask for any of this garbage.

As he carefully made his way to the barn door, he felt relieved having to go to South Carolina. He didn't feel equipped to face what was ahead. So far, Maria had episodes of being upset and she had moments of hating herself, but he felt comforted when his usually boisterous Maria occasionaly shone through and, for a little while, everything would appear to be normal again.

Perhaps…? Maybe Peter was right. Just keep her in dresses, and all will be fine.

"Dad," screamed Maria from the kitchen window. "Supper's ready."

He looked at her moon face framed with his black hair at the kitchen window.

He smiled.

She waved.

He waved back with a smile and nodded. Tonight, for now, he had his little princess, and tonight, he was arranging for her protection.

CHAPTER SEVEN

"THERE'S THE FUCKING HOMO."

Maria looked back as she walked towards the main entrance of the Holy Mary Mother of God Catholic School.

"Yeah, I mean you, slut. Moron."

Maria searched the mingling students milling around in their school uniforms. Each student different in hairstyle, height, shoes, skirts, and pants. Some rolled their skirts up so high you could almost see their underpants. Others wore their sweaters and shirt tails hanging out. Only nerds wore their proper attire to school.

The birds were out chirping, though the morning was chilly, especially in the shade. The early June sun was bringing life back to their surroundings. Tulips had come and gone, as had the lillies and irises. Fiddleheads were uncurling everywhere, especially between the rocks in the sad rock garden next to the front entrance.

More yelling. Maria could finally see where it came from. Selena Ryan.

Little by little, more and more students stopped what they were doing as they sensed a fight coming on. Eyes went from Maria up at the top of the cement steps down to hefty Selena, making her way to the bottom. Selena, the brute; the brute with the long braided, red ponytail lugged herself through the crowd. The monster whose nose had to be reset after Maria beat her last time.

Someone whispered, "Fight."

"Shit," mumbled Maria under her breath. She felt a chill, standing in the shade.

"Yeah, I mean you, pea-brain." Selena finally broke through the crowd and climbed a couple of steps. The same two goons from last time were at her side. One taller than anyone in the school, the other freckled, with severe buck teeth. They looked like their eyes were hungry for something. There was an evil glint to them, more than normal.

Maria didn't like that at all. She looked down at her pants which she wore under her skirt. She had become more protective of herself, having to walk differently, sit differently. In a fight, how was she going to protect her fragile parts?

She watched as Selena looked around the garbage-covered rock garden next to the stairway. She saw her dip between the fiddleheads and pick up a rock the size of a baseball. "You want to fuckin' fight, moron? Queer? You lez."

The challenge woke Maria and she had that old feeling of excitement and anticipation she always felt before a fight. Energy came back to her as she smiled and squinted at her nemesis. She slipped her backpack off her shoulders and let it drop. "Me, lez? Are you serious, shithead?" Maria grinned at Selena. A sweet and meaty *I'm going to womp you'* grin.

Selena held up a 'v' with her fingers and stuck her tongue through it.

"My, aren't we clever today. You practice that much?" Maria took one step down.

Selena flung the rock at Maria.

Maria quickly leaned out of the way, her eyes following the rock as it smashed into the front door of the school behind her, splintering the oak and causing a hollow drum sound somewhere inside. Maria picked up the rock and casually tossed it up a few times with her right hand to feel its weight. "You could've killed me with that, dumbbell."

Selena scowled and blew a red tendril of hair out of her runny eyes.

Maria noticed a uni-brow. "You going into puberty, Selena? Where'd you get that uni-brow? You got hair on your back, too?"

Selena motioned to her goons to follow her as she slowly took the next step. She glared at Maria from under her uni-brow. "I know all about you, you freak. You got balls."

"Oh, I got balls all right."

"Go get her, Maria." Someone yelled from the gathering students. Selena twirled around. "Who said that?"

Someone giggled. The other onlookers searched around and then looked back at the action, not wanting to miss a thing. Either the cold or the tension got to them because Maria could see girls shivering where they stood in the early morning sun. A figure moved through the crowd behind Selena and then stepped out to the side in clear view of Maria.

It was Francesca, a little older, a little taller. She wore the school's navy wool spring coat which made her look neat and trim. Maria nodded at her, and Francesca raised a small hand before putting down her own backpack onto the broken concrete.

Maria took a nonchalant step down. "So, what's up your sleeve today, eh, Selena? You're going to have your goons hold me down again so you can look like some big shot? What a wus you are, Selena. Can't fight your own battles." She tossed the rock back into the rock garden to the right of Francesca. "By the way, how's your nose?"

"Fuck you."

"No, thank you, Selena."

Some of the girls giggled. This was a one-woman show. Or a two-man comedy routine.

"I know all about your Dad. And your uncle," Selena sneered. "Your uncle killed somebody and hid him in someone else's coffin, and he's in jail now for murder."

Maria shook her head. "Gotta get your facts straight, stupid."

Selena pointed at Maria. "You're not only a queer and moron, but you're mafia, too."

Some girls giggled.

"What are you, then, moron?"

Selena glared at Maria.

"First of all, my uncle didn't kill anyone, and second of all, you have no idea what my Dad does. In fact, you probably live in a house my Dad built." She turned and pointed at the doors behind her. "This school extension was built by my Dad. The mall where you hang out was built by my Dad." She pointed out to the onlookers. "Their houses were built by my Dad."

"That's why they're ugly pieces of shit." Selena took another step up.

Maria laughed. "You know, you shouldn't throw rocks when you live in a glass house yourself, idiot. Your Dad was killed by your godfather."

Selena's jaw dropped. "Fuck you, he didn't. And don't talk about my Dad."

"Oh, yeah. What are you going to do about it?"

More giggles temporarily distracted Selena. Then she turned back and sneered at Maria.

One girl yelled, "Selena, you're a wus."

Selena twirled around again. "Who said that?"

No one answered.

She glanced around, then elbowed her friends further to the side. She went up to the fourth step and sneered again. She motioned to Maria to come and get her.

"You want me bad, don't you?" Maria took another step down.

Then Selena did what Maria didn't expect. She yelled, "Get her." The two goons ran up, and each grabbed an arm. Maria tried to kick sideways at them while trying to find somewhere to bite with no luck. "Get off of me." Maria fell back and pulled the two girls off balance. Selena caught up and pinned her down.

Maria heard little Francesca scream at the top of her lungs. In the corner of her eyes, she saw her scramble up the stairs, jump on Selena's back, and hit her head with the rock.

"Ow." Selena, shocked, yanked herself up and away from Maria and grabbed Francesca's arms from behind her. Francesca wouldn't let go but dropped the rock. Selena rose to her feet with Francesca on her back. She twirled and rushed backwards and body-slammed Francesca into the brick wall behind them.

Maria heard a crack. Francesca's arms limply let go as she slid into a heap at the bottom of the wall.

"You fucking piece of shit," screamed Maria, terrified that Francesca was severely hurt.

"Sit on her arms. Keep her still," yelled Selena. With that, she flipped up Maria's skirt and pulled down her pants and underwear.

"Shiiiiit," yelled Maria, kicking her legs and squirming. One shoe flew down the steps.

Selena's eyes squinted as she looked down at Maria's twisting body, and then they widened into saucers. "Ewwww, gross." She scrambled back and looked at her two assistants. They looked quizzically at Selena, then down at Maria's exposed groin. "Fucking shit," yelled one of the goons.

Some of the students craned to see. A few of them ran up to look. "Oh my god," yelled one, covering her mouth and ran back down the stairs. That made some want to see as well, and a few managed to catch a glimpse before Maria, spitting angry, tore herself free and scrambled onto her knees, pulled up her pants, and crawled to Francesca lying on the cement.

Maria touched Francesca's head. She hooked her arms through Francesca's underarms and picked her up. Maria turned and yanked at the front doors. She half carried Francesca down the long hallway and slammed into the same bathroom door she'd been in with her a year before. Maria dragged her into a toilet cubicle, locked the door, and sat on the toilet cradling her. She wrapped her arms tightly as she cried, rocking Francesa. Every once in a while, she looked at the scratched, graffiti-covered door, frightened someone would beat it down. She looked into Francesca's face. Her eyes were closed. Blood ran from her nose and mouth. Two teeth stuck out between her swollen lips. "Francesca, wake up," she pleaded.

Francesca wasn't waking up.

MARIA, FACE SWOLLEN, watched the ambulance speed away from the school, its lights flashing and sirens wailing. Claudia, who had driven Andy to the school and arrived while the paramedics were still working on Francesca, stood to one side of Maria, holding her protectively. Next to her, Andy grimly stood balanced between her two crutches.

Constable Stan was beside his police car, interviewing some of the students.

"I'm going to get to the bottom of this. Come on," Andy said. She hustled Maria and Claudia into the school and led them slowly to the Principal's office. Andy noticed the staff weren't there, so she slipped into a teacher's cubicle room, and Maria and Claudia followed. "What happened?" Andy demanded, as she carefully lowered herself into a chair.

Maria fell back against the wall, slid to the ground, and slowly pulled her legs up into a fetal position.

"You'a wan' something t' drink or eat'a?" asked Claudia, looking down at her granddaughter, concern etched across her face.

Maria looked at her *Nonna* and shook her head.

Andy cracked her knuckles and put her hands on the office chair's armrests. She pointed her nose up to the ceiling tiles and waited.

Maria shifted on her behind and looked at her mother. Then she covered her face and moaned. Moaning led to tears.

Claudia looked at Andy.

Andy sat up straight. "I know this is bad, Maria. She really did a number on that little kid."

Maria dropped her hands. "What she did to Francesca is—I mean, she might die. I heard a crack when she was slammed against that door."

"So, what else did the Irish bitch do?"

Maria crossed her pants legs and straightened out the pleats in her skirt. She looked deathly pale around her swollen cheek and eye. "She pulled down my pants."

Andy's face dropped. "She what…?"

"The whole world saw that I'm a freak."

Andy shot up and balanced on her cast leg. "WHAT!! She pulled down your pants?!" She clenched her fists. "I'm goin' to kill that Selena. You know, I bet you Selena had something to do with our fire, too!" Andy shook her head. "This is the first time in my life that I feel this way, kid, but I'd like to erase that evil girl and leave her under one of *Zio* Pete's coffins."

Someone knocked on the door.

Claudia looked at Andy.

"Open it, Ma."

Claudia turned the knob and stepped back as she opened the door.

Constable Stan poked his head in. "Everything all right in here, Andy?"

Maria scrambled to her feet.

"Shit, Stan. That friggin' Selena."

"I heard, Andy. Just now. And you said some very disturbing things. I could hear you in the hallway." He looked at Maria, then at Claudia and back to Andy. "What's going on?"

Suddenly, everyone heard shouting from the lounge.

"Where's that little bitch, Maria." It was Mrs. Ryan, Selena's mother.

Andy lunged forward and leaned on Constable Stan as she poked her head out of the teacher's cubicle. "Who are you calling a bitch?" Andy leaned back toward the chair and grabbed her crutches. Before anyone could stop her, she hobbled past Constable Stan into the school's office and whacked Mrs. Ryan in the head with her crutch.

MARIA, CLAUDIA AND ANDY sat along the wall at the Vindenza Police station.

Selena's mother came out of Constable Stan's office and gave Andy the hairy eyeball as she left, limping for effect. She spat in their direction.

"Oh, for frigg's sake," muttered Andy. She moved away from the glob of spit on the dirty green linoleum floor beside her feet. "Pig!"

Constable Stan cleared his throat and motioned for them to come into his office. As they filed in, he patted Maria reassuringly on her head. He closed the door behind them.

"I tell you this. Maria's NOT going back to that school ever again," Andy announced.

"Well, both Maria and Selena are expelled until further investigation."

"She's not expelled. I will just refuse to let her come back."

"However, you see it, Andy, she's not coming back for a while."

"Ever," Andy insisted. "Maria, you're never going back to that school."

"As if, Mom. I told you I didn't want to."

"Doesn't matter. Now it's done." Andy eyed Constable Stan.

He cleared his throat and took out his notebook. He flipped through the pages. "I interviewed some of the students who were witnesses to the fight. I think I pretty well have all the details, Maria. All say you did not start the fight. So, you are not liable for what happened to Francesca. However, I do understand that something of a personal nature transpired and I am sorry for that. It's none of my business."

"You're right. It's none of your business," Andy snapped.

"Oh, *Mamma Mia*," mumbled Claudia, as she wrung her hands. Her face was now as grey as her grey velour two-piece.

Andy twisted in her chair. "Any word on Francesca?"

"Francesca. The paramedics only found a weak heartbeat before they finally stabilized her somewhat. They strapped her onto a plank in case of a broken back, and her parents followed them to Emergency in their own car. However," he eyed Maria as his face paled. "You do realize, Maria, you may have caused irreparable damage to Francesca by moving her? She did have a broken back. There is a chance she may die. Or she may come to and we find she can't walk. What you did, unfortunately, was the very last thing anybody should do to someone terribly hurt by an accident such as this."

"It wasn't an accident," Maria hissed. A tear trailed silently down her red, hot cheek.

Constable Stan pulled out a box of tissues and placed it on his desk. He gently pushed it to the edge to where Claudia was able to pull one out and hand it to Maria.

Maria took the tissue and blew her nose.

"We have another major issue on our hands in addition to, er, issues. For one thing, Mrs. Ryan charged you with Assault and Battery. Of course, I witnessed it, Andy. So, I'm sorry. You're going to have to contend with this. Either you find a way for her to drop the charges or you may end up with a criminal record."

"So, shoot me."

"Which brings up other concerns, Andy. Apart from your threat against Selena, which I overheard, I have another concern." He looked down at his notebook and recited what he had written: *Students say Mrs. Adriana Giordani, Maria Giordani's mother, said the following:*

"If I so much as hear that any of you even mention what happened to Maria today, I will search you to the ends of the earth and strangle every last vestige of life left in you after I beat you senseless first."

Andy fidgeted. "Maria's business is private. And you know that family, Stan. Their father was just assassinated. You know darn well they're the West End Gang and you know what they do to, well, young people who may not fall within their..."

"I understand, Andy. But you can't go around threatening people. First of all, what happened to Dunie Ryan is a Montreal matter, not mine. This here, what happened here, in Vindenza, is *my* business. Right now, I have your death threats, your battery charges and another pending for either Selena or Maria. I have a little girl in Emerg who may not make it. It is for me to find out, as much as I can, who will be held accountable. This is quite serious."

"You think we don't know that, Stan?"

Constable Stan leaned back in his creaky, wooden office chair and exhaled. He rubbed his dirty-blond, five-o'clock shadow. He picked up his pencil and tapped his notebook. He tossed the pencil and leaned forward, clasping his hands over his papers. "Well, Maria. Why don't we start with your rendition of what happened earlier today?"

THE GARAGE DOOR whirred open, cracked, and banged into place as Celia drove her Omni past the Stefano Giordani & Sons Construction truck, its wheels sunk into their ancient grooves formed in the cracked blacktop from years of parking in exactly the same spot. In front of the truck, half on the grass, stood another truck with the ends of 2-by-4's sticking out of its cargo bed.

Claudia stopped the car in front of the garage door. She turned off the ignition. All three people in the car heard hammering and banging back of the house.

It had been a very sad and long day for everyone, and they were weary. Their visit to the ICU, after their session with Constable Stan had drained them. In fact, they were devastated when they discovered Francesca was still in a coma and doctors had decided to induce her coma further to allow for thorough testing. There were even whispers of Francesca possibly being "brain dead."

Traumatized, Maria lay flat on the back seat, a wet Kleenex in one hand, and the other hand stuck between her legs.

Andy, cradling her crutches in the front seat, looked back at Maria. She reached back and touched her.

"Don't," yelled Maria. Her face was distorted, swollen, reflecting deep, soulful pain. "I TOLD you I didn't want to go back to that school. If you had just left me alone, none of this would've happened. Now Francesca's going to die."

"She's going to pull through," said Andy.

"But she look'a so bad, no?" Celia weakly offered, looking into her rearview mirror at Maria's swollen and pale face.

"Ma, shut up."

"But—"

"Don't you get it? Selena almost murdered her. And it's your fault. If she dies, it's on you, you fucking bitch."

Andy gasped in shock, lunged toward Maria and slapped her hard on the side of her face three times. Maria's mouth dropped.

The women froze.

Andy slowly slid back in her seat, staring at her daughter.

"How could you do that?" Maria's face crumpled with grief. She lifted her head and screamed.

Andy covered her mouth in shock. She reached out.

Maria slapped her hand away and continued to scream.

Andy panicked and grabbed her purse from between her legs. She searched inside until she pulled out a little bottle of pills. She opened it and shook out two tablets. She spied an open can of Coke in the cup holder and took a slug. "Ma, give this to Maria, will ya?"

Claudia took the can and pills, got out, threw the backdoor open and awkwardly climbed in. She grabbed Maria. "Sit up for *Nonna*, Maria," she said as loudly as she could over Maria's screams. She leaned on the edge of the back seat and held out the can shakily. "Here, take'a these."

"Everything all right, Mrs. di Giovani?"

Claudia got out of the car and stood up.

Andy bent down to get a clear view through the back windshield. "We're fine," she yelled. It was one of Stefano's men. "Ma, tell 'em to leave us alone."

Maria stopped screaming.

Claudia looked at Maria, and then the worker and at his fellow workers behind him. She waved the men away. "Is'a fine. Is'a okay. She'a upset but good now. You wan' something'a to eat'a?"

"Oh for cripe's sake, Ma," Andy muttered.

The man smiled and politely shook his head. "Boss said to keep an eye on you while we're here."

"No need," yelled Andy.

The man motioned at Claudia and nodded, then turned and motioned to the others to get back to working on the barn. "Well, just yell if you need us. And hope everything's okay," he said over his shoulder, as they disappeared around the corner.

"Like we're gonna need their help. Shit. Who can help us with this?"

"*Santa Maria*," muttered Claudia.

"Ma, the pills."

Claudia jumped into action and bent toward Maria again in the back seat. "Maria, take'a these now." She forced the two pills into Maria's mouth. "Keep'a in mouth. Now drink this."

Somehow, Maria closed her mouth around the pills and sipped weakly at the Coke. She shakily held onto her *Nonna*'s hand as she drank. Then Maria let go, dropped back onto the back seat, and curled up into a fetal position.

Andy stared at Maria. She turned and struggled to get out of the car. She leaned on her crutches and hobbled through the garage doors, making her way past the Volvo straight to the door leading into the house. She opened it, struggled with the step up, stumbled over the same shoes that were there every day, then hurriedly swung and hopped through the family room. She held the crutches with one hand and grabbed the railing and yanked herself up the few steps into the kitchen. She made her way to the phone, dragged a chair over, and grabbed the receiver off the wall. She dialed as she leaned her head against the doorjamb.

"Hi, it's Andy. Can I talk to Stef? Oh shit." She slapped her forehead. "I'm sorry. I forgot he's in South Carolina. No, I'm not alright. I need to talk to him. You don't have a number for him, do you? Oh, you do?" She got up, twirled and got herself tied up with the extension cord and reached for a pad and pen she had on top of the fridge next to the door. "Are you sure? How come he didn't give me this number? Oh, it's *Zio*'s. Yeah. I'll give *Zio* a call and leave a message. Okay, thanks."

She hung up. She looked at the number scribbled on the pad. "Shit." She tucked the receiver between her ear and her shoulder and shakily dialed, carefully and slowly, as she kept checking the numbers. Then she let herself slip down the frame of the door and settled on the floor. Her spring coat bunched up around her. She covered her eyes as she listened to the phone ring at the other end.

SEAGULLS swooped and dove as they fought to fly as close as possible to Yvonne on the small balcony. The beautiful, heavy-set woman hummed an old gospel tune to herself, tossing pieces of bread and old hush puppies up in the air.

The surf pounded onto the sandy beach not 300 feet from the balcony. Yvonne finished feeding the massive birds and squinted her beautiful, innocent eyes at the low hanging sun and the myriad diamonds of lights that played on the ocean waters below. She looked down at people dressed against the cold wind, strolling or jogging, most of them looking down at the sand as they went along. Every once in a while, someone bent down to pick something up, perhaps a shell or small shark tooth. One gentleman had a metal detector, and she watched as he went over a specific spot several times before bending down to dig for possible buried treasure, Myrtle Beach style.

She looked over the side, as she rested her right hand on her abdomen. She looked down at a nearby public park with access onto the beach from a small gravel parking lot. She saw two stray cats slink under bushes that grouped around a dozen dust-covered palm trees. A city worker pulled a black plastic bag full of garbage from a large cement garbage receptacle encrusted with shells. Next to it, stood a pole with a public phone. She looked at the clearing blue sky.

Slowly, it dawned on her she was hearing the phone ring faintly from inside the condo. She hustled through the patio door, to the rotary phone next to the old pull-out couch. She flopped down, as she picked it up. "Hello?" They'd been getting strange calls ever since they moved to the condo from Georgia. This time, she heard a desperate, demanding woman on the other end. She was tempted to hang up but the woman said something she recognized, and Yvonne's eyebrows shot up.

"I got this number to call Stefano Giordani. Is this the right number?"

"Honey, yes. This is the right number. Though Stefano isn't here right now. Sugar, he's workin' with Leo now. Can ah take a message?" Yvonne shifted on her ample thighs and looked around for a pen and paper. "Hang on, Honey. Let me get a pen 'n paper." She put the receiver down on the couch cushion and struggled up to her feet. "Now, where is a stupid pen when ya need it," she mumbled to herself. The pounding of the surf outside seemed too loud, so she shut the heavy glass door.

She pulled open a drawer in an old white dresser and fished around. Then she pulled out the next drawer, and the next, and the next. "Shoot." She went to the couch and picked up the receiver. "Just one sec, Honey. Ah think ah know where a pen is." She dropped the receiver and went to the living room corner, to two high chairs in front of a Murphy Bed. Leo had left one of his briefcases there. She dug around and finally pulled out a pen, grabbing a newspaper from the small round glass table next to the couch before settling back. "All right, now ah'm ready." Yvonne cackled and chuckled with deep-rooted gentleness and joy. "By the way, how are you?" Yvonne listened and then frowned. "Oh my, an emergency. Well, Andy Honey, ah'll let Stefano know as soon as he gets back with Leo. What's that?" She looked at her wrist, but she hadn't put her watch on yet. She got up and dragged the coiled telephone wire into a little kitchen and looked at the clock on the stove. "Oh, they'll be heah for dinner soon. Okay, Hun. Ah'll tell him. He'll call you as soon as he gets in, ah'm sure. Uh-huh. Right. Okay. Bye-bye for now." She went to hang up, but changed her mind. "Oh, Andy, 'you there? Ah'll pray for y'all for whatever the emergency is." She hung up and patted the phone. She closed her eyes and bowed her head. "Thank you, Jesus. Ah hope their emergency isn't too bad. Please take care of them. Thank you, Lord."

Yvonne nodded and got up, returned the pen to the briefcase, then walked to the patio door. She opened it and looked out. She stepped to the rail and looked down at the small sparkling, turquoise-colored pool below. She gently put her hands on her little belly. "Lordy, let there be some heat tomorrow. I would love to be out there and get nice and warm beside that nice turquoise water tomorrow afternoon. Thank you, Jesus." She smiled and looked down at her midriff. "And thank you for all your blessings."

Yvonne headed to the little kitchen. Having Stefano Giordani staying with them was a real pleasure. Such a sweet man. A good-looking man with those eyes that outshone the sun and ocean together. She thought Leo was so blessed to have found a family. It helped make him a better person, even more than when he'd lost everything in that twister.

She opened the fridge, took a bowl of batter out, and put it on the counter. She looked down and spotted a wayward cockroach on the ceramic floor. She looked for her sandals and saw them lined up against the wall in the hallway to the door. She quickly walked over, slipped them on, and walked back, stamping down hard on the cockroach with her sandal. She got a piece of paper towel from the corner of the counter and bent down with a grunt to whisk away the evidence. She threw that into the toilet in the small bathroom behind her and flushed.

She returned to the counter, pulled open the oven door and pulled out a big pot of oil she'd hidden there. She placed it on top of one of the electric burners and turned it on. "Hush puppies for mah sweet Leo." She rested her fingers on the edge of the stove and looked into the oil, and thought back at that incredibly frightening and fantastic day over two years before.

SHE WAS STANDING by the deep fryer in the kitchen of the little café Leo owned in Shellman's Bluff down in Georgia. She was looking down into the boiling hot oil. The radio played as it always did. The phone rang, and she turned and answered it as she always did. And, as always, it was for Leo, who was sitting at the counter on a diner's stool closest to the little serving window that led into the kitchen. She reached through the serving window and handed him the phone.

His calls always disturbed her. He was the boss, of course, and she initially didn't like him much. In fact, she had always yelled, "Get thee behind me, Satan," if he said something out of line. But he only laughed. He would also say things that he knew would make her squirm.

She knew Leo said these things just to get a rise out of her. Even so, she still jumped to the bait each and every time, appalled and horrified. Yet she prayed fervently for him to be saved at church every Sunday.

She had been startled by the things he would say, and how he continuously tried to woo her, and how he never stopped complimenting her on her looks, her eyes, how she dressed. And on her cooking.

The man confused her. She struggled and prayed. She couldn't leave because she desperately needed the work, and many times she thought she was being tried by God. Surely, the man was Satan incarnate. But with each day, her feelings toward him changed and softened.

On one fateful day, as she stood over the fryer in Leo's Shellman Bluff café, she was able to catch the odd word of Leo's conversation on the phone, and knew the call had a profoundly evil intent. She remembered saying a little prayer, then waited for Leo to finish. He sat thinking for a moment before getting up to return the phone to her. That was when she gave him a dirty look and made sure he saw it. "Did ah heah you right? You're gonna knock some poor boy off?"

"Don't be silly, *Bella*." That's when the kitchen floor and walls started to shake with a roar. Pots and pans rattled around her. Dishes and glasses tinkled and clanged. She looked down at the roiling oil in the pot and watched a series of concentric circles forming. Quickly, she turned off the burners. "Dear Jesus!"

Leo yelled at her to turn the radio off, and she did.

Then they heard what sounded like a locomotive racing toward them overhead. The floor and walls pounded like drum skins.

She was so frightened, she looked at Leo, her beautiful, big eyes almost popping out of their sockets, and he looked back at her. Time stood still, and she knew then that he was everything to her. She remembered whispering, "Sweet Jesus," just before the restaurant exploded. She felt herself lift up, up, up. Her ears were close to bursting, and she felt the force suck her favorite pierced earrings right out of her earlobes.

She flew into the sky along with most of the kitchen walls and floor. She thought it was the rapture. Or God punishing her. And then she lost consciousness.

She had no idea how much time went by before she woke up in a marsh far from shore. She was surrounded by debris and, so deep into the marsh, she could hardly move her body. It was just before dusk, before she heard and saw firetrucks and ambulances slowly meander around debris and building materials on the highway nearby. She had found a piece of Styrofoam and waved it with all her might, calling out and using her loud, deep gospel voice.

She watched trucks stop and two people step out to remove blockage on the highway. She was relieved when one of them finally looked in her direction, just as darkness fell. Rescuers worked hard, digging her out of the marsh.

Eventually, she was rushed to the city of Darien further south. There, she was looked at by a doctor in an emergency tent. She'd been cut down the side of her head and neck and had a deep gash in her shoulder blade on one side. They stitched her up and bandaged her. She spent that first night alone on a cot, praying she hadn't lost both Leo and her son, Willie.

Early the next morning, a rescuer announced they had found her son. It was a miracle. Hours later, Willie limped into the tent, looking for her. She jumped up and climbed over other survivors on cots to get at her boy.

He hurried to his mother and grabbed her, clinging to her, it seemed, forever. Finally, he let go and pulled her down on the cot. He told her he was out back of the restaurant washing Leo's fiberglass fish bins when he noticed the tops of the ancient Live Oaks around him sway and their majestic all-encompassing limbs dance and rock in protest against the sudden storm. He said he ducked when a heavy limb came crashing down, knocking over a slimy, fish-filled container on top of him. Next thing he remembered, he was fished out of a marsh by two firemen. He didn't have a single scratch on him, though he looked and smelled appallingly vile.

Her son's experience humbled Yvonne, and she remembered her years of prayer for his safety. They had both bowed their heads in gratitude and said a little prayer together, praying that their boss, Leo, would also be saved, along with those who were in the café.

When Yvonne and Willie went about looking for Leo, she was shocked by the destruction she saw. The monster twister had cut a brutal path through the city, plowing through the few old historic buildings which survived the scorching of the earth at the end of the Civil War. The wounded were everywhere. Cars tossed like little toys had been pushed and piled to the sides of the roads. Broken ancient trees stood naked and stripped of their majesty.

They learned that Shellman's Bluff, where the café once stood, was almost unreachable by road. She broke down in tears, crying, "Willie, we've lost Leo. Please, God, forgive me for being so mean to him. He has a good heart and soul inside of him. Oh, Willie, we lost a fine 'n good man."

She remembered her brave, teenage son trying to give her hope that Leo was still alive. As they sat by a survivor message board, he told her all that Leo had said to him about her. "Sometimes, Mamma, he'd ask if I thought you'd ever consider going out with him. He said he was crazy 'bout you. That you were the most beautiful woman he had ever seen."

"He wasn't that bad, was he?" she had cried to Willie. "Just a diamond in the rough." Willie nodded and agreed wholeheartedly.

She remembered the noise of the helicopters and ambulances and trucks and cherry pickers. Then they were told those helicopters were searching for bodies out in the ocean and she had cried at the thought of Leo's bloated body floating out in the ocean's currents.

Desperate to find Leo dead or alive, they managed to borrow someone's old car and drove around. In the center of Darien, Yvonne looked over and saw a crazy man in a ripped shirt, covered in blood, screaming at them from inside a cracked phone booth.

"Willie, look," she had cried. She saw Leo look up to the sky, and pray to Heaven. That did it right then and there. She'd never thought of him as a Godly man before, but there he was, praying up a storm. She felt she had witnessed a miracle.

Then, as a promise to her to never hurt another human being, Leo raced up to Canada to stop the killing he had ordered of that young man called Jack Taylor. Jack, was killed anyhow, but, not by her Leo. And it was there that he found family he didn't even know he had.

YVONNE REMEMBERED IT ALL standing by the stove. She chuckled and shook her head and, seeing that the oil was hot, reached for the bowl of batter.

She thought of how Leo and his nephews were now in business together. No more smuggling or drug running as he did in Georgia. No more beating up people, ordering people to be killed. Instead, he was committed to building up the economy for Myrtle Beach by making that nice theme park to attract tourists. He even promised her a restaurant or two, which excited her to no end. And most beautiful of all, Leo was supporting Willie, at university. Her son was studying to be a lawyer.

She and Leo had talked about marriage. Which was a good thing; she hadn't told her Leo yet, but there was a hush puppy in the oven and as a good Christian woman she didn't want her child, their child, out of wedlock. Not like she did with Willie. But she hadn't yet figured out how to tell Leo.

Her. A little black girl from New Orleans, now a grown, mature woman marrying an Italian immigrant and having a new family. She would never have guessed in a million years that she could be so happy and proud.

She tapped a spoon against the rim of the bowl of batter, and frowned. Sure, sometimes she felt a little uneasy because money seemed to come far too easily to Leo. Where did it all come from? But she had already decided not to meddle—some things you simply didn't question. One thing she knew for sure; all those years of hard times were far behind her now.

But she *was* going to hold Leo to his sacred promise—that he would never hurt another human being so long as he lived to breathe.

CLAUDIA STRUGGLED as she half-carried Maria out of the car. "Come'a," Claudia pleaded.

Maria didn't want to leave the back seat.

"Maria. Get up'a."

Maria slowly attempted to get out of the car. She groaned and leaned over Claudia's stooped shoulder.

Claudia shut the car door and struggled to keep Maria upright as she shuffled her through the garage and into the hallway. Maria's feet caught and dragged the tossed shoes sitting along the wall as she did her best to help her *Nonna* get her into the house. Finally, Claudia lost control of Maria and let her half-fall into Fabrizio's favorite old La-Z-Boy at the bottom of the stairs. The heavy chair bounced and rocked under Maria's weight, and Claudia tried to keep her balance by leaning on the back of it, but it gave way and fell back, fully extending flat, forcing the foot rest against her shins. She half-toppled on top of Maria.

"Ouch," Maria yelled.

Andy, still near the phone, hobbled on her crutches over to the top of the stairs to see what the commotion was all about. She looked down to see the La-Z-Boy fully extended with Maria trapped underneath Claudia whose little legs were desperately trying to find the floor.

"What the frig?" Andy held out the crutch from the top of the short flight of stairs, leaned forward as far as she could, and pushed at the back of the La-Z-Boy to put it back into an upright position. The end of the crutch slipped off the velvet material, and Andy toppled forward and fell, sliding down the few steps of the stairs, onto her belly.

The clatter of a crutch and the sound of her mother falling made Maria look back to see what happened. The shifting of her weight toppled the La-Z-Boy backward. Maria half-slid out onto Andy's back.

Claudia slid further along Maria toward the floor. Now her little legs stuck straight up in the air.

Claudia tried to raise her head. "Help'a. Help'a."

There was a pause as all three briefly listened to the hammering back at the barn.

In unison, all three loudly screamed for help.

CHAPTER EIGHT

LEO GRABBED THE MAN'S WRIST to look at the blood-splattered Rolex more closely. He sat back and stuck his cigar back in his mouth and, with two hands, unclasped the watch and weighed it in his hand. He bounced it around. He took the cigar out and smiled. "I like this. Nice watch, huh, Stef?"

Stefano leaned forward to take a closer look and nodded. "*Si*, nice watch." Stefano quietly leaned back on his crutch, listening to Mandolin Concerto on the large ghetto blaster at his feet. The surf nearby added to his feeling of contentment. The late afternoon sun was bright and the air was spectacular. He held a lime green plastic bowl of crushed seashells he had collected from the beach nearby. He gently played with the pretty shells, appreciating the light tones and notes he created.

He and Leo were in a shaft of light in the middle of a long dark hallway. Stefano looked up the hall. Light poured in at even distances along the south side of the hallway through the abandoned motel rooms' open doorways. He counted the openings all the way down to the end. Twelve on both sides. At some point, the doors had been stolen, as were their frames. Even the hallway ceiling fixtures were either broken or missing—some probably lighting up a lower-income house or two along unkempt sandy roads further inland; the rest surely sold at the local flea markets.

Stefano looked down at his wrapped ankle, noting that the bandage needed to be washed and replaced. He straightened out his leg and leaned back against peeling wallpaper as he quietly watched Leo press a gun against a guy's temple.

"Nice ghetto blaster," said Leo, clamping the cigar between his lips. He smiled tightly. "Though I prefer our music. Happy. Light. Creative. A work of art." He took his cigar out and spat a morsel of tobacco. "Not like that shit you had blaring on the street, asshole. Look at you." Leo motioned at the young man in front of him. "What's this?" He reached over and flipped the bottom edge of a thick, gold chain on the man's chest. "And this? Where'd you get that? Don't you think that kinda looks out of place here on Ocean Boulevard?"

The man muttered through his swollen lips.

Leo grabbed the man's hair and lifted his face. "What did you say?"

"No one gives a shit, man. Da cops leave me alone, alright?" The young man tried to spit but it dribbled over his split, bottom lip onto his blood-stained shirt. The young man wiggled his hands. They were tied at the wrists and his arms were stretched upward by a rope knotted onto a ceiling water sprinkler. His arms shook like branches in a storm, with one hypodermic needle swaying from his right shoulder, stuck through the short sleeve of his soiled white, baseball jersey. They had stuck him on an old chair, its back broken away.

The man's short afro sparkled with sweat, sand, dirt, and blood. Earlier, they had ground his face into the broken pavement under some sickly-looking palm trees in the private courtyard, dragged him into the deserted motel and roughed him up considerably. *Like tenderizing an expensive piece of meat*, thought Stefano grimly. He said a silent prayer, asking that the young man finally give in before they hurt him too much more. He knew the guy would eventually. They always did. He just wished it was sooner. But Leo had taught him, that the fact a man doesn't give in easily was actually a good sign of his character. Like wild animals, once you break anybody like that–once they turned—with a few added perks thrown in, and some love and attention, you had them for life.

They became *family*.

Stefano's elegant nose twitched. He could smell the guy shit his pants. He felt a twinge of guilt every time they had to humiliate someone to get a point across. But Leo had told him; that's how you build an army—one soldier at a time. It was a simple method and very elegant in spite of the mess it generated. It was as simple as the lovely, clean, bright, bouncy piece of classical mandolin music they were listening to.

Leo looked at him. "Stefano, this guy must be hungry. Let's give him something to eat."

Stefano leaned over his crutch with his plastic bowl of pretty shells and stepped from behind the guy. He dipped his paw into the bowl and let a handful of shells sift through his fingers. The sound of the falling shell pieces was almost angelic.

The music stopped, and the tape clicked to the end. "Just a second," Leo politely said, holding up a well-manicured finger. Sweating like a horse, he looked down at the ghetto blaster and bent to place the gun on top. Then he opened the blaster to turn the cassette. He smiled as the Württemberg Chamber Orchestra continued its magic. He picked up the gun again. "That's better." He pulled out a rumpled linen handkerchief from his khaki shorts and wiped the sweat from under his eyebrows. It was hot in the hallway. No air. "Isn't that pretty music? Huh?"

Until then, the man kept his gaze on the gun. Now he slowly dared to look into Leo's face. His one eye was completely swollen shut.

"Stefano, he's hungry." Leo shifted his gnarled milk crate closer to the man's sweat and blood-covered face. "It's a mid-afternoon snack," he sneered.

"Wha-, what—?" The guy's blood-shot eye stared myopically up at the bowl in Stefano's hands. He looked frantically to Leo and then up at Stefano. "Wha—?"

"You're askin', what are we going to do with these shells? I'll tell you what we're going to do with them. You see," he looked at his new Rolex watch, "We've been here at least two hours. I don't know about you, but I'm getting hungry. This is hard work. Isn't it hard work, Stef?"

Stefano nodded.

"So, we made sure we packed a late lunch special for you." He leaned into the guy. "Did you bring a lunch along?"

The man trembled.

"Did you?" He held up the gun and once again pushed the nuzzle into the man's head.

The man tried to lean as far away as he could from the gun. "No."

Leo kept his cold, steel-blue eyes on the guy while he wrapped the guy's collar around his free fist, tightening a choking hold on him. "No?"

"No," the man choked.

"Well, that's okay. Because we brought you something really special." Leo let go of the man's collar. "We picked this just for you." He motioned to Stefano.

Stefano lay down his crutch and carefully went down on his haunches, to the side of the man. He dipped his fingers into the shell pieces and held some out to the man's face.

The man pulled back as far as he could, staring with his one good eye at the shells between Stefano's fingers.

Stefano wiped the pieces onto his filthy, sweaty face. A few fell off while others stuck to blood and sweat. One slightly cut the young man's cheek. A drop of blood formed over the grime on his dark skin.

"Oh, now, look what you did. Your table manners are terrible. Stefano, make sure some of it gets into his mouth. We don't want him hungry. How sharp are your teeth, by the way?"

Stefano dipped his fingers back in the bowl and scooped out more shell pieces. He delicately mushed them against the swollen lips.

The man let out a stifled sob and groaned, keeping his lips pursed, trying to turn his face away from Stefano's fingers.

"You know, if you would just work with us, maybe we can get some of it in your mouth."

Stefano put the bowl down. Balanced on his haunches, he reached out with his other hand and squeezed the guy's face making him open his mouth. He smashed some shells in, and then closed his mouth for him. This created a crunching sound along with muffled groans.

"Swallow it," Leo yelled.

The man broke down entirely. He cried, howled, shook his head. He spat out shells and blood. "I'm sorry. I'm sorry. I'm sorry."

"Maybe it doesn't taste good, Stef. Why don't we get something he really likes. Don't you think we should, Stef?" Leo grinned at Stefano. Then he faked a concerned look. "I guess our shells must taste awful."

"Meatballs and spaghetti," suggested Stefano.

"Yeah, or maybe crab cakes." Leo turned to the guy. "Maybe you'd rather have crab cakes. Italian style, right?"

The guy nodded eagerly. "Yeah. Yeah. Italian crab cakes. Whatever you say."

"Are you ready? What's your name again?" Leo leaned closer to the man's bleeding lips.

"Matthew."

"Matthew." Leo sniffed the man's pungent odor. He pulled back and grimaced. "Matthew, I think we should nickname you Stinky. What do you think, Stef?"

Stefano laughed. "*Si*, Stinky is'a good name." Stefano slapped the guy's shoulder.

"Stefano, this guy needs a bath. We should make sure we help get him clean. Would towing him behind the boat do that, do you think?"

Matthew shook his head. Something caught in his throat, and he gagged. He spat out tiny pieces of shell.

"What did you do? You didn't swallow the shells which, to me, means you don't appreciate our kindness. We have ways of dealing with people like you."

The man cried. "No, please. I told you. I don't mean no disrespect. I'll do whatever you say."

Stefano took out a tissue from the breast pocket of his light-yellow golf shirt. Stinky was the second guy they turned that day. The early morning appointment only generated a little blood, but Stinky liberally sprayed him. He gently dabbed Stinky's lips, then motioned to him to spit out the rest of the shells. He held the tissue until the guy spat out a bit more.

"I swear to you both. I'll get killed for stopping. I've seen others try to leave or deal on their own, and they always ended up as shark bait. Please, oh God, listen to me."

"Stefano, that reminds me, there's really good fishin' here in Myrtle Beach, I discovered. I go out whenever I get the chance. I got a good engine and some gear. You like to fish?"

"*Si*, I do. Very much." Stefano smiled.

"Well, we already have our own shark bait here. So, see? No need to look for any."

Stinky groaned.

The tape deck clicked to a stop again. For the moment, it was quiet but for the sound of the surf and seagulls. Leo closed his eyes and listened to the sounds. He opened them, took out the finished tape, and pulled another out of his pocket. He held it up for Stinky to see.

"This is my favorite piece." He stuck the new tape into the machine and clicked the lid shut. It was the Godfather theme, an innocent strumming of a lovely, gentle string instrument. Leo pulled Stinky's head up by the hair. "Can you hear it?"

Stinky nodded.

"Listen to this." Leo let go of Stinky's hair and held up a finger, listening to the music.

"Oh, man," Stinky moaned. Tears created shiny streaks down his dirty face. That's the Godfather. I knew it. You're Mafia."

"No, we're not Mafia. You have to be Sicilian to be Mafia."

"Who are you then?" Stinky cried.

"We're from Calabria. Some call us the *'Ndrangheta*."

"In drag what?" His voice cracked.

"'*Ndrangheta*. We're the smarter ones. We hide right before your eyes. But guess what? We're more dangerous than the Sicilians. And we're worse than your boss the Hell's Angels." Leo motioned with his hand.

Stinky looked confused for a moment. "I don't work for Hell's Angels."

Leo and Stefano looked at each other. "Who do you work for, then?" asked Leo.

"Irish guys from Canada."

Leo and Stefano stared at him. Leo looked at Stefano. "All the way down here?" Leo looked at Stinky. "Stef here is from Canada, too."

Stinky looked at Stefano.

Stefano nodded silently.

"Canadians are nice people," said Leo. "Aren't they, Stef?"

Stefano shrugged. "Some'atimes."

"Well, these Irish guys aren't so nice," Stinky said weakly.

"Listen, does the name Dunie sound familiar?"

Stinky nodded. "Yeah, but he's dead now. We have a new boss. Allan something."

"Wow," Leo said. "The Weasle."

Stinky's eye opened wide. "That's it."

Leo shook his head. "Well, am I ever glad we got you. Stinky. You work for us, and I guarantee you no one will do anything to you. You know why?"

The guy looked hopeful. "Why?"

"Because once you work for us, we protect you. We value loyal soldiers. You work for us, and you won't be stuck on the street corners selling weed or crack. We have more dignified work for you. You'll be looking *over* those who stand on the street corners, or you work for us directly, see? And we only do weed and pills. We don't do crack."

"No crack? But that's where the money is."

Leo shook his head. "No, we sell the best weed. Comes straight from Venezuela, none of this South Carolina shit. The Irish boys can keep the crack shit. They'll be grateful." Leo rested his elbows onto his knees, still holding onto the gun. "And you know what else we can offer you as a really nice perk?" Leo raised and pressed the gun into Stinky's forehead for effect.

Stinky looked cross-eyed at the gun.

"We get you outta what stinking hole you live in, and we put you in a nice little apartment in a building we just bought."

"A little apartment?"

"Yeah, with a nice queen bed, a small kitchen, a balcony lookin' over the beach. We can all live happily in the same building. Why you will even taste some of my Yvonne's cookin'. Stefano, isn't Yvonne's cooking somethin' to die for?"

"*Si.*" He grinned at Stinky.

"A place? Cooking?"

"Yeah."

"Would I have to die for it?"

"No, you won't have to die. Once you taste it, you'll see what I mean."

"Are you guys for real? You're not shittin' me?"

"No, but you've been shittin' you," Leo laughed.

"Can I put my arms down now?" Stinky's voice broke like that of a prepubescent boy.

"Just don't do anything stupid."

Stinky closed his one eye. It fluttered open again after Stefano loosened the knot at the ceiling and allowed his arms to slowly lower to his lap. Stinky rubbed one arm where they had punctured the skin a number of times with the needle he had with the stash of heroin he was pushing. The needle still hung, limply, forgotten in the mix of events.

"So, no more disgusting drugs," Leo warned.

"I never touch the shit," Stinky said.

Leo and Stefano laughed.

"But how's all that going to help if, in the end, I'm dead?" protested Stinky.

"Listen, you don't worry about the West End guys. Anybody who would try to snuff you we'll get to first. Just that simple."

Stinky squinted his eye shut again. Slowly, silently, he nodded his head.

Leo stepped back and held the gun toward the wall at his side. He shot the wall. The explosion rocked the air around them.

Stinky screamed like a girl.

"See how easy that was?" Leo grabbed one of Stinky's wrists.

Stinky slowly wrestled it back.

"Shhhh. Don't worry. It's okay. Here, help me get him up, Stef."

Stefano stood up and grabbed Stinky's free wrist. They pulled him to his feet but his legs wouldn't work, and he slumped back down. They tried a second time, and managed to keep him on his feet though he had to lean against Stefano. Stefano's golf shirt was smudged with filth and blood.

"You're making a good decision," Leo said. "Not only do you still have a job, but ya got a roof over your head that's much better than whatever piece of shit you might live in right now. And you got protection. You understand? That's how we work here." He motioned to Stefano and himself. "We're actually good people. We're kind. Generous."

"Handsome," Stefano added, grinning.

"He doesn't say much, but, when he does, he's right. Yes, we're handsome guys."

Stinky looked sideways at Stefano and then back at Leo.

"So, you ready, Stinky? We gotta clean you up. Let's have some supper. I want you to meet Yvonne. But don't tell her what we did to you. We're just goin' to pretend you're a homeless man we took home to feed. She loves it when we do that. At least, that's what she thinks we're doin'."

Stinky looked down at his filth. He slowly and gingerly pulled at the back of his pants.

"Oh, don't worry, Stinky. We've dragged in worse-smelling guys than you."

Leo grabbed an arm and led Stinky a few steps down the hall toward the stairs, with Stefano following on his crutch. Leo stopped. "Stay here, Stinky." Leo walked back to the ghetto blaster, turned the Godfather music off and picked up the radio. He walked back to Stefano and Stinky. He jovially took Stinky's arm and continued to walk. "You're gonna just love Yvonne's hush puppies," he said, as he yanked out the hypodermic needle.

"HONEY, LOVE, supper's ready. Stefano, ah hope mah man behaved himself today." Yvonne stood in the little kitchen as they entered the condo with Stinky in tow.

Stefano coughed and almost stumbled over his own crutch. He turned to Yvonne who proudly stood in her white summer shift, sported a pretty white bandana in her black curly hair, and gave them a smile as long as the beach outside the condo.

He smiled back and nodded, feeling a hot flush rising up his neck.

"I always behave, *Bella*," Leo said. "Here! I found another stray from the street." Leo turned to Stinky. "Stinky, this is my lovely woman, the love of my life. I tell you this; you must never let anyone hurt a single hair on that beautiful head of hers. You hear me?"

Stinky wordlessly looked at Yvonne in surprise—a black sister. He then curiously looked at Leo, as he nervously fingered his filthy shirt. He nodded, blinking his one good eye.

"Mah, you been in a fight?" asked Yvonne, putting a hand on her chest.

"You should see the other guy," said Leo. Leo turned and rearranged Stinky's hair before brushing down the front of him. "Do we have anything Stinky can wear, *Bella*?"

"You a good man, Leo. Ah'll get somethin' for him to wear. Show him wheah the bathroom is. He's goin' to have to wash up for dinner." Yvonne scurried into their bedroom.

"You use this bathroom, Stinky, before you stink up the place."

Just as Stinky walked into the bathroom, Leo held his arm and turned him around. Stinky froze, startled.

"Remember, Stinky. You be good to us, and we'll be good to you. But you're going to take care of Miss Yvonne when I'm not around." Leo squeezed Stinky's upper arm, making him squirm. "And I mean it when I say, if you ever do anything to hurt Miss Yvonne, or if you allow anyone else to hurt Miss Yvonne, you will not see the light by the end of that day. *Capisci?*"

Stinky nodded, turned the washroom light on, and closed the door.

Stefano looked down at his own bloody shirt. He kicked off one sneaker and bent down to gently take the other one off his swollen ankle. He went into his room to change, closing the door behind him. He yanked off his top, bundled it up into a ball, and took a plastic bag from out of his closet. He threw the top in and swirled the bag around his wrist and tied a knot into the bag. He tossed it back into the closet, grabbed a sweatshirt from a shelf and threw it on. He inhaled deeply, as he heard Yvonne coming back into the kitchen.

"Honey, ah gotta tell Stefano his wife called."

"Who, Andy?"

"Uh-huh. She sounded pretty upset about somethin'."

Stefano closed the closet and opened the bedroom door.

"Stefano, your wife called. Asked if you could call her back," Yvonne said.

"How long before dinner's ready, *Bella*?" Leo asked.

"Just another couple of minutes, but we can wait."

Yvonne frowned at Stefano. "Stefano, you have to call home."

Stefano looked at the pots and pans of food on the stove.

Yvonne waved a hand. "Oh, don't you worry, you call her right now."

As he walked through the kitchen and followed Leo into the living room, where the late afternoon setting sun cast a warm glow, he wondered what calamity would cause Andy to call long distance to a number he didn't remember sharing with her. If she went after the number, she must've been desperate. "It'a can't be good, if she call'a," he muttered as he dialed.

The bathroom door opened and Stinky appeared wearing clean clothes, far too large on his thin frame. "I wouldn't use that phone," said Stinky.

Leo, Yvonne and Stefano turned to look at him.

"They tap phones here."

Stefano saw Leo's face pale.

"How would you know?" Leo asked.

"Along this stretch. Bad part of town. You don't want to take the chance."

Stefano shrugged and raised his shoulders. "How I talk with Adriana?"

"Public phone booth. Or a Brick."

Stefano eyed Stinky. "A Brick'a?"

"Yeah, one of those portable phones. They can't tap them."

Leo said, "Why are they called Bricks?"

"Because they're big and heavy like one."

"Where do we get one?"

"At the mall. They cost around four thousand dollars though."

Leo turned to Stefano. "We gotta make sure everyone has one of these Bricks."

Stefano nodded.

"Technology is amazing these days. We're in the future, Stef. It's the '80's, for crying out loud."

"There's a public phone in the park next door," said Yvonne. "You have change?"

Stefano checked his pockets and shook his head.

Yvonne opened the cupboard above the fridge and stretched to grab a plastic container with its label stripped. She shook it. "You take this. Lots of change. Enough for long-distance."

"IT LOOKED BAD, STEF."

Stefano listened to Andy, feeling a quiet alarm rising in his chest. He could barely hear her over the surf on the beach.

"I talk to Leo. Get a flight. Tell'a Maria I'm coming."

He hung up and stared at the filthy, push-button phone for a moment as he heard kitchen pots from the nearby windows. He turned and saw Leo sitting on the third-floor balcony, sucking on a cigar. Leo was leaning sideways toward Stinky who was sitting obediently on a chair beside him, and muttering something Stefano couldn't hear.

Stefano stepped away from the public phone and limped to the path that led to the side door of their building. He struggled up the flights of stairs. It was cool and dark in the stairwell with a whiff of urine emanating from the corners. He came back to their floor and entered the apartment.

Yvonne, in bare feet and pink toenails, was setting the table as he entered. She put a hand on her stomach and turned to him expectantly. "Honey, Stef's back. Supper's ready."

Stefano watched Leo guide Stinky to the glass doors and open them for him. They walked in and made their way to the table.

Stefano limped to his chair.

"Everything alright?" asked Leo, squinting over cigar smoke as he sat down. He lifted up his plate for Yvonne to put collard greens, beets, hush puppies and gumbo rice in a pile.

Stefano inhaled the comforting aroma of Louisiana cuisine. He salivated, despite his concern and sense of urgency. As he shifted his body, he watched Leo's eyes devour the food Yvonne was putting on his plate. Leo then looked up at Yvonne with a softness in his eyes that made it impossible for Stefano to keep what happened earlier in the day in perspective. It was a dream; an illusion. Either this man was the false version, or the earlier version was. The man sitting in front of him was melting in Yvonne's presence, as if he was a man who surely didn't have it in him to do what he did today to Stinky—the poor man who sat opposite him at the table, looking scratched and broken. He was tempted to feel remorseful. Was he brushing with something evil? Leo sometimes appeared to be something out of this world; full of generosity and love, bravado and camaraderie, with a love for good food and a good woman, for *family*. And yet, Stefano sensed Leo had a long history from the outskirts of Hell.

Stef inhaled deeply and slowly exhaled as he arranged his thoughts. This was his long lost *Zio*, the new, true patriarch and leader of his *famiglia*. A bright, strong leader—stronger than Stefano could ever hope to be. He watched his plate being taken by Yvonne's hand, her soft, chocolate skin so beautiful in contrast to the white, hard surface of the heavy ceramic plate.

"*Zio*, can you'a help me? I need to buy a plane ticket back to Montreal."

"It's that bad?" Leo placed his cigar onto his bread plate.

"Oh, mah," said Yvonne, ladling food onto Stefano's plate. "Ah hope everything is okay."

"*Bella*, we need to help get Stef back to Montreal."

Yvonne nodded. "Ah will look up the number to the airport." She wiped her hands on her shift.

"I know it," said Stinky.

Leo, surprised, turned to study Stinky. "You know the number to the airport?"

"I've arranged that flight for my dealer."

Leo pointed at the phone by the couch. "Fill your boots. A ticket for Stef tonight if you can find it." He dug into his pocket and took out a fat wallet. He held out a credit card. "Here, use this."

Stinky shifted in his seat and looked at Leo pointedly.

"What?"

"You want this call to be tapped?"

Leo shrugged. "Who cares? So, Stefano Giordani flies back to Montreal to see his family. What's so secretive about that?"

"Okay." But Stinky kept staring at Leo.

"What now?"

"Why am I here?"

Leo slapped his back. "You are here because you have finally found your calling, Stinky. We need you. Now be a good soldier and find a flight for my dear nephew, Stefano."

LEO PLACED A HAND on Stefano's shoulder. He took out his cigar and smacked his lips.

They were standing in the small terminal on what used to be the United States Army Air Force Base, used as an auxiliary landing airfield during World War II. It had recently been converted to accommodate commercial flights.

Leo looked around. "Perfect set-up." It was one of the reasons why Myrtle Beach was so tantalizing as a new base for laundering and drugs. He had already set up a bribery ring, shifting drugs into the area from Venezuela, through the terminal. Easy peasy.

Stefano knew of this, but it was the first time he'd seen it. He saw a Piedmont Airline ticket counter employee looking at them, then quickly look away.

"Let's sit over there, Stef. I wanna talk."

Leo led him to metal and black fake leather seats. He sat down and looked at a wall clock. He looked around the brightly-lit terminal before settling back. He looked to Stinky at the door.

"I'm gonna keep Stinky under my arm for a while. I like him. He could become someone I can count on. Maybe even my own couple of eyes, if you know what I mean."

Stefano looked down at his hands. He felt Leo bend closer. He smelled his breath.

"So, tell me more about this problem with Maria. She gets into fights."

Stefano, his mouth slightly open in deep thought, looked at his *Zio. What was safe to say?* Maria's particular challenge was packed full of unknowns. It could even become dangerous. He hesitated.

"Stef, if it's so bad that you can't tell me, all the more you should. I'm your father, your uncle, your protector. I should know every-thing so that I can figure out how to help. How to protect you and your family. I have to figure out if this could eventually hurt the Consortium's interest in what we do."

Stefano felt an eyelid twitch as he pondered how much he should divulge.

Leo poked him in the ribs. "Do you remember what Jorge said? No secrets?"

Stefano looked into Leo's eyes. They were cold blue. They bulged slightly from their sockets, his bushy salt and pepper eyebrows shading them from the stark fluorescent light overhead. Those eyes meant business.

Stefano swallowed. "My *bambina*. She'a was born as, um, what you call, a *ermafrodita*."

CHAPTER NINE

STEFANO SAT NERVOUSLY in the window seat. The roar of the engines slammed his ears. Looking out over the American Eastern Seaboard, his breath fogged the glass. He swallowed hard. He watched the hills and valleys of North Carolina pass by in the deepening dusk.

The only other time in his life he had ever flown was when Fabrizio and Claudia sponsored him as an immigrant to Canada—over 20 years before. He was newly betrothed to their daughter, Andy, and hadn't even met her. He thought of the times he ignored Andy's pleas to fly to Miami for holidays over the years, simply because he hated to travel. Now here he was, working in Myrtle Beach, and hopping on a plane to fly back home to Montreal. Like some modern globetrotter.

So many changes and not all good. He sat back and readjusted his Myrtle Beach baseball cap so that the visor was just above his eyes. He felt exposed. Not in his element.

He told Leo what Andy had told him; that Maria had been in a major fight with Selena Ryan, dead Dunie's daughter, the Weasel's godchild. He explained how Selena had flattened Maria's little friend, eight-year-old Francesca, against a brick wall, and how she was now in a coma. He talked briefly about Maria's anomalies, watching Leo's face carefully as he did. He was disturbed by Leo's reaction. Shock and dismay covered Leo's face while, at the same time, he tried to be matter-of-fact about what he heard. He also told Leo about his barn fire.

Leo told him it wasn't enough just to have his workers hang around the house as protection. His family needed a personal body guard,

24/7. He announced he was going to talk to Jorge Pesseck about his son, Alessandro Pesseck.

While they waited for Stefano's flight, Leo got on a public phone and called Jorge. By the time Stefano's flight was called for boarding, Leo told him Jorge had agreed to send Alessandro to Montreal next week.

Stefano was impressed with young Alessandro, but he wasn't sure how effective he would be as a guardian. He seemed eager to please, but how was he as an experienced bodyguard? And what would he be protecting them from? Even Stefano didn't know for sure. It was, perhaps, only a matter of a young bully—Selena Ryan. Perhaps it was only she who put fire to his barn. Perhaps it wasn't a turf war, after all.

Stefano glanced over his shoulder at two women sitting; one wore headphones connected to the plane's armrest, the other was an older woman with her eyes closed. He hated to disturb them. He wished he had an aisle seat, but he knew he was lucky to get this last available seat on such short notice. He glanced at his swollen ankle.

He gently unclasped his seatbelt and shifted sideways, facing the younger woman. She sensed his movement, looked at him, and shyly smiled as she undid her belt and lifted herself on her hands.

He had to bend and lightly tap on the older woman's shoulder. She jerked awake. She looked up. She unclasped her seat belt and struggled to her feet. She stepped into the aisle and stood back clear of their seats.

"I'm'a so sorry." His words disappeared into the din in the cabin, so he smiled as nicely as he could.

She looked up and also smiled, politely nodding.

He managed to squeeze by the young lady and step free. He raised his hands against the overheard baggage compartments to keep his balance in the rolling plane, as he made his way to the lavatory. He jolted to a stop. His eye caught the back of a couple of familiar heads midway down the aisle. One had his hair slicked back, shining, perfectly groomed. The other rougher, lighter-colored hair. Wavy, longer. That guy looked to his left across the aisle.

Stefano nervously looked to the back of the plane to see if there was a lavatory sign. None. He looked at the sign in front again and sighed. He pulled his baseball cap further down over his eyes and lowered his head. He made a point of looking out the windows to the right, away from the men he passed on his way.

He slipped through the open curtain up front and hugged the wall with his back. He saw the lavatory was vacant and tried to open it. The plane swayed as he fiddled with the door, desperate to get in before the guys spotted his bulk through the curtain. A woman's hand reached in front of him. He looked to see a blonde-haired stewardess smile. She gently pushed the door in from the middle.

"There you go," she shouted, over the roar of the engines.

He nodded, thinking of beautiful Anita and her blonde hair and bright smile.

He stepped into the lavatory and unzipped his pants, straddling his legs to keep a tight balance. The toilet was so far down that he had to focus carefully on what he was doing. As he watched the stream of urine steam into the noisy steel toilet, he continued in deep thought. He didn't tell anyone except Peter that he had Mario keep an eye on Anita out west. He had sent Mario, now a *vice capo* and his right-hand man, to follow the money and expand into markets ripe for the picking. Through Mario, he tried his hand at the textile market, importing goods from the Philippines, but the Chinese were too powerful, so now they were setting up a disposal business just outside Vancouver where Anita lived.

There were rumors British Columbia was going to invest in the latest fad - recycling. He chuckled to himself. It seemed he had a knack at making big money from the garbage business—collecting and disposing of regular garbage, and recently the lucrative business of collecting and disposing of toxic materials. Now they want to *recycle* the stuff. He tried to anonymously create a job for Anita through one of these enterprises, but she instead acquired a position on the production team for CBC Radio. Now he was looking for strings to pull, to get her the job of her dreams, a radio host. That would make his heart glad, he thought. God forbid, Andy ever found out.

He zipped up his fly and faced the mirror as he ran water over his fingers. He rubbed the stubble on his chin. Then he smelled his armpits and frowned. He looked around for paper towels and found them stuck in the metal console by the sink. He plucked a few sheets, dampened them, and squeezed the fistful of paper under his sweatshirt, dabbing at each underarm. He tossed the paper into the garbage hole. He leaned against the counter for a moment to brush his black locks into place. Then, he turned his attention to the threat sitting outside in the center aisle of the plane.

He pulled at the inside of the door and was pleased to see a waiting line at the lavatory. The line blocked him from view of the men. He nodded, smiled, and carefully limped to the side behind the curtains. He slowly moved the curtains away from the inside of the doorway. He peeked through, taking a good look at the two guys. One of them had his eyes closed, listening to his headphones. It was Nick Rizzuto, the Sicilian. He'd taken over for Vic Cotroni after his death the year before. He knew he lived just south of Montreal. Big guy. Mansion, fast cars. Dangerous. Family man.

The other guy with the longer light hair was Allan the Weasel, Head of the West End Gang, just taking over for Dunie Ryan— Selena's godfather.

Stefano jerked back in shock. His heart quickened. It was a double whammy. With them snooping around, he sensed there was going to be a fight on his hands over Myrtle Beach. And here he was, on the same plane as Selena's godfather, a threat on its own merit.

He jumped at a sudden clatter of dishes in the galley and saw the stewardess. He limped toward her. He dug into his jeans hip pocket, and pulled out a 100-dollar bill from his wallet, folded it and leaned into her right ear. She listened to what he said and looked down at the 100-dollar bill. She smiled, blinked, and reached up to loosen her top button. She took the bill quickly, grabbed a tray, and placed two little bottles of champagne and glasses on top. Stefano watched as she squeezed past the waiting line at the lavatory. Then Stefano lowered his head and followed closely behind her.

As she reached Nick and The Weasel, she bent down enough for them to see down her cleavage.

Stefano squeezed past her, seeing both men stare at her as she graciously offered the champagne.

He limped to his row. He bent down very close to the women, almost in their faces. "Would you like to sit at the window? I'm'a big. 'N I no need to look'a."

The older lady looked at him blankly.

The young woman nodded and smiled. She undid her seatbelt and gathered her things from the pouch in front of her. She moved into his window seat, as the other lady looked around, then back at him.

He pointed at the seat next to her questioningly, then at his swollen foot.

She looked down with concern and nodded. She gathered her magazines and reading glasses, undid her seat belt, reached up to the edge of the overhead luggage compartment to pull herself up, and switched.

"*Grazie*," he said over the roar of the cabin, as he sat down and stretched his leg into the aisle. He eyed his two nemeses near the front of the plane.

Allan the Weasel looked like he was about to look in Stefano's direction. Stefano slouched and covered his brow. He looked up just as Allan's head swiveled back around.

Stefano thought of Maria's life. How things have changed. Once upon a time, years before, he was sure he would have a slew of sons to eventually take over his construction business as he grew old. Instead, they had beautiful Maria. Then, he expected he would eventually have grandsons through Maria and a fine son-in-law. Prospective husbands were slim in their Vindenza *famiglia* and it occurred to him, if everything had been normal, he secretly thought perhaps Alessandro Pesseck would make a good future son-in-law.

The future was now a mystery. Stefano felt as if he were standing at the edge of a bottomless abyss. It made him as nervous as sitting in a plane, 30,000 feet above the ground.

MARIA CURLED UP ON HER BED, numbly watching the light crawl across her bedroom ceiling. She ignored each of her mother's knocks at the door offering food or drink, and her *Nonna's* pleas at the door. She watched the light fade as it traveled over the cutesy pink and yellow wallpaper of unicorns on the walls. She watched it crawl down the closet doors to the shag carpeting. When it became so dark it was difficult to focus on anything, Maria sat slumped on the edge of her bed, picking at the chipping nail polish on her bitten nails. After a while, she looked up and inadvertently saw the shadow of herself in the full-length mirror.

She stared. *Was she dead?* She reached up and touched her messy bob cut.

She saw the dark shadow in the mirror lift its arm and do the same.

She took a deep breath and looked around the room. She leaned to her bedside lamp and turned it on. She let her eyes travel around the sweet little girl's room, and saw Bert and Ernie grinning at her from the bookcase. Once upon a time, they were her friends and her comfort; now they were strangers mocking her.

She looked down at the Barbie Doll House in the corner and saw her Barbie dolls, some in good condition, others pretty banged up. One had a mustache drawn on it, done by one of Peter's twin boys, Andrew. She remembered clobbering him for it and getting punished.

She looked down at the school uniform crumpled in the corner. She felt like screaming. She felt terrified. Suddenly, the images of the morning before, of Francesca's accident, rushed back at her, replaying in her mind's eye. She jumped up, grabbed the uniform and rolled it in a ball. She opened her bedroom window and threw it out as far as she could over the back lawn. She heard chickens protest in surprise somewhere out in the grass.

Tears welled in her eyes. She held her crotch and looked at the bedroom's sickly-sweet walls. She stepped to the closest wall. She felt the seams in the wallpaper. She turned and looked back at the single bed, pushed into the corner ever since she could remember. There she had spent years peeling away at the seams by the headboard.

She climbed on her knees up onto the bed, found a loose edge, and pulled at it. She stopped when it was the size of a quarter. She pulled more until it was the size of a dollar bill. Then, she tore a large portion of the wallpaper from left to right. She flipped the paper over her shoulder and stood up on her bed. She tore piece after piece of paper off the wall, tossing them to the side.

DEEP IN THOUGHT, CLAUDIA SAT peeling potatoes. She stopped listening to Andy long ago. Andy was complaining about Holy Mary Mother of God Catholic School and what she would do and say as a piece of her mind. How it was all their fault, and they should try harder to prevent violence in the school. All Claudia could think of was her poor *nipotina* being exposed and shamed—dishonored by a bully. She remembered that Irish family, all red-haired, freckle-faced. She remembered when these strangers moved into their predominantly Italian-Canadian community a few years before, fresh 'off the boat' from Ireland.

Fabrizio had shared with her the rumors that said the two sons and their father were wanted back in Ireland. That they were members of a militant group with a name made up of three initials but she couldn't remember what they were: IRS, IBS, AAA? Something like that. They killed many people, mostly politicians, and were wanted for murder and planting bombs. They ran away and came directly to Vindenza, Quebec. And now this evil family was causing havoc with her own.

She knew what Fabrizio would've done. Their only grandchild dishonored in such a way. That girl wouldn't be breathing tonight, she thought. She put her peeler down and sighed.

Andy, at the stove, leaning on her crutches, noticed. "What, Ma?"

Claudia shook her curls. "*Niente.* I was thinking of you'a Daddy."

"A good thing he's not here. His heart would be broken by that little—"

The two of them became lost in sorrowful thoughts, both feeling helpless in the face of such an outright evil deed against their Maria.

Andy swung over to the table, sat down carefully, and covered her head with one hand as she kept a grip on her crutches.

Claudia looked over. "Stefano. He'a flying in da plane still, *si*?"

Andy looked at her watch. "He's landing in about three hours." She looked down at her stained black blouse. "Sheesh." She wiped at it and gave up. "I need to stretch my back." She struggled out of the kitchen and disappeared into the dark hallway.

Claudia thought she heard the click of a door upstairs. She put her peeler down and quietly slid the kitchen chair back, ignoring her sore knees. Pushing herself off, she tip-toed from the kitchen into the hallway. She looked into the living room and saw Andy's shadow standing quietly at the window, looking up at the night sky.

Another click of a door caught her attention and Claudia looked up the stairs into the upper hallway. She saw Maria, in t-shirt and blue jeans, appear in the light streaming from her bedroom. She watched Maria slip into the dark master bedroom across the hall. The light went on.

She looked at Andy's shadow. "Adriana," she called.

Andy looked back, her arms hanging limply over her crutches, her back hunched over in defeat.

"Maria." Claudia looked up in time to see the light go out in the master bedroom, and Maria slip back into her bedroom carrying something. Maria's door closed slowly, and she heard the click of the lock.

Claudia reached for the handrail and slowly took the first step. Her knees cracked. She leaned back and looked at Andy, who now held her face in her hands and appeared to be praying at the windows. Claudia slowly went down on her hands on the next step and crawled up the five steps. At the top, she continued to crawl awkwardly in her black dress, the hem getting in the way of her bony knees. Slowly, she crawled to Maria's door. She focused on the light coming from underneath the door. She set her eyes on the moving shadow across the source of light as she came closer and closer.

She reached the door frame and slowly lay on her stomach. She smelled the carpet; years of socks, carpet freshener, powder, and perfumes. She could smell cooking and garlic. Her nose started to itch, but she stiffled a sneeze. She silently breathed and then rested her head to look under the door with one eye.

Claudia saw Maria sitting on the bed facing the door. She had lit a candle on her bedside table. Claudia watched Maria reach up to her hair with something, and she heard a snip. Something fell like a feather from her head onto the carpet. She watched Maria cut lock after lock of hair. Then the scissors went to the blue jeans. Maria snipped into the material and cut slashes. First, a few across the upper thigh. Then one on the knee. Then she shifted her position so she could cut the other leg. Claudia bit her lip as she watched Maria look at the scissors, then put them down on the bed, before looking at the hair on the carpet. Maria brushed some of it under the bed. She got off the bed and on her knees in front of the full-length mirror. The candlelight reflected off the mirror onto Maria's face.

Claudia's heart broke at the sight of her.

Maria leaned out of Claudia's sight. Then, she straightened up and held something up to her head. A razor. Stefano's razor. She gently started to shave part of her eyebrow.

"No, *mia* Maria. *Non farlo. Non farlo.*" Claudia saw Maria twirl to face the door, her mouth open.

"Leave me alone," Maria screamed.

Claudia pulled herself up by the doorknob.

Andy's crutches clattered and banged as she swung herself into position from the living room to the bottom of the stairs.

"Ma, what you doin'?"

"Adriana, Maria cut her hair."

Andy dropped her crutches onto the tile in the hallway and frantically pulled herself up the stairs. Andy leaned against the walls. She winced and hobbled with her heavy cast over to her mother. She banged at the door. "Maria, don't you do anything you'll regret."

"Leave me alone, I said."

"Shoot." She turned to Claudia. "What exactly did you see?"

"I can hear you," screamed Maria.

Claudia pointed to her head.

"She cut her hair?"

Claudia nodded silently, tearfully. Then, slowly, she shakily pointed to her eyebrow.

"What?"

Claudia patted Andy's upper breast and pointed at her eyebrow again, making a shaving motion.

"She's shaving her fucking eyebrows?!" She banged at the door. "Maria, don't you dare shave your eyebrows."

"I'm not Maria anymore."

"God, Ma. What should we do?"

Claudia put her hands together as in prayer. "*Telefono, padre Carloni. Per favore.*"

Andy turned to the door again. "Maria. I'm gonna call Father Carl."

"I don't give a shit. He's not coming in here, and I'm not coming out."

They heard Maria's ghetto blaster turn on, searching for stations. Vile intrusive heavy metal blasted from the room and ugly lyrics introduced language neither woman had ever heard in their lives.

Andy turned and hopped toward the kitchen. "I'm going to get Father Carl to come right away. This is an emergency."

"CARL, MARIA IS HALF WOMAN AND HALF MAN."

Father Carl Carloni stopped sipping his wine. That wasn't at all what he expected to hear.

"Excuse me?"

Heavy metal still played loudly from upstairs.

Earlier, Andy had told him of the fight and what Selena had done. Why exposing Maria to the other girls was so dangerously cruel. "Maria has nuts. They dropped last month." Andy, who never cried, leaned on both crutches and frantically searched for a Kleenex somewhere in the pockets of her pants.

He eyed the stains on her blouse and the state of her hair. Her mascara had run and faded long before. He pushed back his chair, spilling his wine down a pant leg. He grabbed a box of Kleenex on the table and pushed it toward her and quickly stole a glance at his pants. It looked like he peed blood down his leg. He secretly groaned. Andy pulled out several Kleenexes and started dabbing her eyes. She blew her nose.

What Andy had so colorfully said sunk in. He stiffened. He raised both hands to his forehead. Father Carl realized he had been very wrong about a very sensitive subject and concluded he had let Andy down. He eyed her and raised a finger. "Did it occur to you that maybe I was wrong—?"

"Of course, it friggin' occurred to me. What do you think I am, Carl? A moron? What else would this be."

"But I could swear your genealogy said otherwise."

"Carl, it's wrong. It has to be. That ol' lady in Calabria knew shit. Oh, my God."

"I'm so sorry."

Claudia reached over and patted his arm. She accidentally knocked over Andy's crutches. They fell to the kitchen floor.

Andy didn't flinch. "It's not your fault, Carl. It's someone else's friggin' fault." She shifted to position her cast at a comfortable angle.

Father Carl bent over the table, arms outstretched in apology. His fingers spread out. "So, what exactly do you mean by her *nuts* dropped last month?"

Andy twisted and tore the Kleenex. "She had this attack while she was in a fight with that bitch, Selena. The same bitch who hurt Francesca this last time."

"You mean, two fights ago."

"At that time, we thought the fight brought on Maria's first—well, you know, that time in a woman's life. Right Ma?"

Claudia nodded sweetly. "Oh, *si*."

Andy's chin quivered and she had trouble keeping herself calm. "But tests showed that the pain was not her first—you know—time, but that it was her gonads that had dropped. Maria said she felt the pain first when Selena threw her full weight on her. Later, the pain was so bad, she passed out. The doctor thinks the fight hurried them along. She's going into puberty and her body is deciding to be a man instead of the young woman we thought she was going to become." She looked at the ceiling, at a loss for words.

Father Carl tore his eyes away. He absentmindedly looked at a wine stain in the tablecloth.

"Carl, I need counselling. Counsel me."

"Well. Two things; first, I set you up with a pediatric endocrinologist in Montreal, I know."

"A what?"

"Someone who can help you with Maria and her anomaly."

Andy threw up her hands. "There's that word again. Anomaly. As if there was something wrong with her."

"Anomaly only means something out of the ordinary."

Andy stared at him. "She's special, Carl. She's my baby."

"Yes, Andy, she is exceptional. You and I both know that. Perhaps this 'anomaly' helped make her special."

"No, Carl. She is special all on her very own."

Father Carl nodded. "It's obvious to everyone that she is. But you know I'm trained as a grief counsellor and have some medical background. This friend of mine in Montreal is the way to go, I know it."

Andy thought about it. "Okay, give me his number.

"Andy, leave it to me. I'll arrange it first thing in the morning."

Andy sniffed once. Then she nodded twice.

There was a lull in the music, and Father Carl lowered his voice. "Second; I want to revisit your genealogy and do it right, this time. Let me do this, and perhaps I can find where I went wrong."

"Fuck it, Carl. Just forget it. I don't give a shit who did what. I just want to know how to make my baby better again."

Father Carl blinked back tears and nodded.

Then, Andy did what she had never, ever done to him before. She reached out and squeezed his hand. Then she reached out to her mother who took her hand. They stayed in this position for a few more moments, under the glare of the kitchen ceiling light. Hard metal broke out anew up in Maria's bedroom.

AS THE AIRPORT LIMOUSINE pulled into the driveway, Stefano recognized Father Carloni's car parked beside Claudia's Omni. He saw what was left of a pile of 2 x 4's at the head of the driveway. He was startled to hear loud music through the windows of the vehicle. Yet the house was dark. He looked at his watch and saw it was almost one in the morning, and though he didn't expect all the lights to be on, he assumed at least the outside lights would be on for his arrival. They weren't.

"Sounds like a party going on in your place," the limousine driver said. "That's Ratt's *Round and Round* someone's got playing.

Stefano wordlessly bent forward, paid the driver, then struggled out of the car and slammed the door shut. He waved at the driver as the car pulled away. He turned toward the back of the house. Though it was June, it was cold compared to Myrtle Beach temperatures, and he shivered slightly. He felt the brick wall of the back of the house, and leaned against it as he limped to the back door. Soft light filtered around the plywood in Maria's window. To the right, he saw a new light over the barn's new doorway. He could see its new façade.

He looked over to see Luna's dark shadow coming out of her doghouse, sniffing the air. She barked once. Stefano whistled reassuringly at her.

He looked at Maria's plywood rattling like a drum to the beat of the harsh music inside. He saw one light on in the kitchen over the sink. He was upset—one o'clock in the morning on a weekday; the music was loud enough to wake the neighbors, however far away they were.

He reached the back door and opened the storm door. He kept it open with his shoulder as he searched through his jean's pocket for the key. He squinted hard, trying to get the key into the lock. He had to take a deep breath and quieten himself down. His hand shook; he was so agitated. Finally, he opened the door, and stepped into the dark entrance. He searched for the light switch and turned it on.

The walls vibrated with the bass pounding above his head.

He hurried upstairs without taking his shoes off. As he turned into the family room, he saw Claudia, slumped back in Fabrizio's old La-Z-Boy asleep, her mouth open and snoring loud enough to compete with the music. She looked like she'd been in her rumpled black dress and wrinkled stockings for days.

Looking past her into the kitchen, he saw Andy and Father Carl sitting at the kitchen table. Andy sat slumped with her head in her arms, her crutches at her feet. Father Carl was rocking on his chair, his eyes closed, his lips moving soundlessly.

He kept his eyes on Andy as he quietly walked past Claudia to the stairs. It knocked the air out of him to see her look so helpless. It was the first time he ever saw her grey roots.

Andy looked up with swollen eyes.

He nodded grimly and blinked. He went up the stairs and passed her straight into the hallway without saying hello.

"Stef," Andy yelled, surprised.

He ignored her and went straight up the steps and kept going until he reached Maria's door. He tried to open it but couldn't, so he pounded on the door with his fist.

The brooding music lessened in volume, but not much.

Stefano stood, breathing heavily. He felt his heart skip beats. He felt a faint woosh throughout his whole system as his heart struggled. The doctor had warned him about not getting too worked up. He coughed when his heart skipped another beat.

"Dad?"

"*La musica.*" He wanted to kick in the door. He wiped his eyes and stood and listened, hearing her stumble inside, and finally, the music stopped. He leaned his head against the door. "Maria," he said softly.

There was a pause. "I'm not Maria anymore."

Stefano banged his sweaty brow softly against the door. He stood back and shook the doorknob. "*Abri la porta.*" He looked and saw Father Carl standing in the doorway between the hallway and the kitchen.

Claudia's head popped into view beside Father Carl.

No answer.

"Maria, *abri la porta.*"

The door flew open.

Stefano stood back in shock. He scoured the vision he saw in the dark doorway. One candle was burning amongst many spent ones on the bookcase where Bert and Ernie had once perched. The dolls were gone. Then he looked around the room. Shards of wallpaper crudely hung in jagged strips; pieces of it lay over everything. Broken torn-apart Barbie dolls lay scattered over the paper. The purple quilted bedspread had been slashed and lay crumpled on the floor over the slivers and sheets of wallpaper and doll pieces. "Maria," he whispered in shock.

Maria stood tall, chin up, her hair and eyebrows shaved off. A shiny dome with nicks and spots of dried blood where once her blue-black hair grew.

"Maria." He looked down at her slashed and torn blue jeans.

"I'm not Maria anymore. I'm Mario now. You finally got your fucking son."

Stefano dropped his chin. He heard Andy gasp beside him. Somehow, she had appeared.

His chest heaved as he tried to control his emotions. He turned to face Andy, grey and drawn. He looked back at Maria. He saw she had cut her arm. Many times. He lunged and grabbed her arm. "Maria." Her cut skin shocked him so entirely, he slapped her.

"STEF," screamed Andy. She tried to pull Stefano away from the room. He didn't budge.

Stefano grabbed Maria, shook her hard a few times, and then wrapped his massive arms tightly around her.

"Let me go. Let me go," Maria hissed. She fought Stefano who towered over her like a brick wall.

Stefano looked back at Andy. He watched Father Carl appear and look around the room with wide eyes.

Claudia poked her head around the corner of the doorway. She covered her mouth at the sight of her granddaughter and what she had done to her room. "*Abbiamo bisogno di aiuto.*"

Father Carl placed a hand on Stefano's shoulder.

Stefano shook like a leaf. He clung to Maria as she continued to protest, cry and yell in his arms.

Andy joined him and reached out around Stefano's back, barely reaching Maria.

Then Father Carl moved closer and put his arm around Andy.

Claudia remained in the doorway crying behind her hand.

Stefano finally felt Maria go limp in his arms.

"Stefano, we'll fix this for Maria. Real soon," Father Carl said.

"I'm not Maria anymore. You can't fix this. I'm a freak."

Stefano bent his head down over her shaved dome, and rocked her from side to side.

Maria let herself be held. "N Francesca is in the hospital' n she might die—."

"Shush, shush *mi bambina*," Stefano muttered softly, tearfully.

Andy patted Maria's head. "Don't worry, Maria, everything'll be fine."

Little did they know their problems were just beginning.

CHAPTER TEN

ARIA, MISERABLE AND HUMILIATED, stood naked, as Dr. Boucherville took another photo of her standing against the wall of his office. Andy sat in the corner, holding Maria's clothing on her lap, averting her gaze. With her head and eyebrows shaved, Maria looked like a street urchin straight out of Dickens. Andy's heart hurt.

"Okay, Maria, you can get dressed now, *merci*."

Wordlessly, Andy stood up and handed Maria's clothes to her and guided her behind the partition in a corner.

Dr. Boucherville put his Polaroid on the desk and pulled the developing film out. He stood and fanned the paper in the air to dry.

Andy went back to her chair and sat. She had dark circles under her eyes.

Dr. Boucherville peered at the developing photo.

Andy noticed his glasses were slightly greasy. She wiped at her stately nose with her sleeve.

Maria slunk out from behind the partition, in her torn blue jeans and a MUCH Music t-shirt. She quietly shuffled over to the chair next to Andy and stole a glance at the doctor. She looked down at the ugly linoleum floor.

Andy patted her on her knee.

Maria looked over, and Andy smiled at her and winked.

Dr. Boucherville placed the photo on the edge of the desk, went over to the office door, and motioned Stefano and Claudia sitting in the waiting room. He waited for them to come into the office before closing the door. He sat down in his rickety wooden chair.

"So, what's the scoop, Doc?" Andy asked.

He cleared his throat.

"There are a variety of hermaphrodites, and almost as many variations in *zie* physical and physiological syndromes. Some have Androgen Insensitivity Syndrome, which means you remove the testes and reconfigure the clitoris through surgery. But this does not apply to Maria. If it did, it would be a simple solution."

Andy shifted in her chair. "Shit, I hate all this scientific jargon. This is my daughter we're talking about." She looked over at Stefano with large eyes and shook her head.

Maria picked at her nails, still looking down at the floor.

"Klinefelter Syndrome affects some children, but, as males, they typically have smaller testes and do not produce as much testosterone as what is considered normal. This sometimes leads to arrested puberty and female attributes but they could also have testes that do not drop. Maria's did, however. Typically, they have an under sized penis—"

Andy lifted her hand. "Okay. That's enough. This is all fucking gobbly gook to me and it all sounds disgusting." She turned to Stefano. "Do you understand any of this?"

Stefano, beet red, shrugged.

Maria said, "I do."

Andy turned back to Dr. Boucherville.

"Shall I continue with a little more?" said Dr. Boucherville, looking at Maria.

Maria looked at Andy. "We should listen, Mom. That's why we're here."

Andy thought for a moment, shrugged, and shook her head.

Maria looked expectantly at the doctor.

"Congenital Adrenal Hyperplasia is more typical in babies born with predominately male characteristics though, as in your case, Maria, it also applies to female babies." He leaned forward, took out a cigarette and lit it. "Hyperandrogenism shows itself a little later and only in females. This syndrome sometimes includes excessive acne, hair, infertility, and high levels of testosterone. Someone with this syndrome cannot maintain a healthy salt level."

"Okay," Andy said, raising her hand once more. "All I want to know is, what do we do next?"

"Well, we've learned a tremendous amount with all our testing. Of course, you have always been very patient while we put Maria through all tests."

Andy snorted and crossed her arms.

"Maria's body needs help in optimizing growth, and medication will be essential to her health. If she doesn't take the necessary medication, it could lead to illness, stress, vomiting or reduced blood pressure. In extreme cases, even death."

"Holy crap," Andy whispered.

Stefano leaned forward. "You'a say Maria can die from this'a?"

"Let me just say that Maria's bone growth needs the correct medication. And I highly recommend Maria wear a medical bracelet and carry an identification card in her wallet to alert future emergency medical care."

Andy reached out toward him. "Can I have a drag?"

Stefano jerked his head in her direction.

"Stef, I need this. Either a drag or a hammer to the head, which is better?"

Stefano blinked and looked away.

Dr. Boucherville held the cigarette out to Andy who waved it away.

"No, you know what? Give me one. I'm going to smoke the whole damn thing."

Dr. Boucherville picked up his pack and pulled out a cigarette and offered it to Andy.

Andy pulled one out. She held it to her lips where it bounced from the tremor in her mouth.

Dr. Boucherville picked up the matches but Stefano took them away.

Stefano struck a match and held it as he watched Andy lean over to light her cigarette. He watched her trembling hand. She took a deep drag and slowly blew the smoke at the ceiling.

Claudia waved at the smoke, squinting.

"You know, I feel like I've died and I'm on a different planet."

"I totally understand how uncomfortable this all must feel."

"That, Dr. Boucherville, is a fucking understatement."

Maria protested. "Mom."

"Kid, I say it like it is." She faced Dr. Boucherville once again. "So, which of all this fancy-named shit does Maria have? And what do we have to do to make her better."

"She has *zie* Congenital Adrenal Hyperplasia or CAH for short."

"She's a *Cah*. I'll call it the *Cah* syndrome."

Dr. Boucherville shrugged. "Whatever works for you." He squished his cigarette into his brown glass ashtray. "Excuse me for asking, but is there a chance there may be an occurrence of consanguinity in your family?"

"Consang what?" asked Andy. "Do I look like I would know that word?"

Stefano reached out with a paw to comfort her.

"Well, basically if you look it up in any *dictionnaire*," he said, "It means *zie* property of being from *zie* same kinship as another person. In that aspect, consanguinity is *zie* quality of being descended from *zie* same ancestor. A consanguineous marriage is a union between two willing or unsuspecting individuals who 'r directly related. It could be *zie* first cousins, siblings, uncles 'n nieces, aunts 'n nephews, fathers 'n daughters, mothers 'n sons. It extends to *zie* grandfather 'n granddaughter, grandmother 'n grandson." Dr. Boucherville leaned back in his creaky chair.

There was a long pause.

"What the fuck." Andy pushed Stefano's hand away. "That's disgusting. See this?" announced Andy, jabbing her third finger up into the air. "You can shove *zie* finger up *zie* ass." Her face twisted with shame. "Are you telling us incest caused this?" She jabbed her forefinger in his direction. "You watch it, buddy—"

"Moooom." Maria's face was white.

Dr. Boucherville leaned further into his swivel chair. "I expected this outburst because you are a passionate and outspoken woman, Mrs. Giordani. But now your daughter has to witness your outburst." He made a tent with his long, tapered fingers. His mottled face started to turn red, and his grey goatee and hair looked electric white in contrast. "It is best to face this in a sober manner, for the sake of your daughter."

Stefano put an arm solidly over Andy's shoulders.

"It may be 'elpful to inquire as to *zie* makeup of your family first."

"Are you shittin' me?" Andy's voice cracked as if she was about to cry.

Dr. Boucherville sat up straight and held his palms out to her. "Now, I am not implying anything of the sort. But the blood samples of your family members seem to imply…"

"Imply crap." Andy straightened up and tried to grab her Gucci purse from the carpet beside her chair. She couldn't reach it, so Stefano bent down and retrieved it for her. Andy pressed down on Stefano's sturdy lap and struggled to her feet. "We're leaving, Stef. Ma." She tried to pass in front of Stefano holding her crutches but her coat got caught on the arm of Stefano's chair. She accidentally dropped her crutches. She let out a short, soft sob and stood, facing the door.

Dr. Boucherville stood up out of his chair. "*Madame* Giordani."

"Mom."

"No," Andy turned angrily. "I'm NOT staying here to be insulted."

"Now, *s'il vous plaît, ecouté, Madame* Giordani. I'm not suggesting that you and your husband knowingly, as first cousins, or as brother and sister—"

"Knowingly screwed as fucking related people you mean. And I *do* mean the fucking pun."

"Well, I have met many different people in different but similar situations."

Andy didn't stay to hear because she knew all about it. As she herded Maria out the door, leading Stefano and Claudia out into the waiting room, a new word repeated like an evil, distasteful mantra in her frazzled mind: *consanguinity, consanguinity, consanguinity.*

STEFANO DROVE through the narrow, packed, garbage-strewn streets. There was never an end to construction in Montreal. Or garbage strikes. Almost as if Nick Rizzuto and that gang kept the city in their grips, extorting the city by continually holding up garbage pick-up or the repaving and widening of the roads.

Eventually, the Cadillac quietly carried them out of dusty, downtown Montreal onto the packed highway. But there, again, orange cones lined narrow redirected lanes. Drivers in Montreal, having adapted to years of construction and restricted, winding lanes, easily cut back and forth between cars, racing to go home.

Andy sat fuming quietly in the front seat, every-once-in-a-while gasping and giving other drivers the finger.

Stefano looked in the rearview mirror and saw Maria swaying with the motion of the car. She looked miserable and depleted.

"Tonight, Alessandro Pessek is'a coming from Venezuela," he announced.

Andy turned to him. "Alessandro who?" She leaned back against the door to look at him more fully. "And why, may I ask?"

Stefano looked in the rearview mirror again. He saw Maria look directly at his eyes.

"You remember, Alessandro, Maria?"

Maria shifted and frowned.

"Jorge's son?" asked Andy. "That nice young man standing waiting at the car?"

Stefano nodded.

"Why's he coming?"

Stefano glanced at Andy. "*Protezione.*" He looked square in her face before tearing his eyes back to the highway.

Andy didn't say a word. Instead, she settled back in her seat, looking straight ahead.

Claudia, quiet since leaving the doctor's office, piped up. "*Per cosa, protezione?*"

"Ma. Think about it."

"Think'a of what'a?"

Andy turned to face her mother in the back. "Our barn almost burning down? Francesca? Maria?"

Claudia made a funny noise.

Stefano looked at her in the mirror and saw her looking befuddled, shaking her head. "I have to go airport to get Alessandro very late'a," he said.

"Where's he going to stay?" Andy asked.

"Downstairs'a. He use my'a bathroom 'n sleep on the couch."

"No way," yelled Maria. "There's no fucking way a stranger comes into our house."

"MARIA. Your language," Andy yelled back.

"Why? You talk like that. Why can't I?"

"Stop'a," Stefano yelled. He watched the road carefully, put on his signal, and slowly moved into the far lane. He finally came to a stop on the very narrow shoulder of the highway. Someone leaned on their horn as they sped by.

Stefano undid his seatbelt and turned as far as he could to face Maria.

Maria, eyes wide, leaned back in fear.

He lifted a finger in her direction. "You, Maria. You."

Maria looked at the finger. And then him. "What do you mean, *me?*"

He clenched his jaw. "Is'a not your fault," he said, waving up and down at her body, "but you fight. Always, you fight. 'N now, your friend is almost dead."

Maria's face dropped.

"You can't say that, Stef. It's not her fault," yelled Andy.

Stefano's heart beat hard against his chest. He had never in his life felt so angry with his precious princess, his one and only child, his *bambina*. He watched Maria shrivel, sink into the back seat. He watched Claudia lean over to comfort her. "No, Claudia. Don't'a. This time, Maria, *impara una lezione.*"

Andy smacked at his shoulder.

He looked down at her, angrily.

"What lessons are she supposed to learn, Stef? You tell me. What is she learning from all of this shit we're going through now?"

"She'a learn that she causes bad things. She picked a fight with a girl. *Una ragazza stupida.* I know my barn was put on fire by that stupid girl or her brother, 'n look at Maria now."

"It's not because of the fight with Selena that Maria looks like this."

"*Si*, the fight makes it worse. 'N now Francesca." He looked to see Andy picking lint on her skirt. He leaned forward to look at Maria in the rear-view mirror again.

She was glaring out the car window, her mouth set, her chin quivering. She swiped at tears running down her cheek.

He didn't allow himself to feel any remorse for the way he was treating her. He wondered sarcastically if she was really his daughter or did someone do a magical swap, giving him someone who wasn't perfect. Wasn't whole. Wasn't either girl *or* boy.

"I don't want a stranger in the house," Maria protested.

"He doesn't know anything. You will be fine, Maria." He watched her curl up in a ball in the corner of the back seat. He looked in the side mirror as he put his blinker on and shifted back into drive. As he pulled away from the shoulder, he gave his Cadillac a kick in the engine and squealed the tires. Once they were on their way again, all he could hear was the engine purring.

That's exactly how he felt that moment. Under duress, under pressure, but he felt unfazed. He breathed deeply as he thought of Leo and how he did business. He thought of the money he needed to recuperate, his loss because of Peter. He thought of what Peter was going to do once he was out of prison. And he thought of the uncertain future for his daughter.

He suddenly felt determined. Things were going to go the way he wanted them to go. He was going to learn from Leo-the devil's own- and support Leo in all he did. He was determined to recoup all his money plus create a dynasty with Leo's help. He was determined that Peter would grow, finally smarten up and become a solid member of the *famiglia*. He was going to keep him close from the moment he left that jail. And Maria. Maria... He looked at her, still curled up in the corner, Claudia's hand resting lovingly, reassuringly on her shoulder. Then he looked at Claudia.

She looked back at him, swaying with the car. She looked resigned, tired, haggard. She closed her eyes and lowered her face.

He nodded once to himself. They would find out exactly what Maria was going through and then he was going to make sure she stayed *Maria*, his daughter; his precious princess. Even if he had to wrestle hand to hand with the devil himself, even if he had to spend millions of dollars, he was going to do all he could to prevent whatever it was that was taking over his daughter, and put an end to it. He was going to have his Maria back.

MARIA FELT DAMAGED. There was no longer innocence in a damaged person. Not once the sacredness and privacy of one's body had been trampled.

The doctor had told them she would never be able to have children. All the things she turned her nose up at before—getting married, having children—were suddenly things she yearned for, grieved over. Now it was all out of reach. She flopped on her bed, the pill bottles, newly-dispensed, rattled together in the plastic bag she was holding. She emptied it and picked one up, and read the strange term on the label.

What was it now? she wondered. *Was it sports? Football?* She always played and enjoyed sports. But would she be scratching her crotch as she'd seen other athletes do? Would she start smoking cigars like her father and *Zios* Peter and Leo?

She stepped to the mirror. She stared at herself, searched her eyes, her face, her upper lip. She stretched her neck to see if she was getting an Adam's Apple. She stepped closer, so close that her breath fogged the mirror. She saw three little blemishes on her lower left jaw. She frowned. Pimples.

She searched the lines of her arms, her legs, even her fingers. She fingered the waistband of her sweatpants. Slowly, she lowered the waistband and stopped just below the beginning of a line of pubic hair. She remembered with humiliation how Dr. Boucherville had taken photographs of her. It had been a massive assault on her already shattered self-image. She pulled up her sweat pants and shuffled backward, flopping onto the edge of her bed.

What was she going to do with a stranger in the house? How would she dress? How could she be herself, whoever she was becoming? She grabbed her pillow and lay down, placing the pillow between her knees. She looked up and stared upside-down at the sky through her newly-repaired window, wishing she had wings to fly away.

STEFANO PICKED UP JORGE'S SON, Alessandro Pesseck, at Montreal-Dorval International Airport. He helped him with the many suitcases he had taken along. He had told Leo to pass along to

Jorge that Alessandro bring plenty of clothing - he was going to be in Vindenza for quite some time.

"While I am'a in South Carolina, you use'a my car."

"Okay," said Alessandro. He made room on the baggage buggy while they stood keeping an eye out for more of Alessandro's suitcases on the moving belt.

"'N you stay'a downstairs. You can pull out the couch to sleep on. I have'a a shower and toilet down there."

"Okay. That would be fine."

Stefano looked at him and nodded, then looked away at the moving belt. "Anymore?"

Alessandro counted the bags on the buggy and the two larger cases on the floor. "One more."

They waited while Alessandro looked carefully at the bags as they passed. Every once-in-a-while, he'd lean over to look at a tag on a suitcase.

"Your father, Jorge, he happy you are here to help?"

Alessandro nodded. "And I'm very happy to be here, Mr. Giordani. I'm happy to be able to help somehow."

"You are'a now official *picciotto d'onore*, a boy of honor."

"*Si.*"

Stefano studied Alessandro's profile. He wondered what it was like to have a son? Young, virile, polite and with so much presence. A fine young man. He realized it must be very different from having a daughter.

Alessandro leapt at a bag, checked the tag, and yanked it off the belt. He slung one suitcase with a strap over his shoulder, threw a case on top of the pile and, as Stefano picked up the other large suit-case, started to push the buggy toward the exit. He had already gone through customs in Toronto, so they were able to leave right away.

As Stefano drove away from the airport, toward the Honore Mercier Bridge which directed them toward the Eastern Townships, he opened his window to the breeze coming off the St. Lawrence River. He inhaled the early summer aroma and squinted to see if he could see lights reflecting off the water on the south shore. As they drove onto the bridge, its barriers only allowed the odd glimpse of the dark waters below.

He leaned his elbow out of the window, his fingers tapping the top of the roof above his head as he drove. It felt good to have the cool air batter his face and upper chest.

"So, do I simply keep an eye on the house, Mr. Giordani?"

Stefano looked over. He looked ahead again. He was pondering on how he was going to explain to Alessandro the nature of his job.

"My dad told me someone tried to burn down your barn?"

"*Si, pero…*" Stefano pursed his lips. He wondered if he was doing the right thing, including Alessandro in their mess of a life. His mind skirted Maria's predicament. "Maria'a, she has a problem with a girl. But the girl, she come from a bad family in the West End Gang."

"Okay. Wow. So, it's not just the house but also Maria and the West End Gang?"

Stefano blinked. "Maria, she is special, a little sick. She go to doctors many times and Adriana she no like to drive. So, you drive. You watch. You listen. You look around the house all the time. Watch when they go out. You can do that, *si*?"

"*Si*," said Alessandro.

Stefano glanced over to catch Alessandro's head drop and jerk with exhaustion. Stefano sat back in his seat, happy to leave Alessandro to nap on the way home. He had a 12-hour flight from Caracas with a stop-over in Mexico City, and then Toronto. The poor kid needed shut-eye.

He sighed as he watched his purring Cadillac devour the dotted white lines down the deserted highway. The moon was full and bright enough that he could see the surrounding farmers' fields. There was time to go over everything in the morning.

CHAPTER ELEVEN

ALESSANDRO WOKE TO GENTLE SHAKING. He opened his eyes to see Stefano tower over him. He quickly sat up and rubbed his face. "Mr. Giordani."

"You'a get up and Adriana will give'a you'a breakfast. Then we talk."

"Okay." He watched Stefano turn and cross the basement floor to the stairs.

Suddenly, he heard clucking at the window above his head.

He struggled onto his feet onto the mattress of the couch and lifted the blinds. He came face to face with about six hens pecking at the ground. He smiled and tapped at the glass. One chicken lifted its head and looked at him with one eye, then the other. It flapped its wings and scurried off. The other chickens ignored him and continued to search for food.

Alessandro looked for the cord and pulled the blinds to the top, allowing the mid-morning sun to pour through. It warmed his face as he continued exploring what he saw.

He watched Luna come out of her dog house and sniff along the edge of the tall frost-wire fence of her kennel. He looked over at the newly-renovated barn. He looked further to the right to see a pond beyond a fence. Around the pond were a few goats and sheep. One lamb cried like a human baby. A goat nuzzled another goat. Yet another was chewing on the fence post.

Alessandro smiled. Where he came from, they were surrounded by massive walls to protect against the constant threat of intruders. Night time, one could never fully see the sky because of the security lights in every corner and every hundred feet along the walls. Here, upon arriving the night before, he could see the stars, as if someone had pricked the night sky a million times and a bright light shone from behind. And the moon. So, bright, you could see every detail.

Here also was distance. Hardly any trees blocked the view, just wide, open space with vast, majestic skies. Alessandro liked this country called Canada.

Suddenly, he heard the scraping of chairs and voices. He reminded himself he had to get ready. He got off the couch and felt the coolness of the floor under his bare feet. He looked at his bags lined up against the wall. He looked at his watch, grabbed his shaving kit beside the couch, and hurried to the washroom.

"GOOD MORNING, ALESSANDRO."

Alessandro stepped into the kitchen. He saw Andy, smiling from the stove, holding up a spatula. Stefano was at the head of the table, under the window. The sun played on his blue-black hair.

Stefano nodded and motioned to a chair.

Alessandro pulled out the chair and sat down.

"You hungry?" Andy asked.

He looked at the table, where dishes implied others had already finished. He smiled and nodded. "Yes, thank you."

Andy threw some sausages on a plate and heaped scrambled eggs beside them. She reached over for two pieces of toast, already buttered, and placed them carefully on the side of the plate. She put the plate in front of Alessandro. "Coffee?"

"Thank you, yes."

"More coffee, Stef?"

Stefano nodded and held up his mug, and waited for her to get the coffee pot.

She grabbed a mug from the counter, brought it over, and filled it before topping up Stefano's cup.

Stefano leaned toward Alessandro and motioned to his plate. "*Buon appetit*."

"*Grazie*."

"You speak Italian?" asked Andy. She sat in her seat and sipped her coffee.

"I understand it. I speak Spanish because, well, that's what we speak there."

"Your grandfather was German, I hear."

"Yes, so I can understand a little bit of German, too."

"Wow, impressive. And your English is so good, you hardly have an accent."

"My Dad sent me to private school in London, England for a while."

"That's impressive. Your English would be better than mine, then," Andy laughed. Then she looked at Stefano. "Stef always wants me to speak Italian, but I can't be bothered. Maybe I should've because then Maria would've grown up speaking it fluently." She waved her hand. "But she understands it all."

Alessandro smiled. "Where is Maria?"

"She's up in her room. She'll come down later." Andy looked into her cup.

Alessandro sensed a sadness in her demeanor. He started eating.

"So, what do you want me to do, Mr. Giordani?"

Stefano leaned forward. "I show you where the guns are. You know how to shoot?"

"I do," said Alessandro, chewing.

"I also have a special place in the Cadillac. I will show you later. But I wan' to know'a how your grades were in school."

"I graduated with honors. Why may I ask?"

"Maria has stopped going to school. There is only a few weeks or so left, *pero* she need'a help for the exams. You will be her, how you say, tutor?"

"Yes, tutor," Andy said, looking at Alessandro.

"How old is Maria? What grade?"

"She's finishing Grade seven and is 13 going on 50," said Andy.

"I can handle her lessons. She's getting them from the school?"

"We've arranged for the teachers to have her assignments ready at the end of every day. So, one of the things you are going to do is pick them up every day."

"Okay," said Alessandro. "Is this homemade sausage?"

"Stef makes them. You like?"

"Delicious."

"Adriana, tell Alessandro what else'a he is doing," Stefano asked, looking at Andy.

Andy crossed her legs. "You are going to spend four hours every day, five days a week, putting Maria through her studies. You will also drive us to Maria's doctors' appointments both in Montreal and Trois-Rivières. And there's this kid—"

"That girl," Alessandro offered.

"Yes, Selena Ryan. She's trouble. We think she tried to burn down the barn."

"Mrs. Giordani, ever since I learned how to speak, I have been groomed and brought up in the tradition of the *'Ndrangheta*. I am well aware of what could happen at the worst of times while protecting the honor and business of the *famiglia*." Alessandro looked furtively at Stefano, who smiled and nodded in reply.

STEFANO WATCHED ALESSANDRO finish his breakfast. He was beginning to like this young man, even more. He looked over at Andy, who looked back at him knowingly.

She made a face. A face that implied she was impressed by the young man who graced their kitchen table. She pushed her chair back and smiled at Stefano.

Stefano, surprised, slowly smiled back. He picked up his mug and took a sip.

"When are you going back to South Carolina?" asked Alessandro.

"In two days."

"Lots of work?"

"*Si*, we almost finish'a draining the marsh 'n we have everything surveyed. We now'a break the ground."

"That's exciting." Alessandro wiped his mouth and put his knife and fork at an angle on the plate.

Refined, thought Stefano. He congratulated himself for taking Alessandro on, but, good intentions aside, he wondered if in the end, he was unnecessarily exposing him to danger. He sat back and played with his mug as he thought about that a little more. He relaxed and decided not to go there; being born into *'Ndrangheta* was danger in itself, no matter what one chose to do.

MARIA'S HEART JUMPED when she heard Alessandro's voice. She already knew he was to drive them to her various appointments, and that he was to be her tutor Monday to Friday.

Maria stood at her door, not sure whether she should join them in the kitchen. She had a quick shower earlier, ignoring her body's shapes and curves. She had fussed over what to wear; it couldn't be sucky, but not butch, either. Then she fretted over the black fuzz growing on her almost bald head. She had studied her eyebrows and was upset at how slowly they grew back.

She stepped back from the door and looked around her bedroom. She wasn't pleased about the destruction she had caused the week before. She looked at the walls. Andy had already thrown away her purple comforter and cleaned up the debris, and, after a thorough cleaning and organizing, the room was almost presentable. Except for the walls.

She took a deep breath and decided she would do a little more to be presentable. She put on small gold earrings and picked up a little bag from her bookcase. She opened it and pulled out something she never put on before. Mascara. Carefully she brushed it on her long, black eyelashes. She looked for something to cover the remaining bruises and scratches on her face. She found a tube of foundation Claudia had given her for Christmas and opened it. She sniffed it and squeezed a little on her fingertip. She dabbed it carefully on the bruises and scratches and rubbed it in. It didn't do the job entirely, but it was what it was. She looked into her mirror and frowned. She looked ghastly, and the make-up felt like an intrusion on her face.

Maria was initially distraught when her father announced the arrival of Alessandro. But she only thought of the threat of strangers discovering her truth, not the benefit of having someone they could trust to take care of them while her father was gone. Her mother had sat her down the night before and told her there was no need to say anything at all. He was only going to help, to protect them, and do what her father wanted—fill in the gaps; be there for the both of them, and Claudia.

Frightened as heck, she slowly opened her door. She poked her head out into the hallway and listened to the voices before she finally stepped out.

"GOOD MORNING," announced Maria shyly.

Alessandro turned. Her image surprised him. The little girl he remembered in a school uniform and black hair was no longer there. "Good morning, to you, Maria." said Alessandro. He quickly looked her up and down. She was taller, skinnier. Her hair was gone, and surprisingly, in a strange way, it looked okay. She was wearing black pants under a long black, turtle neck woolen sweater. She was pale, but her eyes sparkled.

Andy was at the sink, cleaning up from breakfast. She looked at her from under the hanging kitchen cupboards. "Want some coffee?"

Maria, looking pleasantly surprised, nodded. Nonchalantly, as if she had coffee every morning. "Yes, Mom, thank you."

Andy poured a fresh cup and held it out to Maria. "You look nice, today? I wonder why?"

Alessandro looked sideways at Andy, to read her face. He saw she was teasing Maria. He pretended not to notice. He watched Maria step to the table for cream and sugar. He pushed his chair back. "Well, I guess I will leave you alone. I'll go downstairs and wait until you are ready for me."

Andy motioned him. "Sit, we're not leaving here for another twenty minutes, so let's chat and relax."

Alessandro noticed Maria looking sad. He looked from Andy to Maria, and then at Stefano. "Where are we going?"

"You don't have to, Alessandro."

"*Si*. Let'a him go." Stefano nodded at Andy. "He start right away."

"We're going to see my friend, Francesca," said Maria sadly. She sat down and looked into her cup.

Alessandro played with his coffee cup and traced yellow flowers in the design of the plastic tablecloth with the tip of his finger. "Yes," he said, looking at the design. "I know the story. Your father told me about her and Selena." He was serious, a little sad. He wanted her to know he was ready for this job. He could see that she had tried to cover up bruises and scratches with make-up.

Andy looked at her watch. She went around the counter and carefully sat in her chair, stretching out her cast. "First, I want to know everything about you, Alessandro. I don't trust just anyone with our well-being; I want you to know."

So, Andy grilled a willing Alessandro.

Stefano stayed in his seat, quietly listening, every-once-in-a-while answering with a grunt. Until the moment Claudia finally walked in from the garage.

THE HOSPITAL WAS QUIET. Maria hurried along with her parents, her *Nonna* Claudia, and Alessandro, from the main entrance through the waiting room to the ICU. She stood looking at the little sign above the bell, at the frosted door.

"Go ahead, Maria. Push it," Andy said.

Maria rang the bell. It sounded like an old-fashioned school bell.

They waited silently, patiently. Well, almost patiently.

Andy rang the bell. "Oh, for cryin' out loud. What are they doing? Having a nap?"

"Mom." Maria cast a glance at Alessandro who hung back a little.

"Adriana," Stefano warned. He shook his head slightly.

Andy inhaled loudly through her nose and straightened up.

Maria caught sight of a shadow appearing on the frosted glass door. The door opened.

"Yes? Oh, hi Andy." It was Andy's friend, Teresa, in her kitten-patterned uniform.

"Hi, Teresa. We're here to visit Francesca Tomolini. Is that okay?"

Teresa stepped through the door, closed it behind her, and led them back to the seats in the waiting area. Two people were waiting their turn. One young man with gauze wrapped around his arm, his head back, was napping. The other was a sad-looking older man; gnarled hands twisted by hard work and rheumatism, slumped, staring at a mute TV screen hanging from the ceiling in the corner.

Teresa looked at Alessandro.

"Teresa, this is Alessandro. He flew in from Venezuela and is staying with us."

Teresa smiled and nodded. "Welcome."

Alessandro smiled. "Thank you."

"Well, you can only have so many visitors at one time," she said, looking at them all.

Alessandro held up his hands. "That's all right. I'll wait here in the waiting room."

"No, you should see what Selena did," insisted Andy.

Teresa touched her friend's shoulder. "Francesca is still in a coma, Andy."

"Oh, my god," said Andy.

"They've stopped inducing as they've done all the tests for now. She's stable otherwise. Her parents are with her at the moment."

"Who'a are her parents?" asked Stefano.

Teresa said, "I think her mother's full name is Maria Tomolini, and he's—"

"Ah, *si*. Ceasar Tomolini," said Stefano, nodding knowingly.

"Yes."

"*Si*, I know'a them."

Andy looked at Stefano, inquisitively. He made a rocking motion with his head, then looked at Alessandro. "They moved here'a two years ago. I build their house. Good people. Sicilian."

Maria stared at her father, reading his face. "They live here, in Vindenza? Why not Montreal, with the other Sicilians?"

Stefano shrugged.

Andy looked at her daughter's pale face. She reached out to caress the top of Maria's head. "Look at that, already. Stubble."

Maria pulled back, embarrassed. "Don't." She covered her head with her hand, and glanced at Alessandro. Then she looked away.

Andy ignored Maria's protest. "Maybe they're here because they thought we had better schools than in Montreal. That's a laugh. But Sicilians, *here*?"

Maria looked forlorn. She turned to Teresa. "So, can we see her, please?"

"I'll ask her parents if they don't mind. For a while there, I have to say, we all thought we lost her."

"So, what all is wrong with her?" asked Maria.

Teresa sat on the edge of a seat and motioned everyone to sit.

Maria settled into a seat between her parents across the aisle from Teresa. Alessandro, she noticed, stayed standing. She leaned forward, anxious to hear.

"She has three broken ribs. One punctured her left lung, causing it to collapse. Her pelvis is fractured, as are two vertebrae in her spine. She also has a very severe concussion and is suffering from brain sheer."

Maria was overwhelmed. "Brain sheer? What's that?"

"It's trauma to the skull. In Francesca's case, the sudden and violent slam against the wall shook her brain, loosening it from the sides within the skull cavity." She placed a hand on Maria's hands. She smiled and stood up. "I'll check with her parents."

Maria, speechless, numbly watched her disappear through the frosted door.

Andy, shaken, picked up a magazine and blindly flipped through the pages.

Stefano frowned, leaned back in his chair, and stretched his long legs. He motioned to Alessandro to sit beside him.

Alessandro walked over, hiked his dress pants at the knees, and sat stiffly.

Maria looked over at his dress pants. She looked back at her mother flipping through the magazine. She could hear her blood swooshing through her ears, as her eyes rested on the mute screen in the corner. She watched images of police cars and an ambulance, and a building on fire. A reporter standing in a bright light stood mouthing words, turning and pointing at the drama unfolding behind him.

"What's happening?" asked Maria softly.

Stefano shook his head and shrugged. He stood up and went to the screen, and tapped at the volume button.

"A fire," said Alessandro.

Maria stood and walked directly underneath the TV to hear.

"… There'd been a slew of fires of late, and officials believe arson is the cause. There has been talk that arson is a West End Gang specialty. Why so many of late, is anyone's guess."

Maria turned to see the ICU door whisk open again, and Teresa came toward them. "They said it would be fine so long as you don't stay too long," said Teresa, digging her hands into her tunic pocket.

"What's wrong?" Andy asked, dropping the magazine onto the seat next to her.

"Nothing. I just need to warn you. We keep the room quite dark. And very quiet."

Maria walked over and got a tight hold on her mother's arm, pulling her out of her seat.

Andy patted Maria's hand. "We'll be quiet. I promise to behave. Maria wants to see her. We're all very concerned."

"Follow me, then." Teresa turned.

"I'll wait here," Alessandro said.

"No, you come," Andy insisted.

"He's right. We're already breaking the two people at a time rule," said Teresa.

"Okay," Andy said.

Maria felt her father's strong arm encircle her. She allowed the gesture to comfort her. She put her arm around her father's thick torso, and they led Andy and Claudia through the glass door. They passed the nurses' station. Maria knew most of the nurses. They were her mother's pals from school, over the years.

Andy nodded at them.

Teresa stopped at a dark door opening. Maria let go of her father. She tiptoed closer to look in. The room was quiet save for the slow rhythmic beat of a monitor and a breathing apparatus's swishing sounds. She looked at the little form that was Francesca, appearing to have shriveled away. To the right of the bed, close to Francesca's head, sat a hefty woman in a chair. There was a crumpled tissue tucked into her ample cleavage in a silk blouse. Her right arm encircled the top of Francesca's little head, where her hair spread from under heavy gauze around the pillow. *Like a halo,* thought Maria.

Maria eyed the oxygen mask on Francesca's little face. She looked over at the tubes, monitors, and IV's connected to her little friend. What she could see of Francesca's face was white and translucent. Maria was shocked to see how deep her eyes were.

She felt the heat of anger begin to take hold of her chest. A strong, metallic taste filled her mouth as she looked on. She blinked back tears of awareness because she suddenly recognized it was not the time to be sad, but instead to be stronger than ever; it was time to be a *warrior*. She frowned and looked away. How could she be a warrior for Francesca now? She was damaged goods. No good to anyone. No good to her little friend.

She looked over, open-mouthed, at a man, his head was bowed and his hands clasped in front, standing to her immediate right in a corner. His feet were slightly apart. He was in a rumpled grey business suit, and his tie hung limply from his neck. He looked up, and she could tell he knew her father.

The men shook hands.

Stefano gave it a healthy grip, patting the man's right shoulder.

"Stefano," the man said.

"Ceasar," Stefano whispered. He moved to Francesca's mother and shook her hand. He nodded. "*Signora* Tomolini."

Mrs. Tomolini smiled, but her eyes remained sad, pained. She stood and reached for Andy. "Hi, I know'a you husband. You are Maria's mother?"

Andy took the hand with both of hers. "I'm so sorry this happened." Andy turned and pointed to Maria.

Maria stepped up to Francesca's mother. Maria felt ashamed, as if it were her fault.

Mrs. Tomolini reached out for Maria. She effused a sense of warmth and generosity.

Maria flew into her arms and clung tightly. She finally couldn't hold back the tears, and Mrs. Tomolini comforted her as she cried. Maria felt her mother's hand on her back, and she pulled away. She wiped tears from her eyes. "I'm so sorry."

"No'a need to feel sorry."

Maria felt an earnestness well up inside of her. "But it's my fault this happened to Francesca."

"What the frig?!" piped up Andy. "It's that pig, Selena."

"Mom, please. Francesca was only trying to protect me. Because I had done the same for her the last time." She looked at Francesca's mother. "I know Selena started it, but I'm always fighting. It's my fault. I should've just gone into the school and ignored Selena. But there's something wrong with me," Maria pounded her chest. "I'm a freak. I'm always fighting, and I like it. And now…"

Andy grabbed Maria from behind and twirled her around. Andy looked straight into Maria's eyes. "You, my daughter, are not a freak. Selena did this to *you*. And she did this to *Francesca*."

Maria heard someone shuffling toward her from behind and a strong hand touched her back. She turned to look up into Mr. Tomolini's face. He had a heavy five-o'clock shadow. His eyebrows were bushy like her father's and his eyes were hazel, almost green. She watched his eyes look into hers, searching her thoughts. He appeared to be looking for words. She saw a tear well up, and he blinked it back. He let go of her and swallowed hard. She saw how his Adam's Apple bounced and settled above dark chest hair. She wiped her nose with her sleeve and looked up again, expectantly.

"We don't know if she will make it." He lowered his chin but kept looking at her. "We know Selena comes from a family that's troubled." His face softened slightly, and he looked past Maria at her father. "A child isn't born to be an animal. It comes from somewhere else."

Maria looked back at her father.

Stefano stepped closer to the bed. Everyone sensed he was going to say something in deep confidence. He looked sideways at Mr. Tomolini, then down at Maria. He inhaled deeply and nodded. "*Si*, months ago her father was'a killed. 'N her brother is in'a jail."

"Where Peter is?" asked Andy.

Stefano nodded. "*Si*."

"Are they West End people?" asked Andy.

"Yes, the Irish mob who work with the Sicilians, but they do their own thing in their territories. But this family is worse than the other members of the Gang," said Mr. Tomolini. "Unfortunately, they live on our street." He turned to Maria. "Maria, Selena's father, was the head of the West End Gang. As you probably know, he was killed either by his men or by Hell's Angels. No one knows for sure."

Maria's heart beat fast. She had never heard *famiglia* or Mafia secrets spoken of so openly. She looked at her mother, wide-eyed, and could tell by her mother's expression of surprise and curiosity that it was the same for her mother. She turned back to her father. "Why was he killed?"

"Rumor has it that her father, Dunie Ryan, kept all his money hidden somewhere. He didn't trust banks," said Mr. Tomolini.

Stefano nodded silently.

"Where'd he hide the money?" asked Andy.

"No one knows. He must have hidden tens of millions of dollars away somewhere," said Mr. Tomolini. "But they are very troubled people, the Ryans. Not normal."

"Not normal?" Andy asked.

Mr. Tomolini motioned to his daughter lying on the bed. "They're no good." He turned to Maria. "I would stay away from Selena from now on. What you see is not all there is. She has brothers, Brian and Sean. And now, their godfather, The Weasel, is in control of the gang, and directly, her family. So, she probably believes she could get away with anything right now. They're brazen people."

"Irish mob'a," repeated Stefano.

"Yes, they're extremely upsetting. Selena's mother and brothers are heavy drinkers, too, and their arguments spill out into our street. Last night, we woke up to glass breaking and screaming."

Mrs. Tomolini looked up sadly and nodded.

"I grabbed my rifle and ran out in my housecoat to check it out. As I cleared my hedge, I saw Sean, kicking his younger brother, Brian, through their screen door—blood everywhere on the guys. I mean, he was kicking Brian in the face and the balls. He must have balls of steel because all he did was laugh. They're crazy. Unpredictable."

The beat on the monitor quickened.

Everyone looked over at the monitor, then Francesca.

"She can hear us," said Maria, staring at her friend. She waited quietly to see if Francesca would move. She stepped closer. She looked over at Mrs. Tomolini. "May I touch her?"

Mrs. Tomolini nodded.

Maria gently caressed the top of Francesca's little hand. She willed Francesca's fingers to move. But they didn't. Then she looked at Mr. Tomolini. She clenched her jaw and looked back at Francesca. *I promise to make this good, Francesca*, thought Maria. *I promise with all my heart.* She moved back to the foot of the bed.

Andy said, "You wanna go?"

Maria nodded. She looked at Mrs. Tomolini. "May I come back?"

"May you come back?" Mrs. Tomolini stirred, smiling. "Of course, you may come back." She reached down and gently cupped Francesca's other hand. "She would love it. Please do."

Maria nodded but didn't say anything. She went to Mrs. Tomolini for a hug.

Mrs. Tomolini pursed her lips and smiled gently. "Remember, Maria. This is not your fault."

Andy came around and put a hand on Maria's back. "Let's go."

Maria followed Andy out of the room. Time slowed down. Each step through the quiet hallway was slow and deliberate. And with each step, she became more determined that what happened to Francesca was not going to go unpunished. She swore to God it wouldn't. *No more happy-go-lucky Maria*, she thought. *No more fighting for the sport of it.* As she walked past the nurses' station, she glanced over and caught a nurse's expression as she looked at her. She looked away, at first imagining what that look said: *There goes a lost soul, a ghoul, pale-faced, shaven. There goes a freak.*

No, she corrected herself. *There goes a warrior.*

CHAPTER TWELVE

March 1987

AT FIVE MINUTES BEFORE VISITING TIME, Sandra Giordani slowly walked to their 'usual' table, the one in the farthest corner from the door, from where the guard always stood. She preferred being beside a small window she could look out through while waiting, plus Peter liked to sit in the corner to keep an eye on the room.

Things had become a little iffy for Peter in prison.

She sat and foraged through her black leather purse. She pulled out a little mirror and checked her pale face, then replaced the mirror into the inner pocket of the purse. She went to place the bag back on the floor but hesitated. She sneered disgustedly at crumbs and dried spots of spilled pop on the old vinyl floor, and decided to put the purse on a side seat instead.

She checked the tabletop before resting her elbows. She slid her shoes around under the table to push crumbs away. She looked back at the door and noticed a new sign: *No Smoking*.

Another place falling under the smoking ban, she thought. She was dying for a cigarette.

The door opened, and an older woman, young man, and girl walked in, shuffling directly to a table in the middle of the room.

She disregarded them as she pondered what she was going to say to Peter. She and Peter had conjugal visiting rights, and he'd been pushing for it, but she was still sore with him for screwing things up by getting Jack, a stranger, a non-*famiglia*, involved in one of their businesses. Most importantly, he broke her trust by taking *their* money and that of her parents' savings and gambling it away in Las Vegas.

Thank God for *Zio* Leo. Otherwise, she'd be sitting at home in black.

She looked at Peter's chair to make sure it was clean. She looked down at her dress, brushed pieces of lint off, and sniffed. Like Andy, Sandra loved to dress in crisp expensive clothing. But *'Ndrangheta* tradition required her to wear old and sad clothing and no make-up, so long as her husband was incarcerated. Otherwise, the others would think she was openly advertising for undue attention or, worse, that she didn't care. She sat up straight and raised her meaty chin with pride. She was proud of herself for following their tradition so diligently. But God, may he get out early for good behavior.

She looked over and saw her reflection in the late wintry-morning sun in the window. She studied herself; it was a strong face. Puffy from being overweight, but the eyes were sharp and glistened. She felt strong. After all, she not only ran her signature travel agency, but she also helped with the accounting for the businesses Peter and Stefano shared, plus she was now running the Vindenza Funeral Home and the flower shop.

She sighed deeply. What went wrong? How could Peter not have seen that Jack's tie was sticking out of the bottom of the coffin?

The door buzzed again, and more people came through. She watched them look around and choose seats at other tables. She looked at the young girl at the center of the table. She and her family looked familiar. The girl was rather large, like herself, with a long braided but messy red pigtail. She wondered if Maria would know her as she looked about the same age, and there were only two school systems with one elementary school and high school each. However, she figured it was a good bet; the family's red hair and the Irish lilt in their hushed tones implied they were Catholic.

She blinked a couple of times. Looking around, she realized it was an exciting environment. Why were these people here? What did their loved ones do to end up in this place?

The door buzzed again, and men in grey sweat suits shuffled into the visiting lounge.

Peter was the fifth to come in. He grinned at Sandra and nodded at the guard he passed. Peter wasn't high risk; he could come in without cuffs on his ankles, just on his wrists, but the guard always took them off once he sat down. The guard saw no reason why Peter shouldn't be free to hold his wife's hand.

"Hey, Babe," Peter went straight for a kiss, but she turned her head so that he kissed her on the cheek.

She eyed him warily from under her un-tweezed brows.

He sat and looked around quickly.

"Listen, I don't know how many times I should say sorry. I messed up, okay?"

She gave him a blank face. She raised her hand and pointed to herself, at her face, at her hair. "See this and this?"

"See what?" Peter said, looking as if it was a trap. "What?"

"This? No make-up, can't dye my hair, can't wear my nice clothes…"

"Well, that's because it's an honorable thing to do right now."

"Was it an honorable thing to take all our money and gamble it away?"

"Oh, come on. How many times do we have to go over this? You know, I'm not going to do it anymore. You know I take counseling for addictive behavior."

"I don't remember you ever gambling in all the years we've known each other."

He looked down at his hands. "You just never knew, that's all. I'd do smaller bets."

"On what, do tell?"

"You know. Lotto tickets. The horses. Cards."

Sandra glumly stared at him.

He grabbed at her hand, but she withdrew it. He sat back. He jiggled his legs nervously. "Sandra. I'm sorry." He put his hands together in supplication. "I owe you big time. Leo was a miracle. I believe God sent him to save me and us. And your parents. He saved them, too, from me and what I did. At least I didn't think of touching that dirty money. Not like Jack."

"You lie, Peter. Jack just beat you to it. Oh, don't get me wrong. I'm glad he did. Otherwise, you would've ended in a ditch somewhere."

"Nancy killed him. She had no reason to kill me."

"You dunce. I mean, someone from the drug cartel in Venezuela would've sent someone to wipe you out. How much honor would that be for your wife and children?"

"It was Leo who sent the hit guy. Leo would've stopped it."

"He didn't stop Jack from being killed, did he? He was too late. He would've been too late for you, too."

"Well, let's not get caught up in maybe's. The fact is, Leo and Stef did us an honor by paying the money back."

"Yeah. Both to the drug cartel and my parents. They had to do it for the honor of our *famiglia*. Not for you." Sandra looked out the window with tears threatening.

"How's everything going?"

She flipped her hands a little, a gesture intimating all was well.

"The boys? Do they miss me?"

Her mouth dropped, but she nodded. "Yeah, they miss their father."

"Tell 'em I miss them. I'll be so good, I'll be let out on good behavior."

Sandra dipped into her pocket and took out two photos. She placed them on the table in front of him. "Here, the latest school photos."

Peter picked them up. Tears came to his eyes. "My *bambinos*. I miss them so." He covered his eyes.

Sandra reached for his hand and squeezed it.

"Sandra, please, just take me home. I just wanna go home." He cried, looking around to make sure no one saw. "I have nightmares at night. We have guys here, I know. Without them, I don't think I could survive here. I miss you. Please, take me home."

Sandra's heart broke. She realized her husband was like a little boy; it was that innocence, that love of life and playfulness that attracted her to him. Plus, he was such a beautiful looking man.

"No one fights fair here," he said. "It's like a mind game. I have to look strong. For crying out loud, I'm Stef's brother, but I feel so alone. All the more reason why I need for us to take up on their offer of conjugal rights. Please, Sandra. I need to feel your soft, warm body, your arms around me. Otherwise, I'll go nuts here."

Sandra swallowed. She nodded and smiled through tears. "Okay," she said softly.

Peter rubbed his eyes, smiled slightly, then his face twisted again as he fought more tears.

Sandra squeezed his arm. She bent over the table in earnest, trying to see his eyes. "Peter, this will be over before you know it." She patted the arm gently. "Hey, Mama and Papa say hi. You know they forgive you, don't you? By the way, we're doin' great with the new Pizza joint in the Mall."

"Oh yeah? Great."

"Yeah. 'N I get occasional calls from Stef bringing me up to date on what's happening in South Carolina."

"How is he? I miss his visits."

"He's screwed up over Maria. So, it's a good thing he's busy with something as big as this. They've finished surveying the land, and they've laid the foundations of most of the buildings. They've got one restaurant up and running. Leo's wife, Yvonne, is running it."

"His wife? They're married?" asked Peter, surprised.

"He swooped her away to Paris for a Christmas wedding. Can you imagine? *Zio* Leo, at his age, married with a kid?"

"He keeps on building his dynasty."

"Speaking of which, Leo and Stef are building up quite a work force."

"Great."

"And Leo's got this deal, Pete. It's creative. I mean, the energy of the guy. He's got a contract to buy past due date food in bulk from chain stores and sells it on the black market in Cuba."

"Wow. That's creative."

"I know. Leo used his usual contacts in Georgia."

"Well, he always has the best cigars," Peter laughed, then looked sad. "I miss those cigars." Suddenly, he frowned.

"What?"

Peter nodded slightly at the small family in the center of the room. One of the inmates had joined them. "Dunie Ryan's family."

Sandra's mouth dropped. "Poor things," she said softly.

"I wouldn't feel sorry for them. That's the wife and kids. Those sons are little Dunie's in the making. The older son, he's a real piece of shit. Causes trouble here."

As if they could feel Peter's gaze, the whole family glanced over. The older brother gave him a look of death. He held up his hand and pretended to shoot a handgun.

"Same to you, buddy," Peter sneered. Then he quickly looked at the guard and turned his attention to Sandra. "So, what did Stef say about Maria?"

"He doesn't like it, Peter. He hates it. He feels like he lost his daughter. It's like he's afraid of what she might become. Some monster, even."

"He called her a monster?"

"No, that's my word. He just wishes she'd keep on wearing dresses and stay being Maria."

"Is she doin' okay?"

"Well, it helps that she has company with Alessandro."

"Smart of Stef. Protection and distraction. I bet Andy's happy about that."

"She is. She loves Alessandro.

"Does Alessandro know about Maria?"

"I don't know. What a situation. All these doctors' appointments are driving Andy nuts. But she's concerned about Maria. It's almost impossible to stop this change from happening. Medicine helps, but..." Sandra shrugged.

"Well, Stef's got a real big problem on his hands," Peter said, lowering his voice.

"How so?"

Peter suddenly had a pained expression. "You know what it's like. Everyone we know or work with; they're not going to understand." He looked around. "Us, the Calabrians. The Sicilians." He eyed other inmates at other tables.

"It's none of their business."

"That doesn't make a difference. Remember that boy found in the dumpster out back of the mall around the time of them finding out about Jack at Fabrizio's funeral?"

"Yeah, why?"

"He was found with his manhood in his mouth and dressed in girl's clothes? Hair done, make-up. Remember?"

"So? What has that got to do with Maria? She's a girl. And she's obviously not gay."

Peter shook his head. "They don't know that. Didn't you say last time her body is pumped up with testosterone and that it's inevitable? What happens when she becomes a full blown *he*? 'You think whoever did that terrible thing to that boy-turned-girl, would suddenly understand the complexities of Maria turning boy and walking around like one?" Peter looked down at his hands and nodded. "If I were them, I'd fight tooth and nail to keep her female. I wouldn't care how much drugs it took."

"And here I thought Stef'll have a son, and his Giordani & Sons Construction company would finally come true. Oh, dear."

"Right, *oh dear*."

TWO TABLES OVER, Selena Ryan studied Peter and Sandra. She ignored her mother's tears as she talked to her older brother on the other side of the table.

Her mother slapped her on her arm, "How many times do I have to tell you, Selena, sit up straight."

Selena straightened out slightly. She then scraped her fingernail along the dirty edge of the table as she sat fuming over Maria. Because of that fight with Maria and Francesca, she was taken to the juvenile detention center in Riviere des Prairies. She didn't stay long. Her godfather made sure of that. That little rat's family didn't press charges, and she went home with a slap on the wrist. But the school expelled her and she now attended the public junior high in Vindenza. There, she wasn't the top dog any longer.

She knew that the little snot-nosed kid was still in the hospital. She was out of a coma so, thank God, no one could pin a murder on her anymore. She looked at her brother.

He looked back and winked.

She smiled. She had support from her brother. He understood her completely. He had promised to help her in every way possible to get back at Maria. It was now just a matter of time.

November 1987

MARIA SAT SULLENLY AT THE DESK set up in the family room for her lessons.

Alessandro sat patiently in Fabrizio's La-Z-Boy recliner chair, watching her. Her hair was long enough to style into a bob now, and Maria was in full-bloom of puberty. She had a bad case of acne and was in the habit of wearing a neck scarf. He knew why. He had learned a little more of her *problem* and understood she was hiding an Adam's Apple.

He rocked slightly in the squeaky chair, his nostrils picking up the aroma of cooking. Andy was in the kitchen doing her magic. Living at this house was like living in an Italian restaurant. Andy griped a lot and didn't act like a typical mother or wife, but she sure knew how to cook. He had gained at least 15 pounds since moving in. Alessandro looked down at his stomach roll and pondered how to continue with this unlikable creature sitting in front of him. He went to say something, then thought better of it.

In her tomato-splattered apron, Andy strolled over to the railing that separated the kitchen from the sunken family room.

"Maria," she snapped.

Maria threw the pen she was holding onto the desk. It flew off, as well as a few sheets of lined paper she was scribbling on. "I hate this shit."

"I told you before; you don't get this stuff right, you fail. And you have to start this level all over again."

Maria threw up her hands. "I don't have a brain for this *Factors* stuff. Maybe if Alessandro knew more about it, he could *teach* me."

Alessandro stood up from the recliner with a bang and straightened his cardigan over his roll. His nostrils flared as he stared down at her.

"It's not Alessandro's fault. He has the books. He knows it, right, Alessandro?"

Alessandro turned stiffly to face Andy at the railing. "I do. I studied this at a private school in London."

Andy motioned Maria. "See? What's better than that?"

"Private school, private school. There he goes again about private school. So, you shit gold, who gives a shit, and pun intended."

"Maria."

"'Not doing it." Maria crossed her arms in anger. "Can't I just skip this? Can't I just go and feed the animals. It's feeding time."

"It's not feeding time. Not for another half hour. You know the schedule."

"Shit fuck," said Maria.

"Excuse me?" said Andy.

Alessandro felt like leaving the room. He was starting to feel claustrophobic in this house and wanted nothing else but to escape. Maybe not forever. He needed a break. Perhaps he could ask Stefano for a holiday? Perhaps at Christmas?

As Andy and Maria continued to argue, he walked to the glass sliding doors to look over the snow-covered backyard and beyond. He watched Luna stand stiffly, barking. He wondered why she was barking and looked slightly to the right at the distant fields bathed by a weak winter sun; brilliantly white, the gold branches of leafless trees and shrubs looking like mocha lace along the edges of the pristine fields, the light blue of a cloudless sky imitating a breathtaking painting.

He sighed with contentment. He looked at the backyard in the shade of the house. A little lamb strolled into the backyard from behind the dog pen, foraging through the snow toward the middle of the back yard; its breath created little plumes of steam around its head. *That's what Luna was barking at—the lamb.* "Huh." He stepped away from the doors.

"What?" asked Andy. "Why's the dog barking?"

"One of the lambs has escaped. I'll put it back in the paddock."

"I wanna do it. That's my job," Maria snapped, standing up.

"No, young lady, you sit right back down on your ass." Andy pointed at Maria threateningly. Then she went over to the window at the end of the kitchen table. "Huh, that's funny. How'd he get out?"

"I don't know," Alessandro said. He passed Maria, still pouting like a 14-year-old baby. He cast her a threatening look.

She caught it and looked away quickly.

He didn't care. He went to the side door, slipped on Stef's boots, and grabbed Stef's thick parka off the wall hook. He yanked the door open and stepped down into the cold garage. He shuffled between the Cadillac and Volvo, careful not to scratch them with the coat's snaps and zipper's sharp edges, and slipped out the garage door.

The snow was crisp and hard on the top but soft underneath. Alessandro created fresh footprints in Stef's boots, a little too big for him but quite warm, until he reached the well-traveled snowy terrain, marked by the other workers and by Luna's daily run.

He softly whistled to the lamb. His heart warmed when he had to deal with any of the animals. He stopped to inhale the fresh air, and closed his eyes. This climate was far different from Venezuela. There, they only had two seasons: summer and winter. And winter was nothing but rain from May to November. And the dryness of the air was very different. He was falling in love with Canada. His first fall season was exquisite. Everywhere he looked was a work of art—a symphony for his eyes. The long, endless plains between Montreal and Trois-Rivières continually changed as the seasons passed from summer to fall to winter. Big skies always drew his eyes to the heavens. He had even begun to like the people of Vindenza. He felt at home.

But Maria. *Lord, give me strength*, he thought.

The lamb slowly walked toward him when he reached out his hand. He petted its head and smiled. "How'd you get out, huh?" He took a handful of the curly, thick wool and gently led it back to the gate of the paddock. He found it still locked in place, so he figured there had to be a hole in the fence somewhere. He gently nudged the lamb ahead of him as he leaned forward to open the gate.

Suddenly, a blast like a volcano roar echoed across the land and through the big sky. For miles around, birds burst forth from bare trees, animals brayed, and Luna barked ferociously.

Alessandro was blown back and landed on the snow, the front of Stef's coat in flames and covered in blood. He looked down in shock and swatted at the fire with his bare hands, then twisted and rolled through the snow, leaving an odd trail of black and red. Fence bits and flesh dropped onto the snow around him from the sky.

He looked back to where the gate was. No gate and no lamb. The side of the barn was blown away and aflame. There was debris on the frozen pond, including a large portion of the poor lamb.

It didn't feel like home anymore.

MARIA STOOD OUTSIDE SHIVERING and staring at the mayhem, in her flannel lounge pants and a black t-shirt under her old, heavy school sweater. She watched Alessandro and the workmen fight the barn fire with a garden hose and fire extinguishers. Others picked up burning and smoldering pieces of barn and fencing from the paddock and the blood-covered frozen pond. She saw the blood and soot in the snow. She had gotten to the patio doors just in time to witness Alessandro roll to stop from burning to death.

Andy stood beside her, shivering in the cold shade.

"Not again," Maria muttered.

Andy reached over and squeezed her. "Hang in there, kid."

"Hang in there? We're not normal, Ma."

"Who can say what's normal?"

Maria looked at her mother. For a moment, she thought she was crazy. *What, pray tell, was reality?* Slowly, she became aware of snow falling gently on her face, and looked up. She then looked around. She held her hand out and caught a few flakes and watched them melt. "It's snowing again."

Andy nodded. "They're calling for a big dump from now until early in the morning."

Maria licked snowflakes off her dry lips. "I'm going in, Ma." She turned and crossed her arms, making her way through the crunchy ground and falling snow to the back door that led into the basement. She opened the screen door and tested the inside door. Someone had locked it. "Shit." Alessandro's domain. She rarely used that entrance anymore. She closed the screen door and made her way along the brick wall to the garage door. She looked back one more time, her hand on the doorknob.

Alessandro happened to look back at her. His face was black with soot, the front of the coat burned away to the stuffing. He turned away, as if she was of no consequence.

That hurt.

She knew they were lucky he was still alive. That coat saved him. That poor lamb sacrificed its life for him.

They tried to get a hold of Stefano right away, but even though he had one of those new cell phones, he rarely could hear it ring. Or he had it turned off.

She stepped inside the garage and slipped past the Cadillac. Her eyes caught the sight of the edge of the metal plate that covered the *caverna. Did other people live like this?* She slipped into the house, kicked off her boots, stomped through the family room, through the kitchen, then ran up the stairs to her bedroom. She slammed her door hard. She wanted Alessandro to know she was upset. Her window rattled. Even then, he probably didn't hear.

Or care.

She studied herself in the mirror; a daily ritual. As Maria's body changed in increments day by day, Dr. Boucherville carefully monitored her physical growth. She learned that most babies born such as she, routinely received immediate correctional surgery at birth; the doctor or parents chose the gender. Stefano and Andy didn't do that. In fact, they didn't let the doctors touch her. She was fortunate. They gave her the gift of choice. But how does one choose when one is both?

The anomalies in Maria's case changed startlingly and persistently. Her body was on a stubborn journey and had no consideration for the old Maria living inside her brain. She felt she was going to scream. The upset outside only reflected an ongoing battle inside. She wiped away a tear and went to her bed. She bent down and pulled out the box which used to hold the Italian Rag Time music box, the one given her by her *Nonna.* She lifted the lid and unwrapped a razor blade. She held it up and twisted it from side to side to catch light from the window. It glinted dully. She put the box on the bed and rolled up her pants.

She looked at the scratches on her leg, studying how they were healing. She sighed deeply and put the razor to her skin.

"YOUR FATHER'S NOT COMING HOME," Andy said, as she angrily hung up the phone and went back to scraping the stove.

Maria traced a bit of tomato sauce on her plate with a fork, leaning on her arm. "It's because of me."

"What do you mean, it's because of you?"

"He can't stand me anymore."

"Maria."

"It's true. He doesn't hug me. He doesn't even know how to touch me."

"That's not true," Andy said, not very convincingly.

Maria wasn't sure how to feel. She watched Claudia standing at the kitchen sink, rinsing dishes.

"*Nonna?*"

"*Sì?*"

"Did you ever want a grandson?"

Claudia stopped wiping a platter and looked at her. "Why'a you say dat?"

Maria shrugged. "Just wondering. What if I told you, I could snap my fingers and *voila*." She spread her arms out wide. "You have a grandson."

Claudia blinked. "What'a you say, *bambina?*"

Andy scurried to Maria at the table and leaned toward her. "If you stir this shit with you know who," she motioned slightly in Claudia's direction, "I will kill you."

Maria sneered at her. Then she crossed her arms and stared at her mother in defiance. "Really? Another body. How quaint."

Andy froze and continued to stare at her.

"Maria. You are my little *bambina*. My own Maria. I no care to have more grandchildren. You are my only *nipotina*."

"Okay."

"Why you'a say?"

"Just askin'"

Maria ignored her mother and shoved her chair back.

"Where are you going?"

"To my room. Where ELSE would I go?" Maria yelled. As Maria stomped into the hallway, Andy yelled after her.

"How about lifting a finger to help around the house, huh? Be a naturally functioning *adult* for a change."

Maria stopped at the bottom of the stairs. That bothered her. Those words; it was precisely what she didn't feel—a naturally-functioning person. "I never will, Ma. Remember? I'm the freak." She continued up the stairs. When she got into her room, she slammed the door hard for effect.

"WHY THAT LITTLE—" Andy threw the steel wool back onto the stove and scrambled to the hallway.

"Adriana," yelled Claudia. "Leave'a Maria."

"Ma, I can't stand the rudeness anymore."

Andy lunged up the stairs and ran to Maria's door. She half expected to find it locked, but instead, she was shocked when it gave way, and she almost tumbled into the room. She looked up through the lock of auburn hair that had fallen over her eyes in time to see Maria sitting in her underwear with her sweatpants lowered to her thighs. Maria held a razor blade poised in the air.

FATHER CARL WAS BOTH SHOCKED and excited. He was amused and enthralled. He wanted to tell Andy he had some suggestions as to how it all may have happened. He had just gotten off the phone with a colleague, a Modern Italian History professor at McGill University. He had told him that Mussolini had stirred up trouble and scattered fugitive workers, separating them from their families. Many people died, many were taken away, and many never returned.

Scattered family members either stayed in Calabria or became refugees in other countries. Some moved on as immigrants. To Northwest Europe, Africa, Greece, the Slav nations. Even Russia. Many went to England, Canada, the U.S., and Australia. Consequently, when they crossed paths, their unknowing offspring would recognize something familiar in them and fall in love, not knowing they were related.

He couldn't wait to go to his office and pull out his files on Andy and Stefano's genealogy. He still had to add Leo Mangione's name as a brother to Fabrizio. Of course, also as uncle to Stefano, and also Stefano as a first cousin once removed from Maria. And, all the more thrilling for Father Carl, he knew more tests still had to be done on both Andy and Stef to rule out they weren't brother and sister, either. There was always a chance that Fabrizio may have fathered a child before immigrating to Canada. It was a longshot. But it had to be ruled out.

If Andy knew they were doing these tests, she would be livid. But they had to be done.

Oh, the skeletons in the proverbial closet.

He looked at the clock in his humble little kitchen to see if he had time to call. It was still early, and mid-afternoon mass was an hour away. He shook his head. He preferred to get his file, work on it, do the afternoon Mass, and then give Andy a call afterward. He wanted to write all the information down while it was fresh in his mind.

He stood up, took the keys to the church off the key ring by the back door, opened the mudroom door, and went through. He struggled into his rubber boots and threw on a tuque and gloves from the shelf overhead. It was just a short walk down the shoveled path along the mistletoe hedge to the sidewalk, then a shortcut through the trees to the church's back door.

He opened his door and saw it was snowing heavily. He stepped back inside to get his coat, hung on one of the old, rusty steel coat hooks on the bead-board-covered wall. The jacket was stiff with cold from hanging in the freezing mudroom, but it would keep his clothes from getting wet. He threw up the collar and buttoned it up. He could see his breath in the dimly lit room. He looked out the frosted glass through the snow toward the church's stone walls next door.

He closed his eyes and lowered his head. "Lord, how wonderful. You made a miracle out of Maria. Maria should not have been so bright, so talented, so delightful, and so perfect. Against all odds, you gave her as a gift to Stefano and Andy so they would have a child to love. And you have a grandchild for Claudia. Maria is much loved. How wonderful it is to see Your Hand at work."

Moved to tears, he opened the door. Just as he was about to close the door behind him, he heard the telephone ring. He stood for a moment, debating whether he should answer. He let it ring a few times before he finally shook his head and went back in. He rushed to the old rotary phone and lifted the receiver.

"Father Carloni here. How may I help you?" He sat down on a kitchen chair, his coat bundling up around him. He listened intently. "Oh, my goodness, Andy. Let me call a friend, and then I'll be right over."

AFTER HIS MID-AFTERNOON MASS, Father Carl met with Dr. Stempertown. They sat in a warm, packed café and, over a cup of *café au lait*, he explained Andy had called crying that Maria was suicidal and she was hurting herself with a razor blade. He said he had hurried over and managed to help calm all three women before Mass, and he had seen the cuts on Maria's thighs. He never heard of such a thing.

Dr. Stempertown listened to the details of the case, and looked over Carl's shoulder at some students laughing at another table. He leaned toward Carl. "Father Carl, cutting oneself is not a suicidal gesture. It's a self-hate gesture. Maria needs guidance and support. I recommend she see a specialist friend of mine." He dug into his coat pocket and took out a little note pad with an attached pencil. He scribbled a telephone number. "You want to call this guy right away." He handed the paper to Carl. "The guy's name is Dr. Bob McCrady, a psychiatrist and specialist on consanguineous relationships. He's excellent. He's a card, actually. They'll like him, if nothing else."

"Where is he? In Montreal?"

"No, he's in Trois-Rivières."

ANDY GROANED and leaned her head on her hand. "I hate traffic, Carl. Trois-Rivières is just as bad as Montreal. I almost get a heart attack every time I go."

"'N I have'a one from Adriana," said Claudia.

Alessandro smiled, sitting at the table with his arms carefully crossed, his hands covered in gauze. In front of him lay a new cell phone.

Andy looked at Alessandro, then eyed the phone. She had an aversion for new technical inventions, and no desire to touch it, but it was their new life-line directly connected to Stefano. When that rang, it was his voice and only his voice at the other end. When they called him, sometimes he answered, sometimes he didn't. She learned to hate its presence. "What do you think, Alessandro? Should we get Stef to come home? It's up to you."

"It can't hurt." He went to pick up the phone but couldn't without pain.

"Carl, can you dial for Alessandro? I don't want to touch that thing," Andy said.

Carl reached over and felt the weight of the battery in his hand. "It's smaller than I thought. Isn't technology amazing?"

"Yeah, superb. Alessandro, tell him the number."

Carl pushed the buttons very carefully as Alessandro fed him the number. He held it tentatively up to his ear, then held it out and looked at it closely. "Where do I put my ear?"

"Anywhere. Just hold it up to your ear like you would any phone," Alessandro instructed.

Father Carl nodded, listened, and waited.

Andy drummed her fingers on the table.

Alessandro looked down at his bandaged hands and fiddled with the material.

Claudia stood up and went to the counter to retrieve a little jug of red wine. "*Piu vino?*"

Nobody heard. She placed the jug on the table, sat down and watched Father Carl.

Father Carl shook his head but kept the phone at his ear. "No answer."

Andy dropped her head and pushed her hair behind her ears.

"Don't worry, Andy," Alessandro said. "We've got someone bunking out in the barn for the night. And I don't know how we didn't hear Luna barking earlier than we did today. If we keep an ear open for her…"

Claudia brightened up. She pointed at Alessandro. "I'a remember. She'a bark."

Andy looked askance at her mother. "What time was that?"

"She'a bark when I drive here. *Che*?" She wiggled her head. "*Dieci*?"

Andy looked at Alessandro. "I was in the shower. Where were you?"

Alessandro chewed on his tongue for a moment as he pondered his day. He looked at his bandaged hands. "I was shaving. I had the water running."

"I should ask Maria," Andy muttered. "This is getting too much."

Carl grabbed Andy's arm and gently placed it on the red and white checkered tablecloth. He reached out with his other slim hand and carefully moved a vase of dried flowers over to the side for more room. "I know you are going through a tremendous amount on your own." He motioned to the back of the house. "And what happened this morning was atrocious. I still recommend you call the police."

Andy shook her head. "It's *famiglia* business. I know it. There's no sense."

"Andy, if you like, I will talk to Stefano and see if he will come home right away."

Andy shook her head.

"Why can't he come home?" Father Carl turned to Alessandro.

Alessandro sat up. "I spoke to him. He said he would try but that he and Leo were in the middle of something very sensitive. Something about the West End Gang."

"The West End Gang? Down in Myrtle Beach?"

Alessandro nodded.

"Way down there?"

"Stefano does not need to come home for this, though," Alessandro said with confidence.

"For this? You were almost killed," Father Carl motioned at Alessandro's hands. Sometimes, counseling his parishioners was upsetting and frustrating.

"Just leave it," Andy said quietly, as she fiddled with a fold line in the table cloth.

Father Carl looked down at his lap. He frowned. He was forever straddling a beam with the Giordani family. There was no good versus evil; like mixing a glass of chocolate milk after you add the Hershey's chocolate. Just chocolate milk. Unthreatening. Dangerous.

"I don't want another specialist in Maria's life. She's screwed up as it is," Andy said.

"Precisely. Counseling is exactly what Maria needs." He looked around the table, thinking they should all be going for counseling. "Alessandro does all the driving for you. You just close your eyes and not look at the traffic."

Andy snorted.

"This guy will deal with Maria's psychological problems we haven't addressed."

Andy sniffed and looked at her mother, sitting haunched over like a fragile little bird in black. "What do you think, Ma?"

Claudia raised her thin shoulders and made a face. "If is'a good from'a Carl. You do." She motioned with her hands at Alessandro and nodded, then at Carl. "We okay, we go."

Andy sighed deeply.

Father Carl saw the confusion brewing in her mind. "Why don't I call first thing in the morning and make an appointment, and we can figure that out? I can come along with you some of the time, Andy, but I have my grief counseling sessions every afternoon. We can make appointments either very early in the morning or very late in the day."

Andy looked at him. "Carl, you don't have to do that. Alessandro is a great source of comfort and support. We'll do it. You don't have to help."

Alessandro smiled gently at her. He squinted his eyes and cocked his head.

Andy smiled back and leaned over, asking for his hand.

He held out his bandaged hand and grabbed hers as best he could.

"I don't know what we would do without you here, Alessandro." She pulled back her hand. She brushed at a breadcrumb on the cloth. "Though I wish Stef could be here."

Carl stood up, pushing his chair back. "Well, then. I'll give Dr. Bob a call." He looked questioningly at Andy. "Where's Maria? I should say a few words before I leave."

"I'm here," yelled Maria from inside the dark living room.

"Maria, Father Carl is leaving. Say goodbye."

Maria did not answer, but slowly appeared at the kitchen doorway and leaned against the trim while she crossed her arms and legs. She looked at Father Carl, almost apologetically.

Carl stepped toward her and touched her hair. He looked down at her spotted face and the changing features. He stood back and turned to Andy.

"Maria will help me with my coat. Right, Maria?"

Maria straightened up, glanced at her mother, then turned into the front hallway. She turned the light on, opened the front closet's door, and pulled out Carl's heavy coat. She helped him get his arms in the sleeves.

"Maria, you know that this too shall pass?" he said in a soft voice as he turned to button his coat. "Hat?" he asked, motioning to the top shelf of the closet.

Maria reached up and grabbed the Russian cap with fur flaps. She pulled out the balled-up leather gloves inside the hat and handed them to Carl. She looked down at her bare feet.

Carl looked down and noticed she had used black nail polish. He had never seen black nail polish. He blinked, tempted to think of evil hovering over Maria. His heart skipped a beat as he looked at her and frowned. He held his hat in his hands and cocked his head.

"Maria, you know that God watches over you."

Maria looked up and brushed the hair out of her eyes. She blinked and shrugged.

He smiled reassuringly. "Maria, God would never leave you on your own. There's a reason why you're going through this." He motioned back to the kitchen door. "Why all of you are going through this."

"What could it be for?" asked Maria, softly.

He smiled again and put his hat on top of his head. He adjusted the flaps over his ears. "We can't possibly know at the moment." He took a deep breath, which straightened out his posture. "But whatever it is, it's always magnificent." His eyes brightened as he nodded.

Maria opened the door for him and let him pass into the winter air and snow outside.

He stepped out and pointed at her. "You be good to your mother."

She squirmed, smiled embarrassedly, and nodded at Carl before he turned and carefully navigated the windswept walkway toward his car. The wind had picked up and blew snow into drifts. He was relieved to see by the garage light that his car didn't need any clearing. As he opened his car door, he looked at the road to see a pair of headlights slowly pass by, the thick falling snow highlighted in the tracks of its beams.

It was unusual to see other traffic on this particular road, and he always was interested to know if he recognized a member of his congregation. He squinted against the falling snow and saw a rusty, blue pick-up truck. He recognized it as the truck belonging to the son of Mrs. Ryan, who religiously came on her own every Sunday morning Mass. As he continued to study it, he saw a face watching him at the passenger window. He raised a hand and waved.

The face did not wave back.

Chapter Thirteen

DR. BOB MCCRADY LOOKED at Maria, Claudia, and Andy as they sat uncomfortably on his frayed green couch. They each had a Styrofoam cup of steaming coffee in their hands.

A thin cloud of cigarette smoke hung high against two fluorescent strip lights; one was missing a plastic cover, the other cover shattered at one end. The ceiling tiles were orange-brown and stained; the metal strips holding them up were mottled-grey.

Andy looked at the ceiling, then over at Dr. Bob sitting in a battered stuffed armchair while smoking a cigarette. Andy opened her mouth to say something.

Watching her closely, Dr. Bob's bushy eyebrows rose as he waited for her to speak.

Andy slumped and closed her mouth again.

Dr. Bob smiled and motioned with his cigarette toward the door. "You should perhaps let the young man know we may take a while. He can go for a walk and come back."

"I'll tell him." Maria stood up quickly and left the room.

"He won't go. He stays with us." Andy sniffed. She shifted on the couch, bent down, and smoothed down her wrinkled black stockings.

"I see," said Dr. Bob. "I notice a touch of enthusiasm in Maria. She likes him. A relative?"

Andy shook her head. "No, the son of a friend from Venezuela. He's staying with us." She smiled grimly and looked away.

Dr. Bob leaned forward, and his chair rocked with a groan and scrape. He gave Andy a big welcoming smile. "Mrs. Giordani, I am quite entranced by your daughter. I read all her medical files, and I decided to ask for school records. I was impressed."

Andy snorted and leaned toward him in turn, also to keep her voice low. "Her marks were never great, but only because she doesn't feel the need to work hard at anything."

"I see teachers' comments, and those subjects she does seem to have an interest in, showed her potential. They talk of her sharp intelligence and she appears to have a good heart."

"Yeah, well, we think that could be why she's always fighting. She's always seen herself as a hero, fighting to protect others."

Dr. Bob nodded. He took a noisy drag of his cigarette. "I also read notes given to me by Father Carloni, and I was able to put together a clear picture of her and the rest of your family."

"Great," said Andy, mildly disgusted. She wiped at her skirt. "I hope he didn't divulge too much. We're very private people." She pointedly looked at him.

Dr. Bob looked at Claudia and smiled. "You are her grandmother?" He bent forward, hand outstretched. "Dr. Bob McCrady."

Claudia reached out and eagerly shook his hand. "*Si.*"

Andy motioned to her. "My mother, Claudia di Giovanni."

"Condolences."

Claudia nodded and smiled. "*Grazie.*"

"Was Maria close to her grandfather?"

"*Si*, very."

Maria returned. As soon as she sat down, he took a deep, noisy breath through his hairy nostrils. "So, let's talk about the direct effects of consanguinity, shall we? You know the word consanguinity, don't you?"

Andy snorted. "Boy, you go for the jugular."

"That's why we're here, I believe."

He looked at Maria.

"You understand the term?"

"*Che?*" Claudia shook her head.

Andy impatiently looked at Claudia. "Ma, you've been hearing that word for a year and a half already. You know what it means."

Claudia looked at her questioningly. Then she shook her head, making a little noise.

"She's okay. Keep talkin'," Andy said.

"Well, I'll get right to it, then. Apart from the possibilities of passing on genes that could result in stillbirths, extreme physical anomalies, and learning disabilities—I read about your four miscarriages and one stillbirth, by the way, and I am so sorry—"

Andy bowed her head. "It was hard."

"Yes. An understatement, I'm sure."

Andy nodded.

"History has proven that sometimes the combination of these genes creates extraordinary individuals." Dr. Bob sat back. The movement caused ash to scatter over his stained tie and shirt. All three women watched the ash roll over his rotund belly.

"In fact, many cultures see consanguinity differently from Western Christian morals."

He watched Maria blink twice. She sat up a little straighter and scratched at the stubble on the top of her head.

"What the hell are you talking about?" said Andy.

Dr. Bob squinted and smiled benignly. "Consanguineous marriages were preferred by many societies around the world. Did you know that?"

"No," Maria said.

"Well, it was—and is—widely practiced in Asia, North Africa, the Middle East, and in parts of China." He flicked ash and missed the glass ashtray on a chrome stand to his right. "Once it was practiced in Switzerland and even in North America. Take Hawaii, for example. And in the mountains of the mainland of the US of A; you've heard of the inbred hillbillies." He shifted his weight and chuckled. "You know the old joke about red necks, what do they do on Hallowe'en?"

Andy shook her head and smiled. "I like to tell jokes. Always open to new ones."

"They pump kin."

There was a long pause. "Oh, my God," whispered Maria. "Too much information."

Dr. Bob was pleased to see her jaw drop as she slowly looked wide-eyed at her mother.

Andy, on the other hand, broke out in guffaws. She laughed so hard, tears welled up in her eyes, and her mascara ran. She nodded her head, grinned, and pointed at Dr. Bob as if he were 'the man.' She gave him thumbs up. "I needed that."

Dr. Bob grinned and gave her the thumbs up. He rocked the chair with excitement as he watched Maria squirm in the corner of the couch.

Andy tapped Maria's knee. "Wasn't that funny?"

"Ma, that was disgusting."

Dr. Bob grinned. It was the shock value he was after, and it was working. People were usually overwhelmed by confusion, fear, and emotions when they first came to him. He found using shock cut through his patients' anxiety immediately. Once relaxed, they took his counseling to heart. Right now, Dr. Bob liked the effect he had over Andy and, especially, Maria. He took another deep breath through his nostrils and pushed back a lock of greasy salt and pepper hair from his lined forehead. He had all the physical and personality characteristics of a leprechaun; just a little taller. It helped make him more likable. He was freckle-faced with large brown eyes and a perpetual, self-satisfying smile that rarely left the room. He knew he was the spitting image of one at the end of the Rainbow, and he offered a pot of gold full of hope.

"I have a particular favorite one." Dr. Bob dragged on his cigarette and was utterly oblivious to more ash falling on the fold of his rumpled jacket. He swung his right foot, the one that hung over the arm of his chair, the sock of which slowly slipped down to his ankles to just above the old leather brogues. The movement exposed a large area of freckled and hairy shin just above the sagging stocking. "This one goes like this, though it's the beginning of almost unlimited numbers of gag lines." He cleared his throat. "Okay. How do you know when you are a redneck?"

"Ha. When you go to family reunions to find a date," Andy answered, pointing at him.

Maria looked appreciatively at Dr. Bob.

Dr. Bob smiled and winked at Maria. "Yup. That's one of the better ones." He scratched his nose with his free hand. "You probably already know that the pharaohs of ancient Egypt kept the royal line pure by siblings marrying siblings. They believed they were gods or of a higher rank called *kap*. Their offspring had to continue with the same royal god-like bloodline to maintain their standing. So, consanguinity is not some new invention of modern times. You could consider yourself a bit of royalty perhaps, Maria."

Maria stared at him in wonder. "Wow."

Andy straightened up. "Royalty, huh?" She smiled at Maria and nudged her.

He carefully studied all three faces. There was hope. And these people needed to regain a sense of dignity. He changed tactics and dropped his cigarette into his cold coffee. "But then they did atrocious things with babies born with disabilities or imperfections. Leaving unwanted newborns on window sills exposed to the elements was a common Victorian occurrence."

"Oh my God," whispered Andy.

"The Hawaiians would place disfigured newborns on the beach for the ocean to reclaim."

"That's so cruel," Maria piped up.

"Yes, the human race can be ruthless. Sometimes, however, through innocence and naiveté they seem cruel. People didn't know any better. However, they had to have known they were hiding evidence that consummating these close relationships was an unnatural act. Of course, in the West, most religions consider consanguinity—in this case otherwise called incest—a mortal sin. It still happens, however. A typical example of a consanguineous relationship in the West is when first cousins marry. Sometimes this happens entirely on purpose. For example, because of restrictions against marrying outside of a religion, even into other sects of a particular religion, like the Amish or Mennonites, first cousin marriages are preferable." Dr. Bob swung his leg back and dropped his feet on the floor. He bent over to flick ash into his coffee cup, but most of it fell on the old indoor/outdoor pockmarked carpeting.

Andy and Maria looked at each other.

Maria giggled nervously, covering her mouth. Her eyes sparkled as she watched Dr. Bob.

Claudia, sitting between Andy and Maria, leaned over and put her arm around Maria.

Maria squeezed back.

Dr. Bob sat back and threw his leg back over the arm again. "One in two marriages in Tamil Nadu and Andhra Pradesh in Southern India near Sri Lanka are consanguineous. They have a very high rate of infant deaths. Yes, due to lack of food, medicine and from the challenges of extreme poverty, but certainly resulting in deformities and other physical issues." Dr. Bob groaned as he shifted his behind from one side of the seat cushion to the other. He started playing with his stained tie. "You, Maria, were fortunate, indeed, that you were born so perfectly."

"Perfectly? I'm an ugly freak."

Dr. Bob raised his chin and quietly studied her. Then he pointed at her. "That, dear Maria, is why you are here; because you believe that. If you pardon me, your self-cutting is a sign of self-hatred. It's not a bad sign."

"What the hell," muttered Andy.

"Well, Mother," he said, turning to Andy. "It means she's not suicidal. She cares."

"But I don't' care about anything. I don't feel a thing," said Maria.

"That is why you cut so that you can feel *something*."

Maria's face softened. She looked down at her hands.

"What bothers you the most in all of this?"

Maria tried to find the words. She motioned to the room. "Everything. I hate my life. I hate the way I look. I hate the changes in my body. I hate that I have no friends, and I don't know what's going to happen with me. I hate my pimples and being cooped up in the house. I hate that my Dad's gone all the time."

"Where is he?" Dr. Bob asked.

"He's in construction, and he's helping build something major in South Carolina," said Andy. "He comes back every once-in-a-while."

"Yeah, I hate not having him around every day. And I hate that he doesn't know how to look at me anymore."

"Go on," said Dr. Bob.

Maria continued. "I hate that *Zio* Peter is in jail. I hate seeing everyone in black and how my mother-sorry Ma-picks on me all the time."

"I don't pick on you," retorted Andy.

Dr. Bob shushed Andy. He motioned Maria to keep speaking. "Go on."

Maria shifted in her seat and crossed her arms protectively. "I hate that my friend is in a coma. I hate that the person who caused it is walking around free."

"Who is that?" he asked.

"A girl called Selena Ryan."

"She's trouble," added Andy.

"Yeah, she's crazy."

Dr. Bob closed his eyes. "Okay."

Maria was quiet. Her chin quivered.

Dr. Bob opened his eyes and saw her fighting back her emotions. He leaned forward.

"Anything else?"

"I have no purpose. I'm just dead weight."

Dr. Bob watched her cock her head. Her cheeks took on color.

"Deep, deep down inside, you must realize that you are *not* dead weight? That you are special. No?"

She shrugged. "Life is hell. Or purgatory."

"You know, Maria, as strange as it may seem, there's always something you take pleasure from even in purgatory. Think about it carefully. What do you take pleasure from?"

Maria thought for a moment. She looked down at her thighs and gently rubbed them with the palm of her hands. "I love the farm animals we have. I love feeding them. I love my *Nonna*, I love…" She looked at her mother. "I love my Mom, I guess."

"You guess?" Andy repeated.

Maria smiled slightly and looked down again. "I love …"

Everyone waited patiently.

Dr. Bob glanced at the door. He suspected the young man out in the lobby might be a confusing element in Maria's life. A beautiful young woman is going through terrible physical changes, and a fine young handsome man nearby. His thoughts were interrupted when Maria brightened up.

"You know, someone attached a bomb to the paddock gate. I think it was meant for me. But, instead, it killed one of the lambs and almost killed Alessandro."

Dr. Bob raised his eyebrows. Mafia. He kept a calm face. It was not the first time he had their families in for counseling. They were the ones who needed help the most.

"Maria, he doesn't need to know that," cut in Andy.

"Why, Ma? Why can't I talk about that? Aren't we here to figure out why I'm crazy? Why there's something wrong with me?"

"You're not crazy."

"Yes, I am. And you're crazy. Our family is crazy."

"Maria, shut your mouth this minute."

Maria stood up and pointed at her mother. "You don't see it, do you? Because you're so far gone, you don't even remember what normal is anymore."

Andy shot up and turned to Dr. Bob. "That's it. I don't know what you're playing at here, but I sure as heck am not going to sit through *this*." She stepped to the door, opened it, and hurried through.

Dr. Bob eyed Maria, who remained standing.

He watched as Claudia stood up.

"*Mia Maria*," she cooed, comforting Maria.

Maria patted her grandmother on the arm. "*Nonna*, you're not crazy."

Claudia reached up and gently rubbed the peach fuzz on Maria's head.

"So, are you following your mother out of the office?" asked Dr. Bob. He knew Maria faced a crucial moment.

Maria pursed her lips. She sat back down, and Claudia, holding Maria's hand, sat down beside her.

"Are ya comin'?" yelled Andy from the waiting room.

Maria leaned over and pulled at the door. Just before closing it, she looked at Dr. Bob.

"No, Ma. I'm not finished."

She closed the door.

ANDY FUMED in the waiting room, nervously pacing the worn carpet. She had hissed and whispered her protests to Alessandro for a few minutes before she finally fell quiet. Her insides squirmed with fear. She was afraid of what Maria might say. Secrets of the *famiglia*, secrets she wasn't comfortable with outsiders knowing. Alessandro put her mind to rest when he reminded her they were there for Maria. And Maria was hurting badly.

"Talking is exactly what she needs to do right now."

She knew deep down inside her soul he was right.

"She needs to find a way to heal, and the only way she can is if she has good, professional help." He motioned with his bandaged hand at the closed door.

They could both hear mumbling.

"They're sure talking a lot," she said.

"Precisely. I guess Dr. Bob must be doing his job."

Andy sighed, and sat down to wait.

"I guess we're havin' to come here each week, as well. If someone paid us for the number of kilometers we drove to these appointments, we would be rich."

"You don't need to come every week. I'll drive Maria in."

Andy looked deflated. She shook her head. "Don't mind me, Alessandro. I'm a perpetual martyr. I will always come along. That's what a mother does. And some mother I am," she added sarcastically.

Alessandro touched her hand with his bandaged one. She looked, startled.

"She's lucky to have you as her mother."

"Ya think?!"

MARIA GLANCED AT ALESSANDRO'S EYES from the back seat. She did this surreptitiously and wanted to read what he was thinking. Was he still angry with her?

Alessandro had opted to use the Volvo to keep the Cadillac free from the black, salty slush that always caked on their car when they drove through the city. It was more cramped and so it was a rougher ride than usual, but it had a comforting purr to the engine.

As they passed over the large bridge spanning the St. Lawrence River to Saint-Gregoire, Maria sat up taller to look through the barriers down at the river. It was ice-covered for the most part, with one lonely ice-breaker weaving a thin, curvy trail behind itself through the ice. She sat back when they reached land. Something was missing. It was too quiet in the car, and her thoughts were far too noisy, frazzled.

"Can we have some music on?"

Alessandro reached out to the radio and turned it on. Old-school Italian music played.

Maria rolled her eyes. "Ma, can we change that stupid channel?"

"That stupid channel is your heritage, Maria. And it's my channel. My car."

"I don't care about my heritage, Ma. Right now, I want music. I *need* music."

Andy impatiently turned the knob to tune into a clear local station. Most were talk shows in French. One had rock music as she passed it.

"Go back, Ma. Go back."

Andy turned the knob back. "Rock," she sneered.

"That's it. Leave that on."

Andy looked back at her, making a face.

Maria nodded her head to the beat of Purple Rain.

"Prince," said Alessandro.

Maria was thrilled Alessandro knew the song. And it thrilled her that he finally acknowledged her. She closed her eyes and listened to the words of the song. They talked of *her* story. "Louder, please?"

"Maria."

Maria looked at Alessandro's eyes in the mirror and willed for him to look up.

He glanced up and looked away. He reached out and put it a little louder.

Maria looked through the window at passing distant ski hills on the other side of the river; purple, grey, and brilliant white against a big sky of marshmallow clouds floating in a bright robins-egg blue heaven. She felt Claudia's little hand reach out, keeping the beat on her thigh. Her sore thigh. She looked down and resisted removing *Nonna's* hand. She looked out again and thought back on what Dr. Bob had told her.

Royalty.

She thought of how, against all odds, she survived what could've been stillbirth, deformities, and brain damage. She realized it meant she was a survivor—a fighter.

A warrior.

She cast another furtive glance at the mirror.

Alessandro glanced up and looked down.

She looked away and bit at her almost non-existent thumbnail. She looked at it scornfully. No nail to bite. She shook her hand and continued to look out the window while she listened to the words of the song.

"Screaming at each other.

That was their life. It was their family.

"You got the butterflies all tied up...
"Lonely in a world so cold...
"Maybe I'm just like my father, too bold,
"Maybe I'm just like my mother; she's never satisfied...
"This is what it sounds like when doves cry..."

She watched as the snow-covered fields sped by in rhythm to the music. The words dug deep into her soul.

"...Maybe I'm just demanding..."

She leaned her forehead against the cold glass of the window. She felt pain, a touch of fear. She didn't want to feel so *weak*. Her chin quivered, and tears threatened to well up.

"... Darlin', don't cry..."

She wiped away a tear before anyone would notice.

Dr. Bob had asked about her fighting. As she talked about her fights, especially those with Selena, she realized she had enjoyed them. Was that part of competing hormones? She remembered the sight of Francesca crumpled at the base of the brick wall and her clasping her limp body on her lap hiding in the washroom cubicle.

"Ma, I want to ask Mrs. Tomolini if we can take Francesca out sometime," she yelled over the music.

"Pardon me?!"

"Francesca."

"Excuse me?!"

"She needs a break."

Andy turned the music down. "How the hell is her mother going to trust us? Did you see that wheelchair? What if she chokes while she's with us?"

"We can be taught what to do."

"No, we are not having Francesca in our care without one of her parents with us."

Maria sat looking at her mother, glumly.

Andy faced the front and crossed her arms. "Shit." She shook her head and slapped her forehead. "Crap."

Maria turned back to the window and tapped the window lightly to the quiet beat of the music.

CHAPTER FOURTEEN

STEFANO WIPED HIS SWEATY BROW with a greasy rag as he shook his head. He was disgusted and worried. This was the third hold-up this week, and they were behind schedule. The noise was deafening as he and Leo mutely stood watching one of their bulldozers try to right an excavator that had sunk into the marsh. It wasn't going too well.

"Stupidity," Leo yelled. He spat into the half-dried mud at his feet, disgusted.

Stefano frowned and squinted at the driver of the excavator. He was one of the new guys, a local from north of Myrtle Beach. He looked at Leo who angrily chewed an unlit cigar. He reached out and pulled at Leo's lime-green shirt, motioning to move away from the noise to talk.

The two men slowly walked through the deeply-rutted ground.

Leo motioned at the other men who were watching and roared. "Get the hell back to work."

Stefano looked around at the men slowly retracing their steps to continue their work. One guy climbed up on a roller, flattening the ground; two more continued hand-shoveling a trench to divert water into a nearby ditch. Two others climbed into a truck of fill. A trencher roared back to life and continued to cut a drainage ditch.

Stefano hiked up his work pants as he led Leo about a hundred feet further to a slight rise, dust swirling around them as all the heavy equipment roared into action. Stefano stopped and rolled up his sleeves for the hundredth time that hot, dusty day and looked at the sky. Sun. No clouds. Unusually hot for February. It had rained for two weeks straight, up until a few days before and this particular area hadn't drained. They also knew all three accidents that week were preventable.

"*Zio*, these'a are no accidents."

Leo glared at him, then over to where the bulldozer attempted again to slowly lift the excavator's extended arm.

"Look at that idiot," Leo yelled. "He doesn't know what the hell he's doing."

The bulldozer's bucket slipped away from underneath the extended arm, and the excavator fell back on its side, sinking deeper into the marsh.

"Fuck." Leo squinted up at Stefano, then moved into his shadow. "Someone's doin' this to us, you're right. But who? It's anyone's guess at this point."

Stefano looked around and chewed silently at the inside of his mouth. He mentally reviewed who they had hired in the last month.

"I wanna see all three guys who caused the accidents this week. Tell the foreman I wanna see them at the office at lunch break. Someone's head's goin' to roll."

Stefano spotted a dark-skinned man with a clipboard, wearing a dirty, white hard hat. He raised his fingers to his mouth and whistled loudly.

The man turned to look.

Stefano motioned him to come over just as he heard a cell phone under all the surrounding noise. He patted at the bulging form in his back pocket but saw Leo grab his own cell phone out of his front pocket.

Leo pulled out the antenna and spoke, walking away from Stefano. It took barely a moment before Leo pushed down the antenna and put the cell phone back into his pleated golf pants.

"You take care of this, Stef. Yvonne just called to say there's a problem with the new industrial stove. We're having a hell of a week."

ALESSANDRO'S CELL PHONE rang on the kitchen table. He grabbed it with both bandaged hands. He carefully pulled out the antenna and pushed the answer button.

"Hi, *Zio*."

"Alessandro."

"Everything going okay?"

"*Alcuni problemi*. All good'a there with you?" asked Stefano.

Alessandro saw Andy looking at him intently from where she appeared at the kitchen doorway. He heard a commotion behind him and knew it was Maria running in after hearing the phone ring. Alessandro glanced at her, then bent his head over the phone. He pulled out a chair and sat down.

"We had a bomb go off. You lost one of the lambs."

There was a pause.

"*Zio?*"

"*Si*, tell'a me."

Alessandro eyed Andy, and looked down. "It was a home-made bomb attached with a tripwire across the gate to the paddock. It looked like someone baited us with one of the lambs by letting it loose. They knew we'd put it back in the paddock. The lamb blew to bits."

"The barn'a?"

"They're working on fixing it now."

"Anyone hurt'a?"

"No, not really."

"I come home maybe next week'a. Now is a bad time."

"Oh, okay."

"Da bomb'a. Maybe West End Gang?"

Alessandro eyed Maria, who stared at him wide-eyed from the middle of the stairs leading from the family room. She held out her hand.

"Can I talk to him?"

Alessandro held up a finger. "We don't know, *Zio*. Is there a reason why they would?"

"*Si*, a few'a. Alessandro, keep'a guns ready, leave outside lights on and take Luna into house. You keep a watch in the nights."

"I did that last night, and we have a guy bunking in the barn. I gave the field workers head's up to keep an eye out for anything out of the ordinary during the day."

"Good. Le' me talk'a to Adriana."

Alessandro wordlessly held up the phone to Andy.

"Stef!?"

Alessandro watched Andy as she sat down.

"Wow, good for Yvonne. I bet she's happy to get her teeth into decorating. She finally has her restaurant… You're calling the company what?"

Alessandro looked back at Maria who sat on the stairs, plucking at the carpet's deep pile.

"I wanna to talk to Dad," she whispered.

"I know." Alessandro looked back at Andy.

"Paradise Beach Enterprises, huh? How long will this construction job take?" Andy asked. She looked sad. "A long time." She brightened up. "Our condo? We have a condo?" She lowered the phone and grinned at Maria. "Hey kid. They're building us a condo in the new high-rise Leo and Yvonne's living in."

Maria's mouth dropped. "What?"

"Good," grinned Andy. "Well, it ain't Miami, but Myrtle Beach will do. When?" Andy looked at Alessandro.

He smiled at her, pleased to see her happy.

"When it's finished? Stef, don't finish it completely. I wanna decorate it. Whatever. I'll start shaving my bikini line, and we're goin' shoppin'."

Maria scrambled to the table and held out her hand to her mother.

"Stef, Maria wants to talk to you."

Alessandro watched Maria fervently speak to her father. He looked at her eyelashes, her neck, her long fingers. He looked away. Part of his job was glorified babysitter and he had come to resent that part of his role, but he was concerned that she had become a deadly target; because that bomb took planning and someone put it at that gate precisely with Maria in mind. He stood up and walked to the kitchen window. He saw the light on in the barn and felt comforted there was an extra pair of eyes and ears. He glanced at the dog pen.

He turned to Andy. "I'm going to get Luna."

Andy made a face. "For God's sake, keep the dog in the basement, will you? I don't want her shitting everywhere."

Alessandro went down the stairs, grabbed his coat and, by the garage door, Stefano's boots. He made his way downstairs, then across the ceramic toward the back basement door. He sensed a heaviness lurking in the air. Something was going to happen, but he didn't know what. He looked at his watch and decided to have a nap before Andy and Maria went to bed.

It was the second night for him keeping an eye on things, with Luna and rifle at the ready.

MARIA STOOD IN HER FLUFFY PAJAMAS in front of her mirror. She brushed her hair and fluffed up what bangs she had. She turned her head to one side and studied herself, touching the various blemishes on that side of the cheek. She pushed some hair behind her ear and frowned. She walked over to a light switch and turned it off before stepping to her window. She pulled back the curtains.

The moon hung over the barn, outshining the stars that clearly dotted the heavens. It wasn't quite a full moon, but bright enough.

It was strange seeing the light on in the barn. It shone against her curtains during the night, mildly irritating her, the glow dancing on her closed lids just enough to prevent deep sleep.

Her breath fogged up the cold glass as she looked at the fields beyond the barn. Then she looked at the gate. The snow still showed signs of the aftermath of the blast. It hadn't snowed since, and Maria was anxious to have it all eradicated. The memory of Alessandro rolling in the snow in her father's flaming coat was burned into her brain.

She felt heavy with grief at the thought of what might have happened if it was him and not the poor lamb. She realized she had almost lost someone she had come to rely on, whose presence gave her purpose and hope, however much she may occasionally have hated him.

They had almost lost him.

And the thought of losing Alessandro caused her heart to hurt.

MARIA BURST OUT OF THE DRESSING ROOM and did an awkward twirl in front of the full-length mirror. She wore a black Hard Rock Café t-shirt and expensive torn blue jeans. She made a pose. "Ta-da."

Christmas music blared and echoed in the main mall. People shuffled by from both directions, some in boots, the young ones stubbornly wearing runners. People's coats hung slightly off shoulders or were swung over arms. Everyone carried packages.

Inside the high-end clothing store—muffled by thick carpeting, elegant display window dressings and sumptuous décor—the noise gave way to a quiet, comfortable haven.

Claudia sat contentedly on a luxurious velvet mini bench facing the dressing rooms, listening to lovely Italian music playing overhead. She clasped her hands and frowned at Maria.

Andy sneered.

Francesca smiled brightly from her wheelchair and moaned with delight.

Alessandro was over in the men's section looking at leather jackets. He looked at Maria, then continued touching the delicate leather.

Andy saw a strange look come over Maria's face and followed her gaze over at Alessandro. She noted his lack of interest in Maria, then looked back at her daughter.

Maria dropped her arms and stopped smiling.

As Andy watched Maria turn and look at herself in the mirror, it occurred to her that it was the first time her daughter showed any sign of caring whether Alessandro liked her or not. There was always an underlying sense of hostility in Maria's handling of Alessandro, so the change was noticeable. She thought perhaps Alessandro's brush with death had something to do with it.

Something had changed, and because of the unusual challenges they faced with Maria, she hoped it didn't lead to some emotional upheaval. The last thing she wanted was for Maria to have her heart broken because she didn't have the luxury of knowing how or who to love.

"Get back in there and put my shit on," Andy demanded. She had given Maria a different outfit to try on: a lemon-yellow polo shirt under a black unbuttoned over-shirt patterned in a Klieg-like splatter of paint. She had also added a red canvas belt with brass clips and a pair of cream-colored pants. Andy looked at her watch. She didn't have patience when it came to shopping for anyone else other than herself, and Maria was taking too long.

"Ah, Ma. It's old people's clothes."

"Oh, for frick's sake. Get back in there and put on what I gave you."

Andy watched Maria slink back into the dressing room, and crossed her arms impatiently. She looked around the store, then out the store's entrance into the rest of Vindenza Mall. Her nostrils twitched. Something smelled delicious.

"What do you want to eat later, Ma?" she asked Claudia.

Claudia sat holding Francesca's curled-up fist, but her gaze was on Alessandro. She didn't respond.

"Ma. You deaf? Where were you? You were miles away."

Claudia pointed to Alessandro. "He look'a like Fabrizio when we were in'a Calabria."

Andy looked at Alessandro studying a price tag.

"Yeah, he looks a bit like Dad in some of the photographs you have," she said softly. She bit her tongue. Similarities between people around her now gave her the willies, even though she knew exactly who Alessandro's parents were, and there was absolutely no family connection. She turned to her mother. "What do you feel like eating?"

"Pizza," yelled Maria from behind the dressing room door.

Andy looked out at the busy mall. The *famiglia* owned the pizza place, as they did most of the businesses in the mall. She knew they'd get preferential treatment no matter where they ate, though. "Ma, you want to have some *Pasta Con le Sarde*?"

"I hate sardines," said Maria.

Andy turned to the dressing room. "No comments from the peanut gallery."

Suddenly, the door swung open and there stood Maria, looking years older. Suave. Beautiful and sophisticated.

Andy eyed the outfit. "You can wear that in Myrtle Beach."

"I'm not wearin' this nowhere, especially not Myrtle Beach."

"It looks fine," said Alessandro.

Andy turned and looked at him. He seemed impatient with Maria.

Maria sadly looked into the mirror. "You like, Francesca?" asked Maria, smiling.

Andy looked at Francesca. She couldn't nod or move except for the muscles in her face. Francesca smiled slightly.

Maria walked over to Francesca and bent over her. She stood back. "What do you think?"

Francesca made a soft throaty noise. Her eyes were bright, round, gentle.

Maria smiled, looked down at herself, and turned to her mother. "She doesn't like it."

"Liar. That's not what she said." She turned to Francesca. "She looks great, doesn't she, Francesca?"

Francesca's eyes swiveled to Andy. They blinked twice.

Andy's eyebrows shot up. "See?" She looked back at Francesca and winked. "Well, no offence, but when Francesca buys you the clothes, you can care what she thinks. Right now, it's me. And they look great. Go on. Look at yourself, Maria. You look fine."

Maria looked at herself again.

"Here." Alessandro walked over with a fedora in his bulky hand.

Maria eyed the fedora.

Alessandro placed it on her head and looked into the mirror from behind her.

Maria looked wide-eyed into his eyes.

He looked her over, nodded, and walked away.

Maria took a closer look. She stood up straighter, put a hand in a pocket. Then she tilted the hat over her face. "Look, like Michael Jackson."

"You're the wrong color," quipped Andy.

Maria twirled and attempted a moonwalk. She twirled and faced Claudia.

"What do you think, *Nonna*?" Maria did a Charlie Chaplin walk.

Claudia laughed.

"You're more fun to dress than your frumpy Dad," Andy chuckled.

"He no frumpy," mumbled Claudia, shaking her head.

"Yes, he is, Ma. Goddamn frumpy. And it's not because he doesn't have any nice clothes. We never get dressed up for anything anymore. He dresses up for Peter when he's home."

"Stefano is a good *marito*. He no want's people to see him."

"Yes, Ma. I know he's a good *marito* and doesn't want to be noticed, but what the frig's wrong with dressing up? I like getting dressed up."

Claudia motioned to her black dress.

Andy looked down at her black outfit and made a face.

"Mom. What's next?"

Andy looked at Maria. "Oh, yeah." She went to another bench with clothing draped over it. She picked them up and held them out to Maria who grabbed the whole bunch and rushed back into the dressing room.

Andy's feet were killing her, so she shuffled back to Claudia, gratefully sank into the ample cushions, and sighed. She slumped into the pillow and stretched her legs. "Nice music."

Francesca screamed.

Andy and Claudia looked at Francesca in shock.

Maria jumped out of the dressing room, half undressed, and ran to Francesca's side. Her eyes were wide, dilated. She looked horrified.

Andy quickly looked into the mall's crowd to see what frightened Francesca.

Alessandro raced out into the middle of the mall and frantically looked in all directions over the heads of shoppers.

Andy followed him out. She was much shorter, but as she looked past people milling around her, she thought she saw a glimpse of messy red hair.

"Selena," she whispered.

"Selena?" asked Alessandro. Taller than Andy, he found her and focused his eyes on her figure. "You want me to go after her?"

"Selena?!" roared Maria from beside Francesca's wheelchair. She raced out of the store and was about to run after Selena when Alessandro grabbed her by the waist and stopped her.

"You piece of shit. You're the one who did this to her," yelled Maria. People around them stopped and stared.

Francesca whined, and Andy turned to see Claudia holding her from the side, gently petting her head.

"You should've gone to Juvenile, you bitch. You don't deserve to be walking around."

"That's enough, Maria. Shut up," Alessandro hissed.

Maria struggled to get out of Alessandro's grip.

"Settle down," demanded Andy.

Maria settled down and pulled away from Alessandro. She eyed onlookers as she walked back into the store towards Francesca's wheelchair.

Andy looked around at the gathered crowd. "What are *you* gawking at?" She stood and waited until the knot of onlookers dissipated, then turned and walked to Francesca. "Don't worry. She won't hurt you anymore."

"You shoulda let me get her," Maria grunted, her eyes full of angry tears.

Alessandro looked at her. "She's not worth it, Maria. You may want to cover yourself up, though."

Maria looked down to see her frilly bra and the top of her jockey underwear showing at the open zipper. She gasped, turned red, and raced back into the dressing room.

SELENA STOPPED RUNNING once she reached the center gallery, at the waterfall. It was hard work running in her heavy winter coat and boots. She was sweating from the panic of being seen by the Giordanis. She bent over while she caught her breath.

She straightened out, turned and looked back.

Maria was still alive. But how could that be? Her brother had told her it was a done deal. They didn't expect to hear anything in the news but did expect to eventually hear about her funeral. She shook her head. She couldn't understand it. She knew Maria always fed those animals at a specific time of day and, with her Dad gone, Maria was the only one that went in and out of that particular gate.

She sat on the marble ledge that surrounded the spectacular water display, to wait until her heart calmed. She looked at a bright red Christmas tree below the glass dome, its top just touching the rotunda above the center gallery. At the bottom, stood a tiny Santa's Village, with a little gate, sign, and two elves standing on either side. A short line of children anxiously awaited their turn to sit on Santa's knee.

Santa sat on a gold-trimmed, red velvet throne. A typical Santa.

Selena's breath slowed down finally, as she loosened the scratchy scarf on her itchy neck. She then looked to the side and down into the sparkling water, and eyed the coins people had thrown in for good luck. She briefly wondered how to steal them without anyone noticing. But there were more pressing thoughts fighting for center stage in her head.

She wasn't frightened of that bitch, Maria. Or of that bitch of a mother. And she didn't like the look of the guy. He looked like a bodyguard of sorts. He had to be. Why didn't she know about him? Why didn't her brother mention him?

She looked around carefully. After a moment, she was satisfied no one had followed her. She relaxed a little and pondered what she was going to do next. She looked back to where the Giordanis were shopping. Her day hanging out at the mall was a goner, now that they were there.

She looked to the mall's main entryway and peered through the large glass doors into the parking lot. She slowly smirked.

"SHIT, ALESSANDRO. What should we do about that Selena?"

Alessandro stuck his hands into his dress pants and walked a little closer, but still kept his eyes on the main mall. "Nothing at the moment."

"I don't trust that kid." Andy briefly thought of the bomb. Was it possible? "Do you think she had anything to do with that bomb?"

Alessandro looked at her deep in thought. "She has brothers?"

Andy brushed her black turtleneck sweater. "She has two brothers. Her mother's still alive. Her Dad's not. Her oldest brother's in the slammer with Peter."

"West End?"

Andy looked up and then down again. "I'd rather it's Selena and her brothers than the actual West End Gang. That'd be her godfather."

"The Weasel?"

"Shit, we can't fight…" Andy swallowed and covered her eyes.

"Mr. Giordani mentioned the West End Gang when we were talking about the bomb. But maybe it's only personal, between Selena's family and us. Not business between the Gang and the *famiglia*." He dropped his voice when he saw they weren't going to be alone.

A tall, slim, well-dressed man with a thin mustache came from the back of the store. "*Signora di Giovanni, Signora Giordani,* everything okay?"

"Yeah, we're okay, Antonio."

He nodded and smiled broadly. "Some more *café espresso,* perhaps? *Biscotti?*" He looked at clothes tossed over the top edge of the dressing room door.

"*Si,* a ton more of *biscotti,* Antonio. They're nice and fresh." Andy sat back and gathered herself together. "Oh, and do you have *a cappuccino,* for a change?"

Antonio bowed. He daintily took the little empty espresso cup and saucer from a little table near Claudia, then looked just as Maria's dirty sneaker pushed cream-colored pants under the door. Antonio snatched at the pants, and deftly flipped them into shape with one hand over his arm. He turned back to the ladies.

"A *cappuccino* for *Signora* and a ton of *biscotti.*"

Andy pointed her chin and nose up into the air. "*Grazie,* Antonio. You da *man.*"

Antonio's nostril trembled as he turned and walked to the back of the store.

Alessandro moved closer and settled on the arm of a velvet plush wing-back chair next to the little sofa, still looking back over his shoulder into the mall.

The dressing room door banged open, and Maria stepped out wearing a turquoise polo shirt under a crisp white shirt in red, yellow, red, and blue. The padded shoulders were the newest fad. These were over black pants and a black belt with brass clasps. Maria twirled.

"Ah, beautiful, Maria."

"'You think, *Nonna?*"

"*Si.*" Claudia smiled broadly, looking proud.

Andy threw up her arms. "Antonio. We'll get everything that we tried on today."

Maria turned to her. "The t-shirt and jeans, as well?" she asked, hopefully.

"No, they can go jump in the lake."

Alessandro chuckled.

Maria looked. "What do you think?"

"Your mother has good taste," he said.

Antonio poked his head through the black velvet curtain at the back. "Pardon?"

"We're buying the two full outfits, Not that shitty t-shirt and jeans, though."

"Mom." Maria turned, "They're over $200 each. They're not shitty."

"Well, to me, they are. I don't care if that goddam t-shirt costs a thousand dollars. Okay, Antonio? No t-shirt and jeans. Just the two other outfits."

"*Si, Signora. Subito. Perfezionare.*"

"That's worth a ton of *biscotti*, right, Alessandro?" Andy said as she stepped to him and poked his shoulder. She turned to Maria and pushed at the big padded shoulder in her blouse.

Maria flipped her hair from out of her eyes. "Don't."

Andy smiled at her. Then she shook her head and grabbed Maria, pretending to dance with her. "We'll get you looking like one of those girls in a Rick Astley video. Sporty, but sexy." Andy twirled Maria in circles. She broke out in a Rick Astley song:

> "*Never gonna make you cry,*
> *Never gonna say goodbye.*"

Maria dizzily stumbled, then jumped back. She grabbed her mother by the shoulders. "Stop singing, Ma. That's terrible."

Andy kept singing.

Maria put her hand over Andy's mouth, but Andy poked her tongue into Maria's palm, and Maria pulled her hand back quickly. "Euuuuwwww." She wiped her hand on one of the pants on display in front of them.

"Come on, sing with me." Andy wanted to lighten up the mood. She was frightened to the core by that Selena, by the bomb, by everything going on with Stefano, and the only way to handle that was to either yell at someone or become outrageous.

Maria laughed. She joined her mother and sang the next line.

"Never gonna tell a lie,
"And huuuuurt you."

They both stopped and laughed, and their outburst echoed into the mall.

An older woman passing by the doors stopped to look where the noise was coming from.

Andy saw her and let Maria go. Andy knew the woman. She was also dressed in black, and was the mother of one of the Montreal Sicilians. Andy walked toward her mother.

"Ma," Andy said.

Claudia looked up as Andy sat beside her on the sofa.

Andy discreetly pointed at the lady, and Claudia craned her neck to see.

"Mom," whispered Maria, coming over. "That's what's her name, Mrs.—"

"Mrs. Santorini," Alessandro offered. He stared at the lady, who shifted a large fancy shopping bag from one arm to the other. "Best to leave her alone, Mrs. Giordani. That's not a good scene, either."

Either. Andy felt whoozy and overwhelmed. She took a deep breath. Slowly, she let it out as she watched Mrs. Santorini continue on her way. She pushed hair away from her eyes. She turned. "Hey, we're not finished yet. After we wrap this up and pay for it all, we're having supper, and then we're spendin' more of your Dad's money."

"Eh, *excusez-moi*, Madame?"

Andy turned around to see a stranger standing at the door. The man wore a Panama hat and a light brown suede jacket over jeans.

"Can I help you?" asked Alessandro, stepping in front of him.

The man smiled politely. Pearly whites showed under a well-trimmed mustache. "Please, I am sorry. I couldn't help but hear beautiful singing." He put his hairy hands together as if in prayer. "May I introduce myself? I am James Shapiro."

Andy stood up. "Hi, James Shapiro, I'm Andy. How can we help you?"

James looked at Alessandro and motioned to Andy. "May I?"

"It's okay, Alessandro."

James stepped past Alessandro and held out his hand.

Andy shook it.

He let go her hand, dipped into his breast pocket, and took out a business card. "I'm sorry to bother you and your family," he said, handing her the card. "But I wanted to introduce myself because I couldn't help but notice your very striking son."

Andy looked at Alessandro. "Oh, he's not my son."

"No," James glanced over at Maria and smiled. "I mean, this fine young man."

Andy looked at Maria.

Maria's face paled. She turned and disappeared into the dressing room.

"You changing?"

No answer from Maria.

Andy slowly turned to James and looked at him. She raised her chin. "That's not my son. That's my fine young *daughter*, Maria."

James' face fell. "I'm so sorry. I didn't mean to insult you *or* your daughter. Young people can look quite androgynous these days. Her hair is quite short."

"I know. She had a buzz cut. It's growing back."

"Handsome young woman. May I ask your names?"

"Why, may I ask?"

"I'm a talent agent."

She looked at him curiously. "I'm Andy Giordani. And this is my mother, Mrs. di Giovanni, Maria's grandmother. Alessandro, here, is my nephew," she lied.

James looked at Alessandro after nodding at Claudia.

Alessandro steadily looked back.

Andy looked up from the card.

"Perhaps we can talk?"

Andy shrugged. "Yeah, I guess." Andy quickly looked at the back of the store where Antonio was carefully wrapping the first set of clothing Maria had tried on. "Just a sec." Andy turned to the dressing room. "Maria, hurry. Get changed so Antonio can ring everything up."

"I'm going as fast as I can," Maria answered.

Andy turned to James and motioned to the winged-back chair Alessandro had perched on earlier. She sat back down beside Claudia.

"Well, I couldn't help but notice. Your daughter is quite an exquisite looking young person." James sat down. "How old is she?"

"She's fifteen," offered Alessandro, guardedly.

"And eats like it," quipped Andy.

James laughed. "Well, Mrs. Giordani, I have a proposition to make."

"I'm taken." Andy looked at him, her head cocked to one side.

He held up his hands. "Ha, that's funny. I'm sorry. What I mean is — Listen, I know, here I am, out of the blue. But I've been looking everywhere." He motioned toward the dressing room, nodding. "For a young person to fill a small but crucial role that could lead to bigger and better things." He clasped his hands together. "We've been looking at young people for over a week. We want that special look, someone who looks," he paused, "androgynous."

No one said anything.

Alessandro shifted his weight and cleared his throat.

Andy made a face.

Claudia looked blankly, then looked at Andy for an indication as to what he meant.

"It's becoming quite the look these days, but not everyone can carry it off," he added.

Maria came out of the dressing room holding the new clothes over her arms. "Ma, what's this all about?"

"He's a talent scout."

"Talent agent," James corrected her.

"For what?" Maria stepped closer.

"TV, film, commercials. Even stage." James blinked, studying Maria from the top of her head down to her dirty running shoes.

Andy frowned and turned back to James. "Are you putting us on? You're talkin' maybe's and could. What kind of role are you talking about? And where?"

"Toronto."

Andy shook her head. "Oh, no. I'm sorry. We're not going there." She stood up and straightened out her black pants. "Not the big, bad city."

"Toronto, the good, is what they call it."

Claudia looked from one to the other, even looking at Antonio for clues about what was going on. She turned to Andy finally. "*Cosa sta succedendo?* He wan' Maria in a Toronto'a?"

"No, Ma, it's a come on." Andy turned to Maria. "I'm paying the bill, and we're leaving." She turned to James. "Listen, thanks for thinking about us, but no thanks."

James hesitated and was about to say something when Alessandro stepped toward him.

"That's it, sir. She's not interested."

"Well, if you change your mind, you have my card." He looked sadly at Maria.

"We won't," Andy said.

James turned and left quietly, disappearing into the mall.

"Ah, Ma. I wanted to know what part he was thinking of."

"Who gives a shit? We're not interested."

"I am."

Andy turned to her. "We're not interested," she repeated, slowly. "Okay? We got enough on our plates, don't ya think? Our world already revolves around you, Maria"

Maria frowned and flopped onto the little sofa beside her *Nonna*.

Andy walked up to the counter, with her black Gucci purse and pulled out her black Gucci wallet. Antonio clasped his hands.

Andy looked down at the total on the receipt, then rifled through her wallet for cash.

"We take credit cards if you prefer, Mrs. Giordani."

"Uh-uh. My husband doesn't let me have credit cards, Antonio."

"And my condolences."

"Condolences? My father died almost four years ago. We're still in black. We're actually from the Middle Ages."

ANDY HURRIED EVERYONE down the packed mall in the direction from where her nose said was the source of the beautiful aroma of *Pasta Con le Sarde.*

Maria pushed Francesca's wheelchair as Claudia held onto Alessandro's arm. They raced to keep up with Andy. As they rounded the corner to where the beautiful water fountain splashed against the marble walls in the middle of the grand hall, they stopped and looked at the large red Christmas tree.

"Wow," said Andy.

Claudia swayed, as she tried to raise her face enough to look at the very top.

"Isn't that beautiful?" asked Maria, as she bent over Francesca and pointed upward. Suddenly, she saw a familiar Panama hat at the phone booths by the main entrance.

"Mom, wait."

Andy stopped and looked back. "What?"

"Mr. Shapiro," Maria said, and pointed at him at the phone booth.

"Forget it, Maria."

Maria stopped pushing Francesca and crossed her arms angrily. "Ma, he's interested in me. The least you can do is allow me to find out why he thought *I*," she pointed at herself, "*I* am of interest. I have a right to know."

Andy fumed silently. "Maria, he's a stranger."

"So?"

Andy turned to Alessandro. "What do you think?"

Alessandro looked at Maria.

She stared him down.

He looked at Andy. "It's up to you."

Maria dropped her arms in disgust.

"Adriana, maybe he'a come and talk to us when we eat'a. *Si*? Den Maria know'a."

"Yeah, Mom. Even *Nonna* thinks I have a right to know."

Andy looked at her mother and shook her head.

"ALLOW ME TO PAY for this dinner." James put his hand on his chest. "I guarantee you I am most sincere. I'm going to give you a rundown of all the actors I've had the privilege of representing and those whom I represent now. My clients find work all around the world."

"All around the world, eh?" Andy shifted on the plush bench as she played with the white linen napkin. "You think I want my daughter to go all around the world?"

"May I. Please. Buy this dinner?"

Maria nudged her mother's arm, as she took a large bite of her pizza.

Sitting on the other side of the round table, Claudia nursed a bowl of *rigatoni* and Italian sausage.

Andy chewed happily on her pasta and sardines.

Alessandro had opted for a cup of coffee and was carefully placing fries into Francesca's mouth with a fork.

James sat over a bowl of plain linguini with parmesan cheese. He just finished explaining how he had moved to Vindenza to be close to his widowed mother after working 20 years in Los Angeles. He had a new agency in Montreal.

"So, tell me. What were some of the jobs you sent your clients to?" Andy asked, giving him a direct look. She pointed her fork at him. "Names I recognize."

"Okay." He wiped his mouth with his napkin. A waiter in burgundy and black came over, but he waved him away after seeing no one needed anything. "You've heard of *Growing Pains, Alf, The Wonder Years, Family Ties?* My clients have acted in these series. Maria reminds me of Michael J. Fox—*Head of the Class*, and I hear through the proverbial vine that we're about to do a major Canadian production of *Anne of Green Gables*."

Andy put her fork and spoon down and picked up her napkin. She dabbed her lips. "Okay, impressive, but I only count—what? Half a dozen shows? So, say she gets a job in each one. She's finished for the year?"

James grinned and shook his head. "No, it's not exactly how it works."

"So, tell me." She gave him a side glance before picking up her fork and spoon again.

"There are many other productions you may know. There are pilots of shows, there's also modeling, stage, commercials. I guarantee Maria work. Him, too." He pointed at Alessandro.

"How about a little problem like school?"

James nodded slowly. "Because most of these shows are union, which is ACTRA here in Canada, we have to hire on-set tutors.

Parents can be there as guardians and support. Most productions welcome parents."

Maria tugged at Andy's sleeve.

"Yeah, what?"

"Mom, it wouldn't hurt to try?"

"Listen, your Dad wouldn't allow it. I don't know why we're even talking about this."

"Well, maybe we can try and see if it's any good. Dad's gone anyhow for a while. If it's something that seems good, we can tell him. And if it's something we don't like, then we didn't have to get Dad all upset."

Claudia looked at Maria with wide eyes. "Maria, you father should'a know."

Andy sighed deeply. "Tell you what, Mr. Shapiro, you buy us dessert, too, and we'll set up an appointment. I wanna see where you work. Hell, we spend a lot of time going in and out of Montreal. We can squeeze in an appointment." She looked at Alessandro. "Is that all right?"

Alessandro shrugged. "You're the boss, Andy."

Maria screamed and jumped up, pulling the table cloth with her and spilling her Coke.

Andy covered her eyes. "Why don't you just kill me already." Then she looked at James. "See what I have to put up with?"

MARIA EXCITEDLY CHATTED with Francesca, her breath hanging heavily in the cold air, as she made sure Francesca's winter hat covered her ears.

Alessandro pushed the wheelchair into the parking lot, its wheels crunching through the icy tire tread marks. Overhead, hung giant garlands of lights and heavy tinsel. The Christmas jingles from within the mall slowly faded away. Here, they heard the crunch of surrounding car tires and their own tentative treads through the quickly-freezing slush.

They made their way to a dark waiting van, with its engine running and steam billowing out of its exhaust. The driver's side door opened, and Mr. Tomolini stepped out into the light of a tall lamp stand. He smiled and nodded at everyone. He opened a sliding door and pulled out a ramp. In his long, winter coat, he gingerly stepped to his daughter, almost slipping in his leather shoes. He flapped his arms around to keep from falling.

Francesca found it funny and laughed.

He laughed, as well, as he regained his balance.

Andy held Claudia's arm while they watched Mr. Tomolini push the wheelchair up into the van, then locked down the brakes. He pulled over a seat belt and carefully fastened it around Francesca's body and clipped the end into the floor. He stood back, looking and smiling at Francesca, then waved at everyone.

"Say bye, Francesca."

She looked as far to the side as she could, and smiled.

Maria waved both of her fluffy mitts. "See ya."

"And thank you, Andy. Maria. This means the world to us," said Mr. Tomolini.

Andy went over and padded him on his shoulder, giving him an air kiss near his cheek.

"Our pleasure. Drive carefully."

"Give my regards to Stefano," he said, shivering in the cold. He motioned to the dark, winter sky. "I'm sure he's a lot warmer where he is." He opened the driver's door and slipped in. He lowered his window as he closed the door and leaned out. "If there is anything we can do for you, anytime, please let us know." He waved and closed the window.

As he pulled away, Andy gently led Claudia further into the parking lot. Maria fell in behind them and Alessandro followed Maria. He looked around the parking lot, as he meandered past snow-covered cars.

Mounds of snow lined the aisles, and there was a mountain of soot-stained snow off to the side. Tall lights lined the rows of cars forming a glowing grid that cut through the dark.

"I can't believe it, *Nonna*. He does *Fraggle Rock*. And Michael J. Fox. I LOVE him. Oh, my God, Mom." She tapped her mother on the shoulder. "Can I keep all the money I make? Then I'd buy my first car, cash."

"Dream on, kiddo. Nothing's that easy." Andy laughed, her breath floating away from them in a sudden, cold wind.

"Yeah, but he liked me, Mom. Right, *Nonna*? He wants me."

"That's what scares me," Andy said, as they all stopped at the car while Alessandro searched for the keys.

Suddenly Alessandro froze.

Andy and Claudia stood looking at the car.

Maria looked from Andy and Claudia and down to where they were looking.

Someone had scratched an ugly, jagged "FUCKING QUEER" along the side of Stefano's Cadillac.

CHAPTER FIFTEEN

MARIA LISTENED INTENTLY to Alessandro's end of the conversation with her father, as he explained what had happened that day, about Selena, and the damage done to the car. She looked over at Claudia, who looked bedraggled. Alessandro had done his best to cover the filth on the side of the vehicle with face lotion Andy had in her Gucci bag, but the pain and shock didn't leave them. Her *Nonna* still looked traumatized.

After leaving the Vindenza Mall, they stopped at her *Nonna's* to drop off Claudia at her little house, but as Alessandro helped Claudia out of the car, he stopped. He looked again at the large frozen white smudge on the side of the vehicle and announced that Claudia shouldn't be alone considering what happened that day and the previous week. So, they waited while Claudia packed, then took her to the house.

"Yes, sir, I will," muttered Alessandro. "Thank you. We'll be here, *Zio*." He gently pushed the off button and pushed in the antenna slowly. Then, he turned to look at Maria.

They looked at each other for a quiet moment.

Andy came down the stairs. "I got your room ready, Ma. You can go to bed anytime."

Claudia nodded sadly. "I no'a like not being in my'a house. Fabrizio is'a still there. He will be alone'a."

Andy stood for a moment, not saying a thing. She had taken off her make-up and was in her housecoat. Eyebrows raised, she pursed her lips. "Ma, I'm sorry to tell you, but Dad's gone. He's dead."

"I know'a but'a he is in'a the house. I feel him'a." She pulled out a handkerchief from her narrow black sleeve and blew her nose.

"Well, I'm sure he'll be fine. But you might not be if you stay. So, Alessandro's right; you are better off here." She turned to Alessandro. "So, what's the scoop?"

"He said that the City of Montreal gave the downtown sector to us."

"Garbage contract? Is that smart?"

Alessandro shrugged. "He wondered at first if perhaps the bomb was the Sicilians."

"The Sicilians?"

Alessandro nodded.

"Like we need another hole in the head." Andy sat down, covered her face, and sighed. "Oh, what a soap opera."

"I wouldn't be too concerned, though," Alessandro said, "I heard Leo remind *Zio* that he had sent word they were given a territory for the hard stuff in Myrtle Beach. That we can afford to give it up because of the other areas of business they established."

Maria gazed at Alessandro's profile. *Famiglia* business again. She thought back to a day, years before, when she wanted to play a trick on *Zio* Peter, while he, her Dad, and her *Nonno* were in the *caverna* smoking cigars. She had crept into the garage while her mother was busy cooking, and slowly crawled to the edge of the hatchway, waiting patiently to catch anyone poking their heads out. She wanted to frighten them. She thought it would be funny. But she had heard things. Things about dirty money and drugs and Venezuela and Anita's husband being in trouble. By the time *Zio* Peter finally popped his head out, she'd forgotten to frighten him. She felt guilty having heard their business secrets and saw the thought scared *Zio* Peter; She heard things only adults should know. The first thing he asked was if she had heard anything. She had lied and shaken her head no. Now she was overhearing things again, but as an adult.

The Sicilians. Hard stuff. Territories.

Alessandro shrugged. "It's Selena who scratched up the car. I mean, you gotta be stupid to do that unless you can back it up with balls."

Andy laughed. "Stupid is, stupid does."

Alessandro flipped the phone over and looked at it. "I guess I better charge this thing."

"*Nonna?*" Maria piped up. "Are you okay?"

Andy and Alessandro turned to Claudia. She was deathly pale.

"Today drained her. Didn't it, Ma?"

Claudia nodded.

Maria looked down at her socks. She reached out with her toe to a tiny spill of something on the tile and rubbed it. It disappeared.

"Where's the key to all the guns?"

Maria looked at Alessandro in surprise.

"You've got the rifle," Andy said.

Alessandro glanced at her. "I need more. Just in case." He turned to Maria. "Have you ever used a gun?"

She shook her head. "No." Her father rarely took out the guns in the gun rack. He went moose hunting once a year to Newfoundland and, every once-in-a-while, he'd shoot a bothersome fox or raccoon on their land, so there was no need to use all the guns in the rack. Then, she thought of the secret stash of guns and ammunition under the trunk of her father's Cadillac. "We have some in the car, too.

"I know. We'll leave those for now. First thing in the morning, I'm calling an autobody shop to fix the damage done by that sicko." Alessandro stood up and looked around the kitchen.

"What ya lookin' for?" asked Andy.

"The charger."

"You probably left it near your bed downstairs." She pushed her chair away from the table. "Ma, you okay goin' to bed on your own?"

"*Si*, I'm no *bambina*."

"Come on. I'll help you up the stairs. And then let's take a look at the gun rack." Andy helped Claudia to her feet and led her away from the table.

Alessandro got up and took a few steps down the stairs and waited for Andy.

As the two women left the kitchen, Maria turned to follow Alessandro but wasn't watching what she was doing. She reached for the handrail going down and accidentally touched Alessandro's bandaged hand as it rested on the railing.

She pulled her hand back in shock. "Sorry."

Alessandro silently looked at her.

She held back and waited until her mother appeared again in the kitchen.

She turned and followed Alessandro, with her mother in tow behind her. They went down into the family room and downstairs again, to where the gun rack was located on the next floor below.

They all stood in front of the gun rack just right of the rug-covered stairs. On this level, were the second kitchen, a huge entertainment room with a massive fireplace, the cold cellar for the cheese and wines, and Stefano's bathroom, shower, and sauna. Of course, there was the pull-out couch, which made for Alessandro's bed.

"The charger," Andy said pointing to the table next to the pull-out couch.

As Alessandro looked, Andy pulled out a key from the drawer underneath the gun rack's locked doors. She opened other drawers and showed Alessandro boxes of ammunition.

"Do you know your guns, Alessandro?" Andy asked.

He pulled out a Remington and gently balanced it on his palms. "Here's an old Remington. A 31, I think. Yeah, this will do. The shot won't kill if someone's not too close, but it could mess them up a bit."

"Mess them up a bit?" repeated Maria.

Andy looked at her daughter. "You should go upstairs. This has nothing to do with you."

"Mom, yes it does. The bomb was meant for me. I'm not a kid anymore. If something's going on that forces us to use guns, then maybe I should know a little, don't you think?"

"Don't *you think*? You sound like me now." Andy stared at Maria for a few seconds. Then she shrugged and nodded.

Alessandro turned to another gun and carefully unlatched it. He admired the beautifully-polished cherrywood stock. "Here," he said, resting the rifle over his palms as if to show its beauty. He motioned to Maria.

Maria's mouth dropped open. She looked at the rifle, and her eyes widened. She swallowed hard and gingerly held out her hands.

"It's a rimfire. A good gun for you to learn on. It has less recoil."

He placed the rifle into her hands then positioned her hands on its stock and the fore-end. She slowly raised it and peeked through the scope.

"That's right," Alessandro said.

"Wow." She handed the rifle back to Alessandro. "Can you teach me how to shoot tomorrow?"

"Uh-uh. Not a chance, is he going to do that for you." Andy impatiently jabbed the air in front of her. "Not so long as I'm alive." She looked at Alessandro. "How are you going to do this, Alessandro?"

"Well," he said, as he carefully placed the rifle back in its spot in the rack. "Let's see." He looked at his wristwatch, "It's 8:30, so I'll do my usual quick nap until you go to bed."

"I'll wake you when we're ready to go," offered Maria.

"Okay. But tonight, we turn every single light on outside."

"I'll go and do that now."

Alessandro took down the Remington again and loaded shells.

Maria stopped. "Should I bring Luna in now, too?" asked Maria.

"Yeah, bring her in."

She went to go.

"Be careful out there, Maria."

She looked at him, wide-eyed. "It'll be okay. We would hear barking otherwise, right?" Maria turned and ran upstairs, pounding the floor like an elephant as she traveled from light switch to light switch, turning on every single light outside. Then, she threw on her rubber boots and grabbed a heavy jacket from the coat hook. She hesitated at the door into the garage. Then she took off her boots and carried them through the house and back downstairs, passing her mother and Alessandro to the back door.

"Maria, make sure the dog takes a shit first," her mother called.

"Okay." Maria opened the heavy door, then the screen door. The screen slammed shut. Its clap echoed like a rifle shot in the cold, still night.

Luna came out of her kennel and barked up a storm.

One half of the barn door creaked open, pouring light onto the trampled snow. A head poked out around the corner.

"It's okay. It's only me getting Luna."

The figure waved and disappeared into the gold light of the barn, and the door creaked shut.

A full moon hung high in the dark expanse of the sky above. Fast-moving upper clouds danced by its brilliant, pockmarked face. Under Maria's boots, snow crunched. As she got closer to the kennel, Luna settled down and stopped barking. She stood and sniffed the air. Her tail wagged furiously. She whined, her eyes riveted on Maria. "Shush," Maria whispered as she held her finger up to her lips. Luna understood. She lay down and rested her chin on her paws and gave Maria a sad look from underneath the arch of her brows.

Maria reached for the gate's latch and opened it, bending down to swipe at Luna's back with her mitt as she shot out of the gate. Both Maria's and Luna's breaths floated above them. She allowed Luna to do her long figure eight across the back lawn, right down the length of the driveway, looping back up, and back into the back property the length of the fence of the paddock; then past the barn and back to her kennel. Over and over again.

Maria smiled in the moonlight, feeling as if it lit the world like a strange sun in a black-sky world. She looked down at the new gate to the paddock and the repairs to the side of the barn. It hadn't been very long since they repaired the damage caused by the fire before the bomb. Maria frowned. She thought of Alessandro, how he lay quietly in the snow after he finished rolling out the flames. He lay staring up into the sky, soot all over his face.

His handsome face.

She looked to where he had lain in the snow, and walked over. Traffic by animal and human obliterated where Alessandro had lain, but the soot was still there.

Luna stopped racing and settled down beside Maria. Luna was content to sniff her pant legs. Maria watched Luna, then stared into the snow as she became aware of something unsettling, something quite curious.

She asked herself, if she were to feel something for Alessandro, would it be as a woman? Or is she doomed to end up secretly loving him as a man?

Suddenly, she felt nauseous. Either way, woman, man, Alessandro would not be interested in a freak of nature. She stumbled under the weight of such a blow. She fell to her knees, then slowly, sadly, settled back on the heels of her boots. She looked at the back of the house and saw Alessandro's head and shoulders through the lit window, standing at the gun rack on the rising. Maria rested there, on her knees, and drank in his image, waiting for Luna to finish her business.

"COME," MARIA WHISPERED, as she led Luna into the house through the garage. Alessandro had finally turned off the landing light, so she knew he was well into his nap. She let go of Luna in the garage, and closed the heavy door. There was no need for lights, as there was enough glow inside from the outside lights. She turned and saw Luna sniffing the damaged area of the car. Maria stood and watched, taking off her mitts.

Luna sniffed along the bottom edge of the car, the wheel at the front, then she took her time sniffing along the other side of the vehicle. Maria, intrigued, followed. They went around the back of the car. Maria watched Luna sniff around to the other side one more time before her tail wagged, and she finally headed for the door into the house. There, her tail wagged so hard it rocked her rump from side to side. She smiled back at Maria with her tongue hanging out.

Maria opened the door into the house and looked back one more time. She stopped and squinted at the car even as she heard Luna scrambling over the boots and shoes in the narrow hallway. She cocked her head and walked over to look at the hood. In the dark light of the parking lot of Vindenza Mall, they hadn't noticed anything other than the terrible damage on the side. Now, Maria could see that someone had traced an image into the dirt and dry road salt on the hood of the car. Maria reached back and turned on the light. She blinked and swallowed a cry.

It was a crude drawing of a naked man's torso with breasts.

December, 1987

ALESSANDRO GOT OFF THE PLASTIC-COVERED couch and did his rounds again. It was two in the morning. Everyone was asleep.

He'd been going from window to window since Maria had awoken him from his nap at eleven.

Up until a month before, Luna had rarely been in the house and was still quite frantic with happiness for being with the family indoors. Andy was upset, of course. But she recognized how important it was to have Luna free to roam the house.

It had been a few weeks, but the level of tension hadn't lessened as Christmas drew closer, so Alessandro appreciated it when he was alone with Luna and his thoughts. He had a lot of time to think about reasons for accepting this very personal mission of watching over the Giordani's, like a holy exercise. If he did it well, he would win the honor he craved from the *famiglia*. *Zio* Stefano was second in command in the *famiglia*. He was very determined to impress *Zio* Leo. He had big plans. He wanted to climb as high as he could in the *famiglia*, but, for that, he had to prove himself. That's why he saw his time there as *treasure* days—life and death challenges which he could not have hoped for, so soon in his life.

His mother used to remind him it wasn't a game. Danger lurked in this way of life, and she still cautioned him to be patient. To think; to reason. He looked down at the windowsill and saw a dead fly. He looked at the trim above the window and reached and touched a small spider web. He spied another fly wrapped in spider's silk. Victims of entrapment.

He stepped back. *To think; to reason.* He realized, all this time he stood at the windows willing for something to happen, so that he could be the *hero*—someone whom *Zio* Stefano would think is dependable, unique, loyal, and dedicated. But there was something else that was now part of his every-day thoughts; *Maria*.

Initially, he didn't care about Maria's health and the pills and appointments. So long as whatever it was wasn't life-threatening, it was none of his business. And she was just a kid. Yes, he knew about Maria's anomalies in a general way, but he never thought beyond that. He never went beyond imagining a baby with slightly different body parts. So small, and relatively, so insignificant.

At the same time, he knew he had to marry and have children to pass on the legacy of the *'Ndrangheta famiglia*. So, someone like himself would typically be on the look-out for potential mates. If the *'Ndrina* community was considered small in Vindenza, it was even smaller in Venezuela. So, while at the mall, he had looked around at the pretty faces milling about; faces studied. Were they Sicilian? Calabrian? Pretty faces were nice to catch the eye, but behind the pretty face, there had to be a bright, healthy young woman dedicated to the culture.

He spent all of his time with women, now. Andy, Claudia, and Maria. He never spoke to any of the field workers out back. Yes, he occasionally exchanged a word or two with some of the men who took turns spending nights in the barn. But he spent *so much time in female company*. So, naturally, if Maria, or even Andy, did or said something in a strangely female and appealing manner, he took notice.

Well, at first. And not for long. Besides, Maria was the boss' kid. And she was spoiled.

He woke from his deep and wandering thoughts; something caught his eye in the distance, about a half kilometer down the road, to the right. His senses sharpened and he opened his eyes wide as he kept his gaze on the location.

He squeezed to the left end of the large window and kept the rifle parallel to his body. He felt the gun with his hand. Did he really want to hurt someone? He prayed he wouldn't have to, and perhaps he could just frighten them away. Something flicked in the moonlight behind the trees on the other side of the road. It had traveled closer.

Alessandro heard Luna stir in the kitchen and click her nails on the ceramic into the front hallway. He heard soft noises and looked back to see Luna sitting behind him on the carpet. He watched as she straightened up and sat in the moonlight on the shag rug, quivering with excitement. Her eyes sharpened, and her tail banged against the floor.

"What is it, Luna?" Alessandro whispered.

Luna got up and walked to the window. She pressed her snout against the glass as she focused on the mailbox at the end of the driveway. She quivered and whined.

Alessandro put his finger to his lips and shushed her. He walked to the kitchen carrying the rifle. "Luna, come."

Luna hurried past him down the stairs to the basement's back door. He put one foot into one of Stefano's heavy boots as he unlocked the inner door softly. He turned and grabbed a leash for Luna, off a nearby hook with his free hand, as he placed his other foot in a boot. Before he finished clipping the leash onto her collar, he opened the screen door.

Luna bolted.

"Oh, shit," he spat, scrambling to get the second boot on before he ran outside.

Alessandro turned along the back wall and rounded onto the end of the driveway in time to see Luna sniff frantically at the mailbox, then fly like a plane over the snow-packed road, cutting diagonally across and into the bushes closer to the house than where he last saw movement. He heard a blood-curdling scream and then choking. He rushed through the hardened snow as fast as he could. Not too far along the road, he saw bushes shaking.

He got down on one knee, took the safety off the gun, and aimed it at the bushes. He softly whistled for Luna to come back.

The bushes shook again and Luna returned, panting happily. He petted her and noticed something black on his hand. He looked at it under the moonlight. He rubbed his fingers together and discovered it was sticky—blood. He aimed the gun back on the bushes. His ears rang with expletives and moans.

His heart jumped. He sprung up and rushed down the rest of the driveway, over the snow-covered road, into the opposite ditch. He lost his balance and fell face-first through the crunchy top layer into the soft underbelly of the snow, and the gun flopped into the snow along with him.

He scrambled up on his hands and knees, climbed up the other side, and crawled underneath the bushes. He followed along the road, staying as much as possible in the shadows of the moon. Eventually, his eyes made out snapped branches and dog prints. He went a little further and stopped. His heart jumped in his throat.

Something squirmed and whimpered under the next bush.

He squatted and aimed the rifle. He searched the bush in the dark.

A voice croaked, "Brian, is that you? I can't breathe. I need help."

Brian? Alessandro panicked. He quickly twisted, aiming the gun in all directions. A clod of snow fell off a nearby branch, and he almost shot at it. Where was this Brian guy?

He turned quickly in the person's direction and frantically tried to see into shadows. Slowly, he could make out a form and saw someone's breath. It was rapid and shallow.

"I can't breathe… My neck."

Alessandro bit his lip and wondered what to do. He readjusted his position and looked around. He slowly moved closer to the bush. Whoever it was, was quite hurt. Perhaps he could leave the person there and wait until the morning to call the police, claiming to find the person on a morning dog walk.

But if there's supposed to be a Brian around, he would have to hunt him down, too.

He slowly lowered onto his belly into the snow and crawled toward the bush.

He heard a noise behind him, and his heart leaped. With a quiet yelp, he suddenly felt Luna lick the side of his face. Then, he watched as she sidled up to the bush and disappeared under its branches. Alessandro heard growling and snapping.

He reached the edge of the bush, snow caked up into the sleeves of his sweater. He was without a coat or gloves and quickly waggled his hands and fingers for some circulation. He crawled a little closer. Then, he reached out at what he thought was clothing. He grabbed it and pulled it toward himself. He was yanking at a coat, also pulling the person.

The person moaned. It was a girl.

He yanked at her some more but she was dead weight. Heavy.

Luna remained by her side and panted, the dog's breath ample and hanging amongst the branches of the bush.

Alessandro fished around for a limb and found a heavy leg. He grabbed a handful of corduroy material on the leg and slowly pulled her closer. More of her body came into view. He saw what looked like long red hair in the stark moonlight. The hair was matted and spread around in the snow. He let go. It was Selena.

He got back on his haunches and looked around the small clearing. He watched his breath float away from him and disappear. If there were anyone around, he would undoubtedly see theirs.

And Luna would know.

He relaxed. "Good enough," he whispered. He stood up, slung the rifle over onto his back after shouldering the strap, then bent down to grab Selena's legs. He dragged her out from underneath the bush. She weakly kicked at him, but he had a firm hold on her.

He stopped and stared at the snowy trail her body formed. He squinted. "Shit," he whispered. In the faint moonlight, he could see the trail was black. Blood. He leaned over Selena's legs. Selena's eyes widened with recognition and she howled.

He quickly jumped over her, and covered her mouth with his hands. He had to push hard on her face to keep his hands in place.

He quickly looked around and craned his neck to see the road. He counted to a hundred.

She sniffed and choked under his hands and tried to scream. He looked down. "Shut the fuck up, or I'll kill you. Did you hear me?"

Selena stopped squirming and managed a wet gurgle. He could see the whites of her wide eyes. She was terrified.

He looked around at what he could see in the light cast by the moon. What a mess. Footprints. Dog prints. Blood. Bushes wrecked and flattened. Even if he kept her kidnapped in the barn until he could speak to *Zio*, he couldn't possibly eradicate all the evidence of what had happened. Not if Brian was stumbling about or waiting nearby.

He had an idea. He stood and stooped over her shoulders. "Get up."

"I can't. I'm hurt. Your fucking dog chewed me up," she moaned.

Alessandro looked around feverishly. *Shit.* He heard movement behind him. He twirled and was in the middle of taking the rifle off of his back to aim and shoot when he realized it was Maria hurrying towards him through the snow.

"What happened?" she cried, her voice echoing through the field.

He lunged at her and covered her mouth. He put a finger to his lips and motioned her to get down. He took his hands off her mouth and was shocked to see he'd left blood on her face. "What the hell are you doing here, Maria? It's dangerous."

"You fucking bitch, Maria." Selena managed to hiss, glaring at her from the snow.

Maria jumped back in shock. "Selena?"

"Your dog mauled me. I'm going to tell my godfather on—"

Selena didn't finish the sentence. Alessandro hit her mouth with the butt of the rifle. Alessandro looked back at Maria.

She stood with her hands cradling her face in shock.

Alessandro hiked the rifle over his back again and moved to Selena's shoulders. "We're in deep, Maria. Take the legs."

It took a moment for his request to sink in, before she finally jumped into action. She bent over and grabbed Selena's legs. Together, they half dragged, half carried her along the road to a point opposite the front lawn.

"Wait here," whispered Alessandro. He looked at Luna. He whistled softly and waited until she came to him. "I'll be right back."

Maria grabbed Alessandro by his sweater. "Where are you going?

"She's not alone," he whispered. He let himself slide into the deep ditch, then flopped on the other side, looking over the edge of the mound. He looked down the road in the direction he had seen Selena come from earlier. He whistled softly and climbed up onto the street. He stood still as a statue and waited for Luna to stand beside his legs. "You smell anyone, Luna?" he said softly.

Luna looked at him and then looked around.

He placed the rifle down along the road and scrambled into the ditch again. He made his way back to Maria.

"Okay, we're gonna run for it."

"What about her?"

"She's comin' along. We're taking her to the house."

They picked up each end and moved crab-like to the ditch.

"Wait." Alessandro let go of the shoulders and slid down on his butt. Then he got up and bent over. He was lower than Maria. "Give me her arms." He turned and helped Maria drag her closer to the edge, then he lifted her upper body over his back. He bent further forward and lifted her.

Maria kept a hand on Selena as Alessandro struggled up the other side, then she hurried beside Alessandro as he stumbled with Selena to the front of the house.

He laid her on the snow-covered front walk. "She's covered in blood. I don't want to mess up your Mom's floors. Do you have an old blanket?"

"We have extra sheets and blankets downstairs."

"Anything will do."

Maria scrambled into the house, and Alessandro waited, his heart pounding as he looked in all directions. He shivered and looked down at the blood seeping spider-like over the surface of the icy walkway. There was no movement from Selena.

"Shit."

Maria returned with two sheets. They put one on top of the other and lay them to the side of Selena. They lifted her enough to swing her over onto the sheets.

Luna sniffed Selena's bloody head.

Alessandro gently pushed her snout away. "Good girl," he said, as he briefly patted her.

He stood. "Come on, Maria. Let's get her into the basement."

"MARIA, SHUT THE UPSTAIRS DOOR," Alessandro said.

Maria bolted up the stairs. He could hear her whispering to Luna, and her paws dance on the hallway floor above him. He looked down at the body wrapped in blood-stained sheets. He nervously wiped his brow and caught his hand shaking. He looked at the other one. It also shook.

Maria slowly came back, looking at a few dark spots on the carpet. "Oh my God," she said. "We're trailing blood."

He looked back and then down. Blood was forming under Selena's body. Her heart was still beating and she was bleeding to death from her face and neck wounds. He shook his head. "I never meant to..."

Maria went to touch his face, but he pulled back. "You didn't hurt her, Luna did. Mind you, the butt of the rifle. That didn't help."

"There was no other choice. We were goners."

Maria got down on her knees and slowly lifted the sheet from Selena's face. She froze.

Alessandro looked away. He saw the blinds. "We need to close the blinds." But he couldn't move.

Maria got up and closed the blinds on the window. Then she squeaked over the tiles in her wet socks to the window on the other side of the back door and closed those blinds. It was quite dark in the basement. "I can't see," whispered Maria.

"Find a light."

"Ow."

"What?"

"I stubbed my toe."

"Maria, we just need some light."

"I know, I'm trying."

Finally, the overhead light went on. Alessandro closed his eyes against the sudden glare and took a deep breath. Then he opened them slowly. He looked down.

Luna had mauled Selena's face. Her left nostril had been torn open, and a cheek had a massive slash. Where her mouth was, looked like wayward teeth and tenderized meat. He saw blood pulsing from under the collar of her coat. Luna had done a job on her. She went after her jugular. Like a good hunting dog.

He swallowed back bile. Then firm resolve took over. Life dealt a hand of strange cards this night, and he had to play them the best way he could. He looked up and wondered where Maria was.

She was standing by the light switch staring at Selena.

"You okay?"

She nodded.

He motioned her with his chin, to come over. Slowly, she stepped over the tiles and stopped where blood pooled through the gaps of the sheet and ran along the grout lines. She carefully stepped around them and stood beside Alessandro. She grabbed his upper arm, and leaned her head against him.

It felt strangely comforting, both of them standing beside a mauled body which was still bleeding, close to death, and wrapped in bloody sheets. At that moment, her touching him felt like a natural gesture. He looked down at her. He lifted his arm and wrapped it around her.

"She's not going to bother you or Francesca anymore."

"What are we going to do now?" she asked.

He let her go, moved over to the couch and sat down. His feet were slowly warming up, but they hurt like crazy. He lifted one foot and wrapped it with his hands, rubbing it. Then he did the other foot. Maria came over and went on her knees and put both of his feet on her lap. She bent down and blew warm air on them. Then, she gently cupped them in her hands and rubbed. His feet lost a bit of the achy feeling. Blood was finally rushing back into them.

"Thanks, Maria." He was exhausted.

She got back on her feet.

He looked up and recognized a maturity he'd never seen before. "Right. Brian."

"Brian?"

"Her brother. She called for him. He might be down the road waiting for her."

"What was she going to do to us? Beat us with a branch?"

"I don't know. Maybe she's got something in her pocket. You check, I have to go.

"Don't wake up Mom."

"No, she'll go ape shit." He heard footsteps above his head.

He turned to run upstairs, but Andy met him on the landing. Her hair looked like a fluffy cloud on top of her pale face. Her body appeared to be slenderer than he thought. She had tied a lavender satin housecoat around her and was barefoot.

She looked down the stairs and saw the trail of blood. Her face went grey as she looked back at him. "What's happening? That's blood?"

He nodded, studying her closely. He raised his bloody hands. "Don't panic."

"I'm not going to panic unless you got blood all over the goddam house."

He turned and led her to Selena's body.

Andy looked wide-eyed at the blood-soaked grout between the tiles. Slowly, she pulled her gaze away from the blood, to the body, then to him.

"Selena?"

He nodded.

She nodded and slowly, silently, went back upstairs.

"Right, I have to go." He ran to the stairs and caught up to Andy on the landing.

"Where are you going?" Andy asked, dazed.

"I think someone's waiting for her outside somewhere. I have to get him."

"Who the fuck?"

"She called for Brian earlier." He continued up the stairs, and she quickened her pace after him. "Luna," he called, as he hurried through the kitchen.

Luna appeared.

He rushed to the front door, where he had left the boots and rifle, still off safety. Carefully, he picked it up, opened the door, and followed Luna out. He stopped. He opened the front closet and removed a long coat. He put it on. He tucked the rifle underneath. Then he opened the door and shut it loudly behind him. He wanted to make all the usual noises a guy would make walking a dog in the middle of the night.

He stopped and looked at the closest street light, then felt the rifle's awkward weight. He went back in the house, hurried down to the gun rack, and opened the bottom drawer where he remembered seeing a couple of handguns. He took one out and found bullets for it. He quickly put in six rounds and stuck the gun into a deep pocket of his coat. There, he found a Russian cap. He stuck the cap on his head.

He left the house, slamming the door again, and led the dog along the walk and down the driveway. He glanced at the front walkway and saw one thick dark pool of congealed blood where they dropped Selena the first time. He pulled the ear flaps down on the hat and kept walking. He looked up and down the road. Nothing.

He pulled out the gun and aimed at the street light. The explosion of the weapon echoed over the fields, but he knew anyone who heard it would think someone caught a raccoon or fox. He looked back and wished he had told Maria to turn off some of the outside lights so he would be more protected. *Shit.*

He led the dog along his right and did not look to the bushes where Luna had mauled Selena. He walked into a gulley in the road, then half way up the other rise. He covered his mouth with a glove to filter his breath. He crouched. He looked around and saw he could probably go in the ditch to his left and move into the bushes to get a better and safer view of the road from the other side.

The snow was almost hip deep in the ditch, but Luna helped him move forward as he hung onto her collar. She pulled him out of the depths of the snow. On the other side, they entered the darkness of the bushes and trees. Luna stopped and growled softly. Alessandro could see her sharp, white teeth in the moonlight. "Shit," he whispered. He crouched lower and moved closer to the road. He saw a truck.

Cigarette smoke trailed out of the driver's window. Then he saw a second person, a passenger, take a drag of their cigarette, the embers glowing, giving him, or her, away.

Brian must have taken a friend. Or was his brother out of jail? He squinted, but he wasn't close enough to see any features. Alessandro saw no other outcome than the spilling of more blood. His or theirs. He moved over to the side and gagged, needing to throw up. He realized he was letting fear manifest in his guts.

He swallowed. Slowly, he bent his knees and let himself fall on his behind into the soft snow. He kept his hand on the dog's collar as he pondered his choices of action. If he left them and returned to help Andy and Maria with the cleaning up, there were still two people waiting for Selena's return. And if they drove by looking for her, they'd see the carnage leading to the house.

He reminded himself he had five bullets left in the gun. He patted the dog's head for comfort as he realized his only option. Killing. He felt more decisive. He whispered into Luna's ear. "Stay." He leaned back and held up his hands, motioning the dog to stay put.

Luna sat neatly on her haunches and looked at him.

"Good dog," Alessandro whispered. He got to his feet but remained in a crouching position. He made his way further along the trees and bushes until he saw he had passed the truck. Slowly, on his hands and knees, dragging the rifle, he let himself sink into the deep snow of the ditch again. The snow muffled his movements beautifully. As he crawled up out of the ditch on the other side, he had to climb over a pile of snow left by the snowplow, and realized it meant putting himself in full view of the truck's side mirror.

He sunk to his stomach and crawled until he saw part of a face of the guy in the passenger seat in the mirror. He could also see he was holding a cigarette, keeping his head back; eyes closed. Alessandro looked closely at the truck. It was a GMC, two-toned blue pick-up, somewhat rusty. The license plate had been bent upward, either by accident or design. He was about to continue crawling over the snow behind the truck when the guy lifted his head and opened his eyes to take a drag from the cigarette. Alessandro froze and held his breath. He saw the face turn and heard him talk to Brian next to him.

"Is she still fuckin' around? How long do we have to wait?"

He could hear it clearly, though slightly muffled behind the closed windows. He couldn't hear Brian whose voice was much lower. The engine started up.

It was now or never. He let the rifle drop and took out the gun. He took the safety off and jumped up. The truck began to move. He grabbed at the back of the truck and allowed himself to be pulled along, his boots sliding on the icy road. He carefully raised a shaking hand. He pulled the trigger.

The rear window shattered, and Brian, sitting at the wheel, slumped forward over the steering wheel. The truck rolled to a stop when it nudged into the plowed bank.

"*Calisse*," screamed the passenger.

Alessandro scrambled to the driver's side to aim at the passenger. There, he faced the muzzle of a handgun. His own firearm exploded at the same time as the other guy's. He felt a line of searing fire on his face as he watched the guy's brains splash onto the window behind him.

Alessandro yanked opened the truck door, pushed Brian over, and yanked at his legs to clear the pedals. He jumped into the driver's seat and turned the wheels straighter as he gave it a bit of gas. It slowly made its way along the side of the plowed ridge of snow and was able to creep back up onto the road itself. He gave it more gas. Then he stopped. He looked at a crucifix hanging from the rear-view mirror. It was a plastic affair, painted with red dots along the edges and a heart-aflame painted crudely in the middle. It swung crazily off an inexpensive metal chain.

He reached up and steadied it. "Oh shit." He forgot Luna. He backed up and peered into the dark bushes. He leaned out the window and whistled.

Luna appeared. She jumped up against the driver's door to peek at Alessandro. He put the truck in park and jumped out. He petted her head, led her to the back gate and motioned Luna to jump in—which she gladly did, sniffing enthusiastically at all the paraphernalia stored in the truck bed.

Unexpectedly, the truck jerked forward and raced away from him up the road's incline toward the house. He stood, panting, watching the tail lights and Luna's breath as she struggled to keep her balance in the truck bed. After a moment, the truck tires lost their grip on the icy snow on the incline, and started to squeal and slip. Luna jumped out of the truck and ran toward him.

Alessandro ran as fast as he could in his heavy boots on the icy road surface. The tires whined and continued to sing as he got closer. Alessandro knew he had to get to it before those tires melted through the snow to the road's surface and got a better grip. To his horror, he saw the back, left wheel almost take hold.

He hunched over the gun and aimed carefully at the bit of the man's head he saw at the wheel. He fired.

The truck stopped spinning wheels, and it slowly rolled back, the engine idling. As it reached Alessandro, the incline allowed it to roll back faster.

Alessandro quickly got out of the way as the truck rolled further back. "Shit," he whispered. The truck seemed to head for Luna sitting and watching from the road. As if she were an old experienced soldier, she got up and lumbered a little to the side. The truck rolled right past Luna, all the way back into the dip of the road until gravity kept it from rolling up the other incline. Then it slowly moved back down to the dip in the road and stopped. It was a good 400 yards away.

Alessandro put the gun back in his pocket. It was hot to the touch, burning his fingers. He looked at Luna. "You are one incredible dog, you know that? Come on, we have to get that truck over there."

Alessandro slid on his boots down the slight incline towards the truck. He felt something snake down his face and he touched his cheek. He looked at his hand in the moonlight and saw something black and shiny again. More blood.

He made it to the truck and opened the door. Brian had regained consciousness. Part of his head had splattered over the dash, the rearview mirror and the cross. His body was slumped over onto the other man. Alessandro wiped his bloody hand on Brian's jacket. He bent into the cab and looked more closely at the men. He noticed they looked quite alike, even in the partial moonlight.

He got both brothers.

There was going to be hell to pay in the old town of Vindenza. No wrath such as a woman scorned—especially a mother who loses an entire brood in one blow. He didn't have time to think. He pushed Brian over and ignored the brains splattered across the wheel as he put the truck into neutral. He opened the door and let Luna in. He pointed at Luna and the blue blood and brain-splattered dash. "Don't lick."

Luna sniffed once at the dash and the men she leaned on, then sat back as best she could, excitedly looking forward to a road trip.

ALESSANDRO WATCHED MARIA KNEEL beside Selena, and lower her head to Selena's chest. "I can't hear anything, too many layers on her."

Alessandro fished for Selena's wrist and held it. He couldn't feel a pulse. He looked at his watch. It was only half-past two. Yet, this whole ordeal felt like it'd taken a week.

"We've got a lot of work to do," Maria said. "We've got blood-covered snow outside, trampled bushes. We can clean this later." She pointed at the blood-soaked rags around Selena, and the blood-red spider web spread between the tiles. "And we'll deal with, you know, Selena after, but we've got stuff outside. I mean, blood. Even if it snows overnight, the blood is still there, frozen into the snow."

Alessandro watched Maria stare at Selena. Then, her eyes brightened, and she looked at him. "I like to skate." She smiled slightly.

"Skate?"

"Yeah, I like to skate. I've always wanted a skating rink around the house. I had friends whose Dad used to clear the backyard of snow and flood it with a hose over and over again. They had a nice skating rink every year. I wanted one, but Mom didn't want to mess up the property."

"Even if we flood the snow, you'd still see the blood underneath."

"Not if we put white bedsheets down first."

Alessandro laughed. "Good idea. You think we could do that?"

She shrugged. "Yeah. It's cold enough. And we have time yet."

Selena coughed, and blood spurted everywhere.

Maria and Alessandro jumped back. Blood sprayed them and the floor around them. Selena gurgled and coughed again. Her eyes were swollen shut. Her one arm jerked under the sheet. Then her one leg tried to move.

Alessandro gulped. "Holy shit. She's still alive."

She was drowning in her own blood.

He knew if they really wanted to keep her alive, now was the time to help. She would probably survive Luna's mauling, but, again, things had gone too far—they could not let her live. He sat on his haunches next to Selena, covered her face with the sheet to keep the splatter down, and bowed his head as he listened to her death rattle.

"She's suffering, Alessandro."

"Yes. But not for long."

"She can't breathe!"

"I know, she's drowning in her own blood."

"Drowning?" Maria's eyes widened at Alessandro. "Turn her on her side."

Maria lunged at Selena, but Alessandro held her back, carefully helping her step back between the blood-lined tiles.

"Maria. She can't become our friend. My face, and yours, will end up looking like hers if we let her live. They'll smash our faces in the same way I did hers. Right now, we have a chance to destroy the evidence."

"*Evidence?*" Maria said, her face blank. "You call her *evidence?* She's a human being."

Alessandro shook his head. "She is a damaged, despicable human being. She almost killed Francesca, with no remorse, no apologies. And she's out to kill you. This is karma, Maria."

"Karma. So, will what we do to her come back to us as karma, too?"

Maria's words chilled him to the bone. But he didn't have the luxury to dwell on superstition. "We have no time. Come on, Maria, no one can pin her disappearance directly on us. Not if we're smart. But if we let her live; think about it. What would they do to your Mom? Your *Nonna?* Your Dad?" He watched Maria nod, but her face was set. It was a look he had never seen in all the time he'd tutored and watched over her.

It was the look of someone who killed.

"SO, WHAT DO WE DO NOW?"

Andy, her nose red and runny, stood in a ski jacket and boots, her elegant housecoat hanging down from underneath. They were standing in the garage looking into the truck. Andy had driven the old Volvo out of the garage while Alessandro drove the truck in its place.

Maria stared at the two men in the cab. She'd never seen brains and blood scattered, human skulls destroyed, and she wondered why she didn't feel disturbed or repelled. She shook her head. "Not again," she whispered.

"We either bury them or hide them," Alessandro said.

"Or dismember them?" Andy whispered. "We can call our butcher friend who does our lambs."

"Mom." Maria was appalled. She'd never heard her mother say anything so cold-blooded.

"It's the Sicilians that concern me, Mrs. Giordani."

"Oh, for fuck's sake, call me Andy. We're getting pretty intimate in terms of having secrets together," she said, motioning to the men in the cab.

"Mam, *Zia* Sandra. *Zio* Peter hid Jack. Why can't she do the same?"

Andy looked at her daughter. "You're right. That's what we have to do."

"What do we do?" Alessandro looked at Andy.

"I have to call Sandra on the cell phone. Wake her up." Andy turned to go into the house.

"Wait, Mrs. Giordani. I mean Andy." Alessandro dropped his hands. He needed to keep his voice down. "Why are you calling *Zia* Sandra now?"

"Because she's the one who hides the bodies now. It's her job to *clean up*." She looked at Alessandro. "Okay?"

Alessandro nodded and flicked hair out of his eyes.

Maria went up to him and padded his back. "Maybe we should take them downstairs with Selena. We can put plastic down first. And I can start cleaning up the truck."

"No, wait till we hear what your *Zia* says." Alessandro slowly looked at her. He studied her face.

She saw, and was concerned there were unruly hairs on her chin. She reached up and covered her right cheek. Perhaps he was looking at her acne? "What?" she asked, eyeing him.

He wiped his mouth. He looked down at his pocket and pulled out the gun.

She reached out and looked at him. "Let me. I'll stick it in the manure pile at the back of the barn. Where are the shells?"

Alessandro slapped his forehead. "Oh, man."

She held his waist with her right arm. "When it starts getting light, I'll walk the dog there, and I'll pick them up." She stood back and pointed at him. "You can put on another coat of water on that beautiful skating rink we're making. Dress like Dad. Make it look like he's doing something wonderful for his daughter," she joked. She pointed to herself. "Namely, me."

"Stefano's daughter, you." He smiled at her.

They heard the rooster crow out back of the house.

"Don't worry. It's not light yet, so we got time." Maria left Alessandro standing frozen in the dark garage as she walked to the door into the house. She looked back as she kicked off her boots and could see Alessandro lit by the light from the truck's interior. As she closed the door and walked toward the family room, she could hear her mother up in the kitchen explaining what happened, to Sandra on the phone. She smiled at herself. For some odd reason, she felt cozy. Deep down inside. In the back of her head, she understood there was something very wrong with her; blood, brains, dead bodies, and a massive clean-up with potential violent and deadly retaliation on an enormous scale and, yet, she was calm.

It must be the testosterone.

Or just another *anomary* of hers.

CHAPTER SIXTEEN

A LESSANDRO STOOD BY THE FRONT DOOR and watched Maria skate. Her blades scraped and sang as she pushed Francesca's bulky wheelchair over a reasonably good skating rink ringed by Christmas lights on the front lawn. Luna accompanied them on the ice, having learned to take a run and drop her rear end to slide. He could tell the dog was thrilled with her unprecedented freedom.

Well deserved, he thought, with a shiver.

He slipped on sunglasses from his inside pocket where his firearm rested, then crossed his gloved hands. He felt heat escaping from the house behind him. They were airing out the strong smell of bleach.

"Oooo, nice'a." Claudia appeared from inside the house and carefully shuffled down the ramp from the front door. She stopped and squinted into the sun at the ice rink. She giggled, pointing at Luna, who happily jumped at Maria's back. "Is so'a nice for Francesca." She looked at Alessandro. "Here, I have Band-Aids."

Alessandro moved closer to her. He had lied and said Luna had accidentally snapped at him while playing. She believed him. He lowered his head as he allowed her to put an antibiotic cream onto the backs of the Band-Aids before gently covering his gash. She stepped back and admired her work. She nodded. "Why you no sit? I get a chair," she said as she turned and disappeared back into the house.

"No, *Nonna*, it's—" He grimaced and faced the front again. He heard crashing and scraping behind him in the house. He poked his head around the jamb of the door and saw Claudia shuffling backward, dragging a kitchen chair into the front hallway.

He quickly went into the house. "Here, *Nonna*. Let me. Thank you."

"*Si.*" She waved her little hands at the house. "Adriana, she'a do cleaning. Phew." She rolled her eyes.

"She likes bleach."

"Too much'a." She looked into the living room at the plastic-covered couch. "I sit'a there in sun 'n watch Maria." Her short legs were quick, and she bounced onto the noisy, plastic cover and rested in the late morning sun. She folded her hands and craned her neck to look out over the front lawn.

Alessandro looked from her to the chair in front of him. His weary eyes blinked in the reflected sun off the ceramic floor as he bent to pick up the chair. He swung its feet facing outward and carefully maneuvered it through the door.

Claudia had no idea. No one told her about the night's activities. Because she was hard of hearing and in the back bedroom, she hadn't heard a thing. Thank goodness.

For the hundredth time, as he stepped through the door, his eyes looked to where last night's activities disturbed the ditch and bush across and down the road. *Zia* Sandra had arranged for the town's snowplow to do a thorough job of clearing their road earlier, with the instruction of shoving all snow to that side of the road. A mountain of snow now hid the ditch and surrounding bushes.

She also instructed Alessandro, Maria and Andy to put all three bodies into the Cadillac and arranged for a time during the day when Alessandro would come to her house on the pretense of lending her Stefano's car. She was going to have her car with the hood up in their circular driveway, and she was going to call them on the house phone asking for his help. In case they were being tapped. "Being tapped works for us this time," Sandra laughed over the cell phone.

He placed the chair against the warm brick wall outside and sat down. He shivered in his weariness and quickly patted his chest. The solid feel of the gun helped him stay focused. They'd been up all night, and he felt his eyes and body getting heavy. His face pulsated with pain, but slowly, he started to fade away.

A whistle made his heavy eyes snap open.

Maria skated toward him, giving him the eye.

"What?" he said.

She motioned with her head, then swerved in another direction as if nothing happened.

Alessandro looked as far as he could to his right and immediately caught the sharp glint of sun on chrome. He slowly stood to his feet and watched the vehicle come closer. His heart beat faster. He looked at Maria and Francesca, and immediately wondered how he would protect them.

Maria looked at him knowingly. And the look lingered.

He pondered that look. During the entire grisly ordeal, Maria was a pillar of strength. A complete about-face from the spoiled bothersome creature he learned to barely tolerate. The look said, *stay cool.* He took her cue and didn't show any sign of concern outwardly, pretending not to care about the car. He bent down, picked up his cold mug of hot chocolate, and took a sip.

As a grey Audi passed the front of the house, the driver honked the horn to get their attention. Then the engine burst into life, and the car sped up the road and out of sight.

Maria looked back, then over at him. She stopped herself with her skates and stepped into the mound of snow in front of him. "Who do you think that was? It's not Selena's mother. Maybe the Sicilians." She was almost as tall as him on her skates.

He studied her face. Her cheeks were bright red from the crisp fresh air, her skin almost clear of blemishes. Her eyes were large, brilliant. She wore absolutely no make-up, as usual, and it occurred to him that she was one of the most natural beauties he'd ever met, even though there was a hint of shadow on her upper lip.

He leaned back against the wall and looked into the mug. "I hate to say it, but maybe it was the godfather, The Weasel. I'm sure their mother would put two and two together and send someone along. Where would two brothers and a sister go, right? The first thing their mother would do is call The Weasel."

Maria looked back to where the car had disappeared. She clapped her mitts together as she stood deep in thought.

The phone rang back in the kitchen. Alessandro looked at his watch. "It's *Zia* Sandra."

They silently waited as they heard Claudia talking to Sandra. Then, she called Alessandro. "Alessandro, Sandra, she'a have car trouble."

"Well, it's time for the next phase," he said, as he got up and went into the house.

MARIA STOPPED PUSHING Francesca as they watched Alessandro drive the Cadillac down the driveway.

"See you later, alligator," Maria called, thinking of the three bodies duct-taped in plastic sheets in the car. Maria waved as if nothing was out of the ordinary.

He waved back.

He had the visor down so she couldn't see his full face.

Maria had already been out walking and found three shells on the icy road, which she handed over to Andy. Andy had taken them down to the cellar where the cheese hung, and she pushed each shell into a cheese ball.

Maria remembered the things they found in the back of the truck. They found a saw, a black plastic sheet, and paper towels. When they went through Selena's pocket, they found a copy of a key to their back door, duct-tape, and a plastic handgun. It seemed Selena was going to kidnap Maria on her own. She shook her head. Boy, that Selena had it in for her.

She bent over Francesca to look into her face. "You warm enough?"

Francesca looked at Maria with happy eyes, and Maria saw her nose was running.

Maria took out a tissue and wiped Francesca's nose and face. "Let's go back in and get warm." As she pushed Francesca toward the front door ramp, she looked down at her skates and could just make out the white sheets under the ice, though any onlooker wouldn't notice them. She leaned forward, opened the front door, then pushed the wheelchair up the ramp into the hallway, digging her blades into the ramp's wood for traction. She ignored the ice and snow-covered wheels dripping onto the tiles. She bent over and quickly unlaced her skates. She struggled to get them off without scratching the tiles, and put them on the boot tray. She turned to Francesca.

"Let's get that coat off you, Francesca, and I'll call your Dad," she said. She turned to the kitchen. "Mom." She could hear a chair scrape the kitchen floor, and Claudia at the doorway.

"You'a Mama is'a still cleaning."

"*Nonna*, I'm bringing Francesca in to get warm. I need a towel for the wheels."

"*Si*, I get'a one," Claudia said. She turned and pulled herself up the stairs to the linen closet.

As Maria took off Francesca's hat and gloves, she felt weary. She wondered what Francesca would've thought if she'd known she was part of a cover-up. She looked into Francesca's eyes. She bent down a little and whispered into her ear.

"We got Selena last night," she said. She pulled back to look at Francesca's face.

Francesca's eyes widened. Then slowly Francesca smiled and sighed deeply. She closed her eyes. Almost as if she were at peace. Finally.

ALESSANDRO PULLED UP Sandra and Peter's circular driveway. It was a mansion, built in place of their old house.

Sandra's Mercedes Benz was out of the three-car garage, already parked with its hood up at the bottom of one end of the driveway. Alessandro parked at the front door. Sandra opened the door and stepped onto the cleared cobblestones in her slippers.

Alessandro slowly got out of the vehicle and greeted her, giving her a hug and triple kisses.

"Hi, Alessandro," Sandra said, smiling. She was business-like. Strong.

"Hi, *Zia*, thanks for your help."

Sandra stopped and gasped. "Holy cripes, what happened to your face?"

Alessandro touched the Band-Aids. "*Nonna*. A bullet grazed me."

"Your beautiful face. Another scar, eh?"

"Yup."

"Adds character."

"I'm glad you think so."

"The balls this kid had, though. Figured out why she was hiding in front of the house? What was she doing, peeping? Was she trying to get a look at Maria in the nude or something? Like a paparazzi?"

Alessandro coughed slightly. "She was a little obsessed."

"No kidding."

Alessandro walked down to Sandra's car and bent over the engine under the hood. He leaned both gloved hands on the front edge of the vehicle as she caught up to him. "She had a key to the house." He looked at her pointedly.

"No shit." She squinted. "Fuckin' A." She looked down into the engine compartment. "See, I pulled the wires here and there. I had no idea what to do. But it did the trick. It won't start."

He looked closer at the wires and the rest of the engine. "Well, believe it or not, I'm a guy, but I know nothing about cars. It looks like you did a good job. It's all messed up in here."

"Well, I'll go in and pretend to try and start it." She opened the driver's side and slid in. She turned the ignition, and nothing happened except for clicking sounds.

He looked around the hood and shrugged.

She got out and pulled at his jacket, and led him to the front door. "You're going to have a cup of coffee while you wait for me to get dressed. Then I'll drive you back to the house and I'll keep the car for the day. I'll take care of the rest."

He laughed and followed her in.

She turned to him and smiled. "Peter's being released today. I'm picking him up later."

Alessandro was shocked. "Wow, I forgot what day it was."

"Well, you've been kind of occupied," she laughed.

THE PHONE RANG AND KEPT ON RINGING.

"Maria. Get the phone."

Andy was down in the basement, just finishing cleaning. She got up off her knees and took the cleaners, paper towel rolls, and full garbage bag. "Maria." She lugged herself up the stairs and into the family room as she heard Maria stumble into the kitchen to answer the phone. She stopped to see her mother lying in Fabrizio's La-Z-Boy.

She blinked. Her mother was small, aged about five years, and shrunk since her father's death. She had always heard about elderly couples dying within short periods of each other. She looked closely but couldn't see her mother breathing. She dropped the cleaners onto the carpet and frantically shook her mother's shoulder.

"Ma. Wake up."

Her mother's eyes flew open. "Wha'? Fire?"

"No, I thought you were dead, for crying out loud. I couldn't see you breathing."

Claudia rubbed her eyes. "I'm'a okay." She looked down at Andy's feet and pointed.

Andy looked down at the carpet and saw the bleach had spilled into the shag rug. "Oh shit." She threw a paper towel onto the bleach but got it mixed up with the garbage bag so she couldn't get at the bleach quickly. "What the fuck."

"Adriana, you'a swearing, agin'"

"Well, how would you react?! The carpet's ruined." She got down on her knees.

Claudia leaned over the arm of the chair to get a better look.

"Ma, be careful, remember last time that chair tipped?"

Claudia squinted and moved closer, and the La-Z-Boy capsized forward.

Andy, stuck under the extended foot of the chair, heard Maria yell.

"Ma. It's for you. It's that talent agent."

STEFANO LOOKED AROUND the cavernous, unfinished condo. Workers hammered and scraped nearby. He watched large slabs of marble maneuvered through a massive opening in the building's wall. Stefano wore a hard hat and work boots, a white polo shirt, and tan work pants. He was listening to his cell phone in one hand while he held a clipboard in the other. A young Latino stood near him, watching Stefano's face.

"What you say'a, Adriana?" He tried to plug one ear to hear better. "*Solo un momento*." He gave his clipboard to the man and walked out toward the elevator shaft. There was one elevator rigged up without walls, just netting. "*Un momento*, Adriana. I go where it is quiet."

He grabbed a heavy cable and pushed a button. The elevator started to go down. Stefano cast his eyes along the stretch of Myrtle Beach he could see through the building's exposed walls. He stopped two floors down and got out. It was windy up here but not as noisy. He walked to a half wall and stood looking out over the ocean and raised the cell back to his ear.

"*Si? Si,* Selena." He leaned against a cement structure. "*Si.*" He shook his head. "*Si?*" He covered his eyes with his free hand. "Sandra? *Bene. Si,* if Sandra has control'a, is'a good. How's Maria?" He pulled at some plaster that had dripped on his shirt over his stomach. "'N Luna? In da house?" He grinned. "*Si,* I tell'a Leo. Please ask Alessandro to call when he gets back'a. *Ciao.*" He pushed in the antenna and stood looking out over the ocean.

A few little private fishing boats with outriggers slowly went their way in different directions. He saw dolphins waltz over the surface of the waters, then disappear. Looking at the paradise in front of him, he found it hard to imagine the mayhem of the night before back at home.

He didn't panic, but he certainly did worry. His guts told him it was not the West End Gang in retaliation for their Myrtle Beach expansion, though he did know the disappearance of Selena and her brothers was undoubtedly going to draw attention to his family. After all, the spat between Selena and Maria had been going on for a few years. He remembered very well that witnesses heard Andy threaten Selena, recklessly saying she would kill her. And then her assault on Selena's mother, the widow of the West End Gang's former head, was officially part of a police report.

He went back into the lift and returned to the penthouse. He walked out into the roughed-in hallway and turned to a set of double oak doors opposite the unit they were building. He heard a click and the heavy cherrywood door opened as if by magic to allow him entry.

"Stinky."

"Mr. Giordani." Stinky nodded, his chin almost down to his chest. He looked shyly from under his brows. "How are you today?"

"*Bene.*"

Stinky stood back to let Stefano through.

Stefano eyed Stinky's light grey suit with a white open-necked shirt and tan deck shoes. "You dress like'a Leo, now?"

Stinky grinned. "Miss Yvonne likes me to look cleaned up. She does my laundry and she tells me what to wear."

Stefano chuckled but stopped and turned when he heard the heavy door squeak. The door was designed with massive brass handles and brass plate hinges. Stefano thought perhaps the extra brass trimmings caused it to swing incorrectly. Stefano stepped closer to the door and swung it open and shut a few times, carefully listening to the squeak. He looked at the hinges, then slightly lifted the door and swung it again, and no squeak. He gently closed the door, turned, and bent down to untie his work boots. "I fix dat later." Stefano put his boots to the side on a mat and followed Stinky through the white marble and glass hallway into the main living area.

A great vaulted ceiling above him was indented with four large skylights through which the sun poured and reflected off the polished white cupboards and white marble countertops of the kitchen and island. The only furniture was stools by the kitchen counter, an old couch and a coffee table Stinky had picked up for Leo at some Salvation Army. There was also a small bamboo table with an old TV on top, in the corner.

Everywhere Stefano looked were garlands of silver tinsel. In the other corner of the almost empty penthouse, stood a silver tinsel Christmas tree decorated with bright glass apples and red bows. A few wrapped gifts were scattered underneath. Stefano still had to get used to Christmas without snow.

"Thanks, Stinky," Leo said, from the old couch.

"Okay, boss." Stinky turned and sat on the end stool at the kitchen island and crossed his hands on his lap.

Leo smiled. "Everythin' okay?" He went back to going over architectural drawings on the coffee table.

Stefano went to the other end of the island and sat on an end stool. He pushed his back over the white marble counter, then stretched his leg to turn his foot and loosen up his ankle. "Some'a trouble."

"Big trouble?"

Stefano shook his head and straightened up. "No, just home trouble'a. I think'a."

"You think? Andy and Maria, okay? Claudia?"

Stefano inhaled noisily and grinned. "*Si*, they okay, but they do'a some things."

"Oh, what?"

Stefano made a wave in the air around the room.

"No, I checked this morning. I check every couple of days. No taps."

"You got the time? Long story."

Leo took out his cigar again and sat back. "Sure, I'm always in for a laugh when it comes to home antics."

"Okay." Stefano held up his hand to count his fingers. "*Uno*, they go shopping 'n dis girl, Selena, bully from school who almost kill' Francesca, was there. They later see she scratch'a something not nice into the car."

"Your Caddy?"

Stefano nodded. He felt sick.

"Hell."

"*Si. Due*, in da night, Alessandro see someone in the bushes."

"Good story so far."

"*Tre,* Alessandro sick my dog on that person 'n my dog'a hurt that person badly. She is'a good hunting dog, the very best. She goes right at the neck. So, Alessandro see is'a Selena. Her neck open, her face bleeding, but she makes too much noise. So, he shut her up with the end of the rifle."

"Oh no."

"*Si. Quattro*. He'a look for other people and see a truck with two people inside. They have a fight 'n he kills them because he is afraid they tell someone. He thought, maybe Sicilians."

"Holy crap."

"*Cinque*, Sandra tells Alessandro to drive Volvo out of the garage 'n he drive their truck in. Maria, she cleaned the truck."

"What? Maria?"

Stefano laughed. "*Si. Sei.* Sandra says she takes the bodies. *Sette,* they make skating rink in front of the house to cover the blood in the snow 'n Sandra take care of the road and ditches."

"Did they figure out who the men were?"

"*Si,* Selena's two brothers."

Leo didn't find the conversation funny anymore. "Those guys work for the West End Gang."

Stefano frowned and nodded.

"It's a good thing they're happy with the drug territory we ceded them in Montreal. I hope this doesn't push it over the edge, of all things. The Weasel's their godfather, and he'd want to get to the bottom of their disappearance."

Stefano nodded.

"What do you think? Should you go back?"

Stefano stood up. "I call Sandra' n see." He took a few steps. "Oh. *Otto,* someone want'a Maria in a movie."

"A movie? How surreal can you get? What a life." Leo laughed.

"Someone say somethin' about a movie?"

Stefano turned to see Yvonne appear from the far hallway. She stopped and put her hands on her hips. She wore a beautifully-colored purple muumuu which complimented her beautiful chocolate skin. She'd slimmed down since the birth of their little son, Leonardus. "What's all this about a movie? And what's so funny?"

"*Bella,* Stefano just told me Maria will be in a movie."

"Oh, that's wonderful. Ah was in a James Bond movie in New Orleans. *Live and Let Die.* That Roger Moore was some polite man."

"James Bond." Stefano perked up and grinned. "I'a like James Bond."

"Hmmm. The music. The women. The sexiness of it all," said Leo.

"Well, being in a movie for the first time, no matter how small a part, changes one's life. 'N it's not always a bad change. It opened mah eyes to what ah can do." Her hand slipped on the bamboo arm of the couch and she floundered.

Stefano lunged forward and grabbed her arm with a bit of care, helping her to sit.

Yvonne squeezed Stefano's strong wrist. "Thank you. Sweet baby's asleep now but was up all night." She smiled, shaking her head. "Dat movie changed my life, for shoa."

"Well, it opened your eyes, *Bella*. You got out of that slum."

She turned to Leo and shyly looked from under her false eyelashes. "Hmm, but I still had to put up with shady characters."

Leo laughed and placed a hand on her lap. "*Bella,* why don't you tell us your story tonight over dinner? Stefano has to go back to work."

Yvonne smiled at Stefano. "You up for some gumbo tonight, Stefano? Ah made some cornbread this mornin'."

Stefano's eyebrows shot up. His cheeks turned scarlet, and his aqua eyes danced in the light. He nodded and got up.

"See you later, Mr. Giordani." Stinky led him back to the front door and opened it.

Stefano slipped his feet into boots. He stomped one into position, then left Leo's condo. As the door squeaked closed, Stefano looked to his right at the opening into what would become his and Andy's condo. Within a month, it would be ready, and Andy could come down any time she wanted.

That is, if nothing lousy happened beforehand.

THE GATE BUZZED. Peter, freshly-shaven and in civilian clothes, picked up his bundle from the window and faced the door to freedom.

He waved goodbye to the guards and walked through the steel door. He looked and saw Sandra, in her black mink coat, waiting in Stefano's Cadillac. She waved at him through the window.

Feeling great outside, he held up his bundle and hurried over, careful not to get his good shoes wet from slush. It was still bright and sunny, and birds chirped everywhere.

He got into the car, leaned over, and grabbed Sandra, putting a big, fat kiss on the lips he had missed so much. "You, my Sandra, look fabulous."

She smiled back and turned on the ignition. "Well, finally. The boys are looking forward to seeing you."

"Do they still not know why?"

Sandra shook her head. "Nope. Not the whole story." She turned the wheel and slowly drove through the high, open gate. The guard in the guardhouse stepped out and yelled. "See you later, Pete."

"Not if I can help it." He waved back before he turned to face front again. He pointed over his shoulder with his thumb. "Good guys."

Sandra looked at him, and frowned slightly. She saw he was genuine. She shook her head as she drove her husband back home. He was out six months early for good behavior.

"THEY'RE STARTIN' TO SMELL ALREADY." Peter pinched his nose.

"That's the sheep shit you're smellin'," said Andy. "The bodies aren't here."

"Where are they?"

"Where do you think?" Andy said as she looked at Sandra, shivering in her fur coat.

Peter looked at the open barn door, then at the dog kennel where Luna was jumping at the gate, whining.

"That dog's spoiled. She thinks she can live in the house now," said Andy

Maria shrugged. "Why not, Mom? She worked hard."

"A dog is a dog is a dog," said Andy.

Peter, Sandra, Alessandro, Maria, Andy, and Claudia lined up to admire the barn's rebuilt walls.

Andy pointed. "The bomb blew out this wall, and arson burned the other in the fire." She shivered. "Crap. It's colder in here than outside." Her black sweater and pants were lightweight, but she did wear her boots. She looked at everyone's feet. "You schmucks, you know you walk on sheep and chicken shit coming out here, don't you?"

Sandra looked at her two-inch heels. "I just came back from picking up Peter. We came straight here."

Maria, closest to the far wall, looked at her *Zia's* feet. She looked down at her red rubber boots. She slipped them off, stood in the dry hay, in her socks, and held them out to Sandra.

Sandra, staring at the wall with her one bejeweled hand under her double chin and the other crossed over her bulging middle to support it, did a double-take at the floating boots that summoned her attention. "What's this?"

"I don't need 'em," said Maria.

"Oh, but you're in socks."

"That's okay, I always do this. Or bare feet. Hay's warm."

"And so is fresh sheep shit," quipped Andy.

Sandra looked at Andy, and Andy waved at her. "Go with it. She's not kidding. She likes her bare feet in the snow and shit. Ever since Stef's been working down south, guess who now takes care of the farm?"

Maria put up her hand as if in school.

Peter said, "By the way, where's the truck?"

"It's being painted in Montreal, as we speak," offered Sandra.

"We're sending it with the next heavy equipment run down to Myrtle Beach," said Alessandro.

"No kidding," said Peter. Snowmelt dripped on his shoulder from the door frame above. He wiped it off. Then he did a double-take. He squinted his eyes and frowned. "Holy crap."

Everyone asked, "What?"

Peter pointed to the back of the house.

Andy followed his gaze. "Holy crap. What's our rooster doing on our door?"

Claudia caught on.

"I believe someone's stuck him into the door." Peter moved away and walked to the back of the house. Everyone followed gingerly through the snow and animal droppings.

Peter was the first to come face to face with the rooster stuck into the top of the back door behind the glass of the screen door. A note peeked from under the rooster. He yanked the screen door open only to elbow Andy in the nose.

"Ow."

"Oh, shit, sorry."

"Watch what you're doing, Peter," yelled Sandra. "Oh, Andy, are you alright?"

Alessandro, Maria, and Claudia all pushed Andy, Sandra, and Peter closer to the door.

Peter had to lean slightly back to push them away, to keep from having his face squished against the rooster.

"Oh, poor rooster," said Maria.

"We should take it down, Peter," said Sandra.

"Should we? Maybe we should leave it there and ask Stef to fly home."

"I'm not leavin' no dead bird carcass in my back door," Andy said.

Alessandro looked at the carcass. "Yeah, but maybe *Zio* Peter is right. *Zio* Stefano should see this."

"Take a picture," piped up Maria. "I'll get my polaroid camera." Maria took off in her stockinged feet through the snow.

"And get some shoes on your feet," yelled Andy. "So, who's going to take it down after the picture so we can read the note?"

No one said a thing.

"Alessandro can do the honors."

Alessandro squinted at Andy.

"You just don't want your hands getting bloody," Andy said.

"And I've seen enough blood in the last twenty-four hours to last my entire life, I think," said Alessandro.

Everyone looked at the rooster.

"Maria will do it," said Sandra.

Claudia and Andy giggled.

The rooster jumped as the back door opened and everyone screamed.

"What?" Maria asked, from inside the basement, and holding her camera.

"Shit, Maria. You could warn us."

Maria shrugged.

Andy crossed her arms and looked at Maria, giving her the stink eye.

Maria raised her arms in protest. "What?"

"Get out here."

Maria gingerly passed the rooster and stepped out, everyone moving back to give her space. She aimed the camera and took a photo. Everyone watched as the film pushed out, watching the chemicals do their magic. Slowly, the image of the rooster and the door appeared.

Then Peter turned to the door and let the screen door rest on his back as he raised his hands toward the rooster.

"Peter, your good clothes."

"Oh, yeah, Maria's doin' it."

"What?" said Maria.

"We volunteered you would do it," Andy said.

Maria stepped into Peter's place.

While everyone stood behind the opened screen door, Maria raised her hand to pull out the knife but the bird and note were glued to the door and stayed stuck to the surface.

"Oh," said Andy.

Maria held out the knife and studied the weapon. Then she held it out to Peter and Alessandro to see.

"Sicilians," said Peter.

"No way," said Alessandro. "That's a nickel and dime store knife."

"Well, when did it get there?" asked Andy.

Alessandro looked around the property and back at the door. "It's been there for a while. It was probably there this morning." He turned to Maria. "Do you remember looking at the door last night?"

She shook her head. "No, not really. You were asleep for your nap, so I didn't bother."

"Oh my God," said Andy. "How come we didn't hear Luna again."

"This morning? She was skating on her bum."

"Maybe it happened while I was gone to your place," said Alessandro.

"Oh lord, I hope there's no trouble. I can't break parole," cried Peter.

"Peter, don't be such a woos," said Sandra.

"*Che*?" Claudia asked at everyone's underarms.

"We're trying to figure out who did this, Ma," yelled Andy at Claudia.

"*Mama mia*," whispered Claudia. She genuflected.

"Maria, aren't you going to take our poor rooster down?" Sandra asked.

Everyone took a closer look at the bird while Maria fingered the rooster's leg. "Mites."

Everyone leaned in closer.

A wind picked up and ruffled the feathers, which made the bird drop down.

Maria screamed and jumped back against the screen door. The screen door hit Andy in the nose, and she yelled. Sandra and Peter yelled. Alessandro scurried away and bumped into Claudia, who fell over in the snow.

Maria hurried to help Claudia, hitting Andy in the forehead with the screen door again.

"Shit," yelled Andy.

Maria looked back as she helped her *Nonna* to her feet. "Sorry, Mom."

Peter bent down to pick up the carcass and studied it.

Everyone gathered around the screen door again.

One eye hung out of its socket, and the rooster's little tongue peeked out of its beak.

"Poor Dad," said Maria. "This is the second time he's lost a rooster."

"Yeah, but the last one I shot for a reason. This one didn't deserve this."

Peter grunted and let Sandra hold the rooster as he stepped out of the way.

Alessandro reached up for the note glued to the door and carefully peeled it off. He read it to himself.

"What the heck does it say, Alessandro?" asked Sandra.

Alessandro paled and looked around the property. He looked over their heads and then back to the dog kennel where Luna stood wagging her tail. He looked back at the note and chuckled. "It's the Sicilians." He opened the back door and stepped through. Everyone walked around behind him. They followed him to the cheese cellar. He waited until everyone squeezed in before he shut the door. He turned on the flashlight and looked for the ceiling light. He looked for the cord of the light.

"Oh, that's my fault. I broke it."

"We'll just use the flashlight, then."

"Why in here, Alessandro?" Peter asked.

"*Zio* told me they always look for taps in Myrtle Beach. I thought maybe if they were concerned, we should be."

"In our HOUSE?!" yelled Andy.

Alessandro nodded and looked down at the note. "From this note, they heard everything that was going on during the night."

"WHAT THE HELL."

"*Che*?" Claudia asked.

Everyone ignored Claudia as they stared at the note in Alessandro's hand.

"What does it say?" asked Peter.

"It says, 'We know everything. Tell Giordani and Mangione we want the contract back.'"

Sandra looked at Peter. "What contract?"

"What'a contract?" asked Claudia.

Peter scratched his forehead. "We better give up the Montreal contract. I don't give a shit, if we keep it. I think—wait, can this cellar be tapped?"

Everyone looked around the rafters.

Alessandro put up his hand. "Let's go back outside."

Everyone shuffled out of the cellar and made their way through the basement to the outside door.

"What'a is happening?" asked Claudia.

Outside, Alessandro turned.

Once the screen door was closed, Peter motioned them to go to the dog kennel.

They gathered near Luna. Peter peered at the frost fence for microphones before he spoke. "Stef had already planned to give the environmental waste contract back to the Sicilians."

Peter raised his shoulders and motioned from one to the other. "We have to call him and tell him to pass on the message right away."

Everyone agreed and walked back toward the house.

"Sandra, can we go back to your place? I need to get away from this friggin' place."

"Sure, Andy."

"I'll call Stefano right away, and then I'll bring everyone over," said Alessandro.

"Forget it, I'm goin' with Peter and Sandra right now," said Andy. "Maria, you make sure *Nonna* has something packed for the night. We have to figure out if there are taps in the house."

Maria turned to *Nonna*. "*Nonna*, I'll take care of you, and later we go to Sandra's."

"Why'a?"

"We're staying overnight."

Claudia looked at everyone around her and shook her head.

Sandra touched Claudia on the shoulder. "*Nonna*, you okay?"

Claudia shook her head of tightly-wound curls. "So much going on'a."

"Oh, okay, Ma, come with me."

Andy put an arm around her mother's shoulders and led her into the house. Everyone followed, but Alessandro held Maria back by her jacket.

Maria turned around and looked up, eyeing the Band-Aids. She tried not to smile.

Alessandro looked down at his shoes and licked his lips. "Listen, I just want to say that," he shrugged, "that you were terrific. That you *are* terrific."

Maria blushed as she shoved back hair blown into her face. The wind picked up and blew a bit of snow into her eyes. She blinked and rubbed her eyes.

Alessandro hugged her as tightly as he dared.

Maria's eyes flew open. "Are you okay?"

Alessandro let her go and stepped back. "Yeah, I am now. But I thought, just for a moment there, we were goners. Which would have meant I didn't do my job protecting you, Andy and Claudia. And the thought of allowing you guys to get hurt, the thought of anyone killed because of me, well—"

Maria placed a hand on his chest. She stood on her toes, gave him a quick kiss on the cheek, then balled up her fist and gently tapped his arm. "You don't get it. We're a team, now."

Chapter Seventeen

February 1988

"SO, I HEAR YOU'RE GOIN' for a job tomorrow, Maria?" Sandra said. "For a movie?"

"Yeah, and Mom and Alessandro are coming along as my mascots."

"Escorts," Alessandro corrected.

They sat in the great room having coffee at Sandra and Peter's house. Sandra sat in a plush white loveseat beside Peter. Maria sat with Andy and Stefano on the enormous white couch. Alessandro sat in a wingback chair. He always sat in the far corner facing the front door, near windows, adjoining the massive fireplace.

The sun shone brightly through the tall windows. Elegant sheers hung loosely, creating a heavenly soft effect in the grand room.

Peter looked around the room. Everyone wore black, and they still had an hour before the second of two funerals that day. He looked at his watch as Sandra's mother walked over with a large tray of coffee cups and saucers.

Sandra jumped up and grabbed the heavy tray from her mother. "Thanks, Mom. Have a seat with us."

"No, no, no. I'a do a *Panettoni* now. 'N da coffee."

"I'll go with you. Sorry, Maria. I'll be right back."

"What movie?" asked Peter.

Andy put cups onto saucers and handed them out. "It's called, um." She looked at Alessandro.

"*Outrageous, too.* Or something like that."

"Well, we have an actor in the family," said Peter, making a face. "You'll have to take lessons. Know how to look happy, sad, surprised, dead."

"That's easy enough to do," said Maria. "I've seen enough of them."

Peter looked at everyone with a toothy smile. "Speaking of which, today's the day, eh?"

Stefano grunted.

"It's the first time since before Christmas we could finally break ground," added Peter.

Alessandro leaned forward on his elbows. He didn't mean to, but his eyes lingered on Maria, and she glanced over and caught him looking before he looked away and sat back. He stared at the ceiling. Then at the fireplace. Then again at Maria. "It was quite a cold winter this year."

Sandra, her mother, and Claudia returned with trays laden with *Panettone, Cannoli*, and coffee.

Andy raised her hands. "Ah, I'm dying for a piece of *Panettone*."

Sandra stood back. "Are you making fun of me?"

Andy looked confused. "No, I mean it. I love *Panettone*."

"I never knew that," Sandra said.

"After all these years?"

"What else don't I know about you?"

"Wouldn't you like to know?" Andy laughed.

Peter said, "Stef, you should ask Sandra what happened to Selena's body. What a hoot."

Stefano looked at Sandra, questioningly.

Sandra stood with a flower-design, gold trim coffee pot. She looked down at Stefano, then around the room quickly. "Well, by the time we got to Selena, she'd blown up beyond what the bottom space of our coffins can handle."

"I don't want to hear this," Andy said, covering her ears.

"Then I won't say it," said Sandra, bending over to pour coffee into an elegant cup on a saucer.

Peter turned to Stefano. "We tried to press the top half down by Sandra sitting on it but there was no way that top would shut closed. So, we had to cut a hole into the top half so that her stomach had room. We placed the body over her stomach and the hole. We managed to carry it off, so long nobody looked underneath. Then it would've been clear as day."

"But that's not all," Sandra said, smirking, and handing the cup and saucer to Claudia.

"Her body blew air during yesterday's viewing."

Everyone stopped what they were doing.

"Hope that goddam funeral music was loud enough," joked Andy.

Maria giggled.

Andy shook her head. "Well, Selena was always full of hot air, the shithead."

Stefano clapped his hands. "Okay, das enough. Now'a we talk about Leo and what we do'a in Myrtle Beach."

Everyone sobered up and quieted down to listen to Stefano, as Sandra poured coffee and her mother handed out dessert.

STEFANO NERVOUSLY fingered his tight collar as he stood listening to the same old funeral music, as always.

Andy saw he was struggling and reached out to undo the top button of his shirt. Then she readjusted his tie a little. She patted Stefano on the chest.

He smiled at her.

They stood, waiting to offer their condolences to an elderly couple who stood shakily at the grand doorway into the banquet hall at the Vindenza Italian Canadian Club. They had just returned from the graveyard a second time, where they stood by, solemnly watching two coffins slowly lowered into the ground. Bystanders threw in flowers and clumps of dirt.

Underneath the poor couple who had tragically died together in a car collision, lay the two Ryan brothers. Selena had been buried that morning under an elderly lady who had died of a heart attack at the Vindenza Italian Canadian Nursing Home. All three Ryans were forever safely hidden away.

Andy felt like celebrating. After giving her condolences to the grieving family, she went straight to the cash bar and got a double vodka martini. She picked up the glass and looked back at the crowd.

Maria approached her, in her black dress and leotards.

"Black suits you, Maria. Better than me. Cheers, to my beautiful daughter."

Maria looked around.

"Maria, don't worry. No one knows. We buried the bully."

"Yeah, but Mom, how many actually know?" Maria spotted a couple pointing to her and talking together. "People are looking at me."

"That's just your imagination, Maria," Andy said, giving people a stink eye. The people stopped talking and looked away. "People have a short memory. Just act normal, and people will start to wonder if they heard it right in the first place. Before you know it, someone else will be the pick of conversations under Saturday morning hairdryers."

Maria looked at her Mickey Mouse watch.

"Why are you wearing that stupid thing? Didn't Anita give you that watch?" Andy put her drink down and picked up Maria's wrist. She tapped at the clock face.

"So? I like it."

"Maria, you're sixteen. Too old for Mickey Mouse."

"Well, my Mickey Mouse is saying I should be going home pretty soon to pack for Toronto, Mom."

"Fart. Where's Alessandro?" She looked around the large banquet room and spotted him standing with some other young men, looking at her and Maria. He nodded.

She snapped her fingers in his direction.

"Mom, he's too far away." Maria lifted her fingers and whistled. The whistle echoed through the banquet room. She dropped her hands and pretended not to have done it.

Alessandro made his way to them. "You whistled?"

"I have to pack pretty soon."

"In about an hour?"

"Yes." She pointed at her father over by the food table.

"I still wish we flew, Mom," complained Maria. "Why drive for so long? It's dark already, and what if it storms? What about white-outs? What car are we using?"

"Hold your horses, Miss. Everything's under control. We don't have to be on set until tomorrow morning. I already asked if we can have a late check-in at the Four Seasons tonight, and you can nap in the car on the way, for your beauty sleep." She pinched Maria's cheek. "You sure can use it."

"Ha. Very funny."

"Maria, there's three of us. It's cheaper by car. Besides, I hate flying, unless it's down to you-know-where. My favorite place."

"Yeah, I know. Miami."

Andy drained her drink.

"Or Myrtle Beach." Alessandro shook change in his pocket, smiling at Andy.

Andy cocked her head. "It's not Miami, but I would take Myrtle Beach over Vindenza in the winter anytime. I don't care how long the flight is." Andy leaned over the bar. "Another double vodka martini, please. I've had a hell of a week."

MARIA WAS LED OUT OF THE MAKE-UP ROOM, by a man in a headset and clipboard, to what he said was the "set." Andy and Alessandro followed close behind. Maria looked down at a part of a script she had memorized and folded it up into four as she continued to follow.

People milled around on one side of a large warehouse. Others sat and made notes or chatted at various tables or searched through a pile of clothing and accessories. There was also a table covered in refreshments. At the other end, there stood a more elegant table with a sumptuous selection of food, ceramic plates, and real cutlery. Everywhere else were cameras and paraphernalia she did not recognize. Lights hung from the rafters and stands, and men with tool belts milled around working. Others stood talking into walkie-talkies.

Maria was led to a folding canvas chair. She sat at the bidding of the gentleman, while Andy protectively stood by her side.

Andy looked around and then at the man. "Where's mine?"

The man with the headset looked blankly at her. He reached up with his left hand and pressed the earpiece against his head.

"Excuse me," Andy persisted, raising her voice. She stood ramrod straight. Today, Andy didn't wear black. She wore a tight red stretchy dress that stopped just below the knees and her red hair was swept up into a flowing, messy bun. Her father's handsome large di Giovanni nose did not take away how breathtakingly elegant and feminine she looked.

Maria groaned. "Mom, he's listening to someone talking to him. Don't bother him."

"Yeah, but I'm the one talkin' to him," she roared.

Maria looked back at Alessandro lingering nearby. Everything seemed different from what she expected. Maria thought a limousine would pick them up, but it was just a driver in his own old, dirty car. She thought people would fawn over her. Though everyone was polite enough, she felt insignificant. It was an extremely uncomfortable early start to a day possibly full of waiting, boredom, and a demand for intense energy at will, which she wasn't sure she could provide.

She looked at her script. She had four short scenes and one very long one; a short one that day, three the next day, and then once more a few days later. She bit her fingernail.

A hand gently pressed her hand away from her face. She looked up.

"Look what you're doing. You're bleeding." Alessandro held up her finger.

She shrugged and looked down at her hands.

"Why are you so nervous? You'll be great." Alessandro clasped his hands and perused the activity around them. He looked down at Maria, still looking up at him. He got down on his haunches and leaned on her chair. He wore blue jeans, Reeboks, dressed down for a change wearing a white dress shirt under a stunning sweatshirt.

She reached out and fingered his top. "I like the way you dress."

"Well, I like to dress in quality clothes. Clothes make the man, you know." He smiled and stood up.

Maria heard her mother behind her. "Excuse me? Am I the mother here? We're still waiting for chairs?"

Maria looked up to see the man with the headset look at her mother, but still listening to the other end. He waved at her mother. Then he pulled a little mike from the side of his head closer to his mouth. "And Fritz, I need two more chairs here by the actors' table. We've got *Toni* with us, and she has two chaperones."

Maria then remembered it was her character's name.

"*Toni*?" Andy asked. She was about to correct the man, but Maria pulled at her hem.

"Mom, that's me. I play *Toni*."

Andy's curls shook and bounced with every move of her face and body. "Oh." She smoothed down her dress with well-manicured hands.

"Mom, you act like you're in the movie and not me."

"No, I'm not." Andy crossed her arms and sniffed.

"Yes, you are. You're trying to impress people."

"Who am I supposed to impress? All these losers here. Look over there," she said, pointing to a crowd.

Maria saw people in a variety of shapes and heights. There were men, women, men dressed as women, some outrageously so.

A heavy-set man with a beard and headset lumbered over with two folding chairs. He put them down and unfolded them. "For the mother and her boyfriend." He walked away, talking into his headset.

"Shit."

Andy's mouth drop, and her face turn red. She looked at Alessandro who also turned red. Maria covered her mouth and tried not to laugh.

Alessandro held up his hand and yelled, "Excuse me, I'm not her boyfriend."

Some of the chatter stopped, and people turned to look at them. They studied Andy, then Alessandro. Then, they turned back to what they were doing.

"I'm not standing here," announced Andy. "I'm getting a coffee." Andy strolled to the refreshment table.

"Yeah, and I think I'll stand over at the wall. I'll be right there if you need me," said Alessandro, pointing.

Maria turned back to the set and squirmed in the chair, finding a comfortable position. She looked and saw a young man, also with a headset and a tool belt of sorts. He caught her eye and sauntered over.

"Let me take a look at you."

Embarrassed, Maria looked to the rafters as he held her chin and turned her face one way, then the other.

He took out a brush and powder, and brushed her forehead, nose, and chin. "I'll keep an eye on you. It may take a while before

249

you're called but, for now, this will do. Your make-up is otherwise fine." He smiled.

"Thank you," Maria said softly.

"I'm Jackie," he said. He looked to be in his twenties, small in stature and pleasant.

"I'm Maria."

"I know. You play *Toni*. You've been acting very long?"

"No, this is the first time."

"No kidding? Well, you managed to get a plum role for someone so young and just starting out."

"Did I?"

Jackie nodded.

Maria felt relieved to be speaking to somebody friendly. He seemed effeminate, gentle, delicate in a way.

"Can I ask you a question?" asked Maria. "I only have my bits to the script, so I don't know what the movie's about."

"Oh, I'll see if I can get you a full script. I'll be right back."

Slowly, Maria realized Jackie was gay, that many in the cast and production crew were gay. She looked at the carpenters and watched a woman with a buzz cut hammering at a frame for one of the set walls. She was intrigued, confused, but strangely comforted. Here was a community that would undoubtedly not question her Adam's Apple or whether she would have to give in and function as predominantly male. She sensed a community such as this would be a haven for those who were of more than one spirit in one body.

Andy came back with a cup of coffee in hand. "How are you doin', kiddo."

"Fine. I'm getting a full script."

"About time."

A door opened behind them. Maria turned to see Mae West walk out in a dazzling white gown and long white evening gloves. Her massive hairstyle was immaculate, and sparkled. She shimmied her way to where all the lights pooled and blew kisses at everyone.

Alessandro came close to Maria and Andy, and the three watched as people cheered and applauded.

"What the fuck? Mae West is dead, right?" Andy asked as she sat down beside Maria.

Maria watched, mesmerized, as Jackie hurried to Mae West's side and stood up on his toes to powder cheeks and nose.

"Thank you, Darling," boomed Mae West. "You make me feel so gorgeous." Mae West looked around the set, and her eyes fell on Alessandro. "My, don't we have some fine-looking men here today. What's your name, Honey?"

Alessandro looked around, then at the back wall behind him.

Maria nudged him. "She means you, I think."

Alessandro pointed at himself, surprised.

"Yes, I mean you, gorgeous. Come heah." Mae West put a hand on her hip and motioned with her long fingernail for him to come.

Taken aback, Alessandro hesitated.

"Go, silly," shouted Andy.

Alessandro walked to Mae West, embarrassed. People clapped, cheered, and hollered as Mae West suggestively placed an arm around Alessandro and waited for the clapping to settle down.

"What's your name, honey?" asked Mae loudly.

Alessandro whispered to her.

"Say it loud so everyone can heah who you are," Mae West shouted.

"Alessandro." Alessandro looked back at Maria and Andy, frightened and nervous.

Maria giggled.

"What the hell, Mae West is dead," Andy said loud enough for Mae West to hear.

"Honey, Mae West never dies," yelled Mae.

Andy leaned toward Maria. "Holy shit, she must be in her nineties. She looks terrific." Andy's foldable chair collapsed, and she fell against Maria, who almost toppled over.

Maria grabbed her mother and helped her to her feet.

Andy picked up the chair to try and set it straight again. She couldn't get it entirely unfolded, then gave up and smashed it on the ground.

"Some of us simply don't know when to stop, Honey."

Andy stood straight and slowly turned to look at Mae. "Excuse me?"

Maria tugged at her arm. "Mom, don't."

Andy pushed her arm aside. "What did you say to me?"

Maria groaned and covered her face.

Mae turned to Alessandro. "Hold me, Stupid. Hold me." Mae grabbed his arms and put them around her. She gently pulled back and looked at him suggestively. "What's that I feel? Is that a gun, or are ya just happy to see me?"

Everyone hooted and applauded.

Andy was getting more heated, Maria could tell. She got up. "Mom, sit down."

Andy shifted over and sat in Alessandro's chair with her eyes glued on Mae. "I don't get it. She must be 95 by now. I thought she died?"

Another spotlight turned on with a bang. The sparkles in Mae's dress went on fire. She looked breathtaking. Beautiful.

"Well, nice meetin' ya here." Mae let Alessandro go. "Listen, anytime you got nothin' to do—and lots of time to do it—come on up and see me some time." She wiggled her body and winked at Alessandro.

Alessandro mutely walked back to Andy and Maria, to applause and jeering.

"All right, everybody, quiet on the set," yelled the man with the clipboard.

All of a sudden, everyone stopped talking.

The man went up to Mae and spoke softly to her. Mae nodded, then said something to him. The man looked at the lights.

"Everyone, take five," he yelled. He walked back to a large film camera on a movable platform, talked to the cameraman, then talked into his walkie-talkie.

To Maria's horror, Mae walked toward them during the lull.

"Oh my God, she's coming here," Andy whispered, grabbing at Alessandro's sleeve. "Quick, Alessandro. Let's go. Maria, we're going."

"What?!"

"We're not staying to watch this crazy shit."

"Mom, I have to stay. I promised. I'm playing *Toni*."

Mae reached Maria, Andy, and Alessandro. She winked at Alessandro, then looked down at Maria.

"So, you're playing *Toni*. My lost daughter." She put out her hand. "Nice to meet you," she said in a man's baritone voice.

Maria heard her mother gasp.

Slowly, Maria took Mae's hand.

Mae West turned to Andy and motioned for her to get up. Wordlessly, Andy stood up so Mae could sit down to lean toward Maria. She touched Maria's face.

"I'm Craig Russell," he said. He turned to Andy. "Is this your mother?"

Maria nodded.

Craig pointed behind him at Alessandro. "And is this your mother's boy-toy?"

Maria shot a wide-eyed look at her mother.

"I wouldn't mind having you as my boy-toy." Craig got up and nuzzled closely to Alessandro. He looked closely at Alessandro's scars. "Oh, don't you have a certain masculinity about you. Look at those scars. Let me make them better." Suddenly, he licked Alessandro's face. Then again.

Alessandro, in shock, pulled himself free. "I don't do this shit," he sputtered as he wiped his face and moved away about forty feet.

Andy turned and followed him.

The man in the headset ran to Alessandro and Andy, motioning them to stay where the chairs stood. Both Alessandro and Andy shook their heads, pointing to where they stood.

Craig laughed and leaned over to Maria. "So, what's your story? Where were you born?"

"Vindenza, Quebec." She looked closely at the heavy make-up. She realized there were eyebrows under the white make-up, below long curved penciled-in eyebrows high on the forehead. Someone drew the lips more substantial than they were. She looked at the hair and now saw it was a wig. She also saw stubble under the make-up.

"You wanna touch it?"

"Touch what?"

"The wig. What did you think, silly?"

Maria reached up and touched the great, platinum wig. "Wow, it's beautiful."

"I know. Listen, I can see why you got the part. We were looking for a young, androgynous-looking person. Did you know that? We got you dressed up as a girl right now, but later, your character, *Toni,* dresses as a young man in a tuxedo. It's a small speaking role, but it's a good one, and we'll be working together for a few days. I thought I'd get to know you. It would help for me to know how to act as your father."

Maria didn't know what to say. She looked furtively at her mother.

"Oh, don't worry about your Mom. Have you ever seen me perform?"

Maria shook her head. "Where do you perform?"

"Well, I've toured Las Vegas, Hollywood, San Francisco, Paris, Berlin, Amsterdam, Hamburg, Sydney, Toronto, Montreal."

"Wow."

"When I was young, I was president of the Mae West fan club. That's how I got to know her, plus I was her butler before she died. She taught me everything I know about her character."

"Really?"

Craig nodded thoughtfully and leaned in to whisper. "Yes, and I do other characters, of course. Judy Garland, Barbra Streisand. Are you bi?"

"Bi?"

"Bi."

"What is bi?" Maria asked, looking at the double set of fake eyelashes.

"I mean, have you figured out whether you like boys *and* girls?"

Maria blushed. She couldn't think straight.

"Don't worry. I meet a lot of bisexual people. Sometimes they're born that way, and sometimes they're not. I just want you to know that it's okay. No one tells you up front."

Maria stared at Craig.

Craig patted Maria's knee. "That's okay, Honey. I can tell. We all can."

"But I never, ever," Maria's voice trailed.

Craig waved at her. "You're young, I know. I also know you have two lights shining in you." Craig stopped smiling and cocked his head. "Maria, remember this. You have to find your own frequency.

The world out there isn't all there is. The real world is here." Craig pointed at Maria's heart. "Find your center. Listen to your own voice."

"I don't know what my own voice is anymore."

"Well, you'll find it in the stillness."

"Stillness?"

"Yes, always when you are still. When there's too much noise around you, and in your head, you will never find it."

Maria thought of their lives of constant drama, noise and upheaval.

"Only you can do it. And find your world, your people. Your tribe. Where you belong."

"I am where I belong. I have a tribe."

Craig shook his head slowly. "No, you were born into a family but that doesn't mean they'll ever understand you. Look around."

Maria looked around at the various types of people milling.

"A lot of these people are part of the community where you really belong. You see, they *found* their tribe."

Maria sat back and stared at him.

"What are you comfortable with? What drives you? What do you wish from your life?"

Maria thought of blood. She blinked. She had become comfortable with blood. She felt ill and looked away. "I wish people would stop dying around me."

Craig bent over and carefully placed his arms around Maria. "Kiddo, we all lose someone we love. I have. I've lost many with this terrible epidemic."

"Epidemic?"

Craig sniffed sadly. He gently wiped a tear away from under his heavy eyelashes. "Yes, AIDS. Terrible, terrible." He sniffed again, and waved at the set. "There is much darkness and pain out there. But it's part of the illusion. Don't ever spend too much time looking at that darkness or it will swallow you whole. You have to move on. What you see is just a holographic universe. Create a life you feel comfortable with. Be *all* of you. Not just the part that you think people will accept."

Maria slowly nodded her head.

Craig smiled.

"Break's over. Everyone on set, please," called the man with the headset.

"Director's calling." Craig squeezed her knee and got up. "Kevin, give me a pen and paper." He stood holding his bejeweled hand out to the man with the clipboard.

Kevin walked over with a pen, and tore a corner off one of the pages on his clipboard. He handed both to Craig before turning away and speaking into his headphone.

Maria watched Craig scribble on the little paper, then hand it to her. "Here's my number. We're friends now. But here," Craig said, pointing to his chest, "here, we're family. You hear me?"

Maria nodded.

"See you on set."

Maria watched Craig wiggle back to the set in his high heels and stand in position under the lights.

Kevin looked at a man adjusting a light. "Is that better?" he asked, turning to Craig.

Maria watched Craig study the lights above his head. He peered at his hands and around himself. "Yeah, that's better," he said gruffly.

The man suddenly put up a hand and listened closely to his headset. He looked pointedly at Maria. "Oh, fuck, don't say that."

Maria squirmed as she watched him come toward her. "Um, I hate to say this, but your mother has pulled you out of the production. Please go back to wardrobe and hand in your outfit." He walked away, but not before giving Alessandro a long look. "Where'd you guys come from? Mars?"

Alessandro swiveled his body toward the retreating man and clenched his fists.

Maria looked over at someone laughing, then realized the news must have passed on. She slowly got out of her chair and felt as if everyone was staring at her. Even Craig Russell looked over briefly, then away.

She waved at Jackie who stood looking at her, smiling. She nodded and shrugged. "Nice meeting you," he mouthed.

Alessandro put his hand on Maria's back as he helped her out of the chair and walked her back to the dressing room.

Maria took one last look at the set. She realized Craig Russell saw right through her. He spoke about her with certainty. How could he see? She reached up and felt her neck. Did her Adam's Apple give her away? Was it the way she walked?

Alessandro broke up her deep thoughts, by putting his arm around her protectively.

Maria didn't say a word. Craig Russell knew. If Craig Russell knew just by looking at her, how many other people knew? How could she possibly hide her secret, as a woman *or* man? More importantly, what did Alessandro see?

As they entered the dressing room, the wardrobe women barely looked over, and continued looking down lists and costumes on racks.

Maria broke down in tears.

"Hey, don't be sad," Alessandro whispered.

Maria leaned her head on Alessandro's chest, crying.

The day's experience dug into her very soul. Exposing her deepest secret unnerved her. She grieved over lost dreams everyone seemed to want for her; a normal woman's life, with marriage and children, grandchildren for her parents. Yes, with the help of drugs, and the hope generated by Dr. Bob and ongoing psychotherapy, she had fallen into a comfortable *place*, not worrying about the future too much. It was too much to bear, the unknowing of it all. In the meantime, she managed to feel confident, believing she would always be able to hide her secret. That was now not true.

In a glance, Craig Russell put her body under a magnifying glass, leaving her feeling as if no one would ever be able to love her. She was back to being a freak.

Maria cried harder and reached out to hold Alessandro by the neck. She felt her tears wipe against his chin as he bent his face to hers.

His beautiful face.

"It's not the end of the world," he said.

"Yes, it is." She realized Alessandro was probably her best friend along with Francesca. "Thank you for being my friend," she said.

Alessandro squeezed her just as Andy entered the dressing room with their coats. "Ladies, my daughter isn't staying."

Two wardrobe women turned around, surprised. One turned to the other, and they poured over a list. "Yes, we have a stand-in for *Toni*."

"Geez, we better get her in, quick."

A lady walked over to Maria. "I'm so sorry you're not going to stay with us today," she said. She reached out to Maria and gently turned her around to undo buttons at the back of her dress. She undid them quickly, as Maria watched her mother and Alessandro in the mirror, as they spoke.

"Why'd you get so upset, *Zia*? It's all make-believe," said Alessandro. "I mean, I found it a bit much, but not enough to pull Maria out of the movie."

Maria saw her mother frown. "I just didn't like the feel of it, that's all. I could take a joke. But this guy pulled it off on me. I thought he was a woman. And him licking your face and the way he talked to everyone." Andy made a face and shook her head in disgust. "I didn't like it. I didn't want Maria to be exposed to people like that."

People like that.

"*Zia*, he was a queer having fun on our account. He couldn't help it. He's screwed up and doesn't know which way to go. It's like a circus here. He's a circus entertainer. They all seem to be like that."

Maria's heart skipped a beat.

They all seem to be like that.

"YOU OKAY?"

Maria looked at her mother, who was looking at her over the back of her seat.

They'd been driving on the 401 longer than they needed because of a snow front passing overhead, making it almost impossible to keep pushing for home. They slowed to a crawl with the windshield wipers slapping back and forth as fast as they could go.

"I'm okay," Maria said. She hadn't said a word since leaving the outskirts of Toronto. They were now somewhere near the Thousand Islands, and the snowdrifts blew in from the St. Lawrence, more substantial and frequent.

"No, you're not."

Maria pursed her lips. "Why am I not?"

"Because they all upset you back there."

Something about her mother's certainty in the matter bugged the hell out of Maria. "The only person who upset me was you, Mom." She looked out at the snow flying past her window. It was starting to get dark. She looked at her watch. Almost 4:00.

"That's the thanks I get for being a good mother," Andy said, speaking to Alessandro.

Maria watched Alessandro quietly look at her mother, then back at the road. She could see the welt on his face; like the slash of a sword. It never occurred to her how close to death he had been when that bullet slashed his face. She shook her head and sighed. She didn't care anymore. She raised her hand and looked for a nail to bite. Maria was sick of her mother's overbearing assuredness. "So, what do you think you're protecting me from, Mom?"

"From those creeps," Andy said, nodding with emphasis.

Maria saw Alessandro looking at her in the rearview mirror.

She looked back coldly, remembering what he said back in the change room.

He blinked at her coldness in surprise, then focused on the snowy highway ahead. He looked hurt.

She didn't care. She looked out at the snow. "I can't believe you made us leave."

"Drop it."

"I was looking forward to doing that movie."

"I don't want to hear another word about it."

Maria felt a wave of hatred for her mother. She thought of what everyone must be doing on set, at that moment. What was she missing? Would she have been finished for the day? What else would she have learned from Craig? She was hungry to hear more encouragement. More guidance.

She slumped into her seat. She stabbed at a boot with the toe of the other, to push it off. She pushed the other boot off, kicking the back of Andy's seat in the process.

"Stop that."

Maria kicked the seat again. Then she shoved the back.

"Maria, stop."

She shoved again. "Why the hell are we wasting so much time driving? We could've flown." She felt tears welling up and pointed out the window. "How can you make us drive through this shit? You hate long trips in the car. You're forever complaining about having to drive to Montreal. Forty-five minutes. It's taking us a day to get home in this shit and I don't hear one word of complaint coming from you."

"Goddamn it, Maria, it's still better than going down in a fucking plane in this crap."

"You're flying to Myrtle Beach next month. That's a longer flight." Maria was looking for a fight.

"If it means wearing my bikini on a beach, I would *live* on a plane." Andy turned to glare warningly back at her daughter.

"Exactly. It's back to what *you* want."

"Leave it alone, Maria."

"Ladies, should I put on some nice music?" Alessandro offered. He reached for the radio and turned it on and the women quietly waited as he searched for a station, but static was all he could find. "Too bad. We're kind of in between stations." Defeated, he turned the radio off and settled back to driving.

Maria wasn't finished. "No, they were nice people, Mom. I don't care what either of you say."

Alessandro glanced at her, and then he went back to driving. "What did I say?"

"You know very well what you said."

"Maria, don't be rude," Andy warned.

"What did I say?"

Maria ignored him. She didn't care if she hurt him in the process. She changed the subject. "Dr. Bob said I was to have creative distractions. Well, that," she pointed angrily through the back windshield, "was a perfect creative distraction."

"With freaks."

"I'M A FREAK, MA."

Andy whipped around and glared. "Stop this. Alessandro's driving in this shit. Don't upset him."

Alessandro looked at Andy. "I'm okay. Don't worry about me."

A truck stormed from behind, towering over the Cadillac in the unplowed passing lane. Heavy slush and ice exploded loudly against the windshield and the side of the car.

"Holy crap," Andy screamed.

Alessandro braked, but the wheels didn't catch, causing the car to slide sideways.

Andy clutched at the dash as Alessandro tried to regain control.

Maria gripped the back of her mother's seat as she watched behind them for following traffic.

Slowly, the car slithered onto a straight course again. The windshield wipers sounded like drums in the sudden tense silence. Alessandro turned on the hazard lights as he maintained a slow crawl.

Maria's heart pounded. The last thing she wanted was to be blamed for an accident. She'd never live *that* one down. She remained quiet as she regained her composure. She jumped slightly as another car passed by, honking their horn in protest.

"Shit," muttered her mother.

Maria crossed her arms in anger. She knew she wasn't finished protesting against the injustice of it all. Her heart and soul were still back on the set they'd left behind. She thought of how she finally felt hope for a future that included a happy and whole *her*. However strange and unusual the experience was, she felt she had met kindred spirits. She thought of the gentle and sincere Jackie. She thought of Craig Russell and how he described her as having two 'lights.' He could've been a mentor. A teacher. A wise and experienced counsel. She knew in her heart he could show her a road map through her struggles of gender choice.

She leaned her forehead against the cold passenger window. She saw glimpses of snow-covered fields, of dark rows in the deepening dusk. She imagined herself all alone in the middle of those fields; among the cold, wet corn stalks. She felt so unbelievably lonely—especially since her special bond with Alessandro had snapped. They were besties. They had gone through so much blood and guts. How could he have been so unthinking back there?

She was grieving. She hated her mother. She hated herself. And until that morning, she had learned to find comfort in his curly-haired, handsome profile. She reminded herself he was there to just protect her and her family. He was hired help.

"I hate this world."

Andy slowly turned to look at her daughter. "Excuse me?"

"I hate my life."

"Maria, you don't have to feel that way," said Alessandro, concerned.

She didn't care. What she thought about him was an illusion. She now knew the truth.

"Leave her alone, Alessandro. She's in a *mood*."

"Fuck," Maria muttered.

"You got it good, Maria. Don't push it."

"This is not the life I would choose."

"Oh? Really? You wanna choose another life? Go ahead. Fill your boots."

"I can make it change if I want to."

"You think? Dream on, kiddo."

"I'm tired of feeling like a freak."

"Why do you feel like a freak," asked Alessandro.

"Never mind."

"Yeah, Alessandro. Let's not go there," said Andy.

Let's not go there.

"All I can say, Maria, is if you insist on calling yourself a freak, then I'm a goddamned mother of a freak, okay?" Andy turned to face Maria.

Maria looked at her, then away.

"Hey."

Maria looked at her mother.

Andy smiled gently. "And I'm the luckiest mother in the whole world for having such an amazing, unique beautiful freaky creature as you for a daughter. Okay?"

Maria was nonplussed by her mother's words. She fiddled with the zipper on her overnight bag and looked down at it. "Or son. We don't know, do we?"

She saw Alessandro's questioning eyes looking at her in the rear-view mirror.

"Oh for fuck's sake," muttered Andy. "Put a lid on it." Andy turned to face front and reached her arm back between the front seats. She searched blindly with her hand until she felt Maria's knee. "This is as good as it gets, Maria."

Maria looked up. Andy leaned forward and wiped at the moisture on the inside of the windshield. "Shit, how do you see in this stuff, Alessandro?"

"I'm okay. You wanna stop somewhere?"

Andy shrugged. "Where? We're in the middle of nowhere. Are we even across the border into Quebec, yet?"

"Yeah, we are now."

"Good. Maybe we'll be home by daylight."

"No, it won't be that bad. At this rate, we'll be home in about two hours."

"Shit."

Maria reached into her coat pocket and took out the little slip of paper with Craig's phone number. She knew calling him would be a challenge. They didn't do long distance. Ever.

She held onto the slip tightly and looked out into the dark night. Surely, Dr. Bob would let her use his office phone once he knew about Craig and how he made her feel. Especially after hearing how she had discovered a community of people like her.

Freaks like her.

Chapter Eighteen

March 1988

"STINKY, HURRY. YOU'LL BE LATE," Yvonne yelled from the hallway. A baby cried and, Stinky, standing in the sunny kitchen, looked at his Timex. He shook his arm to lower his cuffs, and turned to a key holder left of where he always sat at the end stool. He took the keys of the Audi. "I'm goin' now, Miss Yvonne."

"Thank you, Stinky. I'm just finishin' up here and should have everythin' ready to go for a nice lunch when you get back."

Stinky hurried through the front hallway and opened the large door. He locked it carefully behind him, walked to the private elevator, and stopped to push the button. He looked to his left at the entrance to another condo. It was Peter and Sandra's and the boys. He was to pick them up at the airport later that afternoon.

He heard Andy yelling at someone and looked to Stefano's door to the right.

He shook his head. That woman was always yelling. He impatiently pushed the elevator button again and looked at his reflection in the brass door. He lifted his chin and studied his small, neat goatee and short afro. He wanted to make a good impression with everyone. It was the first time the whole clan was to be together. He had never met Peter and his family. He met Andy, Maria, Claudia, and Alessandro for the first time, two days before. They had flown in earlier than the others to help Yvonne with the after-christening celebration.

The plan was for Leonardus Samuel Mangione, a beautiful, tan-skinned baby boy, to be christened at St. Andrew Catholic Church the following morning. Then, all the guests were to go to *Yvonne's* for a wonderful meal. Yvonne spent months preparing the menu, right down to Claudia's famous cannelloni.

Stinky smiled. He was happy for Leo. His boss was over the moon: at his age, finally having a baby son. Then, his smile faded. He had been thinking of his own son of late, who was probably around 10 or 11, living in Chicago. He realized he'd been a terrible father and a worse husband for the little time he spent with his ex-wife. Watching Leo and his pride and love made him realize he had been in a type of self-induced coma for many years. He barely thought of his son and his responsibilities as a father. In his remorse, he had quickly located them and started sending money and letters. He desperately wanted to make up for lost time.

He stuck his hands in his pockets and looked down at the gold and navy-blue carpet. Secretly, he planned to ask Leo for a little time off to visit his son during summer vacation. Maybe even fly him down, some time, to enjoy Leo's theme park.

An elegant little bell rang, and the door swung open, splitting his image in two and blasting it apart. Before he stepped in, he heard the door to Stefano's condo open. Alessandro's face peeked around the edge of the door.

Alessandro quietly nodded at Stinky.

Stinky lifted his hand in acknowledgment and stepped into the black onyx and mirrored elevator. He pushed the down button, leaned back on the brass rails, and watched the numbers change above the door. Stinky pulled at a small diamond earring in his right ear lobe, and wondered if Leo would let him have a two-bedroom unit.

He still lived in the little one-bedroom unit assigned to him in the old resort next door. Leo had constructed a landscaped pathway leading from there to a secret door at the side of the new condo building. Most of Leo's soldiers stayed in the old resort, though some were married and lived a little inland, within a minute of Leo's abode.

Stinky straightened up when the elevator slowed down and came to a gentle stop. The door pinged open, and Stinky got the keys ready as he walked through the cool underground garage to the red Audi Quattro. This section was private and, with what technology was available on the market, a monitoring system was already wired into the infrastructure. It was as secure as Fort Knox.

He unlocked the car and slipped into the grey interior. He pulled out his wallet and slipped out a little photograph, and placed it on a bit of chrome ledge in the console. It was a school photo of his son. He smiled, as he eyed it lovingly before starting the engine, then looked away as he carefully maneuvered around large cement pillars, following an aisle leading straight to a ramp and garage door.

The door automatically opened as he approached.

He continued on a ramp to another level, following the exit signs. Stinky glanced at the cars parked on both sides. Most of them were more expensive than the Audi he drove. It was Yvonne's car, but neither Leo nor Yvonne wanted any undue attention while out in public.

Stinky approached a larger garage door. He pushed a button on the opener clipped to the visor and squinted against the brilliant sun as it exploded and slashed through the windshield. Light cascaded over the car. Stinky had to put the sun visor down.

He was finally on his way to the airport to pick up Yvonne's son, Willie, flying down from Harvard—another young African American man he looked up to with pride.

He stopped at the sidewalk and looked both ways, then turned left on Ocean Boulevard for the airport, knowing he had twenty minutes to spare. He looked down and pushed in Michael Jackson's newest, *Thriller*. He chose his favorite number, *Wanna Be Startin' Somethin'*, and relaxed and tapped the wheel to the music's enticing beat.

MARIA SAT PLAYING WITH AN ELASTIC BAND, nodding to the very different beat of *I Want Tomorrow* by Enya. The surround sound stereo in the spacious living room filled the luxurious condo with majestic string instrumentals and Enya's angelic voice.

She quietly watched Alessandro lean over the railing, looking over the park below and to the ocean. She watched the wind play with his hair. She looked at his broad shoulders and his slim midriff.

She closed her eyes and stopped playing with the elastic band while she listened more closely to the lyrics. She felt emotional, deep, far away in another place. The bass in the music comfortingly vibrated her chest, and she felt every word sung.

"You, you may take my life away,
so far away…
Now I know I must leave your spell.
I want tomorrow."

Maria allowed herself to become more boyish, deciding she was only going to dress in pants and shirts. She managed to talk her mother into getting one of her hairdressing friends to give her a quick pixie cut. Maria also stopped chumming with Alessandro, only talking to him at lessons or meals. She looked at the gold-framed pictures her mother had hung the night before. Alessandro was in a lot of them.

She looked at the couch and stroked the plush, tropical-design canvas covering. Everything about the south was new to her. It was weird leaving three feet of snow and sub-zero temperatures behind, to see sand, palm trees and ocean in just hours.

Andy came out of the master bedroom, and walked past Maria to the white marble polished kitchen. She fiddled with an earring as she stepped to the fridge and opened it.

Maria held up the elastic band, stretched it between two fingers, aiming high. She shot the elastic. It flew and landed softly on her mother's behind.

Andy shot up and reached for her back with her left hand. "Shit, what was that?"

Maria turned away, hiding a smile. She looked at her watch and saw she had time before lunch to go for a walk on the beach. She stood up.

"Mom, I'm going for a walk."

"Don't be long. We're having lunch at *Zio's* in less than an hour."

"I won't go far."

"I'll call from the balcony. You better come running."

Maria went to the counter, picked up a set of keys, and looked back at Alessandro standing outside again, before disappearing into the hallway.

STINKY PULLED INTO A PARKING SPOT in the small airport. He turned the engine off and started to slip out of the car when a man got in through the passenger seat. Two others slipped into the back seat from both sides. Something cold and hard jabbed against the back of his head. He slowly put up his hands, his eyes darting to the side and into the rear-view mirror.

"Hi, Matthew."

Stinky glanced at the man next to him. He had a scraggly beard and long hair tied back with a leather strip. The man wore a black leather, sleeveless vest and torn, filthy jeans. On one arm was a tattoo of a skull-and-crossbones. He smelled of smoke and bad breath.

Stinky's insides turned into water. He briefly considered opening the door and escaping.

"I wouldn't do that. We would ruin this nice grey interior."

"What do you want?"

"Nothin'. We missed you, that's all."

Stinky's heart skipped when the man took the school photo of his son and studied it. "Your son?"

Stinky nodded, his eyes glued to the photo, not wanting to look away. He broke into a sweat. A drop coursed down his temple. It was getting hot in the car without the air on, but it was also the fear he felt in his guts.

"Nice looking boy. There's lots of snow in Chicago. Does he like to make snow angels?"

Stinky shrugged. "I don't know."

The man feigned surprise. "You don't know, Matthew?" He turned to the guys in the back. Both were overweight. One wore a tight t-shirt over loose, low-fitting jeans. The other's gut peeked from a short leather jacket. Neither one had shaved in years. "He doesn't know. Maybe we're wasting our time here. He doesn't care."

"I don't care about what?"

"You won't care if anything should happen to your son?"

Stinky's mouth dropped. "I care, very much."

"Well, then. That's great. I'm Boomer, by the way. And this here is Sean and Danny. We're going to get along just fine, you and us."

Stinky breathed through his mouth for a few moments. He felt hot tears burning and blurring his eyes. He would do anything to protect his son. He lowered his head and let a tear drop onto his dress pants. He wiped it away.

"What do you want, Boomer?"

MARIA STEPPED BACK from a foam-filled wave. The surf sprayed her as she squinted up into a roaring flock of seagulls hovering majestically nearby, deftly catching bits of bread an older woman threw into the air.

She looked down at a small black object in the middle of white shells in the fine sand. She picked it up and held it close. It was triangular, about an inch long. Maria put it into the pocket of her new black capris. She held down the hem of her white shirttail, which threatened to ride up her midriff and expose her breasts. She'd become embarrassed by them. Attention was the last thing she wanted.

Retracing her steps, she made her way back to their building, looking up at the top floor to see if Alessandro was still on the balcony.

He was not.

Disappointed, she looked down at the seashells, carefully stepping around clumps of seaweed and the occasional blue dome of a jellyfish, something strange and alien. She'd heard stories of people stung by them and imagined red welts across their legs and faces. She stopped. She remembered Selena's bloody, swollen face, her one eye slightly open, staring at nothing.

Agitated, Maria looked back at the horizon and searched for something. Anything. Something that would take her thoughts away from this planet and all that resided therein. For the first time, she appreciated why people sailed the vast ocean, heading for unknown horizons, where no one threatened or bullied you, where there was no conflict, except with the winds and storms and glaring sun.

Her ears perked up. She focused on a strange sound. She looked at the top of their building and saw her mother in the distance, waving.

She waved back and headed straight for the condo.

Maria sauntered through the protected portion of the dunes in front of their building. She heard a tiny cry. She stopped and squinted into the dark of the myrtle and choke cherry underbrush and saw movement. She stepped forward, and several cats scattered in all directions. Then something mewed. She went down on her knees and peered into the thorny bush. She sniffed cat urine.

A little ginger kitten mewed and hopped out toward her. It stopped and looked straight up into her face, squinting against the sun.

"Well, aren't you cute."

STINKY EYED THE BIG PAPER BAG he had stuffed into the furthest corner of the car's trunk. He pulled out the blue Samsonite suitcase with the new handle and wheel design. He placed it on the cement by the car and went to close the trunk.

"Want me to help with that paper bag?" Willie asked, stepping toward the trunk.

Stinky shot out a hand to stop him. He shook his head. "No, that's okay. It stays in the car."

"Well," said Willie, looking around. "It's nice seeing everything finished finally."

Stinky smiled faintly. "They worked very hard."

"They sure did." Together, they walked to the private elevator, and Willie stood by as Stinky pushed the button. "You've been well since I saw you last?"

Stinky looked at Willie briefly before turning his attention to the display above the elevator doors. He was anxious to get back to the car, and willed the elevator to hurry its descent. "Oh, I've been good. Your mother spoils me."

"I hear you stick to Mom and little Leo?"

Stinky nodded. "Yup, that's my job, now." He smiled and looked at his feet, waiting.

The elevator doors opened, and Stinky allowed Willie to go first. Then, he pulled the suitcase into the elevator and turned to face the doors as they closed. Stinky closed his eyes, hoping Willie wouldn't want to keep chatting about what now seemed insignificant, mundane things. How are you? Doing fine. How's school? Great. How was the trip? Wonderful.

All he could think of was his son.

He was also acutely aware of his underwear, too. During his ordeal with the men, he had lightly soiled them. He got a whiff of urine and hoped the smell wouldn't reach Willie's nose behind him. As soon as he delivered Willie and the suitcase, he would ask to take a few minutes while the rest enjoyed their lunch.

He also had to get that paper bag into his apartment and hide it until the next day. His instructions were to get acquainted with its contents before the entire family's attention was on the christening.

Most important, Stinky couldn't wait to call and make sure his son was alright.

"HAVE MORE FRIED OKRA, WILLIE."

Yvonne stood in a lavender lace dress with a matching turban, and hovered over the guests at the table. A perfect ocean breeze lazily blew through the open windows and glass doors in the dining room off the living room. The brilliant sun reflected off glass-topped furniture and polished white marble floors. It was a perfect day in Paradise, and Yvonne playfully tapped a gold sandal on the cool floor as she stood expectantly with a full spoon of okra in mid-air.

"Like the earrings, Mom," Willie grinned, looking up. Willie had to speak loudly over the din of family chatter and his mother's favorite band playing on the stereo, *Buckwheat Sydeco*. She was playing her favorite song, *Walkin' to New Orleans*. It got everyone slowly moving to the rhythm of accordion and trumpet.

Yvonne put down the hammered stainless bowl of fried okra and reached up to feel the delicate pearl earrings she had on. She smiled and studied her son's face for a moment. "Chil', thank you for the lovely gift." She bent over slightly and rested her cheek on her son's short-cropped afro. "Mah, we've come a long, long way." She slowly shook her head. "You almost' die in those stinkin' fish bins in Georgia as a hard workin' skinny kid, and now you in your first year studying law in Harvard. Lor', this is mah son. My prayers sure do get answered."

"Five years, *Bella*," bellowed Leo, sitting next to Willie at the head of the long table. "*Santa Maria* has been good to us." Leo's eyes sparkled as Yvonne allowed her eyes to linger on his rugged, tanned face. He winked lovingly.

Yvonne touched the pearl and diamond necklace that graced her neck and chest. It beautifully matched the earrings given to her by Willie. She mouthed, *Thank you.*

"I don't remember gettin' no pearls or diamonds from Stef when I had Maria," quipped Andy, laughing as she raised a forkful of fried clams.

"That's 'cause you didn't have a son, Andy," joked Sandra. Almost instantly, Sandra choked on her words. She covered her mouth and looked wide-eyed at Peter next to her.

Peter, in mid-chew, silently shook his head in disgust.

Sandra made a face and looked at Andy, who glared at her.

Maria pretended not to hear. She watched the ginger kitten hidden on her lap. She reached up to her plate and pulled away a portion of her crab cake and offered it to her new-found pet.

Stefano put his fork down and sighed. He looked at Sandra.

Sandra mouthed, *sorry.*

"Maria, take that filthy animal out of her," hissed Andy.

Maria gave her mother a cold look. "This is my new friend." She cocked her head. "You want me to be happy, right? Well, she makes me very happy. I'm keeping her."

Andy picked up her napkin and repositioned it on her lap. Her mouth set angrily, she didn't say another word.

The song ended, and a frantic *Zydeco Boogaloo* started. The quicker beat reflected off the tension in the room. Suddenly, cheerful music felt out of sync.

Leo picked up his cigar from an ashtray next to his plate, and nudged Willie. He motioned to the stereo with his chin.

Willie was just about to get up to change the music when his little half-brother cooed and caught his attention. He watched for a moment as Leo leaned over and made a funny face at his infant son in the highchair. A beautiful baby boy played with a plastic donut, absolutely unaffected by the noise around him. He was chewing his toy in earnest, and both Willie and Leo lovingly watched as his little fist banged it a couple of times on the smudged plastic tray in front of him.

An ocean gust blew ash off Leo's cigar, and it scattered over the white jumper little Leonardus was wearing.

"Oh, shit," Leo muttered.

"Oops," said Willie.

Yvonne spied the ash. She quickly put the bowl of fried okra down on the table and hurried to the highchair. Gently, Yvonne picked off the little clumps of ash with her long pink fingernails, and carefully brushed the remainder away. She bent down and blew at what fell on the plastic toy and tray. She stood up and eyed Leo.

Leo shrugged. He looked at his cigar and put it out in the ashtray. "Sorry, *Bella*."

"Hmm, mmm." Yvonne went back to making sure everyone had enough to eat.

Willie got up and went to the stereo. He turned the music down just a touch, so that everyone could still appreciate its cheerfulness.

People started to talk again and continued eating all that Yvonne had created; dishes straight out of her own *Yvonne's* Restaurant menu— Hush puppies, fried clams, Carolina crab cake (made from Hilton Head Blue Crab) and, in honor of her Italian husband, a spicy calamari. Dirty Rice complimented the hot Shrimp Gumbo, all not to be outdone by the Crab-Stuffed Flounder with slices of baked lemon.

Yvonne waited until Willie sat down again, holding the full spoon of okra questioningly.

"Oh, sorry, yes, please, Mom." Willie held up his plate and happily watched his mother fill it with more okra. He put the plate back on the pink braided table mat and dug in.

"How was your flight?" asked Leo, picking up his glass of Merlot.

"It was fine."

Yvonne went back to her end of the long table, occasionally placing a friendly and warm hand on someone's back or shoulder as she checked to see how they were doing with their meal. "What do you mean, fine?" she asked, looking to make sure Sandra had enough food on her plate.

Leo put his wine down and wiped his mouth with his napkin. He eyed Willie closely.

"Yes. Fine?"

Willie looked up and shrugged. "Yeah, fine. You know. Sometimes you find yourself sitting beside someone who's not used to," he paused and looked around. "Sorry, I was going to say *us*." He grinned, looking around at all the white people.

Andy held up her fork. "People don't like Wops either."

"Yeah, but being Italian isn't as obvious as being black," said Sandra. She looked at Yvonne. "Is it okay, I say that?"

Yvonne inhaled deeply, her eyebrows raised. "Sandra, honey, we're family, heah. We're all God's children, white or black." She pinched her forearm. "Ma skin is black. Yours is white. Saying what's clear to us as the truth is not a bad thing." She picked up her knife and fork and sliced into her crab-stuffed flounder. "At least, ah don't find it to be a bad thing."

"Well, if young Italian men didn't insist on slicking their hair back and wearing gold like it came out their asses, they wouldn't look so obvious," Andy pointed out.

Stefano snorted as he looked at Peter's slicked-back hair.

"What are you looking at? At least I don't have a scar across the face like some Sicilian," joked Peter. He grinned at Alessandro.

Alessandro, beside Stefano, wordlessly looked up from his food. His welt looked angry.

"At least Alessandro doesn't slick his hair back." Andy sat back and pointed to her nephews sitting opposite them. "Neither do your kids," she said to Sandra.

Andrew and Steffy looked at their aunt. Then, at each other's hair.

"They're presentable and civilized. No big gold chains or watches." She looked around.

"Like you said, the Sicilians," Peter muttered, cramming a hush puppy into his mouth.

Andy jabbed at the air with her fork. "Exactly."

Leo chuckled. "Remember the first time we met Stinky?" he asked Stefano. "He had that massive gold chain around his neck. Stuck out like a sore black thumb."

Stefano didn't laugh and kept eating.

"He's a good man and does so much for us." Yvonne pointed her fork to the outside world. "He can't stand seeing the cats go hungry between the buildings and goes out every morning with scraps from our restaurants to feed them."

Willie looked at the empty chair and place-setting opposite him. Then he bent over his plate and looked around and along the length of the table. "Speaking of which, where *is* Stinky?"

"He said he'd give us some family time, seeing that everyone's here together for the first time," Leo joked, stabbing at a hush puppy. "He'll be back soon."

Willie wiped his mouth. "Is there something wrong with Stinky?"

Yvonne looked up, surprised. "He was jes' fine when he left to pick you up."

Leo shrugged as he chewed. "Why do you ask?"

Willie looked down at his plate to think. He looked up as he wiped his fingers on the napkin over his lap. "Well, there was something different. I couldn't put my finger on it. Like he was sad or something. We didn't talk much coming here."

Leo looked at Stefano.

Stefano stopped chewing for a second, as he stared at Leo.

Leo shook his head and made a face. "No, he's okay." Leo's face set.

Stefano slowly started to chew again, but kept looking at Leo.

Leo looked at him and blinked. He slowed down his chewing and stabbed at another hushpuppy before pushing his chair back to walk over to glass that overlooked the side of the old resort below. He opened the sliding door a little and stepped onto the balcony. He looked down at the shaded part of the resort, at Stinky's sliding doors, and saw they were open.

"Honey, you know what happens when you leave those doors only slightly open?" Yvonne called. "We get that howlin' through the place. Either you open them completely or close 'em shut."

Leo turned back to the doors and opened them wider. The howling in the condo stopped. He took one final look toward Stinky's place, then turned and walked to the table.

"He's probably having a nap. We worked him hard getting ready for the christening. He deserves a break." Leo sat down. "Yvonne, any more hush puppies?"

Yvonne got up and hustled down the table with the dish of hush puppies.

Stefano noisily pushed his chair back, stood, and held up his glass of watered-down wine. He hit his plate with the knife in his other hand. Everyone stopped talking and eating and looked at him expectantly.

"I would like to make'a a toast." He waited as Yvonne returned to her seat.

Leo pushed his chair back, as well, and wiped his mouth. He raised his glass and squinted happily at Yvonne on the other end.

Little Leonardus made a gurgling sound, and everyone laughed.

"Leonardus just made your toast, Stef," joked Andy.

"I would like to say," Stefano interrupted, "*Congratulazioni*. To our *Zio*. The *nuovo marito e nuovo padre*." Stefano turned to Yvonne. "'N to Yvonne'a who…" Stefano stopped talking.

"Look at that. The new Godfather used up his words already." Peter joked.

Stefano grinned and blushed. He brushed away a tear. "*Si.* Godfather *again*." He motioned his glass to the young men in front of him.

"Oh," said Sandra. "I've never seen Stef so emotional." She looked askance at Andy.

"You should've seen him when Italy won the FIFA World Cup a few years back," Andy joked. "He cried like a baby."

Stefano lifted his glass again. "I pray'a to the health and safety of *Zio* Leo, Yvonne'a, and *bambino*, Leonardus." He turned explicitly to Willie. "'N our almost *famiglia* lawyer, Willie."

Everyone raised their glasses, toasted, and cheered.

"And may God bless us, everyone," quipped Andy.

"And may *Santa Maria* forgive us all our sins," added Leo.

Maria, having barely said a single word throughout the entire meal, fiddled with the shark's tooth hung on a string around her neck. She eyed Alessandro and quietly added, "Amen."

Alessandro slowly turned his head to her. Their eyes locked coldly.

STINKY WATCHED AS EVERYONE SETTLED INTO THE PEWS. He stood by to make sure Leo knew he was there if he needed him. He crossed his hands and leaned back against the grey and white-trimmed wall, and eyed the raised dais where the altar stood. Silver candlesticks with long white beeswax candles stood elegantly in a line in front of beautiful palms and ferns gracing the large crucifix positioned in the center.

Sun poured through the windows onto the colorful scene and glinted off gold trim, polished silver, and sweaty brows.

He looked at his watch—almost 11:00. The christening was about to begin. He looked at the back of the church where he said he would be watching. The church doors were going to be left open throughout the ceremony and the police were stationed outside the doors and on the street in front of the church.

It was all for naught, he thought, for he knew for a fact that all would be well.

His heart pounded as he chewed the inside of his cheek. He thought of his son and the pact with the devil he made to protect him.

Then, he thought of the two years he'd worked for Leo and Yvonne. He had fallen somewhat in love with that woman; beautiful, warm-hearted, giving, and kind. He spent hours and hours standing by her, happily at her beck and call, watching her do her magic in her restaurant's industrial kitchen. Lately, they were planning a second and third themed restaurant, and she was over the moon with more opportunities to spread the *love*. She was so giving to every human being she came across, and she had never said a bad word about anyone in his presence. She was a saint.

He looked over at Leo in the front pew. He could only see the top part of his chestnut bald head encircled by a ring of hair that was so white, it looked almost luminescent. He swallowed hard and thought back on the day he was tortured by Leo and Stefano. He felt tears welling in his eyes, and quickly blinked them away. He straightened out, amazed at how a human being could be abused and misused and, through fear, end up being a malleable piece of human shit. Yet, didn't the end justify the means? It was a good couple of years, after all.

He looked down at his beautiful, Italian brown leather shoes. He allowed his eyes to follow the crease of his dress pants. He brushed down the front of his suit jacket and straightened the wide collar over his white-on-white patterned starched dress shirt—a shirt lovingly and carefully pressed by Yvonne herself. She had even picked out the beautiful lavender paisley satin tie he wore; specifically, she said, because it brought out the green in his handsome hazel eyes.

There was no doubt about it; his captors became his generous benefactors. Though basically a glorified servant and bodyguard, it was a galaxy away from standing on the greasy, dusty corners along the seedy parts of Ocean Boulevard, handing out bad weed and smack to some of the most troubled, broken souls he had ever seen.

But. But. But. Stinky thought about what happened the day before, in the airport parking lot. He had begged for them not to hurt his son, and when they told him what they were planning to do-to harm Leo, Yvonne, and the baby during the christening if he didn't do what they told him, he broke down entirely. He faced a double-whammy: *Don't do this, and this is what will happen to your son, and to the christening. You do this, and you can keep sending money to your son and keep everyone safe.*

He needed to use a washroom. He looked around to the back and saw the washroom sign and debated whether he should wait it out or go.

He clenched his inner muscles and waited.

It abated.

He had been up all night with watery guts.

To his horror, he realized he had reached that threshold where a human being had to try very hard to justify something deplorable he was about to do. Stinky lowered his eyes, and forced himself to think back on that bloody first day at the abandoned motel. He thought of the threats, the blood, the way Leo kept stabbing him with that empty hypodermic needle and telling him he was a piece of shit. How Stefano crammed broken shells into his split, swollen lips. How he couldn't see because his eyes were swollen from being punched by Leo. Then Stinky started to think of how graciously and lovingly Yvonne took him in that day. Then, he forced himself to stop thinking those nicer thoughts. He clenched his jaw and thought, instead, back to when he hung off the ceiling. To when he shat his pants.

And Stinky. No one except Yvonne had the decency to call him by his real name: Matthew. Except the day before, by his new captors; they called him Matthew.

He stood straighter for he was finally there. *At that place.*

He walked over to the front of the church and respectfully approached Yvonne and Leo. He bent down and put on a gentle smile. "I'm now going to sit at the back. If you need me, I'll be there."

Yvonne smiled sweetly at him, and Leo reached up and touched his padded shoulder. "You do that, Stinky. Thank you for everything you've done for us."

Yvonne squeezed his hand. "We love you, Matthew. You're a good man."

Stinky cast his moist eyes at happy little Leonardus on her lap. They looked like a beautiful, black Madonna holding a black baby Jesus.

He stared for a moment. Perhaps he was helping to save this little life. That, in itself, would make what he was forced to do not seem so evil; something he would do while everyone focused on the beautiful christening that morning.

Stinky nodded jerkily, smiled sadly and hastened his retreat.

"WHAT YA DOIN'?"

"I'm watchin' TV." Peter held up the remote and raised the volume on their TV.

"Peter, too loud. You'll keep the boys from falling asleep."

Peter turned to see Sandra hovering at the master bedroom door. All the lights in the open living area were out except for the hood over the stove and the erratic, jumping blue light from the television.

"Sorry." He lowered the volume and surfed the channels. "Wow, look at all the channels they got down here."

"Bigger population."

Peter shook his head as he watched. "Nothing from Canada."

"It would be weird to see our funeral home commercial while we're down here, eh?"

"Ha."

Sandra chuckled softly and pulled her rose-pink satin dressing gown tighter around her sturdy midriff. Her face shone from that evening's cleansing and, without make-up, looked fresh and young.

Peter settled back into the velour sofa and studied her with a smile. In the soft light of the TV, she looked like a teenager again. He looked away and did a double-take at the screen. "Look at this one." He leaned forward and increased the volume.

They listened to the theme music of a show.

"Love the sound of the guitar in this one," muttered Peter.

Sandra walked over and sat beside him. She rested her hand on Peter's knee and watched, "Unsolved Mysteries."

Peter pointed. "Hmm. Look at that. Some guy called Louis Carlucci. Wanted. Neat."

Sandra sat back and allowed Peter to cradle her as they continued watching.

"Wish we had this show back home." He picked up the TV Guide. "You'd see a lot of mysteries our own *famiglia* created. Missing. Forty-five-year-old drug dealer gone bad. A $10,000 reward, ha."

"Missing, Selena Ryan, red hair, bully. No Reward. Good riddance, eh?"

"Yeah, eh? Geez. She was a number."

Sandra watched for a few moments. "What a beautiful christening that was today."

"Oh, my gosh, yeah."

"Maria was quiet, though."

"So was Alessandro."

"What do you think happened? They seemed fine when we saw them last."

Peter shrugged.

"His scar's getting better. Kinda gives him character."

"Yeah. The sun should help," Peter muttered.

"Yeah. Close call, though, eh?"

"Yeah, eh? Occupational hazard."

Sandra watched TV a few more moments before patting Peter's knee. "Right, I'm off to bed. Finish watching if you like."

Peter allowed his wife to kiss him on the cheek.

Movement on the glass doors behind the TV caught Sandra's eye. It was their reflection. She focused on their reversed images in the glare of the TV. She looked back at the condo and then at the reflection again. "Nice condo."

"Yup."

She opened one of the glass doors and stepped out into the stiff ocean breeze, allowing it to flip the hem of her housecoat. It felt like a luxurious gentle massage over her thick calves. She looked down into the dark, lush palm trees below to a brightly-lit path leading to the smaller building. She saw movement underneath their swaying, noisy fronds. "Ah, palm trees," she whispered to herself. The effect was a delightful dance of luminescent green shades swishing and flitting underneath the dark palm fronds. A gust of wind bent the tops of palm trees toward the Boulevard, and she saw a man standing in the middle of a group of cats.

She stepped back to the door. "I think I see Stinky feeding the cats."

She didn't wait for an answer and went back and watched a few seconds more. "Nice guy," she said to herself. She raised her face to the left and looked along the balcony's length, which stretched as a continuous wrap-around balcony for the building. Here, it went from their unit past Leo's glass dining room and living room doors, the end of which disappeared into the darkness toward the ocean view. The unit was dark. No lights.

She looked to her right at the ninety-degree angle in the balcony at the dining room doors. There, the balcony and the building jutted at an angle parallel to the coast. The rest of the extension was their master bedroom, designed to ensure an ocean view. The other two bedrooms were out of luck; they faced Ocean Boulevard.

It was only then, she realized their penthouse was a mirror image of Andy and Stef's on the other side of the building.

She turned her head back to where the pounding of the surf roared. She took a deep breath, filled her lungs with life-giving ocean air, and closed her eyes against the stars above her.

Over the roar of the waves, she could barely hear the cats below. She also heard a dog bark, and traffic on the distant Highway 17. A car playing an Irish lilt revved its engine and screeched its tires as it sped away. The consequent roar echoed between the two buildings. She opened her eyes and caught a glimpse of the car between the buildings, its rear lights racing south on Ocean Boulevard. She thought of the West End Gang.

Her thoughts lingered on the liquidation end of their work, and knew Leo and Stefano accommodated the Gang and the Sicilians by *erasing* bodies during their theme park construction. She thought of her own work, and was relieved to be away from Vindenza for a little while.

She leaned on the railing and thought back on the incredible numbers she saw that day; what Leo and Stefano had created was almost mind-blowing. As it stood, they could now choose to be on the level—their dirty money invested well had a return rate that was once incomprehensible to her. Indeed, there could not be anything in the *'Ndrina* in Calabria, surely, that could possibly boast to be its equal. With Leo, their *famiglia* business changed their lives and offered terrific mind-blowing benefits such as their condo.

It also, of course, brought different challenges.

More soldiers to keep an eye on.

She glanced down to see Stinky walk to his building, followed by the cats. She shook her head and smiled. Sometimes you found real gems, soldiers like Stinky.

She squinted back at the black ocean and sky and saw a glow on the distant horizon, then turned and went back into the warm apartment. "I see the glow of a tanker out there," she said, as she pulled the door shut, shutting off the cacophony of noise outside.

Peter grunted.

"I wish we could live here. The weather's so not Quebec."

"Uh-huh."

"When's that Grand Opening?"

Peter looked up. "What Grand Opening?"

Sandra was mildly disgusted. "Peter, where are you half the time? It's the last phase. We're all coming back for the Grand Opening of the Time Share Resort and Water Park.

"We are?"

"Don't you ever listen?"

"If it's worth listening to."

She bent down and grabbed a pillow off the couch, and threw it at him.

He fended off the pillow, laughed, and went back to watching TV.

Sandra walked to the bedroom door, turned, and pointed at the TV. "Just make sure we never get on that show."

Peter snapped his head around. "What?"

"Just joking."

"Hey, this guy's a multi-bigamist and swindler. Stole money from a bunch of women and has something like 30 kids."

"You wish," Sandra said.

"That many kids? No way. A bunch of women, maybe."

"You're skating on thin ice."

"I'll shut up."

"You, better," she said, pointing a make-believe gun and shooting him.

He faked being shot and spread out on the couch, tongue out, cross-eyed.

"Right." She closed the door to their luxurious marble-floored, professionally-decorated ocean-view master bedroom with the giant waterbed of their choice. She sighed as she gently lowered herself onto the warm, soft, undulating cloud and quickly fell asleep.

CHAPTER NINETEEN

April 1989

"*ZIO*, WHAT I'M TRYING TO SAY IS, I've appreciated the opportunity of working for you and Andy, but I would like to move up in the ranks. I think it's time."

Stefano stood at the window overlooking a newly-paved parking lot in front of the Park's new resort. He took out an old-fashioned linen handkerchief and wiped the sweat from his eyes. He had just run into the construction trailer, out of the mid-afternoon heat and noise, to hear Alessandro on his cell phone.

"It's been almost three years. And, *Zio*, with all due respect, I'd like to think I've done a good job."

"*Si*," agreed Stefano. *And you've got the scars to prove it*, he thought, keeping an eye on the cement truck spewing its load on a broad sidewalk. He sighed. He had different plans for Alessandro, and this wasn't part of it. But he suspected Maria and Alessandro had not been close an entire year. "Where you want'a to go?"

"I would prefer to work with you and *Zio* Leo. Of course, ultimately, I'll do whatever you and Leo tell me."

Stefano thought of their future plans; they were about to expand south from Vancouver as far as California and north to Alaska's exciting coast and mountains. Then there was Canada's East Coast.

Merda.

"No. I nee' you with Maria, Andy and Claudia."

"But…"

"Maybe in a few months. Alessandro, please. Wait until after the Grand Opening. Okay?"

There was a pause.

"Alessandro?"

"*Si, Zio*. We'll talk about it after."

"Good. *Buono*. Say'a hi to Andy. *Ciao*, Alessandro."

Stefano hung up and was about to push in the antenna when the phone rang in his hands.

"*Si?*"

"*Buongiorno.*"

Stefano looked at his watch. "*Buon pomeriggio.*" He smiled - a morning ritual between Mario and him. It was morning in Vancouver.

"*Doppio guaio atterrato.*" Double trouble arrived.

"*Fantastico,*" Stefano yelled. He chuckled and hung up. The daily contact was the highlight of each day.

Smiling, he opened the trailer door and stepped outside into the heat and dust. He looked over at a dark-blue pick-up truck he had given one of the foremen to drive. It was the Ryan truck Sandra had sprayed and shipped to them after the Ryan debacle.

He looked at the cell phone and went back into the trailer. He dialed Leo and listened to the ring at the other end. They had to think of something that would keep Alessandro on the path they designed for him. But, the idea of someone trustworthy like him working on the East Coast of Canada and just hours away from Vindenza could still be part of their plan.

As he waited for Leo to pick up, he closed his eyes and shook his head. Maria wanted things that were not part of what he planned for her, and she pushed the envelope continuously. She kept begging him to talk to Dr. Bob, but Stefano suspected why already. There was no way he would agree to her considering becoming male.

Absolutely not.

Not over his, or Andy's dead body.

MARIA TOOK A HANDFUL OF PILLS, drank from her glass, and set it down with a smack beside the bathroom sink. She pushed her bangs out of her eyes and studied her skin. Acne was now a bad memory, thank goodness. Still, she forever had to shave a specific part over her lips and chin despite the heavy drugs. She quickly took out a pink Gillette razor and scratched at the spots. Then pushed down on the large bottle of hand lotion and lathered the areas. She snapped two tissues out of the Kleenex box and carefully removed the cream off her face, tossing the soiled tissues into the basket on the floor.

She put away her toothbrush and toothpaste and slammed the medicine cabinet shut.

Quietly, she went back into her bedroom, picked up Myrtle her kitten, and kissed her on the head. Then she put the cat back down on her bed and picked up her little satchel. She stopped to look in the full-length mirror. She wore her favorite torn jeans and sweatshirt, looking quite sporty. Ambiguous. The way she liked it.

She left the room, hurried down the carpeted stairs, and went into the kitchen. Without a word, she picked up a thermos set there earlier by Andy from the kitchen table.

Alessandro came up into the kitchen from the family room and silently stood by.

Maria ignored him, went to her mother at the stove, and kissed her on the cheek. Then she turned and led Alessandro down the stairs through the family room.

Quietly, Alessandro struggled to put on his Reeboks. At the same time, Maria, keeping her balance and in her bare feet, slipped into her new bright blue sparkling Jellie sandals she'd been wearing despite the fact there was still snow on the ground. They both silently put on spring coats, zippers ripping the air.

The hinges of the door squeaked as Maria led Alessandro out of the house and down the wooden step to the garage. She shuffled through the remains of dry road salt, to the passenger side, stubbing her toe against the edge of the metal cover to the *caverna* for the thousandth time.

As she slid into the passenger seat, she looked through the garage window at the barn and thought back on the bomb that almost killed Alessandro, but was meant for her. Then she briefly thought of the blood that fed the bushes' roots across the road and on the front lawn and wondered if human blood was good fertilizer.

She looked over at the steering wheel and wished he'd let her drive. But she was continuously reminded by her father that Alessandro was not just a chauffeur but also a bodyguard. And if anything should happen while driving, Alessandro was the one who would know what to do.

She watched Alessandro stand and push the garage door opener. Her eyes lingered on his form as the band of light spilling into the garage through the opening doors widened and crept over his body. She blinked at the beautiful sight and looked away, pushing what feelings she had for him to the side. She shook her head and waited as he walked past the car to look outside, ensuring all was clear before he came back to the Cadillac.

Alessandro got in and started the engine.

He didn't even look at her.

She looked away to hide tears.

"HAVE YOU SPOKEN TO CRAIG LATELY?"

Maria stopped biting her nail and wiped at it with her other hand. She adjusted her little gold stud in her ear and shook her head. "He's in the hospital." She was worried for her dear friend. He had been dying of HIV, and there was virtually no anti-AIDS drug except for a drug called AZT. Craig was hooked up to an intravenous, but it made him very ill. It broke her heart.

"It's an epidemic of massive proportions," Dr. Bob said, "and we haven't seen the end of it, unfortunately. The numbers of dead are startling. Perhaps this new drug may help Craig. But you must be realistic. Since Rock Hudson and Liberace, they've been scrambling to no avail. I don't foresee any other outcome for your friend."

Maria wiped away a tear. "I can't even visit him."

"No, they're still not sure precisely how it's transmitted. Best to stay safe."

"But it's so unfair."

Dr. Bob sniffed and nervously kicked his foot in the air, sitting, as usual, relaxed with one leg over the worn arm. "All of this is unfair, I agree. Pope John Paul II visited Catholic AIDS patients, including two priests, in San Francisco, but he still won't hide the Church's moral revulsion against homosexuality. Even though many of its faithful, including hundreds of priests, have contracted AIDS. It will take a while before the Church is brought to its knees."

"We are so cruel to our own."

"You mean the human race or the Catholic Church?"

Maria nodded. "Both."

Dr. Bob lit a cigarette and twirled it. "Any news on Alessandro?"

"Yeah, he called my Dad. He wants a change."

"How do you feel about that?" Dr. Bob cocked his head.

Maria shrugged. "I'll miss him, I guess."

Dr. Bob studied Maria for a moment. He inhaled deeply and loudly as he swung his foot around and down on the floor. He adjusted his weight. "Maria, as I've pointed out to you before, I can easily discuss things with him. You say the word."

She shook her head. "No. I don't care anymore. I'm in no man's land. Literally."

"You are going on the belief that he sees you as a freak. Yet, you haven't told him everything. And you were going by one statement of his almost a year ago. I truly feel you may want to reconsider. He has proven himself to be quite an individual worthy of keeping in your life, in one form or another. Or part of your 'tribe,' as you like to call it."

"You're right. There isn't much of a tribe in Vindenza. He's about the whole of it."

"Toronto is actually the second largest gay community in the world. There's quite a support network there, but with this AIDS epidemic running rampant, I would advise you to wait regardless."

Wait. That's all she did, was wait. Maria was tired of waiting. "I want to go away somewhere. Where no one knows me."

"Well, Maria, we still have new options. However, before we do anything else, and before the opportunity disappears along with Alessandro's inevitable departure, I'd like for you to reconsider bringing him in for a talk. At the least, if he is to remain a friend, he should understand the complexities of your situation. You may need the extra support in the coming years."

For the hundredth time, she couldn't imagine what the coming years would be like. Besides, she still couldn't bring herself to exposing the entire lurid truth to Alessandro. Even though Dr. Bob made it all sound so logical and doable, she was still humbled by the fact that she walks around with a man's genitalia between her legs. She would rather die than let Alessandro know *that* sordid detail. Alessandro must never know. And because of that, he would never know her completely.

That fact closed the door on any hope for her and Alessandro.

"YOU CAN PUT THE MEAT THERE, MATTHEW."

Yvonne smiled at Stinky as he bent over Leonardus, wearing a miniature version of one of the new souvenir t-shirts Leo had someone design for the theme park.

"Don't you look cute in your new top," he muttered, smiling. He kept his balance by grabbing onto the blue padded Graco stroller. It had been specially designed with double-balloon wheels, manufactured for Leo and Yvonne, so that the stroller could be used for their walks along the beach.

Leonardus reached up with his little arms and tried to climb out.

"Oh, no, no, Leonardus. Stay." Stinky gently put the toddler's leg back in under the little padded railing across his front. He patted the child's curly head.

Leonardus looked up and grinned, slobbering.

"The chil' wants to run around."

Stinky looked at Yvonne stirring a massive steel pot of Gumbo on the industrial stove. He looked down at the turned-up nose, the hazel eyes. He was delighted with this beautiful boy. "Would you like me to watch him? I could take him for a stroll. He can watch his Daddy's big trucks at the water park."

Yvonne, clad in her blacks and in a large black apron, looked at the industrial clock over the doorway that led into the sumptuous interior of the newest restaurant. "Actually, that would be fine. He does love those trucks, some. A good time before his afternoon nap. Maybe he'll fall asleep on the way back. And the new cooks'll be here any minute for trainin'." She turned to Stinky and nodded. "If you don't mind. Ah'd like that, thank you, Honey."

Stinky smiled and lifted up Leonardus for a hug, and snuggled nose to nose.

Leonardus giggled and gently smacked both sides of Stinky's face with his little hands. Stinky grinned and gently put him back into the stroller. He grabbed the blue, padded handle. "Say bye-bye to Mommy," Stinky said to Leonardus, making a waving motion with his free hand.

Leonardus twisted to see his mother and did a little wave. "Bye bye."

Yvonne laughed heartily, wiped her manicured hands on her apron, and bent over her son. "Bye bye. You go with your nice Uncle Matthew."

Stinky straightened out and looked down at her large, auburn wig. He blinked and swallowed. Then he smiled again.

Yvonne turned to the butcher-paper wrapped package on the stainless-steel counter and loosened up the tape tabs. "Thank you, agin', Stinky for bringin' the meat."

"My heartfelt pleasure." Stinky turned the stroller around, leaned forward to push the door open, and pushed the stroller out into the sun.

"And no need to put the sunroof over him. He needs his Vitamin D."

Stinky allowed the door to shut behind him and looked at the manicured pathway that led to the main cobblestone laneway that wove through the various theme park buildings. He bent over and found a rattle tucked behind Leonardus and shook it before offering it to the tanned little hands that reached up. It went straight into Leonardus' mouth.

Stinky pushed the stroller along the cobblestones, and passed the busy games fairway. Families gathered around Grouper Fishing for Prizes, Toss the Ball, a gun range with prizes and a massive weigh scale where people had to guess weights for prizes. There was a Strength Tester, tall and colorful, lights blinking almost to the top with each swing of a massive, yellow hammer. People whooped, hollered, and laughed around them.

He continued past the Hit the Mole game, a basketball hoop game, and a sizeable open-door space full of the latest video games from which a cacophony of bells, whistles, and bangs emanated into the surrounding throng.

He continued, following a new sign saying, Water Park. It was going to open at the same time as the Time Share Resort scheduled for next month. He followed the Disney-like trimmed bushes—which he knew were a bugger to keep from drying up in the Carolina summer—and quickly stepped away when sprinklers popped up from below the ground.

He laughed when he saw spray over Leonardus' face. He took a tissue out from the pocket back of the stroller, and dabbed the child's face. "What happened here? Got wet?"

Leonardus made a face and shook his head. He grinned.

"Stinky."

Stinky shot up and looked around. His insides turned to ice.

One of the original trio. It'd been closer to a year since Stinky saw them last, trusting that what he had done for them was all they required of him.

"Remember me? Boomer? And Danny and Sean?" Boomer stopped and hiked his bulky jeans by his large Hell's Angel's belt buckle. Sean stepped toward the stroller.

Stinky pulled the stroller back protectively.

Boomer put up a hand as he lowered down to his haunches. "Hey, I'm not going to hurt this little fellow."

"Don't touch him," Stinky hissed. He looked around again. He bent over the stroller and pulled Leonardus out, hurting his legs in the process. Leonardus started to cry.

"Oh, he hurt you, did he? Poor little fellow," Boomer said, reaching out to touch Leonardus' cheek.

Stinky yanked Leonardus away and put a hand on the child's head. Leonardus, crying, struggled to look at Boomer.

"What do you want? I've done everything you told me. Everything works, right?"

Boomer nodded and squinted up in the sun. "Here, let's get into the shade over here." Boomer grabbed the stroller's padded handle and pulled it into the shade of a big theme park sign.

Stinky followed with Leonardus. He felt nauseous and wished they weren't on home territory. But then again, it was safer. But what if someone saw him talking to this man. He swallowed hard. "I said, what do you want?"

"Well, we have a little favor to ask. The Grand Opening is coming up." He tilted his double-chin and rubbed his five-o'clock shadow. He squinted to the side and rubbed his sideburn. "We have some meat for Yvonne. We understand she's making a special lunch for the *famiglia* when they come together." He chewed on his bottom lip as he studied Stinky.

Stinky swallowed. "Meat?"

"Yeah, you know. Like the meat you deliver every day for Yvonne's restaurant?"

Stinky almost had a heart attack. He fought back the panic rising in his throat. "I would die before I let you poison my friends."

"Your friends, as you call it?" Boomer reached up and scratched the back of his neck just under his scraggly ponytail. "Well, rest assured, we're not going to poison anyone. It's simply our gift of exotic meat to them for their grand celebration." Boomer reached out and clasped little Leonardus' arm, who cried anew.

When Boomer was satisfied with Stinky's palpable look of fear, he let go. He pulled a toothpick out from a little vest pocket in his leather jacket, and grinned as he chomped on it. He did a finger salute and turned, motioning Danny and Sean to follow.

Sickened, Sinky watched the men look up the lane, wait for a car to drive toward the arcade parking area, then sauntered across the cobblestones. Boomer turned and pointed at Stinky. "We'll let you know, when and where."

Stinky clung to Leonardus as his heart pounded in his chest. He whimpered under his breath. He turned and quickly, gently, tucked Leonardus back into the stroller. He held up the squeaky toy anew, but dropped it onto the child's little lap. He quickly turned to walk to a public phone near the entrance to the Park. He had to call his ex-wife right away, or he was going to go crazy with uncertainty about his own son.

CHAPTER TWENTY

May 1989

MARIA CRACKED HER KNUCKLES as she solemnly stared out at the green foliage of live oak and palm trees surrounding houses further inland. A thick haze hung over the city, part of which she suspected was all the dust they were churning up at the very back of the Theme Park. She could make out the top of the new water slide and resort, and she thought she could see the tops of colorful flags flapping in the wind.

As she grabbed the balustrade, she stepped through her balcony door to the railing, and looked at Ocean Boulevard below her. The railing felt dusty with grease and sand. She looked at her hands. She wiped her hands on her jeans and went back into her bedroom.

She left her room, glanced into her parents' master bedroom, then looked over at the far bedroom where Alessandro slept. The door was closed.

She looked into Claudia's room next to hers. "*Nonna?*" The room was empty; the bed was neatly made, and the room smelled like her *Nonna's* favorite perfume, Nina Ricci's *L'Air Du Temp Eau De Toilette* spray. In fact, the elegant spray bottle with the brushed-glass doves sat on the window ledge next to the sliding doors. A breeze blew the white elegant lace sheers into the room, like angels' arms beckoning to her.

She took a deep breath. She absolutely loved being back in Myrtle Beach and was looking forward to the Grand Opening in two days.

She turned and walked into the sun-drenched living room. Andy was making coffee in the kitchen under one of the skylights. Wordlessly,

Maria walked through the shafts of warm light from overhead and opened the sliding door onto the balcony. Here, the building was in the shade, the afternoon sun having already traveled to the other side. She had a lovely view of the ocean and a park. She looked with interest at another building under construction next door, a new hotel her father and Leo were building.

She looked to her right, and followed what sunny coastline she could see. Mist gently rolled in from loud, pounding surf. She saw couples walk hand-in-hand. Some walked with dogs. And she had to catch her breath when three horses rode by, followed by hovering seagulls.

Something grabbed her ankle. Maria jumped, kicking back her leg. "Ouch."

She looked down at Myrtle, her ginger cat.

Myrtle sat back on her haunches in the breeze and looked at her expectantly.

Maria bent down and took the cat inside, closing the door behind her. "You can't come out here. You might jump." She let Myrtle jump out of her arms onto the bamboo couch.

"I wish."

She turned to her mother. "Ma, please."

"The cat's not *that* stupid, Maria."

Maria watched her mother close the lid on the expensive Espresso machine, on the counter beside the double-width fridge.

Andy leaned against the marble island and picked up a fashion magazine. She quickly flipped pages.

Maria looked away. It occurred to her, not for the first time, that Myrtle Beach should have a Ferris wheel and a roller coaster right on the beach. Within walking distance for everyone. She had already shared the idea with *Zio* Leo, and he said he'd look into it, though he chuckled at the time.

Though only 16, she'd taken a close look at Myrtle Beach and what her father and *Zio* Leo had developed. She had asked if she could hang around them that day to watch. She wanted to learn how they solved problems and see how the workmen tackled jobs that seemed overwhelmingly difficult at first glance. Maria loved everything to do with the building of things.

But her father and Leo only nodded and treated her as if she were made of glass.

She fiddled with her medical bracelet. Sometimes, it left a black mark on the inside of her wrist. Usually, when her body had phantom menstrual syndromes.

Maria observed her mother's occupation with the magazine. She cupped her groin and readjusted her testicles. Sometimes, Maria forgot what she had down there. She rarely wore pants that would show her bulge, and never wore a bathing suit. She liked it best that way. But the jeans she wore were just a touch too tight.

She heard the front door open and slam closed. She heard Claudia, Alessandro, and Peter talking in the front hallway. She looked at her watch and saw it was later than she thought. Alessandro must have taken her *Nonna* shopping, and Peter probably smelled the coffee from across the hallway.

She, Andy, Claudia, and Alessandro had taken the red-eye with Peter and Sandra the night before. She remembered Claudia saying she needed to buy a new outfit for the Grand Opening. During their last visit to Myrtle Beach, Claudia discovered a little North Myrtle Beach dress shop. She raved about the quality of its clothing and shoes. There weren't many choices when you always wore black, but this little dress shop had the most thoughtful and elegant designs any widow could wear with pride.

Not wanting to face Alessandro, Maria hurried back into her bedroom and closed the door. She flopped onto her queen bed and looked at the stucco ceiling.

She heard the rustle of newspaper and the TV come to life.

There was a knock on the door. "Mariiiiiiiaaaaa." Is *Nonna*."

Maria covered her face. "I knooooooowwwwww. I heeeaaaar you."

"Come 'n have some breeeeaaakfaaaas."

Maria rolled off the bed and took one look in her mirror before opening the door.

"Hellooooooooo, Maria. *Bellissima nipotina*." Claudia's eyes sparkled. She had shrunk a little more in the last year. She was bent and almost had to look up at Maria from under her salt and pepper brows. She wasn't that old; only 68. But she was grey and, of course, always in black. But there she stood, in matching blouse and capris, with cork-heeled sandals.

"Wow, you look great, *Nonna.*"

Claudia smiled happily, turned, and motioned with her finger for Maria to follow.

"I'm coming," Maria said, following closely as they walked into the great room. Maria saw Alessandro having an espresso at the marble counter, slowly looking through Andy's fashion magazine.

He didn't look up as she passed him on her way to the living area.

Zio Peter was on the bamboo couch reading a newspaper. A shadow passed before the sun, and its rays through the skylights disappeared. The temperature in the condo dropped by a few degrees. The marble floors were almost too cold on her feet.

"Morning, *Zio*," Maria said softly as she looked at the skylights, and out the glass doors at the blue skies dotted with fluffy white clouds.

Sandra and her mother were having coffee out at the patio table on the balcony. Sandra was handing Andy a cigarette.

"Morning?" Peter looked at his watch. "It's afternoon."

Maria lifted up the top of the newspaper to read a headline or two. She let it go and looked at the TV by the glass doors. "What's on?" she asked.

"Oh, my favorite crime show," Peter said.

"Maria. I make'a you eggs' n toast," yelled Claudia, from the stove

"'K. I'll go say hi to *Zia.*"

"I call'a you."

Maria walked onto the balcony and saw her mother motion to Sandra to give her the lighter.

"Stay there, Maria, don't move. I don't want *Nonna* to see."

Maria had to stand still as her mother hid behind her, taking a long drag on the cigarette. She exhaled, and the smoke immediately snaked back into the condo. Maria watched it, glanced at *Nonna's* little back, and looked back at her mother. She rolled her eyes. "Can I move now?"

Andy motioned at her. "Yeah, you can. Sleep well?"

Maria nodded and squinted up at the sun. "It's beautiful today."

Andy sat back and looked around at the swaying palm trees, the blue ocean, and blue sky.

"We should be sitting on your goddamm balcony, Sandra. You've got the sun right now."

Sandra looked around the shady balcony. She took a drag of her cigarette, squinting against the smoke. "Well, it was here a moment ago."

Andy pushed her chair from the table and leaned back, closing her eyes. "Hm, I love the sound of the ocean. I wonder what the poor people are doing today?" She opened her eyes and looked at the sky. "Look at this paradise. I wonder what it's like back home right now."

Both Maria and Sandra said, "Shitty."

"Bad spring." Sandra put out her cigarette.

"I got a joke," said Andy.

"Oh, no," complained Sandra.

"Listen to this."

"Oh, Mom."

"So, this guy comes home drunk as a skunk, goes to bed with his wife, and bang, he has a heart attack and dies."

"Oh, dear." Sandra shook her head and smirked at Maria.

Maria rolled her eyes.

"Next thing he knows, he's at the pearly gates. This guy looks at St. Peter and says, 'I don't belong here.' And St. Peter says, 'Well, it's a one-way ticket regardless. You can't go back.' The guy says, 'Oh, come on. There's got to be something you can do. I just don't belong here.' So, St. Peter said, 'Well, there's one way. You can go back as a hen.' The guy thinks about this and decides there's no way he wants to die yet, so he says, 'Okay.' So, he comes back to earth as a hen and ends up in a chicken coop. It's paradise. The sun is shining, there's lots to eat, and beautiful green grass everywhere. He loves it. But then he feels a little unwell, with a stomach ache. He goes to the oldest hen and says, 'I have a gut ache. What's happening to me?' The old hen says, 'Well, dearie, hens lay eggs, you should know. I bet you've never laid an egg before. All you have to do is push hard.' So, the guy pushes hard and pop, out comes an egg. Then he has more pain, and out comes a second egg. He still has a gut ache. He says to the old hen, 'This is bullshit, there's no way I'm laying a third egg.' The old hen doesn't understand, either, but tells him the best course of action is just to push hard. So, the guy goes back to pushing and, wham. His wife wakes him up by slapping his face. She yells, 'Bobby, wake up. You've fucking shit the bed again.'"

Sandra went apoplectic. Even Maria had to bend over, she laughed so hard

"All right. That's enough. I really gotta get the guys out of bed. They really partied it up after we got here. They were down in the Jacuzzi till three a.m., and I could hear them a whole twenty floors up."

"Sound travels near water," Maria said, still laughing from her mother's joke. She flopped into a chair.

Without looking up, Andy drawled, "Maria, stop flopping into things like you're some orangutan."

"That wasn't me flopping. That was my wings flapping. I'm a friggin' hen and I'm about to poop three eggs."

"Maria."

Maria squinted at the beautiful sky, then over at the shoreline. She blinked at the beautiful view. She shook her head. "Paradise," she whispered. She looked around, smiling and, suddenly she was aware of their reflections in the sliding doors on the other side of the patio table. She stopped smiling and tilted her head at her own image, then fluffed up her short hair and watched the breeze blow a few tendrils up and down. There was movement in her line of sight on the other side of the glass inside the condo. Her eyes focused on Alessandro, who walked from the counter to *Zio* Jack on the couch.

Alessandro looked over at her and did a double-take.

She looked away.

They had fallen into a cold but comfortable rhythm. Alessandro had gone out on a date last month, and it totally shook her world. She didn't know how to react. But other than the one time, he was always around. Hovering. Watching. Hanging.

"Holy shit," Peter yelled.

Andy and Sandra pushed their chairs back and rushed through the door.

Maria stepped to the opening and looked in.

"Look." Jack pointed at the TV.

"Put the volume up," demanded Andy.

Peter picked up the remote and put up the volume.

Maria stepped in further. She saw Selena in a school photo. Then she saw mug shots of Selena's two brothers.

"Oh, cripes," Andy whispered as she shuffled back to a bamboo armchair. She sat down and covered her mouth.

Maria walked to Peter and squeezed in beside him and the arm of the couch. He shifted over. All anyone could hear now was the TV and the sizzling of eggs and bacon.

"Wha'?" asked Claudia.

Everyone turned and hissed at her.

> "Fact, fantasy, and history have come together to create a fascinating tale of intrigue. Was it drugs, or was it the Irish Mob, the IRA reaching from the homeland to whisk away three of its offspring? Last seen, Selena was on her way to a party. The brothers, Brian and Sean, were dropping her off and then planned to go out for a night on the town, and then to pick up their younger sister by eleven o'clock…"

"That's bullshit. Selena was hiding in that bush at two in the morning." Alessandro hiked up his dress pants and sat on the bamboo arm at the other end of the couch. He pointed at the TV. "Where'd they get such lies?"

Maria chewed on her thumbnail.

> "New evidence has shown that, in fact, Selena and her brothers did not go out to drop her off at a party. It was to a skating party with hot chocolate and Christmas lights and the brothers were to be chaperones for that night, as the neighborhood was known to be dangerous for violence and drugs."

"Bunch of crap. Where'd they get that from?" Peter laughed.

"It's not funny, *Zio* Pete."

"Of course, it is. It's a big fat joke. The writers on that show don't know what they're talking about. They just put up words on a billboard, and Robert Stack reads them off. Who writes this kind of shit?"

Maria's insides turned to icy water. "*Zio*. It's the same people who killed the rooster." She turned and stared wide-eyed at Alessandro.

He looked at her, frowning deeply.

"Oh shit," said Andy.

"Doesn't matter."

"The Sicilians. They aren't finished with us. They want another pound of flesh," said Sandra.

Alessandro stood up. "I'm going to find *Zio* Stefano."

"He's not here. He's at the park with Leo."

"Even if I have to walk there, I have to talk to him." He looked at Maria. "This isn't good news."

Maria stared at him. "The dead come to rise and torture us."

"Well, let's make sure they don't." Alessandro turned and walked toward the front hall.

"Wait, I'm coming," Maria yelled.

Peter whistled at them both. They turned around to face him. He threw keys at them. "Take our rental. It's a burgundy BMW."

"Thanks, *Zio*," yelled Maria as they hurried out the door.

Unbeknownst to everyone, Myrtle, the cat, discovered something enticing hanging from the back of the plaster floor lamp by the TV. She reached out a little white mitten and tested the little knob hanging at the end of a wire. She became more courageous and slapped it around and banged it against the back of the lampstand.

Andy stood up from the armchair and lunged toward the lampstand. "For cripes sake, cat, leave that alone." She shooed Myrtle away and did a double-take. She bent down and touched the listening device.

"Peter," she whispered over the noise of the TV. She slowly looked back at her brother-in-law.

Peter looked up and saw the fear on her face.

LEO AND STEPHANO LOOKED over a large drawing draped over one of the scratched, old desks they had in their trailer. The air conditioner barely lessened the heat as the sun pounded its rays onto the building's flat roof above their heads. They looked up through the nearest window as a burgundy BMW sailed in, churning up dust and dirt.

Leo took out his cigar. "Who the hell is that?"

"Is'a Pietro."

They both went back to looking at the drawing. "You see, there in the middle of the lake?" said Leo. "It's got to be at least twelve feet deep here in the center, and it's not. That affects the fish, and the bottom churns up every time a paddleboat goes across."

Alessandro barged in without knocking and stood looking wide-eyed at Stefano.

"*Zio*, something's come up."

"Maria?" Stefano whispered.

Alessandro shook his head. Then nodded.

Stefano straightened up and took a step toward him. He looked over and saw Maria standing by the car outside. He reached past Alessandro and opened the door wider.

"*Quello che e successa?*"

"Someone's playin' with us." Maria ran up to him.

"Mr. Giordani, everythin' all right?"

Stefano looked over at two men sitting on a picnic table nearby. One slowly stood up, his hand raised to his jacket pocket.

Stefano shook his head and raised his hand. "Is okay." He grabbed Maria and pulled her inside the trailer.

Alessandro moved to let them pass, and closed the door.

Stefano frowned, bent his head to look at the men at the picnic table, and leaned back against the desk. "Okay." He crossed his arms and feet. He felt old and worn in his torn plaid shirt, work pants, and chewed-up work boots.

Leo sat down at the desk and reached over for an ashtray. "So?"

"Who are those guys?" asked Alessandro.

"Bodyguards. Who do you think?"

Alessandro said. "We just saw photos of Selena and her brothers." He looked over at Maria and she at him. Then they both looked at the two older men.

"Selena?" asked Stefano.

"What's this about brothers?" demanded Leo.

"Dad, a TV show called Unsolved Mysteries just flashed their photos. We saw them. With our own eyes. They're reopening the case. The creepy part is they talked about the skating rink. Somehow, they made up some story about Selena going to a skating party. Her brothers were going to be chaperoning. They said all three disappeared on the same night."

"How would they know of the skating rink?"

"Exactly," said Alessandro. "I remember, though, standing and watching Maria skate around with Francesca in her wheelchair. A black car slowly drove by. I couldn't see who it was. They must have been the ones who killed your rooster."

Stefano's brain raced through all they had done to keep the peace with Nick Rizzuto and their collaboration in Montreal and with the West End Gang over their share of Myrtle Beach. What had they missed? Why did they care about a few thugs?"

"The Weasel," whispered Stefano.

"He's chicken shit," Leo said.

But Stefano wasn't so sure about that. He looked over at his daughter.

Maria's artery in the side of her neck pulsed as she stood staring at Alessandro. The vein looked on the verge of popping. When did his daughter get such a sinewy neck?

"So, we are here to ask what to do now?" Alessandro asked calmly.

Leo asked, "How's everyone at the condo?"

Alessandro shrugged. "Fine. Shocked. Frightened, I guess."

"Don't nobody go out today until Stef and I get back home. Dinner's at six. We'll be home by five. Got shit to do here for the Grand Opening." He got up and reached for the black rotary phone. "I'll give Stinky a call and tell him not to leave Yvonne and Leonardus' side, though she should be leaving for the restaurant pretty soon."

Stefano grabbed his wrist. With his other hand, he picked up the cell phone on his desk. He wiggled his head at Leo.

"Oh, thanks. I keep forgetting they can't tap cell phones."

"Yet," added Alessandro, cynically.

As Leo spoke on the phone with Stinky, Stefano motioned to Maria and Alessandro to come closer. "Did they'a show'a your picture, Maria?"

"No." Alessandro was quietly cautious. "Just Selena, Brian, and Sean."

They heard Leo slap the paper on top of the desk. "Okay. Thanks, Stinky. Only to the restaurant. Nowhere else."

Leo hung up and handed the cell phone to Stefano without pushing down the antenna. "Listen, guys, it sounds like it's something we can't really do anything about right now. Why don't you let your Dad and I finish what we're doin' here, and we can talk about it when we all get together tonight at Yvonne's restaurant? I got a nice booth that's almost soundproof. We can talk about anything there. No taps. But no going out in the meantime. How about that?"

They both nodded and turned to go. Alessandro opened the trailer door and let Maria go first. She looked over and waved. "Bye, Dad."

"*Ciao, bambina.*" Stefano smiled reassuringly. But when the door closed, he dropped his smile. Stefano stared at the closed door for a moment.

"You think that has anything to do with the same gang here who has been sabotaging us whenever they could?"

Stefano stood up straighter and tucked his shirt tails in. "Yup. I'a do."

"It's the shits when they get the kids involved. You wanna tell 'em tonight?"

"Nope'a. Is'a our secret."

"Good enough. So, let's get this sorted out, Stef. We have to get the plumbing in for the fountain by end of the day, but the lake has to be dug out, too." He waved his hands at the door. "That can wait." He stuck the cigar back into his mouth and lifted up the edge of the large drawing. "Now, where were we?"

Stefano stepped to his desk and sat in the wooden office chair on rusty wheels. He opened his bottom drawer and pulled out a framed photograph.

"Stef?"

"*Un momento,*" Stefano whispered as he studied Anita's image. Her beautiful face was framed by longer, blonde hair, and his two little boys looked just like Maria did at their age. It wasn't only on this coast he had to worry about the safety of loved ones. He feared whether their present threat stretched as far as Vancouver on the other side of the continent, to a family he viciously kept secret.

MARIA LOOKED OVER the familiar sight of Alessandro's profile. She looked out the window and wondered what they were going to do. *Zio* Leo was so cool about it. But for her, it felt like the end of the world. She thought of how they had to let Selena drown to death in her own blood, torn face and neck.

Alessandro shook his head, deep in thought.

"What?"

"Shit."

"What?"

"I can't leave with this shit going on."

"Leave?"

Alessandro raised a hand off the steering wheel, then dropped it. "Yeah. I told your Dad. I want to move on." He didn't look at Maria.

Maria, shocked, sat up straighter and faced the front to digest what he had said. She didn't care about Selena and her brothers. "You can't leave. Especially now."

Alessandro looked out his side window before staring out front again.

Maria was dumbfounded. "You're leaving me?"

His face was set.

She frowned. "Why?"

He glanced over. "It's been almost three years, Maria." His voice was dead.

"I don't care. Who gives a shit if it's three or twenty?"

Alessandro's mouth dropped. He looked at the sparse traffic and made the BMW do a quick U-turn on the highway. It settled into a dirt clearing on the other side of the road.

Maria frantically looked around at the other few cars speeding by.

Alessandro put the car in park and turned off the ignition. A cloud of swirling dust hovered and twirled around their vehicle. "Nowhere's safe, Maria. Absolutely nowhere."

Maria felt panic rise from her diaphragm. She raised a hand and covered the pit of her stomach as tears burned behind her eyes.

"I don't know why you're so upset. You haven't spoken to me in almost a year." He motioned between them, his face twisted. "This, here? This is the most we've spoken in a year. Did you know that?" His voice cracked.

Maria sunk into her seat. She bent her head down to stare at her fingernails. Her tongue played with her front teeth as she pondered the myriad of conflicting feelings rushing through her. Her balls itched, and yet her heart ached for Alessandro. She had to put the razor to a specific spot on her chin, yet she still wanted the feel of her lips on his. She agitatedly scratched at her left cheek, feeling sweat and grime scrape off into her fingernails.

"You're screwed up, you know that?

She angrily faced him. "I KNOW I'm screwed up. Everyone knows that."

He snorted and pointed at her body. "I don't mean this, Maria, whatever the hell this is. It's you." He angrily poked at his temple. "Up here. You're screwed up. I can't take the silence anymore. There's nothing left for me with you guys." He took a deep, rasping breath. His voice broke. "I can't take this shit anymore." He threw the door open and walked away from the car.

Maria, shocked, watched him for a moment, then frantically looked around. She saw the keys in the ignition. For a moment, she thought he'd simply stop to think, but he didn't. He continued walking along the highway. Very quickly.

She jumped out of the BMW and ran around the car and got into the driver's seat. She started the car and slammed the door shut. She opened the window wide as she went into gear. He was walking against traffic. How was she going to catch up?

It would be the first time she drove the car alone since getting her permit just months before. She put her head out the window. "Alessandro."

He didn't stop.

She turned with the traffic and looked for the first U-turn. She passed one before she realized it and had to drive another mile before reaching the next U-turn. Her tires squealed, almost colliding with an oncoming truck. It honked its horn as she swerved to get out of its way. She squinted at the opposite side of the highway, in the distance. *Was he there?*

She drove closer and past where they had stopped on the other side. She couldn't see any sign of Alessandro. She did a U-turn at the next opportunity and traced back to the clearing. She stopped the car and jumped out, searching the flat, undeveloped land around her. She couldn't see him.

An engine's roar caught her attention, and she turned in time to see an old, dark blue GMC pick-up truck race by. She shaded her eyes as she looked at it speeding away, then shifted on her feet and twirled. "Alessandro." She ran to the edge of the deep, dry grass. Thousands of grasshoppers exploded around her, and her eyes followed them up and around into the sky.

Like a plague—a portent of things yet to come.

CHAPTER TWENTY-ONE

PETER STOOD IMPATIENTLY AT THE END of the plush half-circle booth motioning at his wife to move over to Andy. "Come on, Sandra, shift those beautiful hips over. Andy's skinny. She doesn't need that much room."

Andy, tapping her fingers to the Zydeco music playing overheard, was already comfortably seated between Sandra and Claudia. She gave him the finger. "Speak for yourself, Pete. You don't have a damn tush. At least mine's perfect." She turned to Claudia. "Ma, can you move over more?"

Claudia looked to her left and down, to see how much space was between her and Leo.

Leo put his arm around Claudia. "Come on, Claudia, you're my sister-in-law. I won't bite." He pulled her closer with a grunt.

"Oh, thanks, Leo," said Andy. "Come on, fat ass. Come closer."

Sandra gave her a look. "Who are you calling a fat ass?"

"What, someone else here with an ass like yours?"

"Adriana, you'a drink too much'a." Claudia fussed with her little hands on the table.

"Ma, I had water. I'm always this rude."

"We need more chairs," said Maria.

"Just a sec, Hon," said her *Zia* Sandra, still trying to shift her hips.

On the other side of Leo, Stefano looked over at Maria. She was sullen, pale, and her eyes were ringed and red. He reached for the linen napkin in front of him on the cloth-covered table and quietly contemplated Alessandro. Maria was afraid Alessandro would never come back. Stefano knew Alessandro just needed some space. He told

Maria, if Alessandro felt he had to go, they had to let him go. There was nothing she could do about it.

He had been intrigued by her reaction.

After being so cool with Alessandro for so long, she did a complete turn-around. She didn't want him to go.

He grabbed a breadstick from the glass holder in the middle of the table and snapped it in half. Leo called, "Suzie. Suzie. We need chairs."

In her late forties, Suzie looked over from where she was taking an order from a couple sitting in a two-seater. She nodded and smiled and took a moment to finish her order.

It wasn't fast enough for Leo. "Stef, ask the guys behind you to bring over a chair to put in front of the table, will ya?"

Stefano looked over the wall separating them from the next booth. "Hey," he said.

A man's voice answered. "Yeah, Mr. Giordani?"

"Leo wan' a couple of chairs, please."

"Will do, Mr. Giordani."

Maria motioned to the booth. "I could probably squeeze in by *Nonna*."

"No stay. I'll get out, too. I get nervous sitting beside beautiful women," Peter muttered. Peter got up and motioned for Maria to stay put. He looked down at Maria. "Make that two chairs."

"Two chairs," yelled Stefano.

"No," growled Leo. "Three."

"Three," yelled Stefano.

Two men approached with three extra chairs.

"Thanks, there, eh…"

"Sammy, Mr. Giordani. Remember?" Sammy smiled and bowed.

Leo pointed to the other man. "And you remember Frankie?"

Frankie placed two chairs side by side, and waved.

Stefano stared at them suspiciously. They were relatively new. In light of the TV program and the pile of listening devices his family found in their condos that afternoon, everyone was a suspect. Especially new guys.

He looked over at Maria who he saw, had the same suspicion.

He looked at Sammy again and saw him studying his daughter. People always did that with Maria.

"We saw you and that young guy earlier today. Remember?" Sammy said to Maria. "We were sitting on the picnic table outside the trailer?"

"You guys are bodyguards?" asked Maria.

"Yes, ma'am," smiled Frankie. Frankie looked to be in his late twenties. A little older than Alessandro.

Leo interrupted. "Okay, enough of that. Let me introduce you to my *famiglia*." Leo started to give introductions all around. The two men politely nodded their heads and shook hands.

Suzie, hurried over with an arm full of menus.

"Okay, you guys, get the screen," Leo ordered the men.

"Screen?" Andy asked.

"Wait till you see what Leo does when you want privacy." Peter pointed to the side where the guys were going into a hallway near the kitchen. Within a moment, they returned carrying a portion of a wall and attached plants. They carefully moved it between the other tables. They positioned it behind Peter, and Maria.

Maria looked at the plants that appeared attached to the screen. She reached out and touched one. "Silk," she said.

Peter, next to her, also touched the silk plant. "Oh, yeah."

Stefano looked at his brother. He had slowly regained his muscle tone since prison but still didn't look his dapper self.

"Wow," said Andy. "It's amazing how cozy it feels here. Like we're not in a fish bowl anymore. Even our voices seem softer."

"Precisely. I didn't want open booths, but Yvonne insisted." Leo picked up a menu, scratched his bald head, then dropped the menu on the table. "This offers some privacy. I had it designed for precisely this reason. So, we can talk. But look." He pointed at the screen. "It's made so that I can see through it at the front door, but no one can see through it from the other side."

Andy leaned sideways through where Leo was looking. "Oh, yeah."

Leo motioned at his two guys who were still looming. "Thanks, guys."

Frankie and Sammy nodded and went back to the next booth.

"Hey, Suzie, how's Yvonne doin' in the kitchen?" Leo called.

"Oh, she's fine. She's busy throwin' that beautiful eatin' together."

"Good, tell her we're all here. She wanted me to give her heads up."

"Fine, shall I take your drink orders now?" she asked.

Stefano listened as everyone ordered drinks from their menus. He grimaced when he heard Andy order two double-vodka martinis. She was going to get drunk. Understandable, he thought.

"Maria?" asked Suzie.

"I'll have a Scarlet O'Hara, please."

Stefano watched as Maria sadly looked at the menu.

He got up from the end of the booth and stood by Peter sitting next to Maria. He motioned to the other empty chair, waited for his brother to get up, then sat down beside his daughter. He patted her on her knee, then looked past her, out the restaurant's large windows. He wondered if Alessandro would still show up to join them. He saw a delivery truck pull up, and drive along the newly-hedged and trimmed drive. Through the young palm trees planted in front of the restaurant, he watched it disappear around to the back.

He heard Leo in the background. "Sammy, a delivery just came in. Go help Yvonne."

Sammy struggled out of the next booth. Then, from behind the screen, Stefano clearly saw Sammy go through the front door, adjust his tie flapping in the hot breeze, and walk along the new front walk toward the back.

He stared at the cobble-stone road in front of the restaurant and out at the distant highway. He looked down at his watch, sighed, then quietly studied his menu.

INSIDE THE HOT KITCHEN, fans roared over fryers and a sizzling stovetop. Off to the side, an enormous air conditioner struggled with uneven blasts of cooler air, its rumble joining in with the orchestra of sounds. Food hissed and bubbled in hot oil, waiters rang bells, a dish crashed to the floor, the sudden whoosh of the ongoing dish-washers as it erupted with another load; happy chatter of cooks and dishwasher chatting over the chaos—all contributed to that familiar feeling Stinky had grown to love.

"Yvonne, your Leo's here with the family. He told me to tell you."

Stinky watched Yvonne smile at Suzie at the ordering counter. "Won'erful, that's fine. Thank you, Suzie." Yvonne turned back to the deep fryer. She gave a side glance at Stinky, who stood closest to the outside doors, in the sweltering heat, holding Leonardus.

In his bulky diaper, Leonardus, stripped down to a simple sailor's shirt, sat comfortably in Stinky's arms, chewing on a plastic ring. Stinky looked down at him and smiled, so pleased that the child sat so contentedly in his arms, quietly watching all the activity in the kitchen.

But Stinky was screaming inside. He was told they'd found several listening devices in the three condos. Everyone knew it was a significant part of his job to do a continual routine sweep, but no one had taken him to task about it. Not yet, anyhow.

Stinky's eyes traveled over to the butcher-paper wrapped parcel he had just delivered. It sat on the stainless-steel island. One edge of it showed a seepage of watery blood. He blinked. What was in there? Why did Boomer give him this package? What trouble was it going to bring to the family? They did a lousy job, if they were trying to pass it off as the usual goat meat package; it was larger, messier. Not beautifully-wrapped as it usually is.

"You hungry, Stinky?"

Stinky jumped. He took a deep breath, tried to control his beating heart, and smiled. "No, thank you, Miss Yvonne; I've eaten enough already today. Thank you."

She eyed him up and down. "Hmmm, well, ah think you can take on more meat on those bones if ya ast me." She went back to dredging fish on the large stainless-steel counter. She hummed to herself. Then, she stopped dredging the fish and stared at him for a moment.

He looked back at her, his eyes widening. He couldn't help but look over at the package of meat.

"Stinky, ah think you're not well. Maybe you should go to the condo n' rest. Call the doctor' n get yourself in there."

Stinky gently lowered Leonardus into his stroller. He brushed away flour on the front of his suit. "No, but maybe I'll excuse myself for a moment. Leonardus could use a nap, and maybe I'll have one at the same time. As you say."

She nodded as she finished dredging, and placed the fish onto a platter. "Okay. Good idea." She looked over at the package of meat and frowned. "That's one big goat," she announced.

Stinky eyed the walk-in cooler. "Shouldn't I put it in the cooler?"

Yvonne shook her head. "No, I'm putting some of it up for stew right after this. It's okay there, though they made a mess of the paper. Look how it's leaking?" She leaned toward the package and sniffed, then looked at the little puddle on the floor. "Sure doesn't smell like the usual goat. Must be one old guy." She turned to Stinky. "You can mention that to the butcher next time." She wiped her hands on her flour and fish-crusted apron. "Anyhow, let me say g'bye."

She walked to the stroller and bent down. She lovingly held her son's chin. "Love you, child. You are a gift from Heaven, did you know that?" She smiled sweetly at her son before straightening up and adjusting her heavy bosom under the front of her apron. "And you, too, Stinky. You are also a gift from Heaven."

Stinky choked, and tears welled in his eyes.

Yvonne frowned. "Oh, now. Stinky. Don't be sad. We love you very much. Ah don't know what ah'd do without you."

Stinky looked away, his heart beating like wings of a dove fleeing the grip of an eagle's claws. He wavered a moment as he grabbed at the stroller for balance.

Yvonne placed a gentle, floured hand on his shoulder. "You, okay, Honey?"

Stinky blinked back tears and nodded. He turned and gently pushed the stroller to the back-kitchen door. He bent forward to open the heavy door.

Leonardus leaned over, looked back, and waved. "Bye bye."

"Bye-bye," she whispered, and blew a kiss.

Leonardus blew a kiss on his little hand and smiled.

Hefty Sammy appeared at the doorway in front of Stinky and the stroller. Stinky jumped.

"Where do you want this crate of grapes, Miss Yvonne?" asked Sammy, a giant compared to slim Stinky. Sammy eyed Stinky as he tried to maneuvere the stroller past him at the door.

"You bring that crate of grapes right over heah. Leave the rest in the walk-in, if you don't mind, Sammy," Yvonne yelled over the noise of the fan.

Stinky pushed the stroller away from the doorway toward Yvonne's van, heard the door click shut behind him, and put the key into the lock and opened the sweltering car. He couldn't wait to get somewhere to think. Somewhere far away. In fact, he wished he could just disappear.

But he couldn't.

There was too much love he still had to spend in his life.

He looked down at Leonardus choking back tears.

"CAN WE TALK about Selena and her brothers?"

Leo leaned over the table and pointed at Maria with his cigar. "Listen, Maria. Let your old *Zio* Leo tell you something." He looked around the table and the restaurant. "When you find yourself in a position where you can't help but have to knock someone off, you don't refer to their names. You follow me? Ever."

Maria looked intrigued.

"Not that you're going to make a habit of knocking people off, right?" Andy pointed at her, making a bad joke.

"I just want to understand what *Zio* Leo is telling me."

"It's time she learned a few things, Andy. Otherwise, she'd go nuts."

Andy sat back and looked at Sandra, then at her mother. "Ma, you okay?"

Claudia nodded. "*Si*, I wanna rum 'n coke'a."

"Ma, we already ordered it."

"Oh, *Si?*"

"*Si*." Andy threw up her hands suddenly, as Suzie came with a platter of drinks. "Here's your rum and coke, Ma."

Suzie put drinks down on one end of the table, then walked around behind the half wall and put the remainder of them at the other end. She smiled, nodded, and left quickly.

Leo raised his Pina Colada. "To *famiglia'* n to my beautiful Yvonne."
Everyone toasted noisily and happily. "To *famiglia,* to Yvonne."
Leo slurped his drink. He slammed the glass down and raised his hands. "Get rid of those menus. Get rid of 'em."
Everybody looked at him curiously as they passed them along toward Leo. Leo collected them all. He handed them blindly over the separating wall to Frankie who took the menus wordlessly.
"Yvonne has a special dinner lined up for you. It's too bad Alessandro's not here. Who knows why. He's got his reasons. And Willie's missing it, but he'll fly in later tonight. But we'll do this again in the next two weeks, right?" He looked around, grinning, and rubbed his hands together. He looked up and saw more people come in. "See that? This place has been filled every single night since we opened." He grinned. "So, let's talk business." He folded his arms in front of him and leaned over the table.
Everyone leaned toward him.
"As you know, when you wanna grow big, there's always some rot you come across. So, we've had to deal with a few cockroaches that have come out of the rotten woodwork." He pointed at the family. "You all know what I mean."
"Not everything, Leo," offered Andy. She looked over at Stefano.
Stefano looked steadily back at her.
"Andy, you don't wanna know everything. You'd shit your pants. Us," Leo lowered his voice, as he pointed at himself and Stefano, "us, and Stinky, 'n Frankie, 'n Sammy, and a whole bunch of other guys you'll never meet—well, we know how to handle these things. I just want you to know that the condos are completely secure. Once you're on the twentieth floor, you guys are totally safe. As safe as if you were in Alcatraz."
"Bad comparison," said Andy.
"Yeah, but it's true, Andy. We're okay."
"What about the listening devices we found this morning?"
"Listen. We have a lot of loyal guys who would put their lives down for us. For you. And these things, you found? They don't hurt us. What can they hear? Stef and I, we talk business at the trailer. In the condos, they hear the dishwasher, TV, and what the ladies talk

about. What shoes they bought. Where to get their hair done. Who gives a shit?"

Peter looked over at Stefano.

Stefano shrugged and nodded.

"But how did they get there in the first place?"

"Maybe Alessandro knows something," Maria offered.

Everyone looked around the table.

Claudia looked up. "Alessandro no here," she announced.

"Yeah, we know, Ma," said Andy, rolling her eyes.

Sandra looked over at Maria. "It's not normal for him to be gone this long. Especially not calling us to let us know what's up." Sandra looked at Andy with grave concern. "He knew we were coming here. Yvonne's worked hard for this dinner."

Andy looked at her. She was resting on her elbows.

Leo had his cigar going. He snapped his fingers. "Frankie, go get me an ashtray."

Frankie popped his head over the barrier. "Sir, there's no smoking."

"It's my goddamn restaurant. And I'm not smoking. It's just a cigar."

Andy guffawed.

Stefano chuckled and shook his head.

Everyone waited for Frankie to hurry over with a saucer and hand it to Leo.

Leo looked at it with disdain. "I ask for an ashtray, and I get this?" He pointed at the dish with his unlit cigar.

"I'm sorry, boss. I'll go ask Yvonne."

"No, the hell you will. She'll say no."

"Wait," Sandra said. She dug into her mandarin orange, soft leather purse and took out a small bean bag contraption with a bright lime green metal top. She handed it to Leo.

"What's this?"

"It's a portable ashtray with a little fan. Here." Sandra put the ashtray in front of Leo and showed how the metal top pushed open. She turned it on, and it made a funny whirring sound.

"Shit." He grabbed it. "That'll do." He sat back, lit his cigar, and puffed at it like a steam engine. "The kid's a nice looking young man." He tapped the end of his cigar on the edge of the little ashtray. It bounced around under pressure. "Maybe he found a nice girl."

Maria sat staring at her hands. "He doesn't want to be here anymore," she announced.

"Don't be silly. He loves it here. We're his family." Andy looked at Maria, perturbed. "He's like a son to us."

Stefano looked around the table and thought of secrets; secrets they shared, secrets they didn't share. He looked at Andy. He never used to share secrets of the *famiglia*. Still, once danger reached their own home, it was impossible to keep *everything* a secret.

He knew Leo kept everything from Yvonne. He had watched Leo play the part of a good, decent, kind man with an amazingly acute business sense. Yvonne adored and worshipped him. Stefano half-closed his eyes, already grieving the day that would change. It was inevitable. He accepted that inevitability and tucked it into his heart, ready for the day Leo would need him. The day what little was left of Leo's heart would break.

"We should get him one of those stupid beepers," said Sandra. "My god, I have one. I don't know how to do our business without it." Her beeper went off. She laughed and looked down. "See what I mean? All I have to do is call whoever beeps me now." She went to get up.

"You can't call someone now, Sandra." Peter motioned to everyone.

"Peter. It's the funeral home. I have to." She motioned to Leo.

Leo motioned for her to go.

Sandra held out her hand toward Peter.

Peter looked up, then slowly pulled out his cell phone and handed it to her.

Stefano blinked. "Where is'a cell phone for Alessandro?"

"Yeah, did you try calling him?" Andy piped up.

"He left it in the car," Maria said sadly.

"A personal beeper on his belt would've done the trick." Sandra looked around. "In fact, we should all have a beeper. Especially now."

Peter looked at his wife hovering by the table. He motioned for her to go. "Go and call. See what's up."

Sandra nodded and walked to the front of the restaurant, and pushed the glass doors open. Almost everyone watched her stop at the front, pull out the antenna, and dial. She tucked it into her shoulder as she pulled out her cigarettes.

Leo squinted at Stefano through the smoke. "You and Peter go find him when we finish Yvonne's special meal."

"Can I come?"

Stefano looked at his daughter. Then at Leo.

Leo nodded.

Stefano nodded.

Maria looked over at Leo. "*Zio* Leo, do you think he's safe?"

With the tip of his cigar, Leo played with the ash in the little ashtray. He looked up briefly, as Sandra came back through the front doors. "I never worry unless there is somethin' to worry about." With that, he squished his cigar into the little ashtray, until it was almost pulp, overflowing its tiny bowl.

YVONNE PLACED THE DREDGED FISH into sizzling stainless-steel pans and stuck them one by one into the massive ovens. She turned and grabbed at a clump of grapes.

Something heavy flopped from between the bunches.

Yvonne stood back to look at what landed at her feet.

A hefty, hairy spider, the size of her palm, struggled onto its feet on the floor.

A BLOOD-CURDLING SCREAM shook everyone at the table. Everyone looked toward the kitchen.

"Yvonne!" yelled Leo.

All the men jumped out of their seats and rushed to the kitchen. Stefano, Peter, Sammy, and Frankie took out guns, as they tried to outrun each other. Seeing all the men and weapons being pulled, surrounding restaurant patrons jumped to their feet in shock.

Some, also, pulled out their guns.

A family with children screamed and noisily scrambled out of the restaurant.

YVONNE FRANTICALLY hefted her body onto the stainless-steel counter, knocking pots and pans off the overhead hooks, accidentally shoving the large bundle of meat to the side. Her breast heaved as she twisted her hips in the little puddle of blood, accidentally knocking the bundle of meat further off the island.

It fell with a thud on top of the massive spider.

She looked down, searching for the beast. She saw its front legs reaching out from underneath the bulky package. Her eyes widened as she saw the spider struggle into view and face her, looking upwards.

She screamed again.

Leo led the large brigade of armed men into the kitchen, with guns pointed in all directions.

"Yvonne!"

Yvonne ogled wide-eyed from her perch. She was desperately trying to stand up on the counter, but knocked the whole potholder from the ceiling. "Sweet Jesus," she screamed, as she tried to push the contraption away from her head and shoulders, but her arms were intertwined with the contraption. She pointed to the ground with a long pink fingernail.

Leo led some of the men around the island to look.

Stefano led the rest of the men around the other side.

Leo looked down and saw the beast climbing on top of the bundle. He gasped, jumped back, and screamed.

Stefano screamed and shot at the spider.

Leo took the gun from Sammy and shot it into the floor.

A series of shots immediately followed, obliterating the spider, the bottom of the cupboard doors, the bundle of meat, and the floor beneath.

Acrid smoke hung in the kitchen, setting off an ear-splitting, mind-numbing smoke alarm, and the overhead water sprinklers jumped into action.

As the smoke cleared in the mist of water spray, everyone gingerly shuffled closer to where the spider once had been trying to mind its own business.

They saw thick spider legs almost hidden within the shredded butcher paper.

Stefano reached out with his grime-covered, dripping shoe and nudged at the legs to make sure the spider was dead. Dust scraped off the digits, and water from the sprinklers cleaned them off.

They were not spider legs. These were fingers from a human hand. And the human hand was at the end of a forearm, sticking out of the butcher paper. What was left of the spider was twitching nearby.

Yvonne, eyes popping, screamed, and fainted. Slowly, she toppled onto her side, then, with a large grunt, rolled off the stainless-steel island onto the shredded bundle, arm, and dead spider.

Leo's eyes widened at the sight of his beautiful, dust-covered wife being rained upon. She lay slumped into a wet heap; her wig having fallen off, and looking like a drowned rat.

His face paled under the grime and dirt. He turned, waved his arms like a madman at everyone, slipped on the flooded kitchen floor, and fell on his behind.

"Shit," he yelled. "The alarm's connected to the police and fire department. Everybody. Get her out of there. We got shit to clean up."

PETER'S BMW PULLED UP TO A GAS STATION STORE. It was raining heavily, soaking everything. He turned the ignition off and looked at Stefano, whose face still showed grime and streaks from their debacle at the restaurant. "I'll ask these guys, so you don't have to get wet."

Stefano laughed. "I'm a still'a wet from da restaurant."

Maria leaned forward. "Alessandro and I didn't stop here. How would they know anything?"

Peter turned to face her. "Someone may have seen him walk by. Maybe he stopped to buy a drink."

Maria looked back at the highway. They were about a mile away from where they stopped the car by the grassy field.

"Maria, you stay'a. We go." Stefano opened his door.

They hurried out of the car and ran into the store.

PETER AND STEFANO entered the store. It appeared empty. Peter looked down at a newspaper stand to the right and pulled out a New York Times. He dug in his pocket for change, and studied it.

He shook his head. "I always mix Canadian and American coins." He looked at a young man behind the counter glass. "'You don't take Canadian coins?"

"No sir, we do not," said the man. He was in his late thirties, skinny, hollow-eyed.

"Stef, you got change?"

Stef dug in his jean pockets and pulled out his flattened, curved bill-fold. He opened it and pulled out a twenty.

"You got no change?" asked Peter.

Stef shook his head. "No."

"You okay with a twenty?"

The man nodded.

Stefano walked up to the window and handed over the twenty. Peter came over and stood close to Stefano, to look through the window. "Say, you know me? Right? I'm here getting gas and the papers all the time."

The man hesitated, then nodded.

"You remember some young man comin' by here earlier today? A scar across his cheek here. Nice-looking kid."

The man hesitated, then shook his head. "No."

They turned away. Peter motioned as he walked to the door. "Thanks."

"You forgot your change, sir."

Stefano said, "Keep'a da change."

IT WAS MIDNIGHT. Leo, Peter, and Stefano sat at Leo's dining room table. The lights were turned off, except for the hood over the stove and the low hanging dining room chandelier. Leo smoked his cigar.

"How, Yvonne?"

"They're holding her just for the night. She'll come home in the morning."

"Who's taking care of Leonardus?"

"Claudia and Andy," Stefano said.

"Maria's pretty upset."

Stefano nodded. "Lots'a going on."

"Did she say what happened with her and Alessandro?"

"Dey fight." Stefano made a face and shrugged.

"I don't know, Stef." Peter tapped his thumb on the surface of the table while his other hand clutched a sweating highball. "I can't shake the feeling he's in trouble."

Stefano stretched his legs to the side, his ribcage against the edge of the table. He had a glass of *grappa* in his hands and rolled it between his meaty hands. "*Si*. Something happened'a. *Qualcosa non ha odore giusto*."

"What's the latest?" Leo winced as he moved, having bruised himself in the fall on the kitchen floor at the restaurant.

"We have a couple of the guys asking in the streets tonight. We should find something. Maybe by morning."

"I told Stinky we're going to have a talk tomorrow around noon. You guys be there." Leo looked grim.

"You know, it could be the cleaning staff," Peter said.

Leo shook his head and blew smoke toward the dark skylights in the vaulted ceiling.

Stefano's dry, burning eyes followed the ascent of the smoke. He blinked and saw stars through the skylight, and wondered what the next day would bring. He hoped all would be sorted out by the Grand Opening, the last phase of their long, arduous push in completing their dynasty. He was looking forward to relaxing, going home, taking Luna out for a moose hunt. He missed the feel of the earth in his hands while he worked in his fields. He missed his sheep and goats. He missed home.

He prayed that all would settle down the next day.

CHAPTER TWENTY-TWO

"LISTEN TO THIS."

Reading the morning paper, Peter sat at his usual spot on the bamboo couch. He turned to Sandra sitting on a stool beside Andy, both in their dressing gowns, having coffee at the kitchen island. "Babe, where are my reading glasses?"

Sandra looked around, slid off the stool, and flopped over to the front hall. She dug into a jacket hanging off a fancy white and weathered-copper coat hook and retrieved Nickle and Dime Store reading glasses from one of the pockets.

She flopped back to Peter.

Peter, without looking up, held out his hand and took the glasses.

Everyone heard a knock at the front door and a clatter before Maria, still in her felt red-plaid pajama pants and black t-shirt, came in scratching her short hair. She yawned. She shook under the physical strain and blinked at Andy and Sandra.

They both focussed on Peter. She looked over at Peter. "What's going on?"

"The paper," Andy said.

Maria spied the coffee machine behind her mother on the counter. She hurried over and grabbed a turquoise ceramic mug, and lifted the coffee pot. It had that satisfying gurgling sound as it poured into the large mug.

Peter snapped the newspaper into position and strained through his reading glasses.

"Last night, in Horry County, Myrtle Beach Police rushed to a popular Myrtle Beach restaurant in response to a kitchen fire alarm. *Yvonne's*, purportedly owned by Myrtle Beach's Yvonne Mangione, is a favorite amongst those who enjoy authentic Southern cooking. There was great damage to the kitchen and part of the main eating area but no person was hurt. Patrons state they thought they heard gun shots and some say they heard screams. Statements taken at the site say that the gunfire did not represent a dispute but was sparked by the sight of an unusually large spider not native to Myrtle Beach. It had apparently stowed within clusters of grapes brought in bulk from a local market.

The spider did not survive the onslaught of bullets. Neither, apparently, did the kitchen floor. The restaurant will be closed until further notice. However, Yvonne does have another opening of a second restaurant, *Southern Exposure*, also in the Myrtle Beach Paradise Park. Tomorrow is the advertised Grand Opening of the Myrtle Beach Time Share Resort and Water Park, apparently the last phase of the massive tourist attraction of Myrtle Beach Paradise Park. Mayor Robert Grissom, will be present to cut the ceremonial tape."

Maria tapped her spoon against the edge of her mug. "Nice. Free advertising."

"Shit, what a hoot," laughed Peter.

"Poor Yvonne," said Sandra. She lifted her coffee cup to her lips.

"But still, spiders aren't good for business, are they?" Maria asked. She walked over to the glass doors to look at the ocean's horizon.

"Not big friggin' dinosaur spiders." Andy picked at her teeth.

"Of course, it is. It's great for business. They'll never forget it." Peter watched Andy.

Sandra held up a finger. "Well, it would've been bad if they found that severed arm."

Peter grunted at Sandra and shook his head.

"Oh, shit. I did it again," muttered Sandra, covering her mouth.

Maria almost choked. "What severed arm?"

Andy put her mug down. "What severed arm, Sandra?"

Maria came closer to her mother, and stood in the middle of the room staring at her with fear, the almost mid-day sun pouring onto her head through the skylights.

Andy lowered her head and sighed. "Maria, no."

"Alessandro," she croaked. "The severed arm Yvonne got."

Andy shook her head. "No."

Peter looked over. "Oops."

Andy slowly put her mug down, and looked at Maria with great concern. "Shit."

Sandra got off her stool and hurried over to Maria. "Maria, it was not Alessandro. It was an older, gruffer man with red arm hair." She looked beseechingly at Maria.

Maria wavered, then fell against Sandra's shoulders.

Sandra patted her back. After a moment, she stood back. Maria covered her face and shook her head. "Unbelievable." She dropped her hands and sadly looked over at the basket full of listening devices they collected, sitting by the TV. She went over, and lifted one up.

"I wonder how long they were here?" Andy muttered. Suddenly, she turned, motioning Sandra for a cigarette from the menthol package next to her on the counter.

Sandra picked up the cigarettes and pulled one out for Andy.

Andy grabbed it, and motioned for the lighter.

Sandra turned and got the lighter. "It had to have been in this condo at least the first time we saw that show. You know, the one you like so much, Peter."

Peter picked up the paper again, then dropped it. He rubbed his chin as he thought carefully. "Good point."

"Unsolved Mysteries?" asked Andy.

"Not here, Andy," reminded Peter.

"Shit." Andy took her mug and hurried to the glass doors, opened them, and held the cigarette out in the open air. The ocean breeze blew smoke back in. "Shit."

"You know, this thing about Selena and her brothers on that show really bothers me," Peter said. "We must have already been bugged the night we saw it for the first time. Or just before. What I would like to understand is, how did they get that thing produced? You know? The script, the production end. I mean, how long does it take to tape a show and actually put it up on air? I mean, on air at a time they KNEW we would be watching?"

"Scary," Sandra whispered.

Maria looked at Peter, thoughtfully. Then, over at her mother at the glass doors. She walked up to her mother and stood beside her, softly waving away cigarette smoke. She looked at the white fluffy frill along the edge of the new patio umbrella dance gaily in the ocean breeze.

A seagull landed on the railing on the other side of the umbrella. It stretched and looked sideways at her and Andy. Then, it did a bobbing dance with its head.

"More important, who put those goddamn spy things all over the place? In our homes, even," Andy said, pounding her chest.

"And how'd they get past Stinky all this time?" Sandra frowned, looking at her husband.

Peter's eyebrows went up as a silent, heavy question. "Yes. That is the million-dollar question, isn't it?" He looked at his watch. "And that's precisely what we're going to find out today. Stinky's coming over to your place at noon."

Andy nodded silently.

"So, what time did Alessandro come back last night?"

"That's just it, Peter. He didn't. That's why Maria thought it might be Alessandro nicely bundled for stew."

"Oh."

"Men. Cotton in their ears."

"My mind was elsewhere."

Maria looked over at Andy, then at Sandra. "It's definitely not him, Sandra?"

"It's definitely *not* him."

Maria stood wavering, holding her cup. She looked away and out toward the ocean. She touched the glass, then looked down past the railing, searching what she could of the park and parking lot below.

A cigarette butt flew through the glass opening past Maria's ear. The seagull seeing its arc, flew away in pursuit.

"Mom, don't do that. That could start a fire."

Andy made an apologetic face.

"You better jump after it."

Andy looked at her daughter and smirked. "Cheeky." She walked out onto the balcony and looked down. She turned to her daughter. "That's a drop. That butt's dead by the time it hit the ground."

"What if it blew into someone's condo?"

Andy threw up her hands. "Would you please shut up about it, Maria? What do you want, a pound of flesh?"

"Ooooooooooo," said Peter.

Andy waved him away as she went back into the living room.

Maria's eyes widened. "Alessandro wouldn't put those things in, would he?" Maria wondered aloud.

"Put what in?" asked Peter.

Maria turned and shrugged, pointing at the basket.

"Him? Nah. Give the guy a break. That man's a saint. You should know him by now."

"I thought I knew him."

"Ah, come on. He would never do such a thing."

"Well, neither would Stinky." Sandra blinked at her husband.

"Well, yeah. If you ask me, both of those guys are way beyond suspicion." He pointed at Maria. "And you should give Alessandro a break. It's not a bad thing he's on his own for a bit."

"Peter, he's supposed to be looking after us."

"Yeah, but he knows this place is like Fort Knox and, while we're here, you have a choice of bodyguards. In fact, you saw Sammy sitting out there in the lobby. You walked right past him."

"Yeah, I know."

"Well, you can go without him for a day."

"What if I don't want to."

Peter slapped the newspaper back onto the glass coffee table. "What's the matter?"

Maria stammered, "I mean, what if something happened to him?"

"Nothing happened to him, Maria. He'll be all right. He'll be back before you know it, getting in your hair again." He got up and walked to the front hall.

"Where are you goin'?" demanded Andy.

"To your condo to see Stef. Which is where I think you live though I see you here more often than not. It must be my beautiful personality you can't get enough of."

"Oh, yeah? Dream on, baby. It's Sandra's coffee."

"My coffee? You have that industrial grade espresso coffee machine Yvonne got you."

"I like your machine better," Andy quipped, shaking her brilliant red hair at Sandra. Andy looked healthy, having gotten a little bit of a tan on her face the day before.

"Well, you ladies stay here. I'm going to see if Leo and Stinky are there yet. We're going to figure out our own Unexplained Mystery."

ALESSANDRO GROANED. He gagged. He felt like he was going to vomit. He shifted his head, but the movement made him wince in pain.

He thought perhaps he'd had a nightmare. He willed himself to wake up because something didn't feel quite right in Dawson City.

A hand grabbed his hair and pulled his head back. He opened his eyes. Or at least as open as they could get. "Wha?"

"Shut up."

The hand let go of his head and pushed it forward. He fell over. He tried to raise his hands to break the fall, but couldn't. His wrists were bound by something. He looked down and saw duct tape around his torso, pinning his arms toward his back.

Shit, he thought in alarm. *Oh, God.*

Something scraped along the ground. Then there was no sound for a few seconds. In the short lull, he heard the surf. In fact, he could feel the vibrations of crashing waves on shore, through the floor below them.

Was he still in Myrtle Beach? North Myrtle Beach? Or an entirely different State? North Carolina?

Someone coughed and spat.

Alessandro became aware of three individuals: One shuffling behind him, one spitting off to the side, and one sitting on a creaky chair in front of him. He heard wheezing. Heavy breathing. He smelled cigarette smoke.

"No, *rimani qui*."

He knew enough Italian to understand. Someone told someone to stay. Sicilians?

"So, we got some fancy schmancy pants here, huh? Open your eyes. Look at me."

His neck wouldn't respond to his thoughts. It took a moment to find the muscles and slowly Alessandro raised his head and peered out from under his cut eyebrows.

As a young boy, Jorge, his father, always taught him the best thing to do if you were ever caught was to say nothing and to wait for your captors to give themselves away. Who the captors were; where they were congregating; what they wanted; and how they wanted it, were all important things to know. And the knowing gave one a sense of control. He was to learn how they clicked; what was important to them; and, then, figure out how to escape. You had to look and act cool, or, depending on their personalities, do your best to act frightened, so they would drop their guard. It was a nerve-rattling game. A game he thought he'd never end up playing. But here it was. He was playing the game.

"Nothin' t'a say?"

Alessandro studied the man in front of him. He was pudgy, in a striped gold shirt, with a gold chain, a gold pinky ring, and a gold tooth.

Sicilian. Soldier.

"We thought you'd like to get to know us. I'm Benny. This is Boomer."

Alessandro tried to look to the side and see the other man.

"We got a proposition for you, pretty boy."

"What kind of proposition?" Alessandro licked his dry, cracked lips.

Boomer chuckled. Then, he bent down so that Alessandro could see his face better. He was a big, hefty, blond. Side burns. Big jovial blue eyes and freckled. Ponytail.

Irish West End Gang or Hell's Angels, thought Alessandro.

Boomer grinned. "Got somethin' going' with that freak of Stefano Giordani's?"

Careful. Careful. Alessandro dropped his head.

"Nothin' to say? I thought you'd have all sorts of stories. You know. What it's like to fuck someone with a vagina and a dick."

"Yeah," laughed Benny. "She must have a *pene* like this, huh?" He motioned with his wiggling pinky.

Shit. Alessandro felt anger welling up. He felt his blood pressure vibrate the fragile bones in his temples. He felt hot tears of fear building behind his sore eyes.

"That's okay. We know you 'n her aren't doin' it. You see," and Benny got very close to his face, "we know everythin'"

"Everything?" He winced. How the heck would they know anything? The condo was safe, the cars were safe. They can't possibly know anything. Unless…

"I see it. You're thinkin', how do these guys know anything? Huh?" Alessandro looked at him.

"Come over here," Benny motioned to the person behind Alessandro.

"You said—," the man started.

"The hell with what I said. I said nothin'. I want this guy to see how we got into this so-called powerful protected *famiglia*. Why we know everything about 'em. And what we heard last night." Benny grinned as he focused on Alessandro, "Got someone very, very upset back home." The guy waved at him, and sat proudly back in his chair. He tapped his finger and chewed his lip as he grinned. He motioned at the man behind Alessandro.

Alessandro went to twist back but Boomer punched him in the side of his head. He hissed through his clenched teeth. He felt panic begin to rise.

"You told me no one would get hurt. You were just going to listen—," the man behind him said tearfully.

Alessandro knew that voice. He angrily mustered all his strength to turn his body. He shifted and winced and look up behind him.

Stinky. *It was Stinky.* "Fuck, shit. You traitor," screamed Alessandro.

Benny kicked his head from behind.

Stinky jumped forward and bent over him, ignoring the blood splattered onto his pants. He held his shaking hands protectively over Alessandro's body. "Stop."

Alessandro looked at the creases in Stinky's pants. He knew very well that Yvonne pressed Stinky's pants with her own hands.

"Yvonne trusted you, you bastard." Alessandro tried to spit at his feet.

Stinky sadly stared down at Alessandro.

"What did you do to Stinky to make him do this?" he asked, keeping his eyes on Stinky's face. He read remorse in that face. Pain. They had something over him, he could feel it.

"Nothing. It's what we said we were going to do to people he loves that upset him a little." He turned to Stinky. "Isn't that so? You remember what we did, Stinky? To show you we meant business?"

Stinky shifted on his feet but didn't say anything. He tearfully stared at the ground. His face muscles twitched.

"Tell him," he yelled. Benny pulled out a knife and held it threateningly at Stinky.

Stinky put his hands up in response.

"Tell him."

"I," Stinky stuttered and gulped. "I saw them take one of Leo's work guys and dump him in here. Here," he shakily pointed to a spot in front of Alessandro.

Alessandro looked down. A dark, stained spot.

"Here, I saw them rip the guy in pieces."

Alessandro thought he was going to lose his bowels.

"Tell him what we did with the pieces."

"They took the pieces and butchered them and…"

"Finish it."

"And they wrapped him up in butcher paper and…"

Benny struggled to his feet and aimed the knife's edge to Alessandro's face. The tip almost touched his scar.

Stinky broke down and cried like a woman.

"Finish it."

"Uh, then I had to bring the package to Yvonne's." He sobbed into his hand.

Benny looked at his watch. "All right, asshole. You better get going, otherwise they're goin' to put two and two together."

Stinky looked down at his blood splattered pants. Then he raised his lanky arms and let them drop, surrendering. "They should already know by now." He shrugged. "They probably already put two and two together and good ol' Stinky did it." Stinky looked up, his face twisted with grief. "They know I did it." He pounded his chest. "They know."

"So, what do you think they'll do to you?"

Stinky stood rocking with each heartbeat.

"Go, Stinky," Benny said.

Stinky stepped away.

Alessandro struggled to turn his body and bite Stinky's ankle but missed. He gave up and lay where he was, and waited to catch his breath. He listened to Stinky's feet shuffle along what sounded like cement dust on cement.

All of a sudden, Alessandro's bladder went. He hadn't even felt the urge come close. He closed his eyes. *Shit. Some tough guy.*

"Some tough guy," laughed Benny. "Look at that, huh? He pissed his pants. Pick him up, Boomer."

Boomer yanked him, but couldn't pick him up.

Benny struggled out of the chair and, with a huff, also bent down. The two men raised Alessandro to his feet. They dragged him back to a plastic patio chair where Stinky had stood. Alessandro plopped into it and eyed the wet puddle next to the dark one. It occurred to him that the human race was disgusting. Frighteningly disgusting.

Benny leaned forward again into his face, grinning. "I love it, when we have a job to do." His brown eyes narrowed. He stood back and looked at his watch again. "You might as well relax, Alessandro. We got time. Close your eyes, if you want. Get some beauty sleep. Your job doesn't start till tomorrow."

Alessandro looked at him, then over at Boomer.

Boomer pulled out a package of Camel cigarettes and took one out. He lit it with a match and stuck it in his mouth. Alessandro watched Boomer lift his hand to take the cigarette out of his mouth and exhale long and slow. His hand didn't shake. Boomer was cool. Confident. Alessandro could tell he'd seen death too many times to think about it twice. Here was a man who felt immortal. Dead end for Alessandro. So, he decided he would go the frightened route.

"Wha'? What do you want from me?"

"Well, it ain't what we want from you. It's what we're goin' to use you for." Benny paused to see the effect his words had on Alessandro. He scratched his thick, bushy eyebrow.

Alessandro saw dandruff.

"Fuck you..." yelled Stinky from very far away, before they heard a metal door slam hard, the harsh sound echoing through the desserted hall.

Alessandro spat and coughed. "You fucking asshole. You fucking pervert."

"Don't worry. I think you'll live a little longer than Stinky. He didn't look too good. Cause he knew, right Boomer?"

Boomer took out a box of Chiclet's and popped some in his mouth as he kept a grip on the cigarette in the corner of his lips. He chewed and smiled. "Yeah, I don't think either of the three *Zios* will let him live after this."

"You gotta watch out for that *Zio* Stefano, though. He's the quiet one. He's the more dangerous, don't you know? At least, I have come to believe that the quiet ones are the ones who are really in charge. They keep a level head. Nothing fazes them. But one thing will, right? You catching my drift?" Benny bent forward and kicked Alessandro's foot. "You follow me?"

Maria. "No," Alessandro lied.

Benny looked at Boomer. "He's not reading me."

Boomer grinned. "Yes, he do."

"Hey, you wanna know somethin'?" Benny looked excitedly at Alessandro.

Alessandro shook his head, pretending to be frightened and overwhelmed.

"Human flesh tastes like goat meat. Did you know that? What a coincidence, Boomer. Did you know that Yvonne's famous restaurant serves goat meat?"

Boomer chewed noisily. "Really?"

Alessandro was so repulsed his guts released vile water.

"NOW I'M NOT SAYIN' THAT WE THINK IT'S YOU, STINKY," said Leo. "But we have to figure this out. You know that?"

Stinky stood shaking in Stefano's front hallway, facing Stefano, Peter and Leo.

Leo eyed the blood stain on Stinky's pants. "We just want to figure out what happened," he added.

Stinky was about to open his mouth when something grating and nerve-shattering slashed the air around them.

There was a wail from the floor at the opening of the hallway into the main living area.

All four men looked down to see Maria's cat, Myrtle.

Leo watched Myrtle hug the ground, wailing as if she was a little fire engine.

"*Santa Maria*," whispered Leo.

"Hey," Stefano said. He reached out and stepped toward the cat.

Myrtle hissed, then catapulted back into the apartment. They heard a smash and bang. A light fell over and crashed somewhere inside. Then Myrtle reappeared and stared at Stinky, her eyes completely dilated. She hissed again and an unnerving grating growl threatening to erupt.

"The cat's giving me the creeps, Stef," Leo said.

Peter grabbed Stefano's elbow and pulled him toward the front door.

Myrtle slunk down and followed. She hissed again.

Leo opened the heavy door. "Let's go to my place. This is giving me the creeps. We can't talk like this."

The men followed Leo out of Stefano's front hallway. Stefano closed the door behind them and followed the others through the quiet, sumptuous lobby.

Sammy, reading a magazine beside the side table and large urn, stood up.

Leo eyed the loose sound device they had found in the urn. He hadn't bothered taking it away. He wanted to remind everyone of the massive and dangerous intrusion into their fortress.

He gave Sammy a warning look.

Sammy folded the magazine in his large paws, glanced sideways at the little device, and looked down.

Leo opened his front door.
Peter grabbed Stinky's elbow and directed him inside
Stefano followed and closed the door.

LEO CLOSED THE GLASS DOOR but left it slightly ajar, allowing the ocean breeze to be sucked through the crack. He walked onto the balcony.

He had checked Yvonne earlier. He was pleased to see she was snoring heavily in a sedative-induced sleep. She had been given pain killers, as well, and he knew she was going to have a dilly of a bruise. He hoped she would be fine for the Grand Opening the next day. His heart mellowed at the sight of her. But he had business to attend to.

Now, standing on the balcony, looking at Stinky, he acknowledged he had a heck of a sticky problem to solve. How was he going to persuade her there was no hand and arm in that package of meat? Would he be able to make her believe it was her fear-induced imagination?

Just another series of lies.

He looked at his watch. He was grateful Andy, Sandra, and Maria were out walking Leonardus along the beach somewhere. Thank goodness for the *famiglia*.

Leo stepped past everyone and looked down from the balcony at a low-lying mist. He could see nothing beyond the mist, though the sounds of surf and voices and traffic were clear, magically coming from nowhere.

He turned and motioned to the patio chairs on the balcony and took one himself. He sat on a white resin armchair with turquoise cushions. He was surprised to see that Stinky remained standing.

"Sinky, have a seat. Relax."

Stinky pulled a chair toward him. He sunk into the cushions as he kept his eyes on Leo.

Leo pulled out a lighter to relight his cigar. He squinted into the bright haze. He felt reasonably confident that no one would disturb them on the balcony; the condo below belonged to a Saudi Arabian who insisted on buying all three condos on that level. He had several wives and many children, and used his unit three weeks of the year. They were not home.

"So, let's start again, Stinky."

"SO WHAT'YA GOIN' TO WEAR?"

Maria looked at her *Zia* Sandra. She shook her head and shrugged as she pushed her bangs out of her tearing eyes.

Sandra reached over and put it on Maria's shoulder. "I would love to take you and dress you. Can't I do that? Will you let me, Maria?"

Maria looked at her aunt, who continued walking with her left hand next to Andy's on the stroller's handle. Genuine concern etched on Sandra's sunburned face.

Maria, sad, smiled.

Andy said, "She already has something. Alessandro helped choose it."

"I'm not wearing no dress."

"You'll never change her, Sandra. She marches to her own drum."

"Mom's right. So, leave me alone."

"Well, the big day is tomorrow. We should look respectable. No torn jeans."

"I know that. Give me some credit."

Andy looked at Maria's torn jeans. "Uh-huh."

Maria pushed her mother to the side. "Let me." She took the handle of the stroller.

"Fill your boots," Andy said, stepping to the side. She stopped, took off her beige sandals, and wandered to the water's edge to watch ripples of water stop at her toes.

Sandra and Maria stopped and waited.

Maria looked over the mist-covered waters. Within a hundred yards or so, she saw dolphins waltz up and into the rolling waves. "Look." She pointed.

Sandra looked and smiled.

Andy looked and shook her head in wonder.

Leonardus made a happy squeal, and Maria bent down to look at him. He saw the dolphins. She pointed them out and smiled. "Dolphins, Leonardus. They're called dolphins."

"Dadda," Leonardus said.

Maria laughed. She looked at their condo building disappear into the mist. The sun above shone through brilliantly. She wondered if heaven was made of such brilliant pure mist filled with intense light.

She closed her eyes and inhaled the moist, crisp air. She wanted to memorize the sounds and smells of the moment. Tears welled up as she, once again, worried about Alessandro.

Andy cut through her thoughts. "Don't worry, he'll show up."

Maria looked at her mother, and tears ran down her cheeks. She wiped them away, but only in time for more to fall.

Andy put her arms around Maria.

Surprised, Maria allowed herself to relax. She snuggled into her mother's neck, realizing she had rarely been this close to her. But it still, strangely, felt like home.

"Love you, Ma."

"Me, too, kiddo."

Andy stepped back and wiped at her nose. "Right. Should we get back? Even over rotting seaweed, I can still smell Leonardus needs a change."

"FIRST OF ALL, I'm not saying you did anything wrong."

Stinky watched Leo tap his cigar over the balustrade. The ash disappeared into the sky.

Leo looked grave. "But it was your job to sweep all three places and the lobby every day, Stinky. You know that."

Stinky looked at Leo sideways, with nostrils flared.

Leo turned to Peter. "You said you talked about that show for the first-time last year?"

Peter nodded. His eyes flickered at Stinky, and Stinky caught the movement.

What were they all thinking?

He glanced at Stefano who rubbed his eyes and sighed noisily before settling back into the cushions. Stefano interlaced his fingers and seemed to be content with just listening, leaving the conversation's direction up to Leo.

Like he always did.

Stinky eyed him. Then he looked at Peter. He couldn't read anything in Peter, other than curiosity; concern. The jury was still out, it appeared. How was he going to explain how it all developed?

"And this show about Selena and her brothers meant they knew you always watch the show when you're here," Leo continued, talking to Peter. He turned back to Stinky. "They knew he would watch it." Leo looked ponderously at Peter as he continued talking to Stinky. "That represents about a year of being tapped. Probably. Right?"

Peter nodded.

Stinky looked down at a tiny spot of blood right on the center of the crease on his thighs. He thought of Yvonne.

"I did it," Stinky croaked.

Leo straightened up in his chair.

Stefano leaned menacingly forward, shifting his body, rustling against the canvas of the cushions.

"You did what, Stinky?" Leo said. Stinky saw a glimpse of the man he first knew. The one who strung him up, hit him, tortured him, jested him. He opened his mouth and then closed it.

"Stinky. Tell us. What exactly did you do?" Peter said.

Stinky swallowed hard. His throat was dry. He looked at Leo. "I put them in."

Leo's eyes hardened. "*You* put them in? You fucking bastard." His voice was low but clear. "You fucking, despicable traitor." Leo's mouth hardened. His eyes looked old, tired, watery. "You shithead of humanity. We took you in, fed you."

Stinky snapped. "No, Yvonne took me in. *She* cared for me. She fed me." Stinky angrily looked at Peter and Stefano, and tried to read their minds. What was the threat here? He remembered Stefano smashing shells into his mouth and down his throat. It was hard to remember why he ended up living with these men. He blinked against the mounting heat in his eyes.

Leo pushed back his chair and stepped up to Stinky.

Stinky looked at Leo before slowly pushing himself up off the arms of the chair. He placed his lanky legs to the side of the chair and leaned against the balustrade on his side.

Leo walked past the chair and stood chest to chest with him, staring menacingly into Stinky's eyes.

Stinky's body shook with shock as Leo bellowed in his face.

"You fucking nigger. You stand there and tell me that all this time you deceived *me*? You deceived *all* of us?"

"Did'a you know about the meat?" Stefano asked.

Leo snapped his eyes at Stinky. "You took that meat knowing Yvonne was going to open it up and see that shit?"

Stinky, frightened, looked into Leo's eyes. They appeared to turn black, even as he watched. He turned and pressed his back against the balcony railing, aware of a sudden point of no return.

No return.

Stinky sneered and finally spoke up. "You son-of-a-bitch." He pushed Leo with his chest, forcing him to keep his balance. "Don't' call me a fucking nigger. Nobody calls me that, you fucking wop."

YVONNE STIRRED, in a sleepy haze. She slowly became aware of a bothersome roar through the bedroom, the whine of ocean breeze being siphoned through a crack somewhere. She groaned as she raised a hand and touched her burning forehead. Then, she covered her eyes as she remembered the fiasco of the day before. She remembered that terrible monster of a spider. But she also seemed to recall human remains in the bundle of meat. Or was that her imagination? It had to be. Where the hell did she get that impression?

In pain, she slowly lifted herself into a sitting position, swinging her legs over the side. She pushed aside the bedsheets and comforter and placed her feet on the sheepskin beside the bed. She slowly stood up, straightened out her two-piece outfit, and looked over at the bedroom doors. They were closed. She walked to the bathroom, to check the sliding doors. They were latched.

She briefly looked into the wall-sized mirror, and studied her short-cropped afro and wiped old mascara under one lid. But that damn noise, it kept whining.

She sighed and went to find what window or door was left open.

LEO STOOD GLARING AT STINKY.

Stinky glared back. He spat off to the side and sneered at Leo. "You have no goddamn right touching that beautiful black sister of mine." He raised his thin arm toward the apartment. "The thought of you touching her makes me sick, man. It just makes me want to puke." He pointed at Leo's head, its ring of grey hair waving around in the ocean breeze.

Leo cocked his head. "Sister of yours? That's my wife, you're talkin' about. She's no goddamn sister of yours." Leo looked as if he threatened to grab Stinky.

Stinky lifted his hands. "Don't you dare touch me, you bastard. You will NOT lift another finger against me."

"Stef, what's he talkin' about?" asked Peter.

Stinky looked over and saw Stefano look pointedly at Peter.

Peter looked at Stinky, then Leo. He blinked and appeared to shrink in size.

Stinky could tell Peter was struggling. But he watched, patiently, as Peter built up the courage to ask what he knew he was going to ask.

"*Zio*, what does he mean, *lift another finger*?"

"Shut up, Peter."

"*Zio*. I'm sorry. But I am confused. What has he done?"

"I didn't do a thing. I didn't ask for this," Stinky spat.

Peter looked questioningly at Leo. Then at Stinky. "I don't understand. How'd you get to be part of all this?" Peter motioned with his hands between the three of them.

"It means that he fucking grabbed me off the street. I was working for the Gang, Peter."

"The Gang?"

"Yeah, Canadians. Like you. Selling smack and everything else anybody wanted." He pounded his the chest. "I was mindin' my own business. My own fucking business." Stinky's voice cracked under strain. "And these guys," he motioned at Stefano and Leo as his face collapsed in grief, "these guys came and threw me into a van. They tortured me. They beat me. They threatened to kill me." He dared look at Leo. He looked sideways at Peter, again. Stinky pursed his lips angrily while a tear dribbled down his trembling cheek, drying immediately in the ocean breeze.

Movement in the living room caught his eye. He looked past Leo and focused on something burgundy moving behind his own reflection in the glass. He realized it was Yvonne walking to the door. He straightened up and groaned and his heart twisted; he didn't want to hurt that beautiful creature. Facing Leo, Stefano and Peter was one thing. But to have to admit his terrible sins to Yvonne was an impossible feat.

He turned to Peter. "Tell that beautiful woman I love her and thank her for everything she ever did for me. And ask her to take care of my boy."

With that, he lifted his leg, pushed off his chair, and vaulted himself backward over the railing.

LEO TOOK OUT HIS SOGGY CIGAR, dropped it, and wiped his mouth. "Shit, I didn't mean for that to happen."

"Oops," said Peter.

They stood dumbfounded, staring at where Stinky just stood.

"Did you know he had a son?" asked Peter, turning to Stefano.

Stefano shook his head and shrugged, looking perplexed.

Yvonne screamed from inside the living room. She screamed again. Leo, standing in shock, turned to see her frantically yank at the door.

He threw open the door and reached for her.

She jumped back away from him and fell against the glass coffee table. The glass slipped off its cement shell base and shattered under her. She continued to scream as Leo jumped on her, attempting to calm her down. "Shhhh, shhh, shhh, *Bella*. Shhh."

Yvonne screamed and bellowed.

Leo, desperately grabbed a cushion and put it over her face, trying to keep her quiet.

She screamed more, now with heart-rending fear, as she fought off the pillow and Leo on top of her.

DISTANT SCREAMS CAUGHT MARIA'S ATTENTION, and she looked up into the mist in time to see a shadow fall through the fog, through the tops of the palm trees, and land with a dull thud somewhere below. She looked wide-eyed at Sandra and Andy.

They, in turn, looked from the mist-covered palm trees to Maria.

Maria bolted, hearing her mother call for her to come back. She struggled to run in the deep sand, falling onto her palms twice. Her leg muscles burned under the effort of scrambling through the soft dunes to reach the sandy grass of the little park between their condo and the building next door. She heard cats meowing as she hurried to where she thought she saw something fall.

She stopped. Cats came out of nowhere and gathered in bushes under the clump of palm trees. She saw a few people coming in from the parking lot, also looking around on the ground.

She hurried over to the bushes, hoping to beat them.

She fell on her hands and knees only to land close to Stinky's head. Cats milled around him, one or two sitting on his chest.

She quickly pushed away the torn fronds. Black oozed from under his body and head onto the torn palm fronds beneath him, and his right arm had snapped, the bones protruding through his suit sleeve. But his face was as if he were still alive, except for his eyes. They bulged out of their sockets, the dark brown irises staring up into the luminescent mist.

Maria slowly stood up and looked around. Andy and Sandra were almost near.

"Mom, give me the blanket. Quick."

Andy saw people coming closer, bent down, dug into the back of the stroller, and ran to her with the blanket.

Maria threw the flannel over Stinky's head and turned in time to face people reaching them.

"Go away, don't worry. We got this. We have a cell phone. We'll call 911," yelled Andy.

Sandra dipped into the back pouch and pulled out the cell phone. She pulled up the antenna and dialed.

PETER'S CELL PHONE RANG.

He stood frozen, staring at nothing, shocked.

Stefano pulled Peter's cell phone out of his back pocket.

"*Si*," he muttered coldly.

"WHAT THE FUCK, STEF."

Sandra cried, turning away from the scene, shaking the cell phone in one hand as she pushed the stroller with the other. She looked up through the mist. "What the hell happened?!"

"STAY AND KEEP PEOPLE AWAY. We send someone."

Stefano hung up and redialed. "Body in the park next to us. You'll see the people. Come with the sirens." He hung up.

He took out his handkerchief and slowly wiped down the railing, the chair Stinky sat in, and the glass doors. Then he went in and looked at Leo, who was soothing Yvonne.

Stefano angrily turned to Peter. "Pietro."

Peter, in shock, looked in from the balcony.

Stefano motioned for him to come in.

Peter came in. Stefano shut the door with a slam. "Come." He grabbed Peter's arm. Together, they took Leo away from Yvonne and bent down to lift Yvonne. They grunted and struggled through the shattered glass to the white couch, and lay her on the cushions. Yvonne had lost her voice but still moaned and cried.

Stefano looked over to see Leo struggle to his feet and hurry to Yvonne's side. His hands were bleeding.

"Shhh, *Bella*. I'm here. Shhhh." Leo leaned on the couch, leaving bloody fingerprints on the white material.

Yvonne's face twisted. "Matthew. Why did Matthew jump? Leo, why did Matthew jump? Oh poor baby. Stefano, tell me, why did he jump?"

Stefano stood back. It was time for another sedative. "Peter, get the needle."

CHAPTER TWENTY-THREE

ALESSANDRO HAD SENT A NOTE.

Frankie had run from his post at the front of the building and hurried Maria, Andy, and Sandra away from the scene, as two of their men ran out from the neighboring building to stand guard over Stinky.

The stroller bounced on its balloon wheels as they rushed to the front doors. There were too many people around near the side. Maria could hear sirens in the distance.

Frankie opened the glass doors for them and pulled out his cell phone. He dialed, and the others rushed through the lobby to the private elevator.

"We're on our way back up," Frankie yelled into the phone. He hung up and motioned for the women to come closer. His eyes searched the lobby and the circular drive outside of the building.

Sandra cried and pulled Leonardus out of the stroller. She held him tightly.

Leonardus whimpered, frightened. He started to cry.

Andy in shock, reached out to comfort Leonardus. "Shit," she muttered.

"Oh, Maria." Frankie looked into his wrinkled jacket and pulled out a slip of paper. He motioned outside. "Someone was dropping this off just as I heard screaming."

Confused, Maria zeroed in on the paper in Frankie's hand. She reached out calmly, and took it. "Who dropped it off?"

Frankie shrugged. "Looked like a mailman."

Maria looked down at the paper just as the elevator door rang open. She opened it as she let herself be hustled in with the others by Frankie.

She heard him talk into the phone again. "They're on their way up."

As the doors to the elevator closed, she read the note.

Dear Maria,

Don't worry. I'll be there tomorrow.

Alessandro

MARIA STOOD AT THEIR DININGROOM PATIO DOORS looking south over the beach and as far into the ocean as she could see. She looked closer to shore and saw dolphins waltzing in the waves. There were more of them today, and she wondered if they were the same ones from the day before, innocently playing, blissfully unaware of what the human race was doing to itself, just a short distance away on land.

She looked down at the note she was holding. She had looked at the handwriting. It didn't look quite like Alessandro's. And yet, she believed it was from him. Why wouldn't it be? She thought of Alessandro's face and his hair. How he stood while waiting for her, always patient, always kind. She remembered how, the year before, the first time she stood in the water and saw fins, she had scrambled out of the surf yelling, *shark*. She smiled at the memory of Alessandro, who also didn't know the fins belonged to dolphins, had run to her and grabbed and clung to her as he hurried her through the deep sand.

As if a shark would go that far on land.

She chuckled at the memory. Then she thought of how it was always Alessandro who got to her first whenever he thought something was wrong. She thought of the bomb and how close he came to death. She thought of how he put himself in danger with Selena and her brothers. He was always ready to take a bullet, if he had to. She thought back on how terrible she was with him as he tutored her.

He never complained. Only cautioned her. Tried to make her understand that she and her mother and Claudia were his sole responsibility.

She knew he would feel terrible once he heard what had happened to Stinky. How he dove off the balcony. Things might have been different if he had been there. She didn't know how. But things were always better with him around.

Alessandro.

She closed her eyes. She tried to remember why she was so upset with him. She thought back on what he said on set when they met Craig Russell. How he called him a queer.

They all seem to be like that...

She reached out and touched the glass in front of her. Perhaps, it wasn't an indication of any deep prejudice. Maybe, it was his culture speaking. *Their* culture; a complicated culture indeed, in which lines were clearly marked in the sand. Women did things, and men did things.

Everyone knew what was expected of them, except Maria.

Nowhere in the proverbial *'Ndrina* handbook did it refer to what she and her family had to face. No references to sacrificing gender-vague children. No guidelines as to how to protect them from others. No rules that said, *do not harm a hair on any that appear to be different from the norm.*

She now believed in her heart that Alessandro did not mean any malice. He had never shown any signs of NOT accepting differences in people. And indeed, he would be sensitive to her and her feelings.

She knew, for a fact, he knew enough, that she was born a hermaphrodite. Indeed, he must realize the tsunami of complications that come with such a birth?

What if he ever had a child such as she? Wouldn't he understand that, at least, the child is a human being, and did not ask for what it was born with?

Maybe it was the whole Craig Russell effect he referred to in his humiliation. The overwhelming disorientation that affected each one of them on set. She, her mother, and Alessandro were naïve. They'd never been on a movie set, never mind see a homosexual in the flesh; it appeared Alessandro had never known of one in Venezuela, either. Indeed, not personally. And to see a man pretending so beautifully, so unsettlingly, to be Mae West.

Craig shouldn't have licked his face; she knew. The overtly sexual gesture threatened and startled Alessandro to the core of his young unenlightened manhood.

She had called Craig the night before, amid the aftermath of the mayhem, needing to feel connected to something at home. Needing to hear his voice. Needing to be reminded that Craig was a person, not the two-dimensional cartoon he portrayed.

And she was in for a shock.

He had told her he was finally succumbing to AIDS and thought he had less than a year to go. There was nothing more they could do. Except more antibiotics. Tons of it.

She couldn't catch her breath for a few moments after he told her. She couldn't stop the hot tears from running—so much death. More to come. She had begged him to come to Vindenza. She wanted to care for him. But he said he was too ill, that he was in good hands.

And he wanted to stay close to his 'tribe.'

After hanging up, she had buried her head in her pillow, muffling her cries. She thought of her life and how it might have changed if she'd finished her role in the movie with Craig.

"Maria."

Maria was startled out of her grief. "What."

"Are you getting ready, Kiddo? Your *Nonna* is fretting; she thinks we'll be late if you don't get dressed soon."

Maria looked at her mother at the kitchen counter. She was wiping down the marble with a sponge. Maria looked down at her red satin pants and pink tunic with a Nehru collar. "I *am* dressed."

Andy looked over and dropped her hand with the sponge. "What, you're not wearing that nice white dress ensemble?"

Maria shook her head and walked into the living room. She squinted up through the skylight and saw a seagull hovering in the breeze very high up. She thought of Stinky hovering in the mist.

"No, I feel less conspicuous wearing this."

"Red satin and pink are less conspicuous than a white dress?"

"Mom. No dresses."

"I'm just sayin'. Red satin pants? Kinda jumps out next to *Nonna's* black if you know what I mean." Andy clicked her tongue and walked around the island. She grabbed Maria's arm and led her to her room. Maria allowed her to be pulled along, dragging her feet.

Andy took her into the room and looked around. Then, she stepped to Maria's messy open closet. "What happened here? A bomb went off?" She rifled through clothes, briskly pushing the various clothes hangers to the side, wire, pink plastic, white plastic, soft stuffed ones in light lavender satin. "Here it is," she said, pulling out the hanger with the white outfit. The price tag still hung from under the arm. She held it out and looked at it. Then she looked back at Maria. "No?"

Maria felt the material, frowning.

Andy looked at her pointedly. "Alessandro chose this, remember?"

Maria looked down at her red flats and licked her lips.

"You want to look nice for Alessandro, right? He. Chose. This."

Maria sighed. Indeed, what she wanted most in the world at the moment was to see a happy smile on Alessandro's face. The note seemed to imply he had forgiven her for their argument. Perhaps all was forgotten and forgiven. A fresh start.

She wiped her forehead and closed her eyes. To wear the dress meant to accept Alessandro's gesture, a gesture that said, very clearly, he preferred her to be female.

She didn't feel ready to commit to what it symbolized. She didn't feel she had what it took to be female. She didn't have the right to be female in this world, even though her family, a team of doctors, various hospitals, and multiple medications helped fight tooth and nail to keep her body female.

But she didn't want to lose him again.

She slowly took the hanger. She looked at it with suspicion.

"Oh, come on. It's a dress, for crying out loud." Andy crossed her arms.

"Is everyone else ready?"

"No, of course not. *Nonna* is always an hour early. You got time. If you start now."

"Okay."

Andy gave her a quick hug. Then she looked at her closely. "You alright?"

"Yup."

"Good. Kiddo, that guy is not going to just disappear, okay? Ever. He's staying. Understand?"

"You think?"

Andy held up her hand, crossing her fingers for luck. "Be strong, Maria. We're here to show support for your Dad and *Zio*."

"How is Yvonne?"

"She'll be fine. I think."

"Too bad she's missing the last of the openings—the Grand Opening of the grand *Mangione, Giordani Dynasty*."

"Listen, they worked hard. Stinky's death has nothing to do with this, this, *dynasty*, as you call it."

"I don't know what happened, but he didn't have to die, Ma."

"People die all the time, Maria."

"That's the problem, Ma."

Andy looked at her for a single beat. Then she closed the door.

ALESSANDRO WAS STARTLED AWAKE by a kick to the head.

"Rise 'n shine, little beauty. It's your big day," announced Boomer.

Alessandro looked up from his blanket on the cement floor. His eyes practically swollen shut and his nose broken; it was the bruises along the side of his body that screamed for relief. He slowly put the blanket to the side and painfully pulled his legs up. He got on all fours and crawled up to the wall to straighten out.

"Bed too hard? We'll have to complain to the establishment," Boomer said.

Alessandro stood and wavered unsteadily on his feet. "What makes today any different than any other day?"

"Because today is the day you were born to live out your destiny. You'll be the new savior to the rightful owners of Myrtle Beach. Today, you are single-handedly going to wipe out Leo and the gang."

Alessandro swallowed back rising fear and tried to act nonchalant. "And why would I want to do that?"

Boomer stepped closer, swung him around, and yanked his arms to the back. He put wire strapping over Alessandro's wrists and tightened them. "Well, it has nothing to do with what you want. You actually have no choice."

He pushed Alessandro through the metal door.

"Wait. I have to take a piss." Alessandro craned his neck to look at the bucket in the corner.

"Come with me, and I'll let you use a real toilet."

"Wow, I'm coming up in the world."

"You better believe it." Boomer pushed him through the cement nook they had first interrogated him, then pushed him to the end of the hall.

Alessandro had never gone this far since being captured. His heart beat hard at the thought he'd perhaps see daylight again. Surely, the others were going crazy looking for him.

Boomer stopped him, and took out a grimy red and black kerchief. "Here, I'm gonna make you pretty looking. You like red?"

"Love red," Alessandro quipped as Boomer tied the kerchief over his eyes.

"You're set. All pretty. Let's go see your visitors."

"Visitors?"

Boomer dragged Alessandro along.

Alessandro tried to figure out how he would catch sight as to where he was or where he was going. The only thing that came to mind was to accidentally fall on his face, hopefully, push the kerchief off to the side long enough. Just enough.

"I like visitors. Any good lookin' females?"

Before Boomer could answer, Alessandro, put one foot in front of the other and fell over his feet sideways into a wall. He scraped his face on the ground.

To keep Boomer from helping too soon, Alessandro swung his feet in front of himself, then bent his knees. Deftly, he got back to his feet and laughed. "Holy shit, Boomer, I've had too much *vino*."

He stumbled ahead, then let Boomer catch up. He kept his face looking to the right because, on the right, he could just see his feet below the kerchief.

"All right, watch. There's a step right in front of you, and it's about three steps up."

"Thanks, you're so gentle with me. When we're all finished, do we share a cigarette, like lovers do?"

He let his foot stub against the first step as if he was still blinded. Then, he felt for the next step with his toes.

At the top of the short flight of stairs, they walked into the warmth of sunshine, and he felt his cold bones relax. The heat was comforting. He could hear gentle surf and the call of seagulls nearby.

"Feels nice on the back."

Back.

"What time is it, Boomer? I've lost complete sense of day and time."

"It's about noon."

"Am I getting lunch now, too, along with a nice stroll through the sunshine?" If the sun is on the back, and it's around noon, and it's late spring, the sun is still low in the sky. So, he was walking away from the beach. He became aware of light traffic.

Wait. No.

The direction of the waves' sound didn't jibe with the sun's angle, so he must be hearing feedback bouncing off a giant wall to the right. He heard small birds sing and a cat meow to the left. The could be any one of a few public parks that led from grassy parking lots for the public. And if Boomer was not afraid of people seeing him drag a man with his hands tied behind his back, that could only mean they were either in a courtyard or on a lower parking level of an old motel.

But it wasn't totally abandoned. It had plumbing and power, so it wasn't a motel slated for demolishing. That could mean it was one of two places.

Suddenly, he could see they walked over broken pavement onto a grassy area.

Then large, old tires came into view. A truck. A filthy, dark blue truck.

He was slammed against the truck. It knocked the air out of him. "Hey, watch the nose. It's already been broken once, and I like the effect."

"Smart-aleck."

That was Benny. He laughed.

Someone checked the plastic ties on his hands, then he was led to the other side of the vehicle. A heavy door creaked open, and he was pushed in. He fell into a smelly, mud-encrusted well in front of seats.

Boomer swore and grabbed him by his shirt. It almost choked him. Boomer threw him onto the seat.

Alessandro immediately righted himself up in a sitting position. "Tough love," he said. Then he heard a cell phone ring. Someone answered it and spoke in French. He knew it. It was the Montreal crowd. *Shit on a panda.*

He could tell Boomer got in at the driver's seat and started up the engine. Then the passenger door opened, and someone climbed in beside him. Someone who he could not recognize by smell.

The doors slammed, and the engine started with a rumble and went into gear.

Under his kerchief, he saw a dust-covered dashboard. It was a truck. There was something familiar about the dash. As he bounced around between the two men, he looked at the glove compartment. At the radio. He tilted his head and caught the movement of something swinging. He tilted back a little more and his heart skipped.

A swinging crucifix he'd seen before off the rearview mirror. A plastic cross painted with red dots along the edges and a heart-aflame in the middle, on an inexpensive metal chain. The very cross he'd seen in the truck when he killed the Ryan brothers.

He gasped.

"Look familiar, eh?" said a thick, gravelly voice.

Alessandro sat quietly for a moment and trembled.

"*Sacrament*, what a predicament Alessandro finds himself in."

Boomer laughed.

Alessandro's eyes swerved to the man's wrinkled khaki pants. A slim man, with a slim veiny hand, the hair on which lay curled and sparkled blonde in the sun. It reached up and yanked off the blind.

Alessandro sat looking at a stranger with slicked-back light brown hair, longish at the back, and wearing a black and red polyester shirt. The man pulled out a package of Players cigarettes, tapped one out, and lit it with a Bic lighter.

Canadian cigarettes.

He had a good idea as to who it was. The godfather to Selena Ryan and her brothers. He stared at him.

The man laughed. "*Vous avez les yeux plus gros que le ventre.* Oh yeah, you're from Venezuela," the man said, enjoying each syllable of the word. "You don't speak French, eh."

"The Weasel?" whispered Alessandro.

The Weasel squinted against the smoke as it curled into his eyes. He bit down on the cigarette, put the cigarettes and lighter back into his pocket and threw his left arm around Alessandro's swaying shoulders. He pointed out the dirty windows as he looked at the traffic around them.

"I've always liked it here. *Mais*, the last few years, it changed. Undesirables have moved in."

Alessandro swallowed hard. He tested his tied wrists.

The Weasel dug into his other pocket and took out a syringe, took the sleeve off, and pushed the plunger up enough to squeeze out a thin shot of liquid. It squirted up against the ceiling of the cab.

He turned and squinted at Alessandro. "This is for you and that bitch."

Alessandro leaned away from him, against Boomer.

"This has nothing to do with Leo or Stefano. This," he said, sticking the cigarette back into his mouth and wrapping his arm around Alessandro to pull him closer. "This, is entirely personal."

"No," yelled Alessandro.

The Weasel plunged the syringe into Alessandro's shoulder.

ANDY WAS THE FIRST to struggle out of the elevator. "Whoa, hate to get stuck in that thing with you guys."

Claudia struggled out next.

"Ma, how do you like the white set on Maria?" she asked as she turned, walking further into the private underground garage.

Claudia kept on walking, checking sleeves.

"Ma?"

Claudia kept walking toward the cars.

Andy looked at the others pouring out of the elevator. Sammy kept the door open until everyone was out. He let go of the door.

"You know, I think her problem is not dementia. I think she's deaf."

Andy caught up to her mother. She held up her hand and snapped her fingers. "Ma." Then she full out yelled, "MA." Her voice echoed through the underground garage.

Claudia turned, startled. "*Che cosa?*"

Andy put her arm around her. "Ma, you're getting deaf. I thought you were getting senile, but I think you need hearing aids."

Peter walked behind them, in a crisp navy-blue suit with a light blue and white striped shirt and white-collar. He wore a dark blue silk tie. He shot his sleeves for the tenth time and readjusted his tie for as many.

Leo walked out after Sandra and stuck close to Stefano, brooding.

Andy walked toward him and took his arm. "You okay?"

Leo padded her arm. "Sure, kid."

Andy turned to look back at Maria, the last to leave the elevator. She followed them to the cars without saying a word, looking somewhat awkward in her short heels and feminine attire.

Andy let go of Leo and reached out to squeeze Maria's arm.

Stefano pulled out his keys, but Leo placed his hand on Stefano. "We're not drivin'," said Leo, "We're goin' in style."

Stefano whistled at Peter, who was at his BMW, opening the door for Sandra.

Peter looked up.

"You don't drive'a," yelled Stefano.

All of a sudden, they heard tires squeal outside of the garage door. An engine idled as the door slowly clattered open. Then a long, white limousine slowly drove down the ramp.

"Holy shit. I've always wanted to be in one of those. Is that for us, Leo? All of us?" Andy looked with wide eyes.

Maria looked up. "Wow."

"See what Alessandro's missing? Ha," yelled Andy.

Maria blinked and smiled.

"Soon, you'll see him again, Maria."

Maria nodded.

Leo spread out his arms. "You are my *famiglia. Capisci?*"

Sandra and Andy clutched each other, and jumped up and down, squealing, making fun of the very girls they used to hate during high-school years. They stopped and laughed heartily at their own pleasure.

Frankie got out, nodding. He walked over to the side and opened the door with a flourish. "Ladies?" He motioned to the interior.

Andy stood back and motioned Sandra to climb in first. Then, at the last moment, she pushed her away and jumped in. Sandra laughed so hard, she bent over double. Peter tried to manually push her in. Then, he turned and offered to help Claudia.

When Claudia finally got in and sat down, her eyes widened. She looked at the interior and caressed the white leather seat. She stared at the ceiling of the limousine and looked over at the bar. "*Santa Maria Madre di Dio.*"

"Yeah, eh?" Andy grinned.

Sandra and Andy laughed.

"Eh?" mimicked Sandra.

Andy punched her arm.

"Ow," joked Sandra.

Peter jumped in next and waved at the others to climb in.

"Where do you want to sit, Leo? Beside the bar?" asked Peter.

"Next to the window so I can smoke my cigar," yelled Leo.

Peter moved over beside the ladies on the side bench. "Well, this is even better," he said, as he eyed the bar.

"Are you the bartender?" asked Andy.

"Yes, madam, what can I get you?"

"Double vodka."

Stefano, still standing outside the limousine, watching everyone joke, motioned to Maria to get in.

Maria bent in and looked around. "Where do you want me to sit?"

"Come on, there's lots of room over there," Andy said.

Maria looked toward the front of the limousine as she climbed in. She shifted her body so that she sat next to Leo, allowing her father to squeeze in beside her and the side of the car.

Frankie closed the door and sat in the driver's seat. He opened a little window between the front and the rest of the limousine. "Everything all right in there?"

"Yeah," yelled Andy. "We should toast Yvonne, Willie, Alessandro, Andrew and Steffy." Andy held up her vodka drink. "To Yvonne, Willie, Alessandro, Andrew and Steffy. Glad you're not here. No room in the inn!"

Everybody laughed.

"Ready, Boss?"

"Yes," yelled Leo gruffly.

The limousine started. "Any particular music, Boss?"

"Anybody?" asked Leo.

Stefano shook his head. "No'a, you choose'a *Zio*."

Leo shook his head. Then he nodded. He looked sad, and sighed deeply. "It's time for some sunshine, everyone. For Stinky's sake, let's have fun. Play "*Tarantella*."

Stefano laughed and shook his head. "Tha's so old."

"Yeah, Stefano. Like the old comics." Peter grinned.

Claudia yelled, "*Si, Tarantella*." She clapped her hands with joy.

"Alright, Boss. *Tarantella* it is." Frankie reached sideways at a fancy CD holder and looked for a disc. He took one out and held it up for everyone to see.

They cheered.

Frankie stuck it into the player and adjusted the volume.

Everyone laughed as Calabrian traditional music played.

"Louder," yelled Leo.

Lively accordion music and snare drum played so loud they couldn't hear themselves think.

Peter pretended to dance in his seat.

As did Andy, kicking her legs up in the air. At one point, she kicked so high she slid off her seat, and fell on her bum, to everyone's laughter. There, she tried to dance on her knees in front of them.

Leo laughed so hard he almost swallowed his cigar.

Even Maria laughed.

The music stopped far too soon, as they cruised along Ocean Boulevard, and another tune started to play.

"Play it again, Frankie. This time keep it on repeat."

Frankie stopped the song and went back, playing *Tarantella* again.

They clapped to the bells and mandolin and accordion, as they drove the ten-minute drive to the Grand Opening of the Myrtle Beach Theme Park Time Share Resort and Water Park.

ALESSANDRO COULDN'T FOCUS. His body jerked and swayed with the movement of the truck as it stopped and sped through three traffic lights before it turned onto Highway 17 heading north.

He fell sideways against The Weasel, in the turn. The Weasel pushed him back against Boomer who laughed.

He closed his eyes against the blinding light. The noise was deafening. Everything was louder, brighter, faster, slower. He opened his one eye slightly for a brief second. Were they going up Highway 501? Or was it Highway 105? Where was he and Maria going? Why was he in water?

He felt the truck stop, and heard a door creak open. He saw The Weasel climb out of the cab and turn.

"'Ave a good trip, eh? Say *allo* to your queer bitch." He slammed the door shut and hit the truck.

Boomer put the truck into gear.

THE LIMOUSINE BOUNCED under the weight of seven dancing, bobbing people as it made its way along Third Avenue South, then right on Highway 17.

Tarantella kept everyone hopping, laughing, chatting, and clapping.

Peter opened the window behind him and screamed for help at a passerby, as a joke. "Help, there are nutties in here. Save me." He howled along with the others.

Travel was relatively quick, just after Myrtle Beach lunch rush hour. It was a perfect day for a Grand Opening.

They turned up Highway 501, and the limousine sped without much trouble, having fewer lights to pass. They were five minutes from the theme park; two restaurants and a merry-go-round, with a beautiful waterfall park at the head of a gorgeous lake, with three pairs of swans. And the beautiful Time Share Resort, half sold as of that morning.

Maria looked out the window, past her father nodding to the music. She looked forward to seeing Alessandro. Where could he be? Did he know where to go?

She shifted in her seat, to look out more clearly. It was a beautiful day and such a happy occasion. *So many ups and downs.* But she didn't want to think about it too deeply. Life had an uncanny way of righting itself.

She turned in her seat to face the others and clapped along, laughing at the antics. She watched, smiling, as they went through an intersection, then looked the other way, past *Zio* Peter at the window, keeping beat to the light, happy music.

Frankie turned and grinned at them, keeping the beat with his fingers on the steering wheel.

Just as they entered the intersection, she saw a dirty, blue truck doing a U-turn in front of them. She thought it odd when the driver dove out of the vehicle, rolled and got up to run. Then she realized the truck was racing ahead.

She sat up straight. The truck was on a collision course with their limousine coming through the intersection.

She looked at Frankie, who was so very slow at looking back at the road.

She looked at Peter and her mother who she intuitively knew were both in the cross-hairs of the truck, if they didn't get out of the way in time.

"Frankie. Watch out," she screamed, but the words weren't out of her mouth before they were T-boned, smack in the middle. The truck pushed the limo through cars, across two lanes, into a gas station, smashing it into the same store Peter bought his paper.

Maria heard glass shatter, felt bodies fall over her, and heard *Tarantella* play a few more bars before it, and all the other explosive noises, came to a sickening halt.

CHAPTER TWENTY-FOUR

SIXTEEN-YEAR-OLD ANDREW AND STEFFY jumped out of a taxi in front of the Myrtle Beach Hospital on 79th North, into a brilliant mid-day sun. They pushed through a small group of reporters with cameras and a film crew, then raced through the front doors. They looked around frantically in the dusk of the interior, and ran to the information kiosk, banging against the rim and shaking the protective glass with a rattle.

"Hi, we're Andrew and Stefano Giordani. We're here because our parents have been in an accident?"

"Say wha?" asked a perturbed, heavy woman behind the glass. She had long pink fingernails and her face was lit up by a desk lamp. A phone rang behind her but she seemed to not care.

"You need to get that?"

She waved at the phone behind her. "Reporters. You were sayin' the name was?"

"Giordani?"

"All right. Giordani." She pulled over a huge ledger and flipped through the pages. "Let's see now. Gio…" She used her fingernail to carefully go through the handwritten lines. "We already have a Stefano Giordani in Intensive Care. Are you related?"

"Yes, that's our uncle. I was named after him," said Steffy. He looked over at his twin, Andrew. "Our parents are Peter and Sandra Giordani. We flew in from Canada as soon as we could." He wiped his mouth impatiently. He jumped and turned when someone tapped him on the shoulder.

The taxi driver stood with a briefcase and two suitcases on wheels. "Young men, you forgot your things. And here's your change." He held out his hand, coins between his fingers.

Steffy waved the money away. "Sorry about that. No, please. Keep it. Thank you very much."

The man nodded, lifted his cap, and gave a big, toothy smile with a gap in the bottom front. "Well, ah hope all is well with you boys. Ah'll pray for you and your family."

Andrew and Stefano nodded and tried to smile.

Andrew held out his hand, and the taxi driver grabbed it with both of his. "Thank you very much for being so kind," Andrew said.

"Well, ah hope your parents are fine and dandy." He pointed at the sky and winked.

Andrew watched him leave, then turned to join his brother to watch the attendant continue reading the directory. She looked over her counter, through the glass, at a security guard waiting by the wheelchairs. She knocked on the glass and motioned him.

He looked over with big, expectant eyes, and came with a jingle, both hands on his belt, a gun in his holster. His shirt was of hefty material covering his midriff. "Yes ma'am?" The guard had a short afro and a kind face. He looked at the boys and nodded.

The attendant waved at him to come close for her to whisper to him.

The guard squeezed through the door with scrapes and a clatter, into her cubicle, and bent down and listened gravely. Her desk lamp highlighted sweat along the side of his dark, meaty face.

Then, the guard stood and nodded.

"This here's Joshua. He'll be able to help y'all."

Joshua motioned the two brothers to step over to the side. They followed him away from the information desk. "If you don't mind waitin' there, we have police who would like to come down and talk to you briefly. They'll probably take you right to your parents."

"Are they okay?" asked Andrew.

Joshua smiled, jiggled his head and shrugged. "Your parents survived the crash, and that is a real miracle. It's a miracle more people didn't die. It was all over the news las' night. The biggest crash we've eveh had in Myrtle Beach."

Steffy frowned. "How many were involved?"

Joshua held his chin as he looked at the stained ceiling tiles above him. "Well, now, I think there was a truck and the limousine your parents were in." He pointed to the boys as he continued to think. "And the limousine then got in the way of three other cars goin' the same way. And then the limousine smashed through gas tanks at a gas station and went through the window of the store. Ah think there were more than twelve people involved. This hospital is entirely full."

Andrew and Steffy's faces fell.

"Oh my god," cried Andrew, covering his mouth. "Did anything catch fire?"

"No, ah can honestly say, there was no fire." His eyes widened as he shook his head in disbelief. "As ah said, it's a real miracle."

Andrew looked around and sat down in a wheelchair.

Joshua looked from one to the other. "You guys are twins, huh?"

"Anyone die?" asked Steffy, ignoring the question. His brows knitted tightly, as his sad eyes widened.

Joshua took a deep breath and hooked his thumbs onto his belt. "Well, now, you'll have to ask the police about that, but they haven't told us nothin'." He looked around nervously. "No, sir. Usually we all know everythin' tha's goin' on, but not this time." Joshua's voice cracked. "Your parents important people or somethin'?"

"No, not really," Andrew bleated.

Joshua got nervous. He pointed to the main lobby. "I'll go see what's takin' them, yeah? You can *ast* them everythin' they know."

Steffy looked around and sat on a chrome and orange naugahyde chair close to Andrew.

They watched as Joshua walked to the desk first, to pick up their luggage. He brought them over and put them down near their seats. "I'll be right back."

Steffy and Andrew sat shaking.

Andrew broke down in tears.

"So, this thing happened just after lunch yesterday, according to the taxi driver. How come we didn't get the call till ten o'clock last night?"

Andrew wiped his face with his cardigan sleeve. "I don't know, but I'll never forget *Nonna's* scream."

"Yeah, I thought that meant Dad and Mom had died."

"Well, we still don't know what happened to them. I mean, are they in a coma? Are they awake? Are they talking?" Andrew searched for a Kleenex.

"Here," said a female voice from behind Steffy.

Steffy looked up to see the Information Receptionist holding a box of tissue.

"You wanna soda or somethin', boys?"

Andrew reached for the box. "Thank you."

Steffy shook his head. "No, but is there a phone I can use to tell our grandparents we arrived?"

"Is it long distance?"

"Yeah, Canada."

"Canada? Where's that?"

Steffy blinked. He pointed to the sky. "North of the United States of America?"

"Oh yeah? Y'all have a strange accent. I just wondered." She looked back. "I see Joshua prob'ly went up to get the police." She turned and smiled reassuringly. "If y'all need anythin', just say, okay Hon? The police will help you with the long-distance call. I can't do it here."

The boys nodded appreciatively.

JOSHUA GOT OUT of the elevator and walked over to a couple of constables outside a hospital room. One of them looked over.

"Hi Joshua," said the tallest one. "How can we help you?"

Joshua stopped and hiked his pants by the belt. His blue shirt billowed over his stomach, and his badge shone in the overhead lights. "Ah've got two young men, Andrew and Stefano Giordani. Twins. They're sayin' that their parents are here, but they're in ICU. Thought because of the situation, you should talk to 'em first."

"Shit," said the tall one, looking at the short one.

The short one shrugged and got up. "'You gonna be okay here?"

"Ah doubt gimpy in here is going to break free," said the tall one grimly as he pointed into the room they were guarding.

The short one motioned the guard. "Ah'll go back with you, Joshua."

The two made their way to the elevator.

ANDREW AND STEFFY looked at the two men in uniform heading in their direction from the elevators. They eyed the guns in holsters, a strange sight to their Canadian eyes. They stood up.

Andrew wrung his hands, and Steffy pushed bangs from his eyes as he nervously blinked.

One constable took off his cap and tucked it under his arm. "Hi, ah'm Constable Washington; ah'm the one who called. Ah think it was your grandmother I spoke to?"

The boys introduced themselves and nodded.

"Ah'm sorry ah got your grandmother all worked up. Ah couldn't understand her at first, 'n ah don't think that she understood me. She thought ah meant your parents were dead. You live with your grandmother?"

"No, we live next door to our grandparents' house."

"Uh huh. Wow, she had to run over to get you guys?"

"Well, yeah, I guess," said Andrew. He thought of her racing through the underground tunnel screaming. Tunnels were secrets.

"Good woman. Okay, um, ah'll take you into ICU. Both your parents are there." He turned to the guard. "Thanks, Joshua."

Joshua nodded, reached out to shake the boys' hands, nodded again. "Ah'll watch your bags. You go on ahead." He turned and walked back to his corner, past the wheelchairs.

Constable Washington put his cap back on and led the boys to a frosted glass doorway with the letters ICU painted dark red. He buzzed the door. Shortly, a young nurse with a beautiful pile of braided black braids precariously tucked underneath a cap opened the door.

"Constable Washington, *hai.*"

Her large eyes darted to the two handsome young men. She batted thick, long mascaraed eyelashes.

Constable Washington pointed to Andrew and Steffy. "These are Mr. and Mrs. Giordani's sons from Canada. They came as soon as they could."

"All the way from Canada? You got Eskimos there?"

Andrew looked confused. "Well, not where we live."

"A lot of snow?"

"Yeah, actually, a lot sometimes." He tried to smile. He looked at the constable questioningly.

The young nurse finally opened the door. She motioned for them to come in.

Andrew looked over at her to try and read her face. She seemed so young; so exotic. So pretty. And he saw gentleness. But nothing in her mannerisms gave any hint as to how his parents were faring. He turned away and followed the constable and his brother.

The constable stopped at a doorway and motioned them to go in. "Here's your mother. I'll let the doctors know you're here, and someone will take you to your father. I'll come back and we'll talk some more."

Steffy touched his shoulder. "We have to call our grandparents back in Canada to let them know we arrived."

"Don't you worry none. Ah'll do that right now. Y'all go see your Mom."

Slowly they walked up to the doorway. Steffy was the first to look in.

Andrew watched to see if Steffy would show anything before he dared look through the door. He saw his brother's eyebrows go up. Immediately, he looked in.

Their mother, Sandra, appeared to be fast asleep, hooked up to a variety of IVs and machines. Her blonde hair was flattened, greasy-looking. The left side of her face was heavily bandaged and she had two black eyes. Her left arm was in a sling and hung from a contraption above her.

They walked closer to the bed, one on each side.

The light was overly bright in the room, and Andrew looked on the wall for a switch. He found a dimmer and put it on a lower setting. He pulled over a chair and sat on the edge, his face close to his mother's.

Steffy looked around and spied an old wooden chair in the corner. He scraped it along old linoleum to the side of the bed. It scraped some more as he sat on it and shifted it as close as he could to his mother.

The noise stirred Sandra slightly. She moaned.

Andrew bent and looked at his mother's face. "Mom," he whispered. "Mom?"

"I don't think she'll wake for a while. We had to heavily sedate her earlier. She was in tremendous pain."

They looked around to see a tall, dark doctor in a white lab coat holding a clipboard and sporting a stethoscope around his neck. He pointed to them with his long fingers. "You're the twins?"

"Yes, hi, I'm Stefano."

"I'm Andrew."

"I'm Dr. Perry. Good to meet you. Sorry about the circumstances, however." They quickly stood and shook his hand.

He pointed at Steffy. "We have a Stefano Giordani here in ICU. Don't tell me, you were named after him?"

Stefano nodded, pursing his lips to keep them from trembling. "He's our uncle. And our godfather."

"Then Adriana Giordani is your aunt?"

They both nodded.

The doctor looked away for a second before nodding.

"Your father is still in the operating room. Once he settles down, perhaps tonight, you can see him briefly."

"Wha'? What is wrong with our father?"

"I'm afraid, your father's right leg had to be amputated above the kneecap. And he has several cracked ribs and a punctured lung." He blinked at the boys' immediate violent reaction of grief and watched them comfort each other. He placed a hand on Andrew's shoulder.

Andrew looked up. A quick sob escaped before he quelled it.

"Listen, he's alive. He's going to pull through. There is much one can do with prosthetics. It takes time, but the main thing is you still have your father." He looked over at Sandra on the bed. "You are lucky, boys. They survived a terrible accident. Remember that, and take some solace from that fact, if you can."

He allowed them a moment to digest his words. He looked at his clipboard and went through a few top pages. He read his notes. "Leo Mangione is related to you, and," he looked down at his clipboard, "Maria Giordani?"

"Leo is my father's uncle, our great uncle," offered Andrew.

Steffy looked up and nodded. "And Maria's our cousin."

"Well, it was quite a rush when all dozen people were taken in from the accident at once yesterday afternoon. Some with minor injuries. Your family, however, were the ones suffering the more severe injuries."

"What's wrong with our mother?" asked Andrew.

"She suffers from a very heavy concussion, a broken arm, she has a collapsed lung on the left side, also a couple of fractured ribs. She spoke to us not long ago. She asked about you."

"How come it took so long for someone to contact us?" Andrew asked.

"Your family had each other as an emergency contact, except for your mother who had her parents listed. For some reason, we couldn't get through on the phone. Though technology in the '80s is quite advanced, long-distance can still be iffy around here, at times."

Andrew looked out into the hallway. "Where's the rest of the family?"

Sammy appeared in the doorway. His shirt was crumpled and had coffee stains and crumbs on the front. His eyes were bloodshot and his face grey. He had a heavy five-o'clock shadow. He hiked up his pants and nodded sadly.

Andrew slowly walked to Sammy who held out his arms. He allowed Andrew to hug him for a moment, then let him go.

Sammy nodded at Steffy.

"I understand," Dr. Perry said, turning to the boys, "that this gentleman works for your great uncle." He turned to Sammy. "Would you mind helping these young boys? Are you okay with that?"

Sammy sadly nodded and motioned for the boys to follow.

They looked at their mother.

"We'll come back in a minute," Sammy said wearily. "Let's go have a coffee or soda, or somethin'."

The boys followed Sammy. He shuffled through the ICU and led them out the frosted door back into the lobby and down the main hallway to an open cafeteria where he sat them down.

He stood back and said, "What you want?"

Andrew shifted and looked around. "A juice, I guess."

"You?"

Steffy shook his head.

Sammy walked over to the counter to arrange for drinks.

"Why aren't they telling us everything, all at once?" Steffy was angry.

Andrew shook his head.

They watched as Sammy placed an orange juice on the table in front of Andrew, and set a steaming black coffee on the table. He sat down with a grunt.

"So?" asked Steffy.

Sammy looked down at the floor, then touched his lips with his pudgy fingers. He hesitated, then looked at them. "There's a lot to tell you. So, here goes."

MARIA HEARD A VOICE on an intercom, then fell back to sleep. She stirred when she heard her mother's voice. "Maria." Maria fought to wake up but fell asleep again. Maria heard Enya singing her favorite song, *I Want Tomorrow*. She dreamt things that didn't make sense.

Finally, she slowly woke up to someone touching her hand.

"Mom?" she whispered. She moved her fingers.

Someone said, "She's waking up."

"No, she's not. It's just a nervous reaction."

"'Heard her say something."

"No, you didn't, idiot."

"No, look. Her eyelids are moving. She's listening."

Someone patted her hand. "Maria, it's Andrew and Steffy. Can you hear me?"

She tried to move her lips, but only a croak came out of her throat.

"She's trying to talk."

Maria opened her eyes. The light was too bright, and she had to close them again.

"Steffy, turn the ceiling lights off."

Maria sensed gentle darkness, and slowly opened her eyes. She tried to focus on two figures, one on each side of the bed, but couldn't. But she knew the voices.

"Steffy, Andrew," she said. She licked her dry lips.

"Yeah, there you go. We're here."

She opened her eyes wider and tried to move. Then she lay back and closed her eyes. "The truck."

"Yeah, the truck. It T-boned you."

"How? Mom? Dad?"

Neither one answered.

She didn't like that. She opened her eyes even wider and focused on their faces. She felt her face twist in fear.

"Mom? Dad?"

"Your Dad was just here. I'm going to get him," Andrew said, leaving.

Steffy leaned over. "Your Dad's doing okay. He just got a big cut with stitches. He was released last night. He was here a moment ago, but went lookin' for Frankie."

"Oh, good." She tried to move and gave up. "Frankie's okay then?"

"Yeah, he's in a neck brace and broke a finger, but he's been released, too. He's gone home to clean up, and had to pick something up for your Dad."

"And *Zio* Leo?"

"He's in the next room. Yvonne's with him now. He's smashed up. A broken collar bone and pelvis."

"Oh my god," Maria croaked. She tried to touch her head but saw that she had an IV in her hand. "Shit." She looked and saw the IV stand. "Get me sitting up. I need to sit up."

Steffy jumped into action. There was a handle to turn, to tilt the back up or down. After a few seconds, he figured it out. He cranked it up all the way.

"Ow," yelped Maria, as she doubled over.

"Oops." Steffy cranked it back a little.

Maria tried to shift her legs around but saw a big bundle under the blanket. One leg was heavy. "What's wrong with me?"

Steffy said, "You have over 70 stitches down the right side of your body."

Maria pulled the blanket back. She gazed at the gauze down her side, where the hospital gown was slightly yanked up. Iodine stained her bottom sheet. She thought to straighten out her gown, to hide her secret. Her terrible secret. Her cousins must never know her terrible secret.

She lay back on the pillow and covered her eyes. "Shit. What about everyone else?"

"You'll have to wait till the doctor comes in." Steffy looked away.

"What? Steffy. What?" Maria pulled herself up further, wincing in pain. She looked angrily down at the IV taped and wrinkled on top of her hand. "Why are you crying?"

Steffy kept his eyes diverted, and fiddled with the edge of her blanket. "Dad lost a leg," he said woodenly.

Maria covered her mouth with her hand. "Oh, no." Her face collapsed. She grabbed at the remainder of the sheet over her body and angrily yanked it away. She fell back and threw an arm over her eyes. "That's awful. Your poor Dad."

"But he's alive. So's Mom."

Dr. Perry came in with his clipboard. He lightly knocked on the open door. "I see that Maria is awake."

Dr. Perry stepped in and touched Maria's toes. "Maria, I'm Dr. Perry." He turned to the door, startled by Stefano filling the doorway.

"DAD," Maria croaked. She held out her arms, pulling the IV tape away from her pillow. "Dad. You're okay." Her eyes watered.

He was big, strong, tired, beautiful, dirty, crumpled. His eyes shone like lights at her. Stefano nodded slowly, then looked over at Steffy and motioned with his head.

Steffy looked at Maria and she at him. She watched him quickly get up. She looked on, as he grabbed Stefano and clutched him briefly before letting go.

Andrew appeared behind them, his eyes red and swollen.

Steffy let go of his *Zio* and disappeared with his brother, their arms around each other.

Maria heard their footsteps down the hall. Her eyes clamped onto her father's face. There was something amiss.

Stefano looked pointedly at Dr. Perry. His blue eyes were lit from somewhere within.

Dr. Perry calmly looked at Stefano.

Stefano walked into the room and closed the door behind him. He looked grave. Destroyed. Quietly angry. He hiked his crumpled pants and pulled a chair to Maria's bed and sat down. He rested a bandaged hand on his thigh.

"Your hand," she said.

He looked at Maria, then at his hand, then jiggled his head. "Jus' stitches."

Dr. Perry walked to the other side of the bed and pointed at her medical bracelet. "I will come back and leave you two. But in the meantime, I want to point something out to you. It's a really good thing you wore that bracelet. Believe it or not, the combination of medications you're on could have caused real havoc with your health, if we hadn't known. Let me just say, it saved us a lot of guesswork, and you would've been far worse off than you are now."

Maria looked at her bracelet. She looked down at her side, then up at the doctor's dark, lined face. Her eyes widened at the realization that he knew her grave secret. She blinked back the humiliation.

The doctor's soft eyes and a thick set of curly eyelashes gave him a youthful look and expression. He had grey dots at his temple. He looked away, sadly. "I'll come back later and let you be with your daughter for a little while."

He put a gentle hand on Stefano's shoulder. He opened the door and quietly left.

Suddenly, everything seemed to be in a vacuum. Her father slumped toward her shoulder.

"Maria, *bambina*." He reached for her hand, and deeply sighed. He patted it.

"*Nonna*?" asked Maria. Someone died, she could tell.

Stefano shook his head. "No, *Nonna,* she's okay."

"And *Zio* Peter lost a leg."

"*Sì.*"

"Dad, did anyone die? Someone died, right?"

Stefano's hulk silently rocked with each beat of his heart, as he numbly stared at her.

She looked around the room for her mother. She had heard her mother. "Mom."

Stefano lifted his chin, and his eyebrows slowly raised.

"No...." Maria's mouth dropped open.

Stefano covered his eyes and nodded. "*Si*," he whispered.

Maria's head jerked like a bird. Her eyes darted around the room. Where was her mother? *Wait, it was a dream.*

She looked back at her father's bowed head until he slowly looked at her. She searched his brilliant, moist eyes. He cocked his head slightly, and she saw the deepest grief she had ever seen on her tough, immovable father's face.

Her body jerked forward, and her face fell against his forehead. She jerked back. "Noooooo..." Maria kicked with her good leg. She tried to get out of bed, but slid to the floor instead, her hospital gown riding up, and the IV stand toppling over the bed. She almost fainted with the pain. Her thick bandaging crushed high against her one testicle, but she ignored the intrusion. She needed to run. Run anywhere.

She scrambled to get up, clutching at the gurney, but the wheels weren't on brakes, and it shoved against Stefano. She fell on her hands and her palms hit the cool tiles. She grabbed at what was left of the sheet on the bed, but it slipped off. She clutched at the sheet, then the mattress with her other hand.

"Noooooo," she cried, and kept screaming the word until all the breath was pushed out of her lungs.

Stefano pushed his chair back against the wall, denting the plaster. As he grunted around the bed, a nurse ran into the room, almost colliding with Stefano.

Stefano quickly covered his daughter's nakedness, while he and the nurse attempted to pull Maria back into bed. Maria was dead weight.

She wasn't breathing. Her eyes stared at the ceiling, her short hair sticking in all directions, her mouth agape in mid-cry.

"Maria..." Stefano yanked her on the bed. The bed flew against the chair, denting the wall further.

"Maria. *Respirare.*"

The nurse put the brakes on the bed's wheels as Stefano finally lifted Maria like a baby, and fell on the bed with her.

The nurse quickly grabbed the sheet on the floor, yanking it free from under the wheel of the bed, and covered them both and ran for help.

He clung to her, rolling and keeping his body on the bed by pushing at the floor with his feet. His shoes kept sliding away as he tried to twist and see Maria's face. He slapped her face and shook her. He held her as tightly as he dared.

"*Respirare!*"

CHAPTER TWENTY-FIVE

"**S**O, THAT'S WHAT HAPPENED."

The chapel was quiet as everyone stared at Sammy sitting at the front, facing them. He had just finished laying out the sequence of events, as the police recounted.

But it wasn't quiet in Maria's head. Drums clashed, glass crashed, nothing was in sync. She saw blood, her mother flying forward against the other side of the limousine, the drink jettisoning out of her hand, spilling as it twirled in the air. The front of the truck loomed through the side of the limousine as it plowed into the seating area. She could still smell the dry, dusty heat off the truck's radiator near her head. She saw Peter pancaked against her father. She saw cars coming at them, as their whole world was shoved across the highway toward the gas station.

"So that's why Alessandro's under arrest?" Sandra sat bundled in a wheelchair. Her hair was flattened against her skull, and she still had black/red circles under and around her eyes. "I don't believe it."

Maria looked at her and shook her head. She turned to her father in the corner and winced as she slightly moved her leg. Sitting in a wheelchair was difficult with stitches all down her side. There was no real support for her heel except for resting it on the ground. She needed to scratch her crotch but didn't dare. She was still attached to an IV for her much-needed antibiotics. She felt trapped. Everything bothered her, all at once, and she wanted to throw something, anything. She wanted to scream and yell and destroy. She wanted to be dead.

She turned the other way, expecting to see her mother. She looked at the cross hanging at the front again. "Alessandro wouldn't do that. Alessandro wouldn't kill my mother." *He wouldn't kill me.*

Stefano looked at her through slit eyes.

"I want to see him."

"He's still in a coma." Sandra looked at her, her face pale, weary.

"It's not fair. How can Alessandro be charged for something while he's in a coma? He can't defend himself."

"According to the cops, the evidence and witnesses say it all, Maria." Sammy was respectful, sad.

Maria stubbornly shook her head. "Don't cry," she whispered to herself.

Sandra wheeled herself with one hand, closer to Maria. She reached out for her hand on the armrest. "We just have to wait."

Sandra turned to Andrew and Steffy sitting in the front pew facing Sammy. "Did you remember to bring your father's shaving kit from the condo?"

"Yeah," Andrew nodded.

She exhaled heavily. "I'll give Peter a nice shave. Do him good. He's not doing too well." She looked at Stefano. "How's Claudia?"

Stefano sighed. "Bad'a."

"It's not natural outliving your own child."

Maria's eyes filled with tears. She looked at the stained-glass window. The sun was slowly rising over palms, threatening to burst through with unbearably happy colors.

"I want to see him," muttered Maria.

"Fuck the kid." That came from Leo. He was reclined on a gurney. He hadn't wanted to go further than past the doorway. He was miserable. His face looked haggard with two days of silver growth.

There was a knock at the chapel door.

Everyone looked up to see a constable standing in the doorway.

"Your man's finally awake."

MARIA CLUNG TO HER HOSPITAL GOWN while she held her IV stand. Steffy pushed her wheelchair as they followed the constable to the elevators. Her eyes dashed around the halls, rushing to where Alessandro was kept under guard. She leaned forward in her chair, reaching out with her hands to help hurry the chair into the elevator.

Sammy pushed Sandra's chair into the lift, and Stefano followed with Leo's gurney.

Andrew stood by the constable as he pushed the button. Everyone was quiet, everyone's breath shallow and brisk.

Maria brushed dirty hair away from her eyes. She looked at finger streaks on the stainless-steel walls. She glanced at the yellowed plastic over the fluorescent lighting above her. The elevator creaked and swayed and was far too slow.

"Come on," she whispered. Her nose ran, and she wiped it with the inside of her wrist. "Steffy, do you have any Kleenex on you?"

"I have some." Sandra pulled a tissue out of her hospital housecoat and placed it on Maria's lap.

"Thanks." She blew her nose and wiped her eyes. She was going to see Alessandro. She needed to see him. He was terribly hurt and should've died. The fact he was high on heroin during the crash saved his life. His body was so relaxed he rolled, bounced, smashed with the truck, and somehow came out of it alive. But he hadn't come out of a coma.

Until now.

He had a list of charges against him as long as his arm, including manslaughter.

The elevator doors finally ground open. As Steffy wheeled her along the hallway, she looked at another constable sitting guard outside one of the rooms. He looked up from a newspaper and quickly stood.

"All of 'em?" he asked of their escort.

"All of us," growled Leo.

The two constables looked at Leo on the gurney.

They looked at Stefano, and he nodded.

One of the constables opened the door as wide as it would go.

Steffy hesitated to push Maria's chair, waiting for Leo to go in ahead of them.

Maria bounced impatiently in the chair, but he wouldn't budge. She pushed him away and tried to move the wheel with her free hand.

"Let her go first," growled Leo.

Steffy quickly pushed Maria's chair through. She reached forward, wishing the chair to go faster.

An orange and brown plaid curtain hung from the ceiling. Behind it, somewhere was a window allowing the sun to make it glow from within.

The curtain hid Alessandro from view.

"Alessandro," she called.

Steffy pushed the curtain aside.

Alessandro lay facing the window, seemingly asleep.

"Alessandro," she whispered.

Slowly, Alessandro turned his head.

Maria clutched at the side of his bed and pushed herself along toward his head. She ignored the pain from stitches. "Alessandro," she cried.

With two black eyes and a new cut across his face, Alessandro slowly reached out the hand closest to her.

Maria cried. She cradled her cheek onto his hand and allowed his fingers to caress her skin, feel her tears. She kissed the palm and laid her cheek into his hand once again.

"HE'S SAYIN' HE WAS KIDNAPPED and was made to look like he was the driver. None of the witnesses mentioned seeing anyone else in the truck. No one jumping out. You're the first."

"Maria said she saw him jump with her own eyes," Sammy said.

Leo's steely eyes drilled into Sammy.

"Did she see Alessandro at the wheel?" croaked Peter.

Leo, Stefano, and Sammy gathered in Peter's room where he lay with a massive heap under the blanket where his leg once was.

"No, she only saw the truck left driverless to come'a at the limousine," Stefano answered.

"Listen, somebody stole that truck. I wanna find out who," roared Leo. He turned to Sammy. "Goddamn it, I want my cigar. Is that too much to ask? Shit."

"You can't smoke here, boss."

"I know that, God dammit."

Stefano shook his head. He pointed to a warning sign. "You'a have oxygen here, *Zio*. Den we die."

"What else is new?" Leo growled.

Sammy fought back a smile, then looked embarrassed before going on. "One of the guys said the truck simply went missing." He shifted his bulk and raised his arm, testing the joint. He let his arm drop.

"Where was it parked?" Leo snapped.

"Where we park all the heavy equipment. Up behind the construction shed."

Leo snorted. He irritably scratched the back of his neck. "God dammit. We should've had security cameras installed. Where was the goddam security guard?"

"He said it must have happened when he went for a crap."

"A crap," Leo snorted.

"Should'a had a Johnny on the Spot right there. Or let him in the construction shed and use your can."

"You're fucking kidding me, Sammy. That's where we keep our papers, right? Why should we let any idiot use our crapper?" Leo covered his face with both hands. One was seriously bruised.

There was a frantic knock at the door.

"No," roared Leo.

"It's me. Maria."

Stefano looked at Leo and motioned with his head.

"Come in," roared Leo, giving Stefano a stern look.

The door banged and scraped as Maria forced it open with her wheelchair. She went without her IV, now able to use both hands. She leaned forward.

"Hi *Zio*, how are you?" She looked at Peter, concerned.

"I'm having the time of my life, thanks for asking."

"What do you want, Maria?" Leo snapped.

"I got more information from Alessandro."

"It better help. He's now charged with the second manslaughter."

"What?"

"Maria, dis'a morning a woman from another car'a die."

"He didn't tell me." Her face went white.

"I told them not to tell him yet." Leo leaned both elbows on the chair's armrests. "The last thing we need is more distractions. We need to sort this out first, because if it wasn't Alessandro, it was somebody out *there*, and still out there, trying to get at us."

"Well, it definitely wasn't him, *Zio*. And my story of seeing a guy jump out of the car jibes with his story that the driver jumped out. A guy named Boomer."

Stefano watched his daughter closely as she explained what happened to Alessandro. He sensed a change in her demeanor. She looked radiant despite being bandaged up the whole right side. Despite having lost her mother. She had a presence. A steady presence. She looked at him.

"And Dad, he knows who it was and why."

"Tell us, for fuck's sake," roared Leo.

"It was The Weasel. And he did this because of what Alessandro and I did to Selena and her brothers."

Leo slowly looked at Stefano.

"Just our luck, right? The leader of the West End Gang, and he's their godfather," muttered Peter.

"So, it's personal," Sammy said.

"How the hell do you buy that off?" asked Peter, wiping his forehead.

"You don't buy that off," said Leo. He pulled out his cigar, lit it quickly, and took a long drag. Everyone watched as he pulled bits of tobacco off his bottom lip before squinting at them through the smoke. "You kill it."

THE CONSTABLES STOOD outside Alessandro's door as Maria sat at Alessandro's side, flanked by Stefano.

Leo, now allowed to sit slightly higher, had his gurney positioned on the other side of Alessandro while Sammy stayed beside Peter's gurney at the foot of the bed.

"So, kiddo," Leo said, leaning toward Alessandro, "you think it's the Strand Motel?"

"Well, this is what I know. It's on the beach, not far from Highway 501. There's power, water, a neglected parking lot on a lower level that may be an old courtyard. There's a little park nearby, I know, because I heard birds and cats. And, I smelled and saw grass and turf nearby."

Leo looked over at everyone.

Everyone's eyes were glued on him.

He sighed deeply.

"And Stinky was there."

Peter cleared his throat. "Stinky. You know he jumped, right?"

"Maria told me. I'm sorry."

No one said anything for a moment.

Leo did the cross, and everyone followed suit.

"They threatened Stinky's boy," said Alessandro. "I heard it. And I think they threatened to kill Yvonne and the baby if he didn't follow their God damn orders. They held me at a spot next to where they slaughtered the guy; the guy whose parts Stinky had to bring to Yvonne's for goat stew. The blood stain was still there."

Stefano snorted derisively.

Leo turned red and shook his head. He covered a smile.

"What?" asked Alessandro, looking around.

"Is'a long story."

"Did she actually cook the meat?"

"No, we were saved from getting that far by a friggin' monster of a spider." Peter smiled as he winced with discomfort. He reached for his leg. "Goddam, my toes hurt, and they're not even there. Weirdest shitty feeling."

Leo said, "I want that Strand Motel burned to the ground."

"But what if innocent homeless stay in it?" asked Sammy.

Leo shook his head. "No. It's a headquarters of sorts for the West End Gang."

"Okay, Boss, we'll take care of it." Sammy turned to go.

"Wait a minute," roared Leo.

Sammy looked at him.

"Whatever you do, dammit, don't tell Yvonne."

IT WAS PAST MIDNIGHT, and the day's breaking news was still about the massive blaze on Ocean Boulevard; the defunct Strand Motel was on fire. According to the newscaster, no one expected any deaths, as it was officially out of business for two years. If anything, she said it looked like somebody saved a future developer from having to tear the structure down to make way for yet another new fancy resort.

Maria's eyes were getting heavy from staring at the ceiling-mounted monitor. Instead, she looked over at Alessandro and studied his face. Life had been very cruel the last year or so, with his pretty looks. She reached up and touched the older scar. Then, she pushed against the edge of the bed and kissed his newly-scarred cheek.

He looked at her and blinked, smiling gently. He slowly raised his arm and rested it on her shoulders.

Maria snuggled as best she could. She looked at her father who was also watching along with Leo and Yvonne, cradling a sleeping little Leonardus on her lap.

At the foot of Alessandro's bed sat Jorge, Alessandro's father, looking up at the TV. He had finally arrived from Venezuela.

Maria, grief-stricken, pursed her lips. She wiped away a tear and looked at Jorge's back. His way of dressing was old-world, and elegant. She looked on with interest, and not without a slight amount of fear. This powerful man was going to be part of her life now. Their *famiglia* was changing. Lose a mother, gain a father-in-law. And Rose. Jorge had announced he was marrying Rose, so a mother-in-law in the making.

She sadly looked around at flowers and a few balloons they had received from nurses since her and Alessandro's engagement announcement the day before. It was bitter sweet. She couldn't be happier with the decision. In fact, it was the most natural thing to do. She needed Alessandro. Especially now. But it was still a very, very sad occasion.

Maria so desperately wished for her mother to be with them in that room. Instead, her mother's body lay resting in the basement morgue while arrangements were being made for her funeral. They also needed a few days for everyone to recuperate enough to travel back to Vindenza with her mother.

Leo had Sammy organize all the flights. Sandra had been on the cell arranging space at the funeral home and for extra security for their homes and businesses.

Yvonne's voice cut into the heavy air. "Mah, that's such a big fire. Ah hope no one gets hurt."

"*Bella*, it's good riddance. It's a piece of junk."

"But those firemen, didn't ah just see one go inside?"

"*Bella*, firefighters know what they're doin'. Look they're savin' the old resort next to it and the park. So, it's a good thing."

"They're probably enjoying fighting the fire," said Peter.

"Look at it this way, lots of barbecued rats for the wild cats," quipped Leo.

"Speaking of cats, what's happening with Stinky?" asked Alessandro.

"He's cremated, and we're shipping his ashes to his ex-wife and son in Detroit," Leo said as he patted his shirt pocket for the cigar he couldn't smoke. He pulled it out, looked at it, and sniffed it.

"Leo," warned Yvonne, casting her beautiful eyes at him.

Leo didn't look up, but put the cigar back into the pocket.

"We're gonna take care of things properly for him, aren't we?" asked Peter.

"*Si*, he *famiglia*." Stefano stretched and straightened his legs. "Sandra, she send money."

"How?"

"One of da guys," Stefano said.

"Will they be getting it monthly, too?"

Stefano nodded.

"You sending his family money, Honey?" Yvonne looked at Leo, hopeful.

"Yes, *Bella*. It's part of his benefits package of workin' for me."

"You are such a good man, Leo." She reached over and touched his grizzly chin. "God loves you very much."

Leo shifted his bulk. "I wouldn't go that far, *Bella*."

Maria looked at Yvonne's dark beauty and wondered how she could remain so innocent, so blind to what Leo really did on a day to day basis. How did such an angel come into his life? Into *their* lives? She felt bad for Leo, for she knew there had to be a day of reckoning. They all couldn't sugar coat everything forever.

She smiled but wasn't quite sure as to why. Was it the keeping of secrets that the family enjoyed having in common? Was it the thread that tied them together, forming their uniqueness as a family? Good or bad, she felt very proud, even though everything sensible within her continuously reminded her they lived perilously in an acutely dysfunctional world.

The strange reality was that she loved it. And wouldn't have it any other way. She was proud of the *famiglia*. Their honor and dedication to one primary goal, a goal with no real name, propelled them forward. They grew stronger with every new crisis—they were unbeatable.

But there was always a cost. This time, it cost them her mother's life; Adriana Giordani, the wife of a *Zio, killed*.

There was going to be hell to pay. And she was ready.

She looked back at the TV and thought of the intense power represented in that cramped room. It wasn't just a few people sitting in a little hospital room somewhere on the coast in South Carolina. It was power that stretched outward across the United States, into Southern Canada, Western Canada, Mexico and South America. Soon it was to be the East Coast of Canada, virtually tying up the country. Who knows where they went from there.

She turned to Alessandro and kissed him on the ear lobe. "I love you," she whispered.

He squeezed her with his arm as she settled down once again, holding his hand. For the first time in her life, she took full stock of where she stood in the world. She saw clearly where she belonged and where she was needed. In this scenario, she chose to be a Queen. She was going to talk to Dr. Bob and the other physicians for she had made up her mind. She would begin the long, arduous process of fully becoming a woman.

CLAUDIA WAS POWERFULLY UPSET.

Three days after the accident and the shock of Andy's death, Claudia emerged from a deep sleep of grief, and rose from bed an entirely different woman. Usually old ahead of her time, she woke up looking 10 years younger—closer to her 68 years. She had walked onto her balcony into the balmy, warm tropical air, and looked over the city of Myrtle Beach, far beyond the intersection where Andy had died.

Claudia realized that Andy had died in vain, and that made her spitting angry.

It was different with Fabrizio. She wasn't angry with his death. He had ruined his lungs by smoking three packs of cigarettes a day since he was nine years old and she always knew he couldn't live long. She understood he brought on his own death, despite what Andy had said about Anita and Rose killing him. They simply hurried the inevitable, by probably only days. Yes, she was upset and grieved. No doubt about that. But it was part of life. Men in their Italian Canadian community always died younger than their wives, and many widows were known to wear black for over 40 years.

She also knew she didn't have to fight to be strong when Fabrizio died. Andy was always the strong one and remained so after Fabrizio's death. It was that way in their family since the day Andy was able to speak at the age of two; she took full, tempestuous control over her parents and everything they did as a family. She was the anchor.

After Fabrizio's death, Andy cooked as usual; Andy bossed her around, as usual, Andy organized everything, as usual. The normalcy generated by her daughter helped distract her from the potential depth of her loss.

Now, Andy was gone and Claudia's anchor had been swept away in a terrible gale.

But instead of floundering, even more, Claudia emerged reborn. She was now the Italian Matriarch.

As she shivered in that updraft from Ocean Boulevard with the pounding of the nearby surf roaring in her ears, she could feel the loving, holy hand of *Santa Maria* Herself rest upon her frail shoulder. It was a spiritual awakening.

The world became clear. She had awakened from a different, strange reality.

She turned from the railing, walked through her bedroom and out into the grand open space of the bright, clean, spacious, luxurious penthouse. She sighed as she looked out toward the ocean and up at the sky. She thought at least her Adriana had known what it was like to own a beautiful penthouse overlooking an ocean. She thought of how her daughter had never reached as far south as Miami—Adriana's dream since before her wedding day, not ever having gone because of Stefano's fear of flying. *But that's okay*, thought Claudia. *I will bathe you in love and spoil you in spirit whenever I possibly can.*

It was time to worship her daughter, her son-in-law, and her *nipotina.* Stefano was going to be her *cocco di mamma*, the son she never had. And Maria, her special *nipotina,* will be as if she were her own daughter.

She saw Sammy at the couch. She studied Sammy's big, short-cropped head and double neck. "Sammy," she called, her thin voice barely discernable over the subdued sounds of the baseball game Sammy watched on TV.

He didn't hear her.

"Sammy." She stepped into Sammy's view.

Sammy looked up, surprised. "*Nonna.*" He tried to get up, but his gut got in the way, and he only managed a rocking motion. He gave up. "You okay?" He gave it another try and finally pushed himself up off the couch, his pant legs stuck to his socks over his ankles.

"I'm'a fine. You wanna eat?"

Sammy looked bug-eyed at her. He looked over at the messy kitchen. "Um."

"You'a eat. I'a make," she announced, jabbing a little thumb into her chest.

"Are you sure you're up to it, *Nonna?*" Sammy followed her to the kitchen.

She marched around the island, the top of which almost reached her underarms. She clucked her tongue at the mess as she grabbed a towel off one of the cupboard doors and wrapped it around her light-blue fuzzy housecoat. She shook her head at the bologna slices drying along the edges, dirty dishes piled in the sink with flies buzzing around old bacon on a plate smeared with egg yolk.

"Who'a make'a this mess?" she demanded, sounding like Andy.

"I, uh, me, I guess, *Nonna.*"

"Hmmm. You no'a touch no more."

Sammy's eyebrows raised sky-high. "Um, okay. Maybe you want me to take you to the hospital to see everyone?"

"*Si*, but not yet. First, I clean. Then you take me shopping. I make'a a big meal." She turned to declutter the counter-top.

Sammy nodded at the back of her little head.

"So, you wanna coffee?" she asked, putting jam in the cupboard.

Sammy thought for a moment. "Okay."

Sammy watched silently as she flitted between her step stool, reaching up into the cupboard for coffee, and the tap. Click, click, bang, bang, she put together a pot of coffee to drip and rolled up her bulky sleeves at the sink, standing on her step stool. She stopped, turned to face Sammy, and waved at the TV. "Sammy, you watch you'a football. I clean this."

"It's baseball."

"Whatever."

Sammy took a step back, turned, and sat back down keeping his eyes on her.

Claudia began to hum. Her mind had clicked into motion with beautiful funeral arrangements for her daughter. She was going to make it the most spectacular funeral their little Town of Vindenza had ever seen.

June 1989

SIGNORA SABRINA GIUSEPPINA MORETTI, a longstanding member of the Vindenza Italian Canadian Club, dared to die just before Andy's funeral. Her family had released a white dove for each of her 99 years, thereby using all the available white doves in Quebec and the neighboring state of New York.

Father Carl reassured her the doves were trained to return and Claudia would have the 46 white doves she would need for Andy's service. But in the end, only three doves returned, the rest having gotten lost, killed and eaten by other birds, or simply died on their own in the wild.

Three solitary white doves.

She was spitting angry.

Claudia had unlimited resources behind her. She pushed Father Carl to scour Italy where the custom of raising white doves for these occasions was prevalent. But earlier that year, Sergio Leone, Italy's famous writer and director, had died in Rome, and his death caused a wave of people releasing white doves in his memory. Consequently, even the Pope couldn't find a pure white dove to release from the Vatican as his Peace Dove.

When she heard that even the Pope couldn't find a white dove, she felt satiated and stopped complaining. In her mind, at least she had three pure white doves representing the Father, the Son and the Holy Ghost, to rise to the heavens ensuring her daughter's soul would reach the throne of *Dio Omnipotente* Himself.

So, on the day of Andy's elaborate funeral at the packed Holy Mary Mother of God Catholic Church in Vindenza, amply endowed by a massive police force rented from nearby Montreal, the large crowd left for the graveyard with an angelic children's choir singing God's praises. The long, snake-like line of cars with mourners and police escort made its way to the Vindenza Holy Mary of God Cemetery. There they stood or sat, gathered around Father Carl, standing elegantly in his whites and purples, pouring praise on a woman who everybody either loved or hated.

Peter sat in his wheelchair on the family's platform, a heavy plaid blanket over his lap, despite the mild Canadian June weather. Sandra sat in a chair next to him flanked by Leo, Yvonne, and a restless Leonardus. Taking Leonardus off Yvonne's lap was Willie, who had flown up from New England and was sitting next to his mother. Stefano, now the grieving widower, sat with Maria, Alessandro, Jorge, and his new wife, Rose, on the other side of Father Carl. Claudia sat between him and Maria. Behind them stood Sammy and Frankie, and Mario and Guido and their families hovering nearby. All of Vindenza had gathered that day, all in black, all quiet.

In front of them was Fabrizio's grave and headstone. Next to that, hung the gold-sprayed cement sarcophagus that entombed Andy's coffin. Sturdy straps attached to an excavator's bucket helped balance the sarcophagus on two long two by fours laid across the dug pit. Piled high on top of the sarcophagus, lay a mound of white orchids. Below, overlapping the hole's edges and lining the grave's bottom, was fake green turf swept clean of dirt, flower, bug, or leaf.

On the lid of the tomb, Claudia had ordered a brass engraved plaque reading,

"Here lies beloved wife, mother, and daughter,
Adriana Maria Lisabetta Giordani"

Below that engraved in Italian was,

"*Qui si trova amata moglie, madre e figlia,*
Adriana Maria Lisabetta Giordani".

It was time for the releasing of the three pure white doves—one for the Father, one for the Son, and one for the Holy Ghost.

Claudia nervously reached out and took Maria's hand. Maria looked over at her *Nonna*. Alessandro also looked over at her. Claudia nodded back and wiped her eyes with a tissue. She felt she was doing good. She thought she had indeed done a fantastic job of sending her sweet Adriana off to Heaven.

There was a pause.

Claudia looked over at Father Carl who glanced at her from under his eyebrows. Sheepishly.

She frowned. She looked at the dove cage behind him—a white wooden box, trimmed in gold, punctured with holes for the doves to breathe. She motioned him to release the doves.

Father Carl cleared his throat, turned, and picked up the wooden box. He placed the large box on his podium and carefully placed his hands under the lid.

"We honor and celebrate the life of Adriana Maria Lisabetta Giordani by releasing this beautiful white dove in a serenely beautiful, meaningful way. To symbolize the hope that her departing spirit may find freedom, peace, serenity and a new beginning."

Claudia stood up. "Stop'a."

Everyone looked over at her, surprised.

Father Carl tore his eyes from the skies to her. He looked down at the box and turned red. He let the lid close and took his hands away.

She scurried over to the podium. She peeked through the holes in the side. There was only one white dove clucking and looking back at her, this way and that. Then it stood quietly and cooed at her.

Wide-eyed, she angrily looked up Father Carl's nose.

He shrugged and whispered apologetically, "Claudia, I had to make the gesture. It's the Pope, for crying out loud. The Heavenly Father. He needed Peace Doves. We couldn't cheat him of that."

Claudia stared at him and blinked. She didn't know whether she wanted to bite him, scratch his eyes out or push him into the grave and have Andy's coffin dropped on top. She shook her head vehemently. "Why not'a? God cheat me of Adriana."

"But Andy would've loved to help the Pope."

"No, she would not'a. She no care about the Pope," she screamed loudly.

A gasp rippled through the onlookers. The trees around them swayed in a strong gush of wind. New green leaves spiraled off branches, loitering over the orchids, the green turf, and on everybody's heads and shoulders.

"I do'a dis dove." Claudia wanted to make sure that the one and only precious little pure white dove flew without a hitch.

Father Carl bent his head and stepped aside. He motioned to her to go on with the planned release of, albeit, a single dove.

Claudia, her face grim and set, reached under the lid with both hands. She blindly searched for the dove and wrapped her little hands around its soft little body. Slowly, she withdrew it. The lid slid and landed on the dove's little head. It struggled in panic. Claudia tightened her wiry fingers around the dove but, in her need to control the bird, she squeezed too tightly so that when she finally threw the bird up in the air, the little thing did not have time to unravel and spread its wings before it plummeted head first straight down into the pit and landed beneath the suspended sarcophagus.

Everyone gasped. Someone said, "You could never tell Andy where to go." Some laughed.

Claudia ignored them and gingerly stepped close to the edge of the pit and looked down.

The little gentle dove lay with wings sprawled, its neck broken and its little eyes closed.

Claudia almost dove into the hole, in shock, but Father Carl grabbed her in time. "There's no way we can get that dove, Claudia.

Unless we tell everyone to go home and we take the sarcophagus away. This will take hours, perhaps. We must leave it where it is."

She motioned to the sarcophagus. "But it will squish the dove." She swallowed back bile. "Like a pancake'a." She looked through hot tears at the mass of people around them, all whispering, all pointing at the pit. "*Mama mia*," whispered Claudia.

Father Carl cleared his throat. "I don't think Andy wants to go," he whispered gently.

Claudia looked to see Maria reaching for her, and she let her granddaughter lead her back to her seat. She sat and pondered what it all meant as she watched the sarcophagus sink into the ground. She was the first to throw a red rose down onto the lid deep within the pit.

As people lined up to throw a rose, she sat in her seat knowing what the whole of Vindenza knew.

Andy wasn't going anywhere.

Chapter Twenty-Six

June 1990

LEO TIPPED HIS HEAD BACK and blew cigar smoke upwards as he studied the garage rafters. They sat around the open hatchway of the *caverna* instead of within its bowels, keeping Peter company in his wheelchair. They'd moved out the old Volvo, and the Caddy was at the car wash getting spruced up for the wedding the next day.

"We should figure out how to set up a hoist from the rafters and lower you into the *caverna*," joked Leo.

Everyone laughed.

With a drink in hand, Stefano shoved his stool back and walked over to the open garage door. He nodded at guys posted at the end of the driveway. He leaned against the wall and sipped as he listened to the birds chirping in the trees. He listened to his chickens. He heard a goat bleat.

"Or why not just drop Dad in and keep him there forever. He could be that relative who is secretly locked away," giggled Steffy.

Stefano turned and looked at the men of his *famiglia*. Steffy, and his brother Andrew, 17 years old, were getting drunk on *Grappa*. His godsons. He grinned at the sight of them. Handsome young men. Men in training.

Peter looked reasonably healthy in his electric wheelchair, his pants tucked in at the knee on the one leg.

Leo, deeply-tanned, was a little portly due to Yvonne's fantastic cooking.

Sammy and Frankie had flown in with Leo and Yvonne, the night before.

Early that morning, Frankie had picked up Willie from the airport.

Mario had flown in with his wife from Vancouver and Guido-well, Guido was always there, overlooking their business in Montreal, helping to balance the tensions between them and the Sicilians.

Then there was the bridegroom and his father.

Stefano had noticed Alessandro had gained weight over the previous year. Was it possible he had the beginnings of a receding hairline at the age of 25? A chill traveled along Stefano's arms when he realized he was about to acquire a son-in-law.

And one of the most powerful men in the entire Calabrian Mafia outside of Italy, Jorge Pesseck, was going to be his in-law.

A true Calabrian dynasty.

"Very funny," retorted Peter. "'Why not just drop Dad.' Soon, they'll come up with bionic prosthetics, and I'll join in with marathons and I'll leave you behind in the dust. So, don't worry about me, boys. You too, *Zio*. I'm already taking over some of Sandra's load."

"Me, worry about you? Ha," quipped Leo. He coughed. Then hacked. Sammy bent over and slapped Leo's back.

Stefano walked back to his stool and waved at the cloud of smoke hovering around their heads. He dragged the stool closer to Alessandro. He slapped his future son-in-law on the shoulder.

Alessandro lowered his head as he grinned back. He blushed.

Steffy and Andrew nudged him.

Willie grinned and looked on.

Everyone was delighted.

"So, now. Let's get down to business." Leo cleared his throat and turned to Steffy and Andrew. "You guys, you're both still in school. You," he said, pointing to Andrew, "you're goin' for your Masters in Business. We pay for it all. You would do the *famiglia* well to continue 'cause we want you to go West eventually and help your *Zio* Mario. It's ballooning out there, right guys?"

Perched on a crate, Mario nodded and looked at his brother, Guido. "Yeah, no kiddin'. We're pullin' it in like'a we go fishing." He motioned a fishing pole.

Mario laughed and nudged his brother.

Leo grinned, then got serious. "You," he pointed to young Stefano, "you're studyin' law. That we need, too. Like Willie here." He pointed at Willie.

Willie, a year older, a year more mature, smiled at his stepfather while holding his own cigar aloft.

"He's finishin' up at Harvard," continued Leo. "We need as many lawyers in the *famiglia* as possible. *Ragazzi, capite?*"

Stefano picked up his cigar from a tin ashtray on the cement floor. He tapped it on the edge of the old coffee can they used for the communal ash. "We have'a job for you'a, Alessandro."

Alessandro looked up, his eyes watering from the smoke. "You mean, I'm not Maria's babysitter anymore?"

The men laughed.

"You 'n Maria are movin' down to Myrtle Beach. I need you there," said Leo. "I want you taking over the running of the park. The day-to-day stuff. I'll watch over the money part."

"Oh, okay, I'm fine with that," said Alessandro.

"You live'a in the condo." Stefano jerked his head as he sighed. "I stay here now. With Claudia. I'm finished in Myrtle Beach." He looked at Peter and cast his eyes at Guido. "We still have a problem'a here."

"What do you mean?" frowned Peter.

"Rizzuto, he happy we pull out from Montreal." Stefano looked over at Leo to continue.

"Rizzuto agreed to keep The Weasel at bay. This thing with Selena and her brothers." Leo hesitated and looked at Stefano.

Stefano felt his eyes burn, and he looked down at his cigar. He twirled it as he fought back his grief.

"We lost someone extraordinary." Leo straightened his back, and slapped his gut hard. "All for goddamn personal reasons. Not even business. What a damn waste. Tragic."

Stefano looked at Alessandro and watched him wither under the reference. It was so tempting to blame Alessandro. So tempting.

"But now we have this." Leo turned and nodded at Sammy.

Sammy leaned over, pulled a piece of paper out of his back pants pocket, and handed it to Leo.

Leo unfolded it and read before handing it to Alessandro.

Alessandro squinted at it, then leaned forward. "Shit," he whispered. "Not again."

"Read it, so's the others can hear." Leo chewed his lip.

Alessandro blinked at the paper.

"You pieces of shit. You'll all burn."

"Charming. That's it?" asked Peter.

Alessandro looked up and nodded.

"It's a good thing we got an army watchin' over us." Peter shifted in his wheelchair.

Alessandro looked over at his father.

Jorge joggled his head and slowly caressed his smoothly-oiled hair, pushing it back into place behind his ear. "Nothing to worry about. They're vermin here. They think they're bigshots." Jorge looked at Leo. "We're making sure that the wedding will go without a hitch."

Suddenly, everyone heard an oncoming roar.

Everyone got up, moved to the open doorway, and stood in the sun, looking at the cloudless sky in time to see a helicopter race overhead. The noise was deafening. They could feel the air currents from under the blades.

"Wow," yelled Andrew.

"What's happening?" yelled Steffy.

They moved to look around the back of the house. The helicopter swung to the right and sped over the acres of tilled and planted rows back of the barn.

"One of ours," yelled Jorge.

The kitchen window was thrown open with a bang. "What the hell was that?" yelled Sandra from the window.

"*Ma*, it's one of ours," Andrew yelled as he ran out onto the back grass to look up at the window. "They're keeping an eye on things."

"Thank God someone is," she yelled back before the window was slammed closed.

Stefano raised his face to the sun as the others continued to mill about on the warm blacktop of the driveway.

"There's no end to it. You burn 'em out like rats and they still come out of the woodwork. These guys are nuts," Leo muttered as he turned to go back in. He hobbled back into the coolness of the garage and sat on his stool. "Shit, these stools hurt my ass, Stef. Is there no room for some plush armchairs here in this lousy garage?"

Stefano laughed as Frankie stepped over, took off his light suit jacket, folded it, and handed it to Leo to sit on.

"Yeah, you laugh. At least you got meat on your ass."

Stefano motioned to Mario and Guido. Hands in pockets, they wandered closer. "You make sure der are no bombs' in all de cars as they come to the church."

"And the reception," roared Leo. He turned to Alessandro. "I figure if they're going to try somethin', it'll be on your weddin' day. That's what I would do. So, we all have to check the cars, the church, the reception."

"Well, we'll just have to be diligent. What do we look for?" Steffy looked at his great-*Zio* Leo keenly.

Stefano looked at him and the three other young men. They were all so keen to learn. Leo turned and looked at him. They locked eyes.

"What a *famiglia*, huh? Look at these four wonderful, young, beautiful soldiers." He jabbed his cigar back in his mouth and raised his hand. "Stick with us' n you'll all learn. One day, you'll take over."

"CLAUDIA, IF YVONNE wants to make some of the meal for tonight, let her. She's got two goddamn restaurants for cryin' out loud." Sandra stood with her arms spread outward, beseechingly. She was covered in flour, standing at the kitchen counter by the sink looking over at Claudia who stood at the stove stirring a massive pot of sauce.

Claudia wore a smeared and stained white apron over her widow black. She had to hold her arm up high to be able to stir. "She'a make things I no wanna eat," she said stubbornly. "Not Italian."

"I hear you, Nonna," yelled Yvonne from the dining room where she was setting the table for that night's wedding rehearsal dinner.

"Claudia, it doesn't have to be all Italian," Sandra said.

Claudia turned to Maria at the kitchen table. "Is'a Maria's wedding. She Italian." She walked to the kitchen doorway and faced the dining room. "We Italian. Food should'a be Italian."

"*Nonna*, Leo likes ma food. Ah love your Italian food, but ah want to make my stuff, too. Ah love you, Honey, but you gotta let me do this."

Maria watched *Nonna* standing with her little arms crossed, looking toward the dining room. Claudia pointed at something. "You no use da purple napkins?"

"Where are da purple napkins? I only saw these pink ones."

Nonna raised her arms and dropped them. She disappeared.

Maria continued to listen to her *Nonna* berating Yvonne who, in turn, stubbornly but politely jousted back.

Maria could smell the beautiful aroma of Yvonne's cooking wafting up from the basement kitchen. She shook her head and looked over at Sandra.

Sandra looked back at her from under the hanging cupboards. She smiled and also shook her head. She rolled her eyes.

Maria grinned at her and shrugged. There'd been nothing but arguments about the wedding preparations, and she basically left it up to the three older women: Sandra, Yvonne, and her *Nonna*.

Sandra wiped her hands on a towel on the counter and slapped it back on the surface before walking around to the table. She pulled out a kitchen chair and heavily dropped into it beside Maria, shaking the kitchen table in the process.

Maria immediately threw her arms over scattered almonds to keep them from rolling off the table.

"Oops, sorry." Sandra helped keep the almonds from rolling over the edges.

Maria was finishing making *bombonieres* for the reception.

"How are ya feeling?" asked Sandra, looking at her closely.

Maria jerked her head. "Fine. Though I always feel nauseous."

Sandra nodded her head. "Well, it's a change your body's going through. When's the operation?"

Maria sat back and swallowed. "It will take another year before I'm completely made female." She smiled faintly and sighed. "It's taking so long." She sadly looked at the table and fiddled with a ribbon.

Sandra reached out and reassuringly squeezed Maria's wrist. "Time flies. Just wait." She squinted lovingly at her niece. She withdrew her hand.

"What's time's Francesca coming?"

"We're meeting them at the church for the rehearsal, and then they come back here for supper."

"Good thing you have that ramp. Peter's made good use of it. Who would've guessed," Sandra said.

Maria looked over at her and remembered that wintry, sunny day and their skating rink. She blinked, sat up straight, and continued to stuff a little bag with five candied almonds. Then she silently tied a short white satin ribbon with a little white and silver card around the mouth of the fine net bag.

Off a pile, Sandra picked up one of the little ribbons with a card. Maria watched her read the text; Maria and Alessandro's names and the wedding date. Maria smiled and quietly hummed to herself.

"This would've driven your Mom crazy," Sandra quietly muttered as she studied the card.

Maria snorted. "You're not kidding." Maria smiled at what her mother would've been doing. Screaming, yelling, bossing everyone around. "She would've loved every single second."

Sandra laughed.

"Now you know'a how you *Nonno* 'a me felt'a about you Mamma's wedding," yelled Claudia as she returned from the dining room and went back to the stove.

"I can only imagine," Maria teased. She held up a little bag and shook it. The five almonds signified five wishes for the bride and groom: Health, wealth, happiness, longevity, and fertility. She laughed. No one would guess that the latter could never be a possibility.

"What are you laughing about," asked Sandra.

"The fertility part will never apply," Maria said, as she looked sideways at her *Zia*.

"Well, you can have fun trying, right?"

Maria laughed and blushed. If Sandra only knew the challenges. But Alessandro had been up for the challenges, going with her to Dr. Bob for consistent guidance and support.

"So, there are five hundred guests. How many ya got here so far?"

Maria looked down on the floor where she had two large cardboard boxes. "Let's see, um, I've already got this box full, so that's two hundred and fifty, and I think I still have about fifty to go."

"Alessandro helped you do those last night?" Sandra said.

"Yup. Most of 'em."

Sandra looked at her niece. "You look like the cat that swallowed the bird, Kiddo. Happy?"

Maria looked at her and grinned. She felt her eyes glisten. "Yup."

Sandra slapped at the kitchen table before getting up to go back to work at the sink. "Happy days, Maria. These are happy days."

FATHER CARLONI, DRESSED IN HIS WHITES AND PURPLES sporting a white and pink carnation on his breast, stood in the sunlight pouring through gold, textured glass along the upper reaches of the cathedral ceiling. The entire space was filled with a thick mist of sweet-smelling carnations, pink and white blossoms hanging from the end of each row of pews. Sizeable white floor vases overflowed with pink and white on both sides of the simple altar. White and pink ribbons hung everywhere. Pink, white and yellow rose petals were scattered on the plush red carpet.

A children's choir sang from the upper gallery, their white tunics reflecting the gold sun rays.

In her beautiful white lace gown and veil, Maria stood holding her heavy pink and white carnation bouquet, having just been walked down the aisle by her father.

Sandra stood to the side as the Matron of Honor. Francesca, a bridesmaid, sat in her electric wheelchair, grinning next to her. Both wore pink and coral satin and had small white Baby's Breath throughout their coiffed heads.

On the other side, beside Alessandro, stood Andrew and Steffy, all handsomely clad in grey tuxedos and ruffled white shirts.

The children finished singing, their pure angelic voices echoing a little longer in the rafters.

Stefano let go of his daughter's arm. She impishly looked at him through her veil.

He felt his face heating up. He nodded briefly and turned to sit in the front pew. As he did, his eyes swept over the packed congregation. Over 500 people were there. All wishing the two *Zio's* well, all coming to help celebrate the princess marrying her prince. All respecting their standing in their community. All attentively staring at Stefano.

He blushed again. He raised his pant legs at the knees and sat down beside Leo. He wiped the sweat from his upper lip, then wiped his hand on his grey tuxedo pants. He shifted his shoulders—he wore so much clothing. He settled down and looked at his daughter.

Father Carloni raised his face and looked over the congregation. Then he smiled down at Maria and Alessandro who now stood beside her.

Maria turned and handed her bouquet to Sandra.

Everyone was quiet. Someone coughed.

"We are gathered here today to celebrate the union of two very special people."

Stefano looked up into the rafters and saw delicate spider webs gently moving in the currents of heat. Andy always complained about those spider webs.

As Father Carloni continued the sacred service, Stefano glanced over to the side. He had men stationed along the sides of the congregation area, in the front hallway, and at each entranceway. Stefano also arranged for a couple of men to stand with walkie-talkies in Father Carloni's office. He could hear the helicopter in the distance. He glanced up at the gold glass windows. He knew there were police cars here from neighboring Montreal and Trois-Rivières. Maybe overkill. He didn't care. They had reasons for concern, especially after receiving that note.

Many in the church sniffed and coughed. Stefano, himself, was tearing up. After all the years of worry on Maria's behalf, it looked as if they were finally going to have a happy ending for her.

Stefano looked over at Claudia sitting between Leo and Yvonne, wringing a handkerchief in her hands. She had just finished telling Stefano that Andy's spirit was with them.

He took a deep breath and closed his eyes. Stefano imagined what Andy would say at that moment and smiled: *I can't stand this. This is killin' me.*

A distant roar made him open his eyes, and he squinted at the sky. In the distance, he saw the helicopter.

Stefano glanced across the aisle at Jorge and his wife, Rose. He remembered Rose and Anita fighting on top of Fabrizio. The memory caused him to almost laugh out loud.

He settled back against the pew and thought of Anita. She would've loved to have seen Maria looking beautiful, glowing, happy, ecstatic. She would've gotten a kick out of little tomboy Maria wearing make-up and looking like an angel in a white, sparkling gown. Yes, she would've even cried to see the innocent and hopeful love in Alessandro's eyes.

He looked away and thought of Anita in his arms in the barn so many years before. He wondered if there would ever be a time when he could see Anita again. No one would raise an eyebrow, of course, if he eventually remarried.

He looked down and pushed one of his cuticles with a manicured fingernail as he realized, if it ever happened, it wouldn't be for a very long time.

She never tried to reach him after leaving Vindenza.

That hurt a little.

For now, he was happy just to keep an eye on her and the boys while he made sure they would never go without. He'd seen recent photos of her. She was a little older. She now had a production job at CBC Radio Noon in Vancouver, occasionally stepping in as the host. He was proud of her. She'd become quite the voice on current affairs, a far cry from when she was a Special Events Announcer for little Vindenza's radio station.

She had remarried, which Stefano didn't see as a problem. After all, she was a beautiful, bright woman. He was going to play that one out with patience.

Claudia sobbed loudly, and Stefano looked over. Father Carloni, Maria, and Alessandro also looked at her with concern.

Stefano watched Father Carl smile and look down at his Bible and notes once again. It was time to exchange the rings.

He watched Alessandro take the wedding ring from Andrew, his Best Man. He placed it on Maria's ring finger.

"Maria Giordani, receive this ring as a sign of my love and fidelity. In the name of the Father, and of the Son, and of the Holy Spirit."

Maria turned to Sandra, her Matron of Honor, and took Alessandro's ring.

"Alessandro Bethusdo Pesseck, receive this ring as a sign of my love and fidelity. In the name of the Father, and of the Son, and of the Holy Spirit."

She gently pushed the ring over Alessandro's finger, then looked at him, grinning that mischievous grin.

A shiver of happiness flowed through Stefano.

SAMMY AND FRANKIE checked underneath a car with mirrors. They were sweating through their dress shirts.

"Clear," mumbled Frankie.

"Clear," said Sammy.

Frankie walked around the car and stood beside Sammy.

Sammy squinted up at the sun. It was a glorious day. They had listened to the children's choir earlier and occasionally could hear Father Carloni's voice over the birds and traffic outside.

Sammy looked over at Stefano's Cadillac. "I guess I'll go into Stef's car and recheck it."

Frankie shrugged.

Sammy walked over and opened the driver's side of Stefano's Caddy. He sat inside and checked around, opened the latch for the trunk, and got out. Sammy opened the trunk and looked closely. He frowned and reached for something poking out from below the false bottom. He looked for the hidden latch and opened it expecting to find a home-made bomb.

Instead, all the weapons were still there. Sammy looked around and slammed the trunk shut.

He walked to the silver-grey limousine in front of the Cadillac. He opened the long trunk. Nothing. He checked the tin cans that hung off the back fender. He kicked one of them to the side, listening to its hollow noise as it rolled.

He sighed and looked over the packed parking lot, as the helicopter circled above. He looked over at the road, at the blinking police car lights. Cops everywhere.

This was getting on his nerves.

And the day had only just begun.

"LADIES AND GENTLEMEN OF THE CONGREGATION," Father Carloni smiled, "I am proud to introduce you to Mr. and Mrs. Alessandro and Maria Pesseck."

The congregation cheered as Father Carloni led Maria and Alessandro back from signing the registry at the side of the altar.

Maria felt faint as she and Alessandro faced the congregation. She could feel the sun pour through the high windows onto their heads.

Alessandro pulled at her arm. "Come on. Let's go." Together, with arms entwined and she carrying her large bouquet, they went up the aisle to the sound of *Tarantella* blasting through the church.

Maria had chosen the music. Everyone had been upset at first, but she insisted it was the last piece of music her mother heard before she died and it was something she, Maria, needed to do. That traditional Italian song, so crucial to her *Zio* Leo, had become a part of the tragedy of their lives because of the West End Gang. There was no way she was going to allow them to influence their lives in any negative way. That song had to become a symbol of something more beautiful and wonderful than tragic loss.

Not knowing her motivation for the music, everyone laughed and clapped to the joyful, bouncing music.

CLAUDIA THREW UP HER ARMS. "Now we're doin' photos, but everyone can go to'a club for reception."

"Open bar is waiting for you," yelled Peter.

Some men cheered. Some people laughed. Most ignored him as they strained to watch the couple walk up the aisle to the back.

MARIA LOOKED BACK when they finally reached the main doors to the front hall. Behind them, Sandra was held by Andrew. Steffy was behind them, pushing Francesca in her wheelchair.

She looked on, as she stepped to the side to allow them to pass. She wanted to make sure her father and Claudia were already beginning to follow.

She took a deep breath and looked over at Alessandro.

The front doors were wide open, and a beautiful, balmy June breeze blew her dress around. She closed her eyes. "Love you, Ma," she whispered.

She vowed she would never forget a single moment of this day.

YVONNE LEANED BACK in shock and gave Leo the angry stink eye. They were sitting at the beautifully-decorated head table at the Vindenza Italian Canadian Club. Everyone had been drinking heavily, and Peter had just said something that made her heart skip a beat. In fact, it shocked the heck out of her.

Leo looked back at her beautiful face and saw the surrounding candlelight flicker in her dark eyes. He blinked and frowned.

"*Bella*, he doesn't know what he's saying. Peter's drunk for crying out loud." Leo looked past her and gave Peter a dirty look.

Peter's mouth dropped. "What'd I say?" He wavered in the wheelchair and looked at Stefano beside him for emotional support.

Stefano yanked at the white napkin tucked under his chin. He slapped it on the table beside his half-eaten meal and shook his head.

"What?" asked Peter again. "I was just sayin' what Stinky had said, right? How else do we get soldiers, right?" He looked over at Yvonne staring at him. He shook his head and shrugged. "Yvonne, how else do you think we do it?" He pointed at the packed reception hall. The lights were down, and candlelight burned from tables, wall sconces and chandeliers. Everyone was eating, drinking, laughing, chatting, and the band played beautiful old-country Calabrian music. He had just finished saying how wonderful it was that they were so successful and the *famiglia* was growing, both in terms of family members and soldiers. And he had blurted out how even Stinky had to be recruited the 'hard' way, yet they had found a gem in him.

He jumped in his wheelchair when a helium balloon burst behind him.

Stefano pushed his chair back and looked over at Leo past Peter. He pursed his lips.

Leo rolled his eyes.

Yvonne turned back to Leo. "Leo, you made me a promise, and you swore to *Santa Maria*, that you would never hurt another soul. That's why I took you. And now ah heah, you hurt poor Matthew? Is that whah he jumped?" Her voice got shrill. Yvonne's chest heaved as she breathed heavily. She raised a manicured hand and covered her ample cleavage. "Mah heart," she whispered, tears forming in her eyes.

"It's all part of the business. Like your restaurants. Part of the *famiglia* business." Peter tried to reach out to Yvonne to comfort her.

Stefano stood up and started to unlock Peter's wheelchair.

Peter looked over at what his brother was doing. "What are you doing?"

"I take you away. To the bar."

Peter tried to focus on Yvonne's face.

"'N are you tellin' me that mah restaurants are not just mah restaurants, either?" She turned back to Leo. "What's Peter sayin'?"

Stefano wheeled Peter away from the table, accidentally bumping into Claudia's chair.

"*Scusate.*"

"Where you go?" asked Claudia, surprised. Her mouth was full of wonderful *Fileja Pasta alla Silana.*

"Bar."

Claudia shrugged and continued to eat. She was half-listening to Yvonne's conversation with Leo and briefly glanced over.

"What's your nephew tellin' me, Leo? You're cleanin' dirty money by usin' *mah* hands? Is that it? You're usin' me? Now ah knows why you won't let me see the books." She pointed at herself dramatically. Her long pearl white fingernails contrasted her dark skin beautifully. She was radiant, gorgeous, wearing a wig of curls with gold tips that highlighted her beautiful eyes. She had a purple gem surrounded by diamonds on a choker, and earrings to match. Her purple gown was explicitly designed to highlight and accentuate her beautiful curves.

Leo held up his hands and tried to cradle her face.

She pulled back. She held up a finger and wagged it.

"Leo, baby, ah don't like that. No, no. Not one bit. Ah feel like gettin' up right now and find mahself a plane to go back home. But ah won't because this is Maria's day." She sat back, looking at Leo angrily.

Leo smiled bashfully. "*Bella,* I promised I would never put these hands to someone," he held out his palms for her to look at, "and take their life. I have never done that, and I never will. But that's the only promise I made."

Willie, beside his mother, looked away at Andrew. They exchanged glances.

"It's true, Momma," Willie said to his mother. "Those hands of his have never touched a single human being with the intent of killing them. I'm a lawyer. Almost. I can attest to that."

Yvonne searched her son's face. "But Matthew jumped for a reason."

"*Bella.* Peter's drunk. He doesn't know what he's talkin' about," Leo begged.

"You know what ah'm gonna do, Leo? So, you don't pull this kind of shit over mah eyes? Ah'm gonna take accounting. Ah'm gonna do the books for mah restaurants." She was about to say more, but she was distracted by the sound of cutlery being tapped on wine and water glasses. She looked over Leo's head at Alessandro and Maria as they stood up to kiss. She pointed at Leo and at herself. "You and ah, we're not finished heah."

She pushed her chair back and threw her napkin onto her plate.

"Where are you going, *Bella*?"

"Ah'm goin' to the hotel." Her chin trembled, and her eyes filled with tears. "Poor Matthew. How could you, Leo." She got up and left, squeezing behind Alessandro and Maria as they kissed, not even aware of her departure.

Alessandro and Maria sat down again, grinning.

Leo turned to Willie.

Willie, dark, handsome, blinked.

"You better go after your mother,' he said.

Willie went to get up.

"No, wait. I'll go after her." He pushed his chair back, pulled his napkin from under his chin, and got up. He hobbled past Alessandro and Maria, bending over Maria to give her a squeeze on her shoulders.

Maria looked up and smiled.

Leo followed Yvonne in her wake as she snaked through the 50 fully-decked round tables to the front of the large reception hall.

MARIA WATCHED *ZIO* LEO and Yvonne head for the front grand hall. She frowned. There were washrooms by the coat check, but there were more in the back of the reception hall. She turned to Alessandro. "Where do you think they're going?"

Alessandro looked over the crowd and shrugged.

"Speech, speech, speech," someone yelled.

"Let's hear from the father of the bride," someone else yelled.

"*Si, sentiamo il padre della sposa.*"

People clanged their cutlery against wineglasses once again.

The band stopped playing amidst the cheers.

Maria looked around for her father and spied him at the bar. She looked over at Sandra.

Sandra looked back and pushed her chair out of the way. She ran over to Stefano and pulled at the back of his tuxedo jacket.

Stefano twirled around.

"Come on, Stef," yelled Sandra. "This is your one and only time you'll be doing the father of the bride speech. Make it good."

Stefano nodded and glowed. He walked back to the table as the crowd fell quiet. Stefano looked around the room. He could tell everyone was well aware of Andy's absence. He looked down at the table setting made just for her. Her place card stood in front of her empty plate. The wine and water glasses were in their right spots. The cutlery sat waiting to be used. He looked at the pink and white carnations sitting on her plush chair. He looked down at the back of his chair. He reached out and leaned on the gilt-wood backing.

Everyone was quiet. Someone coughed softly.

Claudia reached over to Stefano and lightly touched the hem of his tuxedo jacket.

He looked at her. He had tears in his bright eyes. He sniffed, wiped his nose, and picked up his napkin to wipe his eyes. He then rolled the napkin into a ball and tossed it back onto the white linen table cover. He smiled at the well-wishers, then directed his eyes to his daughter. He saw that Maria was crying quietly and he held out his hand. "No'a, Maria. If you'a cry den I do."

Everyone laughed.

Stefano mumbled something, and Sandra elbowed him.

Maria smiled through her tears. "Come on, Dad, spit it out." yelled Maria.

"Yeah, Andy would've," someone joked.

People laughed. Some clapped.

"Hey, Andy," someone cheered.

People applauded, many broke out in cheers. Some men shook their heads. Older women in black clasped their hands and nodded their heads knowingly. Some wiped their eyes and noses.

Stefano wiped away a tear and shook his head as he played with cutlery on his plate. "I don' know what to say'a. I try to write'a speech. *Ma*." He shrugged and looked around.

"That's because you're the strong and silent type," Sandra yelled.

Everyone laughed.

"*Ma*, Maria is Adriana and my special daughter. She is'a very, *very* special. As some may'a know, Adriana and I could not have *bambinos* for a long time, n den, here come Maria." His voice broke.

"Oh dear," someone said softly.

Stefano covered his eyes. "I never thought'a we would. Ever. See. Dis. Day." He patted the table in front of him to accentuate each word of what he said.

People clapped and cheered.

He held up his hand for silence. He waited. He raised his glass of wine and water and looked at Alessandro. "I am very blessed by God'a to 'ave such a perfect son-in-law. Alessandro."

He motioned to Claudia, who smiled back through her tears. "We are very happy to have'a you'a take care of *mia figlia speciale. Molte benedizioni*." He raised his glass and took a sip.

The whole room stood up to raise their glasses, to toast the bride and groom, and to toast Andy.

Claudia held up her glass. "See'a, Adriana? Maria is'a happy."

THE NIGHT SKY WAS PACKED FULL OF STARS. A full moon hung watching over the proceedings, but there was a red tinge to its edges.

Sammy walked over to join other men standing around looking up at the moon.

"Weird, huh?" he said.

"Yeah. Weird." Frankie shrugged his shoulders. He was still chewing on a Calabrian lamb chop, tomato sauce dripping from his fingers.

Sammy looked on with disgust. He reached into his pocket and took out his handkerchief. He handed it to Frankie who took it gladly. Sammy watched as Frankie carefully wiped his mouth and chin. Then he checked the front of his shirt and jacket.

"Shit," Frankie said, as he dabbed at a spot of sauce.

Sammy looked at the Club building behind them, then over to the parking lot. There were cops lined up along the street adjoining the enormous lot, full length. Here and there, he saw the red tips of cigarettes where guys were keeping watch.

He walked across the laneway to the parked limousine. He could just make out the 'Just Married' sign taped to the back windshield. Stefano had instructed them to take the large, gold-leaf Thai goldfish, used as a repository for money gifts in the reception hall, to the limousine's trunk. But something about the sign caught his attention, and he went over. One of the corners had let loose, and, leaning over the car to press it down, he straightened out the poster.

He looked at the car under the parking lot light. He kept polishing the car so if someone touched it, it was a clear giveaway. He walked to the back to the car and bent down carefully over the trunk lid. He stood up and looked around. He whistled to three guys who looked back at him and hurried to join him.

"Did you guys touch this trunk?" Sammy asked.

Everyone shook their heads.

"Pop the trunk, will you please, Frankie?" He threw the keys at Frankie, who moved towards the driver's seat.

Frankie unlocked the car and was about to get in.

"Don't start it," demanded Sammy. "Don't put the keys into the ignition, either. Just pop the trunk." He stood by, waiting to hear the click of the lock. He gently opened it and found nothing in the trunk. His heart jumped. "Shit, look. Someone already stole the money." He looked around frantically. "You guys see anything?"

He turned and ran to the Vindenza Italian Canadian Club's grand front doors. He yanked the heavy door and hurried across the marble front hallway, past the coat check and the grand, splashing waterfall. The music boomed through the hallway. The chatter's noise rose as he stopped at the brocade curtains draped over one of the archways into the main hall. He poked his head through and looked around the smoke-filled hall to see if he could catch Stefano's attention.

Alessandro happened to look at him from the head table at the other end. Alessandro waved.

Sammy blinked and stepped through the curtains. He motioned to Stefano.

Alessandro looked over at Stefano and saw that his father-in-law was chatting with a guest, joyfully pumping his hands in congratulations.

Alessandro stood up.

MARIA LOOKED AT ALESSANDRO. "Where are you going?"

A mandolin song came to an end, and the band started another.

"Alessandro, they're going to play our favorite song soon."

"Which one? We have so many."

"The one we fell in love with in Myrtle Beach. Remember? Johnny Dee?"

Alessandro looked at the band. "They're playing something else. I'll be back before they finish this, song. Okay?"

Maria smiled. "You better."

Alessandro's eyebrows shot up. "Oh? I better? What are you going to do if I don't? Hurt me?"

"Yup, I can be formidable," she said mockingly.

"I've seen you in action. I believe it." He bent down and kissed her on the lips. "I'll be right back. Sammy needs me."

She grabbed him by the collar and pulled him closer for a deeper kiss. She let go. "Okay." Maria looked over at Sammy at the front of the hall and saw him disappear back into the front lobby. She frowned. Sammy looked perturbed. Almost frightened. Her eyes carefully followed Alessandro's back as he weaved his way through the dancers on the floor, every-once-in-a-while having to stop and let someone congratulate him.

ALESSANDRO FINALLY MADE IT to the front of the hall. He pushed the brocade curtain to the side and stepped through. It felt cooler in the marble lobby. He wiped the sweat on his forehead with his handkerchief, then tucked it back into his breast pocket.

Sammy motioned him to come over by the coat check. A pretty girl stood by, leaning against the counter.

"What is it?" He had to speak loudly over the noise and the waterfall.

Sammy pulled him to the front doors. "Hey, I hate to be the bearer of bad news, but you know that big Goldfish that everyone was putting cards with money in?"

"Yeah," frowned Alessandro.

"Well, someone's stolen it. It's not in the limousine's trunk. Did you have it moved?"

"Shit. No, unless *Zio* Stefano did. I mean, Dad. I'll go check." He turned to go.

"You looking for a big goldfish?" the coat check girl bleated.

Alessandro turned to her, surprised. "Yeah, did you see it?"

She pointed to the back of the coat check. "Some guy took it to the big walk-in safe in the back."

"Oh, thank God," Sammy yelled.

They both walked to the side of the coat check counter. Alessandro lifted up the swinging countertop to step into the back.

MARIA WATCHED THE BAND come to the end of the song. She looked questioningly at the bandleader, who looked at her and stepped up to the microphone to sing. The first slow bars of "Suddenly" started. The singer began to croon.

> *I used to think that you could never be for me,*
> *Until that fateful day. I saw your special way…"*

Maria quickly got up and hurried along the table behind all the chairs. Sandra had to shift her chair forward. She looked over and saw that her father was with Peter at the bar at the back.

Her *Nonna* reached up. "You go to the washroom?"

"No, I'm getting Alessandro to dance. This is our song," Maria yelled.

Claudia nodded and tried to get up. Maria helped Claudia push her chair back. "I be right back," Claudia mouthed as she made her way to the washrooms at the back of the hall.

Maria yanked at her long gown and swished the hem back with her white satin shoes. She almost twisted her ankle as she hurried. She stopped beside Francesca at a nearby table.

Francesca looked sideways at her and grinned. "Not used to the heels?" she slurred, grinning.

"I hate these things." She bent down and took off her shoes. She put them on Francesca's lap. "Here, you hold them till I get back." She laughed. She lifted up her dress and began making her way through the dancers toward the front.

> *Girl, we're more together than when we're apart*
> *The thought of losing you is far more painful than the start,*
> *Watching dolphins waltz along the shore,*
> *Under sun and sky,*
> *Now I understand the 'why'…*

One of the elderly guests grabbed at Maria to dance.

"Oh, I'm so sorry, Mr. Taddeucci. I have to find my wayward husband," she yelled, laughing. "This is our song." She continued to the front but had to stop while slow dancers blocked her way.

ALESSANDRO FACED THE WALK-IN SAFE. He knew the combination as they were allowed to use it for the duration of the reception. All the gifts had been moved into the safe, and he knew, for a fact, that the money was placed in *Zio* Stefano's trunk already. He didn't like the feeling in his gut when someone changed plans. He needed to make sure that Fish was there.

He thought of their upcoming plans. He had opened an account under an assumed name in Old Quebec City, and they were going to deposit the money there, before their honeymoon. Then, they were going to wire the money into a Bahamas account in which he had been saving up his wages.

He frowned as he fingered the combination lock. He was sure everyone was well versed in what the plans were. He felt nervous. Uncomfortable.

The lock clicked. Alessandro grabbed the handle and opened the door. There, amongst the wedding gifts, stood the large Goldfish. He grinned. "There you are. What are you doing hiding in—"

EVERYONE JUMPED AND SCREAMED. A massive red ball exploded and ripped through the back wall of the coat check. Cement dust, smoke, plaster, ceiling tiles, and objects filled the Hall.

Fire alarms wailed overhead, the sprinkler system jumped into action snuffing out candlelight. Yellow emergency lights came to life, sweeping and slashing through the dense wall of particles in the air.

Some guests ran. Others ducked and hid under their tables, yanking off tablecloths. Glass shattered, plates smashed. Wine, water, *grappa* spilled everywhere.

Those left at the Head Table stared - their mouths open - at the massive cloud and dust before them.

At the bar, Stefano and Peter turned back in shock.

Sandra, blood dripping from her chin, stood and cradled her face.

Willie and the twins scrambled over each other to get around the table.

Willie gave up and flew over their table and looked around frantically. He squinted through the dust and roiling humanity, looking for Maria. He couldn't see where he last saw her making her way to the front. Willie crawled forward, desperately trying to hurry through the throng, grunting as he pushed a toppled table to the side. He quickly glanced around at screaming people. Some covered their faces while others fainted. Everyone was covered in wet dust. He searched frantically, wiping his eyes against the cold, sprinkling water.

Finally, Willie caught sight of her wedding dress. "Maria," he screamed. He battled forward and finally reached her.

He looked down. Maria's dress was covered in blood, and a shard of gold-covered wood was embedded in her chest. He tried to protect her face as he raised his head to look around for help. His eyes widened, searching for Stefano at the back of the Hall.

Stefano loomed by the Head Table, squinting through the mist and watery deluge.

Willie frantically waved at him.

STEFANO PLACED A WHITE ROSE on an ebony-wood coffin and stood back to look at the second coffin.

Jorge and Rose stood by and watched. Rose was crying softly into her handkerchief while Jorge remained grim-faced.

Claudia quietly sat in a chair, stoic, grey, miserable. Angry.

Leo stood quietly next to her, livid.

Yvonne sat on the other side with Sandra. Willie and Andrew stood behind Sandra while Steffy sat bandaged in a wheelchair beside his father.

About 200 people showed up. Many more would've come but were afraid of ongoing violence between the two factions: Vindenza's 'Ndrangheta and the West End Gang-the *Gang de l'ouest.*

Stefano watched the coffins slowly descend into the double cement tomb. Once the caskets were neatly ensconced, the heavy lid gradually dropped. On it, a brass plaque hurriedly ordered and completed:

> *Here lies Alessandro Pesseck, Beloved Son, Beloved Husband.*
> *Also, here lies Maria Giordani Pesseck, Beloved Daughter,*
> *Beloved Wife, Beloved Granddaughter*

While Father Carl finished his Biblical references in a soothing but broken voice, Andrew went over to a cage while Willie stepped to the other. They released doves simultaneously: 25 for Alessandro and 18 for Maria. As they flew up into the brilliant blue sky below high, gigantic popcorn clouds, everyone's eyes followed their journey.

They flew off in different directions, many disappearing into the tall oak and maple trees of the Vindenza Holy Mary of God Cemetery.

One, however, flew in a full circle and winged its way back to the grave.

It landed on the crypt.

Father Carl swallowed hard. "Who is that now?"

Claudia put her hands together and whispered, *"Santa Maria Madre di Dio."*

Stefano looked over at Leo.

Leo looked at Stefano.

Stefano heard a distant explosion.

"What was that?" Sandra whispered as she looked around.

"Don't worry about it," muttered Leo, "It's only in Pointe-Saint-Charles."

"Pointe-Saint-Charles? Isn't that where—?" Sandra's eyes widened. She looked around at the *famiglia*.

Jorge looked at her sideways, then looked away pointedly.

Stefano glanced at her and took a deep breath.

Leo took out his cold, wet cigar, sighed, and stuck it between his thin lips. "You're absolutely friggin' right, it is." He looked over at Yvonne. "The headquarters of The West End Gang," roared Leo.

Yvonne reached over and held his forearm. She nodded, placed a hand on the crucifix hanging from her neck, and then looked down at the pure white dove preening itself on top of the crypt.

CHAPTER TWENTY-SEVEN

2005 Pearson International Airport,
Toronto, Ontario

ANITA TAYLOR GRABBED THE HANDLE of her carry-on and shifted her heavy coat a little higher over her shoulder. She looked up the Terminal hallway, then down the other way. Anita spied vacant seats in the waiting area and made her way toward them. There was time for a tea and a Tim Hortons Boston Cream. She had just sent Steve and Pat to get them.

She sat down with a sigh and organized her coat, heavy purse, and suitcase. She sat back, spied a newspaper on the opposite side on one of the side tables, and hopped over to grab it just as a young man sat down beside the table.

"Oh, I'm sorry. Were you about to read this?" Anita asked him.

The young man shook his head pleasantly enough, shaking what curls he had along the rim of an otherwise slightly bald head. "No, go right ahead."

She noticed he studied her closely. "Thank you," smiled Anita, as she settled back into the chair and shook the paper straight. She stopped and bent over to get a pair of bifocals out of her purse. She checked they were clean and perched them on her nose. She raised the paper and gave it another shake.

"Excuse me?"

Anita lowered the paper and peered over the top. "Yes?"

The young man leaned forward, eyes twinkling. "Aren't you Anita Taylor?"

Anita was surprised, and yet not. She'd been stopped before, mostly when she was a host for CBC Radio Noon in Vancouver. Anita lowered the paper and took off her glasses. "Yes, I am." She smiled.

"Wow," he said. "I've read both your books. I love your writing."

Anita sat back in surprise. "You read both my books? They're on the Italian Renaissance. Are you a student of European History?"

"No, I wouldn't say that. I'm of Italian parents, yes. They know you." He grinned.

"No kidding?" Anita smiled. "Who are your parents?"

MARIO WAS PLEASED. The conversation was going exactly as planned.

"Do you remember Andy and Stefano Giordani?" He smiled as he watched Anita cover her mouth in surprise.

"Oh, my." Anita pointed at him. "Yes, I can see the resemblance." Her happy look was replaced by a hint of sadness. "If you don't mind, what exactly did they talk about?"

Mario straightened up and looked at the ceiling 30 feet above them. "Oh, no," he laughed, "good stuff." He grinned. "For the most part."

"Oh, my God. How are they? Are they still at the farm in Vindenza?"

"Well, yeah, still in Vindenza. At least, my Dad's doing okay. He's retired now. Just."

"No kidding. How wonderful. And your mother? Is she the same old firecracker she used to be? I've never known a more intelligent and, well, bossy woman." She laughed. "Well, at least you always knew where you stood with Andy."

Mario looked at his hands. "Well, Mom passed away, as a matter of fact." He watched her sit back in sincere shock.

"Oh. My God." Anita grabbed his hand. "I'm truly sorry to hear that. The world is a far sadder place without your mother."

"Yes, I agree. The world has lost a star."

"Yes. The world indeed lost a star. Do you mind me asking, how did your mother die? I mean, she was far too young to die of natural causes. What was she, 60?"

"Just," Mario lied. Stefano had told Mario not to go into any *famiglia* details too soon. "She died helping Dad. She drove the lawnmower into the pond. Nobody was around. The machine fell sideways and pinned her."

Anita covered her face, and started to cry.

Mario jumped up and sat beside her, putting a comforting arm around the woman. He drew a handkerchief from his jeans pocket and handed it to her.

She wouldn't take it.

"No, I know. It's old-fashioned giving you a handkerchief, isn't it? But no, you keep it. By all means."

She took the handkerchief and wiped her eyes and nose.

He leaned back and studied the fine lines on her face and deep grooves between the eyebrows. Anita had difficult times, he could tell, but she was beautiful. He figured she must have been into her late fifties, as she was younger than his parents.

"I don't understand," Anita said. "Your Mom hated everything to do with the running of the farm."

Mario laughed. "Ha. Don't I know it. She only went so far as to mow the lawn, and sometimes she helped him with the weeding in the garden." He leaned in conspiratorially. "But she still hated the chickens."

Anita's laugh echoed gaily through the Terminal as she wiped away more tears.

"Mom?"

Mario looked up to see a tall young man of about 21 years old. He met his suspicious gaze.

"Mom, are you alright?"

Anita grabbed the young man's hand. "Yes," she beamed. She pointed at Mario and struggled to find the right words.

Mario stood up and held out his hand. "Hi. I'm Mario Giordani. My family knew your mother in Quebec."

The younger man accepted his hand, pointing at him.

"Yeah, Mom always talked about the Giordanis. Your mother and father were Andy and Stefano. Oh. I'm sorry. I'm Steve, son to this lovely lady," he said, smiling at his mother. He spied her tears. "Oh,

Mom," he said teasingly, turning back to Mario. "My Mom has a big heart, as you can tell."

Mario recognized Steve from the photographs his *Zio* Mario had sent him from Vancouver. "Nice to meet you, Steve." He blinked. *Steve. Stefano*

Steve turned and looked up the hallway and pointed at another young man coming toward them carrying a tray of cups and donuts. "And that gorilla there is my brother, Pat. Hey Pat. You'll never guess," he called out.

Pat took a couple of significant strides and came up.

"This is Mario Giordani," Steve said.

Pat balanced the tray on one arm and held out his hand.

Mario shook his hand and pointed from brother to brother. "Twins."

"Yup," said Pat and Steve simultaneously.

Anita turned to Mario, and he smiled sweetly at the familiar face.

"I'm so glad to know you. Your father always wanted a son. Not that he didn't worship Maria." She laughed. "How is your sister? I tell you, I love that kid. I'm surprised she isn't Prime Minister. I don't know how often I spoke of her to these guys." Anita turned to her sons. "Do you remember me mentioning Maria to you over the years?"

Steve rolled his eyes in jest and laughed.

Mario leaned forward. "Do you remember? Mom always described Maria as being *special?*"

Anita nodded.

Suddenly, a ray of sunshine burst through the clouds and through the massive windows overlooking the airport's tarmac. Light danced in the twins' brilliant aqua blue eyes. It caught Mario's breath. He looked knowingly at Anita.

She smiled shyly and nodded. "Yes, I'm so sorry. It means…"

Mario grabbed her wrist and smiled reassuringly.

She fought back tears. "Your father wanted so much to have sons."

Mario let go of her wrist.

She blushed, stood, and looked at the three handsome men in front of her. "Well, he's got three, I guess. Too bad he retired. He actually *is* Stefano Giordani & Sons Contractors."

An announcement said their flight to Vancouver had been delayed because of technical difficulties.

Anita looked at her boys. "Wow, that's interesting." She looked at Mario. "I guess we have lots of time to talk." She looked at the boys again.

They looked at each other and shrugged.

Mario caught the motion and was pleased. "That's great, right?" He feigned surprise. He looked at the flight schedule on the monitor above their heads. He saw the *Delayed* flashing next to their flight. "You're flying west?"

"We're going back home to Vancouver," Anita said.

Pat turned to Mario. "And you're going back to Quebec?"

Mario paused. "Would you consider spending a bit of time with us? Delay your trip home a little?"

Anita's face drained of color. She blinked twice. "Steve, could you please go and see if there are any vacant seats going to Dorval International Airport? I think it's time you met your father."

"Oh, my God," said Pat.

Steve nudged Pat and they turned slowly, looking back briefly before heading through the terminal.

Mario watched the brothers retreat. He knew they would come back saying there were no seats. He had other plans for them. He leaned closer to Anita. "It's now called the Pierre Elliott Trudeau International Airport."

Anita blinked. "Since when?"

"A couple of years ago."

Anita smiled. "Oh, jeez. Little Dorval. It must be so different back home."

"Some things don't ever change," said Mario.

"Well, certainly obviously lots do! It's been a long time," she laughed, looking at him. She reached out and pulled him over to the seat next to her. "Oh, tell me more. Will your father be alright if we come for a visit? Will Maria be there?"

"Both will love it." Mario looked at his watch. He figured the boys would be about ten minutes, so he had some time to kill. "Do you remember how Mom was always full of the neatest jokes?"

"Oh my God, I have no idea how she remembered them all."

"Have you heard this one?" He grinned and licked his lips. "An Irish priest is driving to New York and gets stopped for speeding. The cop smells alcohol on the priest's breath and then sees an empty wine bottle on the floor of the car. He says, 'Sir, have you been drinking?'

'Just water,' says the priest.

The cop says, 'Then why do I smell wine?'

The priest looks at the bottle and says, 'Good Lord. He's done it again.'"

Anita howled. She slapped Mario's shoulder.

"Anita," Mario said, more seriously. "You won't find any vacant seats flying to Montreal."

Anita looked surprised. "How would you know? We just might." She smiled.

Mario shook his head. "No, you won't." He scratched the curls at the back of his head. "In fact, I'm not here because I was flying to Montreal, nor did we bump into each other by accident."

Anita frowned. "What do you mean?"

Mario held up his palms. "Now, don't get upset, okay, Anita? You're flying to Vancouver and this is your gate, right? I wouldn't be sitting here if I was going to Montreal. You follow me?"

Anita sat back and swallowed. She said nothing for a few seconds. Her voice lowered. "You mean you've been lying to us?"

Mario squinted at her. "I had to make sure you were open to this discussion first. I hope you understand."

"Open to this discussion? I don't get it." She clutched her purse and looked back searching for her boys. "I want to understand something. How did you know we'd be here in Toronto?"

"You were here to speak at a women's function, were you not?"

Anita straightened her back and studied him. "Yes."

"And the invite came out of the blue with an enticing fee attached to it. And they promised to pay for all expenses, including an extra room for the guys."

"You're saying this was planned."

Mario looked at her silently. He raised his chin slightly.

Anita looked away, somewhat angrily.

Mario let her think without interruption. This was when Anita either decided she wanted nothing to do with him and his family, or she took the plunge and accepted what his father had carefully planned for them all these years. His eyes flicked to the twins returning in the distance. He looked back at Anita.

"So, there are no seats available to Montreal, you're predicting. What did you intend to do with us, then?" she asked.

"I've rented a minivan to take you, Steve, and Pat, to my father."

Anita raised her chin defiantly. "Why would we want to do that?"

"Because Dad wants to see you. He needs you, Anita. And he needs the boys."

Anita blushed and looked down at her hands. "And why a minivan. Why not fly?"

"Because we have to arrive somewhat under the radar." He sat back as the boys were about to reach them. He quickly added. "And we have a lot to talk about before we get there."

"Mom, no vacancies." Pat and Steve looked down at their mother.

Mario leaned toward Anita and whispered. "I promise. I won't kill you."

Anita read his expression. "You Giordanis. You're all the same."

AS HE DROVE, MARIO LOOKED in his side-mirror for tails. He then looked in the rear-view mirror at his half-brothers.

"Tell me more of what you've been doing all these years in Toronto," asked Anita.

Mario kept his eyes on the 401 traffic ahead of them. "I've been hiding out. Staying away from trouble back home, which I'll explain, in a bit, why. I've been working as a carpenter on film sets and I've got a little house in Cabbagetown— a little place I renovated." He glanced at her. "You know, I took your last name."

Anita jolted. "You took my name?"

"Yup. I'm Mario Taylor. And I'll explain that, as well." He slowed down to allow someone to cut in front of the minivan.

Anita looked down at her lap sadly.

"Are you okay, Anita?" Mario asked. "Is this too much?"

Anita shook her head. "Yes." She covered her face. "Shit." She dropped her hand and looked at the passing city scenes of Scarborough east of Toronto. It had started to rain and the minivan's wheels hissed and sucked at the wet surface of the highway. The windshield wipers kicked into action.

"I always knew your father's hand was in everything. How could I not? Especially now that I look back. Whenever I was in a bind, something miraculously happened to fix whatever it was." She twisted in her seat and looked at her boys. "I never kept any secrets from you guys, I don't think. I always mentioned that maybe your father may have had something to do with the odd thing."

Pat shrugged. He grimaced.

Mario caught the look. "What?" he asked.

Pat shrugged again and shook his head.

Anita turned in her seat to look back. "Pat."

Pat threw her a warning look.

"Pat, we spoke about this. You can't change the fact that he's your father."

"Yeah, but Mom, why now? Why at all?"

"Is there a problem?" asked Mario, looking at Pat's reflected image under hooded eyes.

Pat caught Mario's look, leaned away out of view toward his window and muttered to himself.

Steve cleared his throat and leaned forward between the two front seats. "So, Mario Taylor, why now and not before?"

Mario focused on the road. "It's perfect timing."

Anita looked. "How do you mean?"

"You retired from radio to pursue writing. And you just got another book deal."

"Yes."

"You could write anywhere."

"Yes," Anita said cautiously.

"You've been recently widowed," Mario said.

Anita blinked twice.

The obvious and suddenly curious question hung in the air about the timing of her husband's death. It wasn't a happy marriage, Mario knew.

"Fuck," Pat whispered behind Mario.

Anita looked at him.

"Condolences," whispered Mario.

Anita frowned.

Mario looked into the rear-view mirror again and saw Steve but only part of Pat's shoulder. "And Pat and Steve just graduated with a Business degree in Vancouver."

"That's right." Steve looked over at Pat and then at the rearview mirror at Mario's dark eyes. "How'd you know?"

Mario ignored the question. "You have, literally, nothing to tie you all to Vancouver now. At least, nothing important."

"How the fuck would you know!" retorted Pat.

Anita looked at Mario, shocked. "How presumptuous of you!"

He saw Steve frown and scratch his chin.

"I know. Girlfriends." Mario saw Steve look out his side window and nod slightly.

"How would you both like to go on and do MBAs?" Mario asked into the rearview mirror. "Both of you."

Steve looked at him. "We've always talked about the possibility. That's a lot of money, though. For the two of us."

"Dad's paying."

"What?" Anita and Steve asked in unison.

"Why am I not surprised," muttered Pat behind Mario.

"But Dad has a couple of conditions," Mario said, ignoring Pat as he signaled a lane change.

"Here we go," said Pat.

"And what are the conditions?" asked Anita.

"A pound of flesh," hissed Pat.

"Pat!" yelled Anita.

Mario sighed deeply. He swallowed. "That you pretend I'm your nephew and, therefore, Steve and Pat's cousin. And we all become part of the *famiglia* as a whole."

Anita's mouth tightened. "Oh, I get it," she hissed. "You're in some kind of trouble and you're using us?!"

"Yes, me personally, maybe. And, no, not at all. Business is big, and business stays in the *famiglia*." He looked over at her pointedly. "You must remember that very well."

She stiffened. "How could I forget?"

"*Famiglia*?" asked Pat, cutting in.

"Yes. *Famiglia*." Mario sat up in surprise at Pat's interest. "Dad and *Zio* Leo have plans for us."

"Who is *Zio* Leo?" asked Steve.

"I'll let Dad explain that."

They drove in silence listening to hissing tires. The windshield wipers quickened their pace.

"Will Maria be there when we arrive?" asked Anita, looking stiffly ahead.

Mario tightened his hold on the steering wheel and remained ominously silent.

Anita snapped her head around to study him. She frowned and leaned toward him. "Is she alright? What happened to Maria? Did someone hurt her?"

Mario cocked his head and looked at her. "There is a gravesite."

Anita's face fell. "Oh, my God!"

"But do you really think someone like Maria can just fade away?" he asked with a smile on his face.

Anita shook her head, tearfully. She covered her face. "No, never. Poor Maria."

He looked over. "Maria didn't die."

Anita looked up, surprised. Then frowned. "I'm confused."

Mario looked pointedly into the rearview mirror at the two young men who looked like himself—like his father. Like Maria. Mario leaned sideways and swiveled his eyes to Anita.

"Anita. I *am* Maria."

Coming Soon by Tina Assanti:

Italian Bones Scattered East
Italian Bones of Contentions Pride Series Part Three

Andy's Ghostly Revenge
Italian Bones of Contentions Pride Series Part Four

GLOSSARY

Abbastanza: (Italian) *Quite*

Abbiamo bisogno di aiuto: (Italian) *We need help*

Abri la porta: (Italian) *Open the door*

Ah: (American Southern Slang) *I*

Alcuni problema: (Italian) *Some problem*

Allo: (French) *Hello*

Ast: (American Southern Slang) *Ask*

Bambina: (Italian) *Baby, female*

Bene: (Italian) *Good*

Benvenuta: (Italian) *Welcome*

Biscotti: (Italian) *Cookies*

Bomboniere: (Italian) *Wedding favors*

Buon appetit: (Italian) *Good appetite*

Buon pomeriggio: (Italian) *Good Afternoon*

Buongiorno: (Italian) *Good Morning*

Buono come il pane: (Italian) *Literally, As good as bread*

Café au lait: (French) *Coffee drink*

Café espresso: (French) *Coffee drink*

Calisse: (French Canadian) *Holy Fuck*

Capisci: (Italian) *Do you understand*

Capos: (Italian) *Captains*

Capobastone: (Italian) *High-ranking 'Ndrangheta who is in charge of a 'Ndrina*

Cappuccino: (Italian) *Coffee drink*

Che cosa: (Italian) *What*

Cinque: (Italian) *Five*

Cocco di mamma: (Italian) *Mama's boy*

Come va?: (Italian) *How are you?*

Congratulazioni: (Italian) *Congratulations*

Cosa sta succedendo?: (Italian) *What is going on?*

Dieci: (Italian) *Ten*

Dictionnaire: (French) *Dictionary*

Dio Omnipotente: (Italian) *Omnipotent God*

Doppio guaio atterrato: (Italian) *Double trouble arrived*

Dov'e: (Italian) *Where is*

Due: (Italian) *Two*

Excusez-moi: (French) *Excuse me*

Ermafrodita: (Italian) *Hermaphrodite*

Famiglia: (Italian) *Family*

Fantastico: (Italian) *Fantastic*

Faccio un brindisi: (Italian) *I make a toast*

Gang de l'ouest: (French) *West End Gang*

Grazie: (Italian) *Thank you*

Hai: (American Southern Slang) *Hi*

I Siciliani: (Italian) *The Sicilians*

Impara una lezione: (Italian) *She learns a lesson*

Kap: (Ancient Egyptian) *Of the Royal school*

La musica: (Italian) *Music*

Ma: (Italian) *But*

Madame: (French) *Mrs.*

Mais: (French) *But*

Mal di stomaco: (Italian) *Stomach ache*

Marito: (Italian) *Husband*

Merci: (French) *Thank you*

Merda: (Italian) *Shit*

Mi bambina: (Italian) *My baby girl*

Mi dispiace: (Italian) *I'm sorry*

Mia: (Italian) *My*

Mia figlia special: (Italian) *My special daughter*

Molte benedizioni: (Italian) *Many blessings*

Mon pere: (French) *My father*

Naiveté: (French) *The state of being naive*

'Ndrangheta: (Italian) *Italian/Calabrian Mafia-type organized crime syndicate, semi-militarized organization, and criminal empire originating in the region of Calabria, dating back to the 18ᵗʰ century. Prevalent in the Eastern Townships of Quebec, Canada.*

'Ndrina: (Italian) *A basic unit in the 'Ndrangheta*

Niente: (Italian) *Nothing*

Nipotina: (Italian) *Granddaughter*

Non farlo: (Italian) *Do not do it*

Nonna: (Italian) *Grandmother*

Nonno: (Italian) *Grandfather*

Nuovo marito e nuovo padre: (Italian) *New husband and new father*

Otto: (Italian) *Eight*

Padre: (Italian) *Father*

Pasta Con le Sarde: (Italian) *Pasta and Sardines*

Pene: (Italian) *Penis*

Per favore: (Italian) *Please*

Perfezionare: (Italian) *Perfection*

Per porgere le mie condoglianze: (Italian) *To offer my condolences*

Perdono: (Italian) *Pardon*

Picciotto d'onore: (Italian) *Honorary position in the lowest rank of the Mafia*

Per lo piu un omo: (Italian) *Literally, Mostly homo*

Pietro: (Italian) *Peter*

Piu vino: (Italian) *More wine*

Protezione: (Italian) *Protection*

Qualcosa non ha odore giusto: (Italian) *Something doesn't smell right*

Quattro: (Italian) *Four*

Quello che e successa?: (Italian) *What happened?*

Qui si trova amata moglie, madre e figlia: (Italian) *Here find beloved wife, mother and daughter*

Quid pro quo: (Latin) *Something for something*

Respirare: (Italian) *Breathe*

Rimani qui: (Italian) *Stay here*

Sacrament: (French Canadian) *Dammit*

Santa Maria Madre di Dio: (Italian) *Saint Mary, Mother of God*

Scusate: (Italian) *Excuse me*

Sei: (Italian) *Six*

Sette: (Italian) *Seven*

S'il vous plaît, ecouté: (French) *Please, listen*

Sidersi: (Italian) *Sit down*

Signor: (Italian) *Mr.*

Signora: (Italian) *Mrs.*

Sono fiero: (Italian) *I'm proud*

Stugats: (Italian) *Male genitalia*

Subito: (Italian) *Immediately*

Telefono: (Italian) *Telephone*

Tre: (Italian) *Three*

Vous avez les yeux plus gros que le ventre: (French Canadian) *You guys have bitten off more than you can chew*

Un momento: (Italian) *One moment*

Una donna: (Italian) *A lady*

Una ragazza stupida: (Italian) *A stupid girl*

Vino: (Italian) *Wine*

Voila: (French) *Here it is. See that?*

Zia: (Italian) *Aunt*

Zio: (Italian) *Uncle*